I0740327

KEEPING ZITA

RESCUE ANGELS
BOOK 3

SUSAN STOKER

CHAPTER ONE

Obadiah Engle, known as Obi-Wan to just about everyone, shook his head in amazement as he drove through the security checkpoint at the entrance to the movie set just outside Norfolk. He was arriving for his first day on the job as military advisor. It felt a little surreal that someone like him—a regular lower- to middle-class boy from North Carolina who grew up loving helicopters—was in this position.

He'd been hired for award-winning big-shot Hollywood director Henry Grubbner's new film, about a helicopter pilot being shot down in North Korea. Obi-Wan couldn't say it was a dream-come-true job, as he was already doing that as a Night Stalker pilot for the US Army. But it was certainly a high point in his life. It was exciting and a change in his usual routine.

At thirty-three, Obi-Wan wasn't exactly old, but he felt as if he was in a bit of a rut. Doing the same thing day after day. Attending meetings on the naval base and being deployed to various places around the world to shuttle special forces teams to and from the various top-secret, highly dangerous missions they were assigned.

He loved flying. Was obsessed with planes and helicopters

from a young age. His parents had indulged him, even encouraging his interest. He wasn't super-close with his mom and dad, but he owed them for what he'd become today.

Butterflies swirled in Obi-Wan's belly as he parked his Jeep Wrangler and headed for the large hangar that had been built for the movie. From the itinerary he'd received, day one was mostly about meeting the staff he'd be consulting with. He was excited to see how the rest of the morning would unfold and to get a feel for how things worked.

His Night Stalker team had given him a rash of shit for not telling them what he was up to lately, when not sitting behind the controls of his chopper and between missions. But they were also intrigued. He'd signed an NDA, so he couldn't talk a lot about the actual movie, but he was looking forward to sharing as much as he could about the new experience with his best friends.

Though, Obi-Wan also knew he'd be very busy for the next few months. He wouldn't have a lot of down time. Between work for the Army and this gig, he'd probably be getting very little sleep, what with traveling between the naval base and the movie set regularly.

Making sure his badge was prominently displayed, he walked back by the security checkpoint, respectfully nodding at the men and women working there, and opened the door to the hangar.

To his surprise, it looked and sounded much like the hangar back at the naval base, with a lot of people milling about. But *unlike* on the base, there were also cameras mounted on what looked like train tracks everywhere he looked. Men and women wearing headsets scurried around as if loaded up on caffeine and stimulants...which they probably were.

Obi-Wan had no idea where he was supposed to go or what he was expected to do. He felt out of his element, which wasn't a feeling he usually experienced when he was inside a hangar.

Just when he was about to stop one of the people rushing by, Obi-Wan noticed a woman walking toward him.

Everything faded into the background as she came closer.

He'd never seen her in any of the Zoom meetings he'd had with various producers and assistants. He would've remembered if he had. She was shorter than his five-foot-nine height—he estimated she was around five-five or six. Her auburn hair was pulled back into a bun at the nape of her neck, and she wore a pair of navy cargo pants with several items in the pockets on the sides of her thighs. Her blue polo shirt had some sort of logo on the left breast. He couldn't make out the color of her eyes yet, but would guess they were probably some sort of shade of green, just based on the color of her hair.

She was lean and obviously fit, her expression intense—and she was completely focused on him, which made Obi-Wan stand up straighter.

He had no idea who she was, but he couldn't deny that he was relieved. It looked as if he wouldn't have to wander around looking like an idiot, trying to figure out where he was supposed to go, after all.

When she got close enough, Obi-Wan saw that his suspicions were correct. Her eyes were a deep shade of green. Like the waters he'd seen one week while vacationing in Maine. Green with flecks of tan. Her lips were full and shiny, as if she'd just applied lip gloss or ChapStick. She wore very little makeup otherwise—and she didn't need it anyway, because her skin was flawless. She was beautiful just as she was.

His heart was beating faster than normal, and Obi-Wan had only a split second to be a little worried about the effect this stranger was having on him before she spoke.

"Hi! You must be Obadiah Engle, yeah?"

"Obi-Wan," he corrected immediately.

"Excuse me?" she asked with an adorable frown.

"No one calls me Obadiah. I go by Obi-Wan."

"Oh...that's your call sign, right?" she asked.

"Call sign, nickname, tac name, whatever you want to call it."

To his surprise, the woman grinned. It was a mischievous smile, one that made Obi-Wan wonder what she was thinking.

She didn't make him wonder for long.

"I can picture it now. A woman in the throes of ecstasy yelling out, 'More, Obi-Wan! Right there, Obi-Wan! Harder, Obi-Wan!'"

Stunned, he was at a loss for words for a moment. Her joke was totally something his teammates would say. But before he could respond, the woman turned an intense shade of pink, then grimaced.

"Oh my God! I'm sorry. That was so rude and completely inappropriate. I'm not usually so crass. I just...it's been a hectic morning. The first couple of days on a shoot usually are. Can we start over? I'm Zita. Zita Darlington. I don't have a nickname, unless you count 'hey you' or 'Doc.' I'm not a doctor though, I'm the set medic. I'm in charge of making sure things are safe, and if people get hurt, I'm the one who sees to them. I'm pretty much invisible until someone breaks a hand or gets their nose bloodied. Not that those things happen a lot, as Henry's a stickler for safety on his sets. But since we're not filming yet and I have some downtime, I was asked to meet you this morning and give you a tour. So, it's very nice to meet you, Obi-Wan. Welcome to the set of *Broken Wings*."

She was babbling now, and for some reason, Obi-Wan didn't think it was as annoying as he might have with anyone else. He was a get-to-the-point kind of guy who normally hated when people made small talk, always preferring for others to say what they wanted to say and move on. Part of that came from needing intel fast and furious when he was flying. And part of it came from the fact his mom could talk the ears off anyone and everyone. The person checking them out in the grocery store, parents of his friends, his teachers during parent-teacher meetings.

His mom was friendly, but it always annoyed Obi-Wan when she felt the need to tell her life story—and his—to everyone she met.

But listening to Zita—he loved her interesting and unusual name—babble on and try to cover up her inappropriate comment about his nickname was hilarious.

"Growing up, some people called me Sage," he told her. "It's my middle name, and around fourth grade I got sick of being picked on because of my name, so I decided to start using Sage instead. It took a while to catch on, but after shoving a few kids when they called me Obadiah, they decided for their own well-being to go ahead and call me Sage. I don't usually condone violence, but changing my name made my life a whole lot easier growing up."

"Okay. Sage. That's cool. Great. Um...look, I'm sorry about being inappropriate earlier. I'm used to hanging around other medics and EMTs. We have kind of a warped sense of humor. We use it as a defense mechanism, I guess. When things get intense or go bad on a call, we tend to make jokes rather than fall apart."

"You've seen some bad shit."

"Yeah. You can't be a paramedic and go on nine-one-one calls and *not* see some pretty horrible things. But thankfully, most of our calls are routine. Lift-assists, sick people, falls, things like that. I'm sure you've seen your share of bad stuff too."

Obi-Wan nodded and said simply, "Yeah."

"Now that I've totally embarrassed myself and put my foot in my mouth at the earliest opportunity, how about that tour I'm supposed to be giving you?" She looked at the watch on her wrist. "You're scheduled to meet Carmen and Logan, the main actors in the movie, which of course you know, at six a.m. That's in about thirty minutes. Although, we probably have more time than that, since Carmen's rarely on time for anything. And I'm not gossiping when I say that. Anyone will tell you the same thing. She's always told anything she's involved in starts a half hour before it actually does, so she can be on time. Come on, I'll show you where everything is."

Obi-Wan found himself grinning. He nodded and fell into step beside the dynamo of a woman who instantly made him feel more comfortable in the unfamiliar surroundings.

As they walked both around the hangar and the areas immediately outside, and she pointed out different things, including the break room full of snacks, the smoking area—unnecessary for him—and trailers where the stars and the director hung out between takes, it wasn't lost on him how many people greeted Zita. She was friendly and outgoing, and everyone they passed or she stopped to introduce him to seemed genuinely happy to see her.

She was one of those rare people who were universally liked. Obi-Wan assumed some of that was because she wasn't there to tell others how to do their job or critique them. She was there to help if someone was injured or got sick.

By the time the tour was over, Obi-Wan was struck anew with awe that he was even there. And overwhelmed with the responsibility on his shoulders. He wanted to be sure this movie was as accurate as possible. If he messed up anything, it could reflect poorly on the Army, and the Night Stalkers, and possibly even his own team. Which was unacceptable.

"You ready to meet Carmen and Logan?" Zita asked.

"Sure. Anything I should know before I meet them?"

Obi-Wan could tell Zita wanted to say something, but she simply shrugged.

He respected the fact that she didn't want to spread gossip or say something out of line. Which was amusing, since the first words out of her mouth were pretty much just that. But Obi-Wan wasn't a man to take offense easily. He was more amused than offended by her observation of women using his nickname in bed. And honestly, she wasn't wrong. He wasn't promiscuous, but the few times someone *had* actually called out his nickname in the middle of making love, it was definitely weird. And that was saying a lot, since he'd gotten used to everyone using his call sign over his given name years ago.

"Seriously. I don't want to start out on the wrong foot with either of them. If there's a topic I should stay away from, please tell me," he cajoled.

"Okay. Do *not* compare Logan to Hugh Jackman. He hates the man. I have no idea why. And don't comment on his name either. Logan Striker is cheesy as hell, and of course it's made up, but he loves it. So whatever you do, steer away from those two topics."

"Got it. Don't mention the *Dead Pool* and *Wolverine* movie, and don't talk about nicknames. Easy enough. What about Carmen?"

If he hadn't been watching Zita so closely, he would've missed the slight wince before she smoothed out her expression.

"I don't think you need to worry about her. She's gonna take one look at you and bend over backward to make a good impression."

"Me? I'm a nobody. She's Carmen St. James. All of her films have been huge hits."

"You're male. A hotshot Night Stalker pilot. Gorgeous. And at the end of the shoot, she'll go back to Hollywood and you'll stay here. You're perfect for her."

Obi-Wan couldn't help but feel a jolt of satisfaction that Zita thought he was good-looking. But he pushed the thought down. He wasn't here to fall into bed with anyone. He wasn't looking for a fling. No matter how rich and famous a woman was...or how intriguing and cute.

"I'm not here for any kind of relationship," he said firmly.

"Doesn't matter. Carmen gets what Carmen wants. And she's totally gonna want you."

The last part was said under her breath.

Obi-Wan stopped walking, forcing Zita to turn around and look at him in question.

"Sage?"

He couldn't deny hearing the name he'd used growing up, that so few people used these days, made him feel...special. He didn't understand the feeling. But now wasn't the time or place to figure out why this blunt, say-what-she-was-thinking woman had him so intrigued.

"Don't leave me alone with her," he blurted, sounding slightly desperate.

Obi-Wan had recently endured a bad experience with *another* woman who'd decided he was going to be her next fuck. She'd spotted him at Anchor Point with his friends...and proceeded to pester him incessantly for weeks. It was annoying as hell, and she'd almost ruined his pleasure in going to the team's favorite hole-in-the-wall bar. She seemed obsessed with bagging a Night Stalker, and it was only because her family moved to the other side of the country that he'd actually gotten a reprieve.

Not that he thought a world-famous actress would take one look at him and decide she just *had* to have him. In fact, most people might think he was being conceited, assuming it could happen twice...but Obi-Wan didn't want to take any chances. He'd been told often enough that he was good-looking, and that, plus his job as an elite helicopter pilot was apparently enough to make some women lose all common sense.

He was a man who liked to do the pursuing. He preferred taking the traditional role in a courtship. He enjoyed dating, holding hands, getting to know a woman. Not that he didn't like to know a woman was interested...but there was a definite line between interest and obsession.

To his relief, Zita didn't laugh. Or roll her eyes.

She simply said, "I won't."

Obi-Wan nodded. He was glad for Zita's warning. There was always the possibility that she was jealous, that she didn't like

Carmen because she was beautiful enough to get any man she wanted. But he didn't think so. Zita was gorgeous in her own right, and she seemed down to earth. Grounded.

She also hadn't been eager to share her thoughts.

All things that led him to believe what she was saying was worth taking to heart. And that he needed to be extremely cautious in what he said and did around Carmen St. James.

Looking at her phone after it chimed, Zita said, "They're waiting for us. We need to go. The last thing we want is to throw off the first day's filming schedule."

"Lead on," Obi-Wan said.

Zita looked at him for a long moment, then nodded and turned, heading for the director's trailer.

CHAPTER TWO

Zita wanted to kick herself. Why was she such an idiot? She was always putting her foot in her mouth when she met new people. Especially when they made her uncomfortable. And Obadiah Engle *definitely* fell into that category. She'd read up on him—as much as she'd been able to find, which probably wasn't even a drop in the bucket.

He was a true hero. The missions he'd been on were full of danger and his skills as a pilot were unmatched. Not only that, but the man was freaking *gorgeous*. And that was saying something, considering she spent her life around men and women who made at least part of their living on their looks.

But Sage's vibe was completely different from the actors and actresses she knew. Even the stuntmen and women had an air of...superiority about them? She wasn't sure if that was the right word. But they all knew how good they looked. How revered they were on set. How special.

Sage? His wide-eyed wonder at seeing everything on the set was refreshing. It didn't matter that he was an *actual* hero. It made her smile at how excited he was to be there, and to be sharing his knowledge.

And him saying he was a nobody? What a joke. Carmen was going to pounce on him; Zita knew that without having to think twice. She'd see how different he was from every other man on set, and she'd immediately set her sights on him.

Zita actually felt a little sorry for Sage. What he was in for.

It was surprising that, instead of being excited over the idea the famous actress might want a fling, he seemed almost *panicked*.

He'd asked her to not leave him alone with Carmen, and Zita had no problem with that request. For one, she needed to escort him to the assistant director afterward, anyway, who wanted to discuss the end scene being filmed that morning.

The thing about movies was that they were never filmed in chronological order. Today, Carmen and Logan were actually starting with the touching reunion scene that takes place at the end of the movie. Logan had spent the last three months losing thirty pounds to match what his character would look like after spending time in the wilderness without much food and after walking miles each day. He'd get a month-long break after all the forest scenes were done, to bulk up before coming back to finish filming the early scenes in the movie, where he was muscular and healthy and living with his family.

The helicopters they were using in the film were on loan from the US Army. They weren't the actual choppers the Night Stalkers flew, for security reasons, and Sage would be giving his thoughts on those as well, when the time came. For now, he had a fairly busy morning ahead of him, and the last thing Zita wanted was his time on set starting off on the wrong foot due to any delays.

They arrived at the trailer and Zita knocked on the door. She heard someone call out, "Enter!" and looked over at Sage.

"Ready?" she asked.

"Ready," he confirmed.

She opened the door, and he held it open as she went up the two stairs into the small space.

Henry Grubbner was sitting on a plush couch with a large sheaf of papers in his lap and Carmen sitting next to him. She wore a pale yellow dress printed with large white flowers. Logan was standing off to the side, leaning against a small counter, and he'd obviously already been through wardrobe and makeup, because he looked like hell. He'd had what looked like dirt spray-painted on his arms and face, and his clothing consisted of a ripped and stained pair of coveralls and worn-in boots. He had a scraggly beard, and his hair was long, greasy *and* dusty, and hanging over his forehead.

It was Logan who moved first. He smiled and held out a hand to Sage as he boomed, "Welcome to the set!"

His tone was completely at odds with his appearance, and while stuff like that used to startle Zita, nothing much fazed her after all her time working in the business, and seeing actors and actresses move in and out of the roles they were playing. Not to mention the sci-fi movies she'd worked on, when the actors and extras were all dressed as various forms of aliens.

Sage held out his own hand to shake Logan's. "It's good to be here."

"Hi. I'm Carmen," the actress purred. She'd stood up, smiling flirtatiously at Sage as she sidled up to him and held out her hand.

To Sage's credit, he didn't sound any more or less welcoming as he shook her hand and said hello. His eyes didn't stray to her chest, and even though it was obvious Carmen was in actress mode, putting her best...*assets* forward, Sage wasn't reacting the way she was used to when men met her for the first time.

"Your suggestions on the script have been dead on," Henry said, as he also stood.

"Thank you, sir."

"I'm not a sir," he said immediately. "It's just Henry."

"And I'm Obi-Wan," Sage told the group.

"Let me guess...*Star Wars* fan?" Logan asked.

Sage smiled and nodded.

"Sweet. Hey, Henry tells me you've been through that evasion school thing, right?"

"SERE training. Survival, Evasion, Resistance, and Escape, yes."

"Cool! I have some questions about that, if you've got a minute at some point."

"I'll probably have more minutes than you," he said, with a polite grin.

Zita was relieved the two men were getting along. She'd worked on one of Logan's movies where he and his costar did *not* get along. It was painful for everyone because of the tension on the set. While Sage wasn't one of the stars, he'd be around a lot for filming, and things could get very awkward if Logan decided he didn't think any of Sage's suggestions were helpful or needed.

"I've got some questions too," Carmen said, leaning in and placing a hand on Sage's arm.

"Sure," Sage said diplomatically, turning toward Henry at the same time, smoothly dislodging her hand as he did so. "I have some suggestions for that scene, specifically the dialogue, where the hero's hiding feet from where the bad guys are standing. The North Korean soldiers wouldn't use the lingo that's currently in the script. I have a few ideas on how to make it more authentic. More militaristic."

"All right. Get with my script supervisor and she'll make the changes, check with me on what was updated, and then the actors involved in the scene will get them."

"Sounds good."

"Right. It's good to meet you. Now, we all need to get on set and get this show on the road," Henry said in a no-nonsense tone.

Logan shook Sage's hand once more and followed Henry out of the trailer.

Zita wasn't surprised that Carmen hung back. She stared at Zita, as if waiting on her to leave too, but Zita had made a promise to Sage that she wasn't leaving him alone with the woman, and she never broke a vow if she could help it.

She leaned against the counter, staring at the actress with more bravery than she would've thought possible. At thirty-five, Zita wasn't an old-timer in the movie industry, but she had enough experience under her belt to know that even if the actors and actresses got irritated with her, there wasn't much they could do about her presence on set. She had an ironclad contract with her union, and unless there was an egregious breach of protocol on her part, she couldn't easily be fired.

Carmen's eyes narrowed as she stared at Zita, but when it became clear she didn't seem inclined to leave, the actress huffed out an annoyed breath before wiping all irritation from her expression and looking at Sage. At five-ten, Carmen was actually taller than him, her heels making her even more so, so as she crept up beside the man, she was looking down into his eyes as she spoke.

"This is your first time on a movie set, right?" she asked.

"Yes."

"If you want, after my scenes are done this morning, I can show you around. Give you a tour. Show you the things that most people don't have access to."

Zita wanted to roll her eyes. There weren't many places that were off-limits to her as the set medic. But it was obvious Carmen was trying to impress the man. It was likely the tactic had worked for her in the past...and she assumed Carmen was insinuating that she'd show him her personal trailer. Those spaces were off-limits to all but a handful of people on the set.

"I appreciate the offer, but Zita's shown me all the places I need to see. Besides, I'll be gone by the time you're done with work for the day. I've got to get back to the naval base."

"Oh," Carmen said with a pretty pout. She ran a finger over the patch on his left shoulder. "I'd love to get a tour of a real-life naval base sometime. I'm sure it's fascinating."

Jeez. The woman wasn't even trying to be subtle.

"Actually, there aren't public tours available, I'm afraid. Although you can see most of it via the Victory Rover, a narrated cruise that lets you see a lot of the naval ships up close."

Zita wanted to laugh. Sage was either being incredibly obtuse, or doing an amazing job of keeping a straight face by pretending to not understand what Carmen was fishing for... namely, a personal invitation to tour the base with him.

"I thought maybe you could show me your helicopters personally," Carmen simpered, giving up on being coy.

"Sorry, but that won't be possible. The hangar is off-limits to civilians," Sage said simply.

"Darn. Well, maybe we can come up with something else to do."

"You're obviously a beautiful and successful woman, but I'm not looking to date anyone right now. I'm sorry."

Once again, Zita was impressed with Sage's matter-of-fact tone—and that he was being incredibly blunt without being rude about turning down Carmen's advances.

"That's too bad. But I've found that men change their minds all the time. Have you ever dated a famous actress?"

"No."

"It's an experience. A good one. I'll see you around, Obi-Wan," Carmen said.

It wasn't Zita's imagination when the woman leaned into Sage a little more—did she actually *smell* him?—before giving him a sexy little smile and turning to head for the door of the trailer. She put a little more sway into her step than usual, showing off her perfect ass and calf muscles, which flexed because of the high heels she was wearing.

Then it was just her and Sage left in the trailer.

Zita wasn't sure what to say after Carmen's embarrassing, but not surprising, attempt at seduction. But she didn't expect Sage's shoulders to sag, or for him to step back a couple of steps and lean heavily on the same counter she was currently resting against.

"Holy crap. She's a barracuda."

It took a moment for his words to sink in, but when they did, Zita could only giggle in relief that Sage was smart enough not to fall for Carmen's sweet talk. This was only the second movie Zita had worked on with Carmen, but she and the actress hadn't gotten along that well the first time, and it looked like this movie wasn't going to be any different. Not if the glare the woman had shot her when she'd refused to leave was any indication.

Not that Zita cared. She was past trying to get people to like her. She was a damn good paramedic, and she wasn't here to make friends.

"Are you okay?" she asked Sage, since he looked a little pale.

"Thank you for not leaving me alone with her," he said in response.

"I told you I wouldn't."

"Well, I appreciate it all the same." He shuddered.

Zita couldn't help it. She chuckled under her breath. "I told you she'd take one look at you and decide you were her next conquest."

"Was it my imagination or did she actually *sniff* me?"

Zita giggled anew. "I saw that. I don't think it was your imagination."

"Next time, I'm totally coming on set after PT. Casper, our team leader, loves to make us roll in the sand after running for miles. Reminds me of the time I screwed up something on my uniform during inspection, and I had to run into the surf, then roll around in the sand...then walk around like that all day. The effect's known as a 'sugar cookie.' Trust me. It sucks. I'm totally coming on set covered in sand and sweat. That ought to discourage her."

Zita shook her head. "Don't bet on it. It'll probably turn her on more. You know...the big bad helicopter pilot, looking all manly after working out."

Sage snorted. "It's uncomfortable as hell. And trust me, smelling like butt after one of my team's workouts is *not* sexy in the least."

"Oh, I believe you. But Carmen and her ilk are a different breed. I'm afraid you made yourself a challenge now. She's not going to just give up."

"Fucking hell," Sage muttered.

Zita wanted to laugh again, but honestly, it wasn't really funny. Carmen could be charming and sweet as pie, but she could also be vindicative and a total bitch. Thankfully, most of the movie focused on Logan's character, and she was in the background as the wife waiting for any word on her husband while he was MIA. But still, she'd be around the set, especially here in the beginning, while her end scenes were filmed. Once Logan gained the weight he'd lost for authenticity, she'd film her parts from the beginning of the movie, before her "husband" left for his mission, with Logan back in California.

Remembering that Henry wanted him to speak to the script supervisor, Zita said, "After you talk to the AD, I can take you to the person to discuss the script issues you told Henry about. If that's okay."

"That would be great, thanks."

"All right. When you're done with the AD, just come find me on the set I showed you earlier, where they'll be filming this morning. And if you've got time after discussing the script, maybe you can watch some of today's scenes."

"Is that what you'll be doing?"

For some reason, Zita's heart beat faster at his question. Pleasure swam through her veins at the way he held her gaze as he asked. As if her response would decide if he'd stay or not.

"Yes. I'm always on set while filming's going on. Just in case."

"I'll probably have a little time to hang around and see what this movie thing is all about then. I'll find you when I'm done with the script supervisor."

Something arced between them at that moment, and Zita wasn't exactly sure what it was. Only that it felt good to be seen for once. She was kind of a ghost on the sets where she worked, at least until someone got hurt and needed medical attention. She hung out in the background and watched what was going on. But this man...he was looking at her as if he truly saw her. Was interested in what she said and what her plans were.

It was a heady feeling.

But it wouldn't be smart to fall for him. She was a nomad. Her life was wherever the job took her. And he was a military man. Heading off on missions to who-knew-where, doing dangerous things that could very well get him killed.

No, she wasn't interested in dating someone who worked in such a dangerous profession.

But a little voice deep down inside her was screaming that she was a liar. That if Obadiah Sage Engle asked her out, she would say yes before the words had finished coming out of his mouth.

But he wasn't going to ask her out. She'd heard him tell Carmen that he wasn't looking for a relationship. So she was being silly. Fantastical. She was dreaming.

He exited the trailer ahead of her and held out his hand to help her down the stairs. As their fingers touched, Zita swore she felt a jolt of electricity from the contact. He made no indication that he felt the same, but his fingers tightened on hers for a split second before he dropped his hand, once she'd stepped down from the last stair and had both feet on the ground.

Zita couldn't help but look up at Sage as they walked toward the AD's trailer. He had a strong profile, and his gaze constantly roamed the area, as if he was looking for danger in every nook and cranny. His shoulders were back and his head was up. He was full of confidence, and way more masculine than any guy she was used to being around.

And Zita had never been more attracted to a man than she was to the one at her side.

Shit.

CHAPTER THREE

"How was the movie set this morning?" Casper asked, when Obi-Wan walked into the conference room shortly after eleven.

"Good."

"You get to meet Carmen St. James?" Edge asked, with a shit-eating grin on his face.

"Yeah, is she as beautiful in person as she is on screen? Or is it all makeup and editing that makes her so gorgeous?" Chaos chimed in.

"She's pretty," Obi-Wan told his friends, being as diplomatic as he could.

"What did you do? Did you meet Logan Striker? Did you get to see any of the movie being filmed?" Pyro asked.

Obi-Wan grinned. His friends' excitement over his work on the movie was a huge relief. They could've resented the time he was taking away from his job. They could've given him a *way* harder time than they were about rubbing elbows with celebrities. But some joking aside, they were pretty supportive, and obviously looking forward to hearing about his experience on the project.

He was also relieved that his boss, Colonel Burgess, was

allowing him to take time off in the mornings to go to the set. Yes, the man had recommended him for the military advisor job in the first place, but he was still appreciative that he was able to take so much time away from the base nonetheless. Of course, if an urgent mission came up, he was expected to report in, but Henry Grubbner knew his job as a Night Stalker pilot came first.

He spent the next ten minutes or so answering everyone's questions and telling them how filming that morning went, and how he'd watched Logan crawl through underbrush on the indoor set over and over again. Wincing at makeshift sounds that would be recreated in post-production. It was actually a little more...*tedious* than he'd expected. Henry was an exacting director, and he wanted everything to be as perfect as it could be, which often meant redoing the same takes multiple times, until they were to his liking.

Eventually, Casper redirected the conversation to work, and the men began to research the area of their next mission. Occasionally they didn't get advance notice of where they were going, but many times they had a few weeks to learn as much as they could about the terrain they'd would be flying over and through.

After a short break for lunch, the meetings continued for another couple of hours before everyone headed to the hangar for some flight time. Even though they were the best-trained pilots in the country, they were required to keep their skills honed by ensuring they had the hours needed behind the controls of their choppers while not deployed.

Obi-Wan's copilot was Buck. Their most recent mission was down in South America, where the latter had met Mandy. In the middle of a rescue in the jungle, Buck had left the chopper to chase her down, and rebels in the area had forced Obi-Wan to take off without his friend and teammate.

The subsequent two weeks were extremely stressful. Obi-Wan second-guessed leaving Buck behind every day that he was missing. He'd had every confidence his teammate would be able to navigate the rainforest and make it back to Guyana with Mandy, but it was still a very difficult time.

Thankfully, the two had safely evaded the rebels and shown back up across the border...with a four-legged companion they'd picked up along the way.

Then *everyone* on the team was horrified when, just a few weeks later, Mandy was severely injured because of her association with the orphanage and school down in Guyana, where she'd volunteered.

But she was doing great now, and Buck was getting back to his old self.

Obi-Wan was thrilled for his copilot. Buck deserved to have a woman like Mandy at his side. Someone loyal, strong, and independent. Someone who could handle her man heading off on top-secret missions for days or weeks at a time.

It was a bonus that she and Laryn, the team's head mechanic, got along so well. And nice to see Laryn opening up to another woman, since she spent most of her time around men.

Speaking of Laryn...when they walked into the hangar, for once the mechanic wasn't instantly fixated on her boyfriend, Casper. Instead, Obi-Wan could practically feel her gaze on *him* as they walked over to the three choppers waiting for them.

"So?" she asked with a lift of an eyebrow. "How was it? Are you making sure those Hollywood idiots get their shit right with the choppers?"

Obi-Wan grinned. "Today wasn't a day where they were filming with the birds. That'll come later."

Laryn harrumphed. "Well, be sure they don't use any AH-64 Apaches."

"Of course. I've already made that very clear."

"Good. So...meet any girls on set?"

Obi-Wan blinked in surprise. That was the *last* question he expected from Laryn.

She didn't give him a chance to answer before exclaiming,

"You're blushing! You *did*! Who is she? Was it Carmen? She seems likes a bitch from the interviews I've seen her do on TV. *Please* don't tell me you have a crush on her."

Obi-Wan immediately set her straight. "No. Although I *did* meet her. And several other women. Why, you need another friend?" He relied on the good-natured ribbing he was used to with his teammates, trying to deflect.

"I have all the friends I need right here," Laryn returned without hesitation. She shook a wicked-looking wrench that could easily take someone down with one crack to the head, as well as a huge screwdriver.

Buck laughed from next to him. "I wouldn't mess with her, for sure."

"Easy, Rambo," Obi-Wan joked, holding up his hands and taking a step back.

Laryn grinned and slid the tools of her trade back into the toolbelt she frequently wore around her waist. "It's just that you and the others don't get out enough. You go from here to Anchor Point and back home. It's unlikely that you're gonna meet someone to spend the rest of your lives with at the bar."

"Who says we want anything other than a casual date?" Obi-Wan asked.

"Well, no one. But I want all of you to be as happy as me and Tate."

"You guys are a statistical anomaly," he said. "Perfect for each other."

"Mandy and I managed to fall in love even under unusual circumstances," Buck piped up.

Obi-Wan rolled his eyes. "Not everyone is like you guys. We can't all meet the loves of our lives under extreme stress."

"Right, which is why I'm asking about women on the set. There have to be a ton of them around. Makeup artists, camera operators, production people, extras, designers. You should do what you can to meet some of them. Talk to them. You never know what could happen."

Obi-Wan's mind immediately went to Zita. There was no doubt he was attracted to her, but her life was so different from his. She was part of the Hollywood scene. She knew all the actors and actresses, and even the director and his assistants. Her life was in California, when she wasn't on the road working on a movie set. Hell, she probably traveled more than he did. There was no way a relationship between a military guy and a set medic would work out.

He shrugged and said, simply to appease Laryn, "I'll see what I can do."

The mechanic narrowed her eyes at him. "I hate when people patronize me. Don't tell me what you think I want to hear."

Obi-Wan mentally sighed. It'd already been so long since he'd been with a woman, his dick had forgotten what it felt like to be inside anything other than his fist.

Buck slapped him on the back and said, "Come on, we've got flight checks to do. And I have a woman to get home to."

Now Laryn grinned.

Obi-Wan rolled his eyes. "Whatever."

The truth was, he was envious of Casper and Buck. He'd had no siblings growing up, which meant that he was used to a very quiet home. But lately, his apartment seemed even emptier than usual. It was also getting tougher to remain satisfied with his life. Going from one mission to the next with nothing else to really occupy his time, no one waiting for him at home.

That was part of the reason he'd taken the job of military advisor for the film. He was bored. And while he'd never take a woman to his bed solely out of boredom, he couldn't help but admit that having someone in his life would certainly break up the monotony.

But...was that fair to anyone who caught his interest? For

boredom to be the catalyst for a decision to date? He didn't think so.

Not to mention, he felt horrible that he was bored in the first place. He had a high-adrenaline job. One that many people would kill to have. He got to do what he loved most, fly, almost every day. Not only that, but he got to serve his country in a way that made him proud.

It felt shitty to be even the slightest bit dissatisfied with all that he had.

Thankfully, the flight checks took his mind off his gloomy thoughts. He was a professional, and no way would he get behind the controls of the multimillion-dollar chopper without having all of his attention on what he was doing.

When he and Buck got in the air, all his worries disappeared. He reveled in the feeling of flying. Of sitting next to one of his best friends, doing what they did best. By the time they landed, his good mood was restored and his morose thoughts from earlier were pushed to the back of his mind.

That night, when he arrived at his apartment and checked his email, he had a message from the script supervisor, asking for his approval of the changes he'd suggested that morning. It read much better now, more believable. Obi-Wan was pleased. It was fascinating to be on the inside, to see how movies got made. It was a lot more work than he'd envisioned and involved way more people than he ever imagined.

To his surprise, he also had an email from Carmen St. James.

Obi-Wan hesitated to open it, an uneasy feeling swirling in his belly. Most people would be thrilled to have an email from a famous actress...but he wasn't most people.

Reluctantly, he clicked on the message...and winced as he read it. It started polite and unremarkable, but she quickly moved on to what she *really* wanted—him.

. . .

Hi Obi-Wan. Lol! Your name is cute. It was very nice to meet you today. I'd love to get to know you better over the next couple of weeks. I'm only in town for my scenes, and then I'm headed back to California. I have another film to prepare for, one where I'm in every scene, unlike this one. I'm told that there's a good chance it'll get nominated for an Oscar.

It seems as if I'll have some down time while I'm in Virginia and would love to see some of the sights around here. But I need a guide. Someone who can protect me when I'm recognized and can keep my fans from becoming too intrusive. I'm sure with your training, you can easily do that. I think the two of us could have a no-pressure, mutually beneficial, no-strings friendship while I'm here. I'm putting my unlisted phone number at the end of this message so you can contact me. What goes on between us will stay between us.

Yours, Carmen

Obi-Wan pressed his lips together in irritation. He'd told the woman he wasn't interested in dating. And yet, she wasn't listening. Which only annoyed Obi-Wan even more. She wasn't being subtle about her intentions either.

Once upon a time, Obi-Wan might've taken her up on the offer. Would've loved to spend a couple of weeks having no-strings sex with a beautiful woman. But that no longer appealed to him.

And just like that, his thoughts turned back to Zita. The paramedic.

For some reason, *she* appealed to him more than he understood. He'd seen the appreciation in her eyes when she looked at him, but she certainly hadn't acted on whatever she was feeling. She was professional, and he appreciated the warning she gave him about Carmen before they'd met with the actress.

In short, if he was interested in dating anyone, it would be her.

Obi-Wan also wanted to be the pursuer. Not the pursue-ee.

It was old fashioned, especially in the current day and age, but he liked the challenge. He also liked the anticipation of a slow courtship. The dance of attraction. Of flirting. Of getting to know someone before falling into bed.

Maybe it was because the first serious girlfriend he'd ever had growing up had made him work *hard* for her attention. He'd given her notes, and flowers, and taken her out to lunches and walks and dinners. Hell, it had taken him two months of asking just for her to agree to a date.

But the satisfaction he'd felt when she'd finally said yes had been so emotionally powerful. And he'd spent the rest of their relationship doing everything he could to make every moment they had together meaningful in some way.

Of course, he was older and wiser now, and he knew relationships weren't nearly as easy as they were when he was a kid. Adulting often got in the way of the grand gestures. And while he still *enjoyed* the grand gestures, there was something to be said for the smaller ones too.

He saw how Laryn smiled when she'd reached into her pocket one day and found a sticky note from Casper. Or how happy Buck was to wake up to a simple pot of coffee that Amanda had made the evening before, setting the timer so it was ready for him when he got up for PT.

Obi-Wan wanted a confident woman—but not a pushy one. A sensual partner, not a promiscuous one. An independent companion who was happier sitting at home in sweats or meeting friends in a bar, than getting dressed up for fancy social outings.

And he had a feeling Zita was all of the former, while Carmen was all of the latter. Which wasn't exactly fair, as he didn't really know *either* woman. But Obi-Wan had pretty great intuition, and the email in front of him simply confirmed most of what he'd already thought of Carmen St. James after only one meeting.

He deleted the email without a second thought, then went on to delete the other forty-seven spam and scam emails he'd received during the day as well.

Tomorrow would be another long day. Hell, most of the next month would be long. Morning PT with the team, then home to shower, and then off to the movie set. Afterward, he'd drive straight to the base for meetings and flying time, then back to his apartment to do it all over again. It was a grueling schedule, but nothing he wasn't used to, especially while on a mission. At least he'd get to sleep in his own apartment every night.

As he got ready for bed, Obi-Wan couldn't help but feel a bit of anticipation for the upcoming weeks. Despite the monotony of watching take after take of the same thing, he still enjoyed being on the set of *Broken Wings* today, and he couldn't wait to see the rest of the movie unfold. He was especially looking forward to going to western Virginia and the mountains, where the scenes with the choppers were being filmed. The most intense parts of the film featured the crash and the rescue of the main character. That was where his expertise would be needed most, and he was looking forward to seeing it all play out.

He was taking a week's leave for that time period, and as much as he enjoyed his job and his teammates, he was excited for a bit of time away from his routine on the base.

And if a tiny part of his brain said that he was also looking forward to getting to know Zita a little more—because she would surely be traveling to the second location as well, because of her job—Obi-Wan wasn't ready to admit it to himself.

CHAPTER FOUR

Zita was more excited to be on set this morning than usual. It was the fifth day, and she'd spent part of each morning with Sage. It was silly, but she felt special that she was the only one who called him by his middle name. She would've felt weird calling him Obi-Wan. To her, the name simply didn't fit the man she was getting to know. She understood it was a nickname, and that most pilots had some sort of call sign, but it felt odd for her to use it when addressing him.

Sage was also an unusual name. But then again, his first name, Obadiah, was even *more* unusual. The man was interesting in just about every way. Smart, funny, and very observant.

He was also doing everything in his power to avoid Carmen St. James. He'd admitted to her yesterday that she'd sent him a super-suggestive email, but didn't say anything else about it, just that he was there to do his job and nothing else.

She admired him for that. Because it was Zita's experience that most men presented with a sure thing like Carmen would've jumped at the chance. Not only because she was beautiful, but because she was famous. Zita never understood the appeal of sleeping with someone because of their job, but that was just her.

Still, she couldn't help but feel a pang of...something—remorse?—at hearing Sage's firm stance on professionalism. On not wanting to date. Zita had never had the urge to go out with anyone she worked with...until now. But then again, she and Sage weren't exactly coworkers. He was a contract employee, and only on set for part of each day as it was. But there was something about him that drew Zita.

This morning, he'd shown up with two cups of to-go coffee. She'd been shocked when he'd handed her one, saying, "Heard you complaining about the break-room coffee yesterday, thought you might appreciate this."

And she did. She loved a fancy, sugary, carmel-y cup of coffee as much as the next girl. And for him to bring her one was... kind. And very sweet. He'd wandered off immediately after, before she'd even had a chance to thank him properly.

Taking another sip of the coffee, Zita smiled. It was perfect. Exactly how she liked it. Which was impressive, considering how picky she was about her coffee.

During the last hour, he'd met with the script supervisor, and then Logan, and now he was ambling back toward her, ready to watch the scenes being filmed that morning. Thankfully, Carmen wasn't on the schedule, so they both had a reprieve from dealing with her not-so-subtle flirting and almost desperate attempts to catch Sage's attention.

"Thank you for the coffee," she said the moment he sat beside her.

"You're welcome."

"How'd you know that I like the caramel stuff?" Zita asked.

Sage shrugged. "Lucky guess. My teammate's woman loves it, so I took a chance that you might too."

"She's got good taste."

"Yup."

"Can you tell me about your teammates? I mean, I know you can't say anything about your missions, but I'd love to hear more about them."

Sage spent the next twenty minutes telling her all about the men he worked with. They all had interesting call signs, but Zita wasn't exactly surprised. Casper, Buck, Pyro, Chaos, Edge...she was curious about the meanings behind their names but didn't interrupt Sage to ask. It sounded like the men were as close as brothers, and she supposed they were. If you spent your career relying on them to keep you alive, a special bond had to form.

"What about you? You work with anyone on a regular basis?" Sage asked.

Zita shrugged. "When I'm not on set, I work part-time for an ambulance service, and I guess I'm somewhat friendly with some of my coworkers."

"I'm guessing working in your profession, some people are better at handling the stress than others."

"Sure. And some people you click with, while others can be a chore. Some medics and EMTs are lazy. They'd rather drive the ambulance and stand back and let others do all the decision-making than jump in and get their hands dirty. It's annoying, but part of the job."

Sage shook his head. "That's hard for me to wrap my head around. I mean, pilots and copilots each have their specific jobs. But we can all do just about everything when we get behind the controls. We just know who's supposed to do what, so we don't trip over each other when things get hot. What's your most memorable call...if you can talk about it without breaking any privacy laws?"

"We were called to a residence for a man 'bleeding.' That's all the information the dispatcher could give us. When we got there, he was in the bathroom and there was literally blood *everywhere*. On the walls, the floor, dripping down his legs. Apparently, he'd had a colonoscopy the day before and had gotten up in the middle of the night to use the restroom, and something inside him ruptured. He was literally bleeding from his anus…not to be crude or anything. As a paramedic, there's not a lot we can do for that except get him to the hospital as fast as possible. But it's daunting as hell to walk into a room and see that much blood."

"I bet."

"You? I mean, again, if you can say."

Sage stared into space, clearly thinking about the question. Zita appreciated that about him. That he took the time to really consider how to answer. "We were called in to extract three teams of special forces in a hot zone. Meaning, the bad guys were everywhere and using any fire power they had to keep us away. Casper and Pyro took point, using their ammo to try to give us a window to land and load up the teams.

"Everything was going according to plan…well, as close to a plan as we could get in a fluid situation like that. Just as we were taking off, our chopper took a few bullets to the radar system and FLIR system located on the underside of our chopper. We had twelve souls onboard, some of whom were severely injured and needed medical attention ASAP. And we were essentially flying blind. There was smoke and dust everywhere, and the wind was doing its best to fly us into the nearest mountain.

"I radioed Chaos and Edge, and told them they were going to have to be our guide. We flew right on their six…their ass… swerving to miss all the missiles being shot at us from the ground while navigating the tricky terrain.

"It was the most harrowing twenty minutes of my life. Buck's too. Somehow, we made it back to the ship…and after we landed, I puked. Buck wasn't doing very well either. We both knew that we'd cheated death. And we frequently cheat death when we fly missions, but this was a whole different level. I honestly think the fact that we had so many men in the back of our chopper was the motivation we needed to keep calm and do what had to be done to get the hell out of there."

Zita was riveted on Sage's every word. She could almost smell the smoke, hear the missiles whistling through the air. Goose bumps covered her arms by the time he finished. "Tell me you both—all of you—received commendations for that mission."

Sage grinned, shaking his head. "All part of the job."

"That's kind of bullshit."

He chuckled. It was low and rumbly, and sparks shot down her body at the sound.

He shrugged. "The AAR—after-action review—was interesting, to say the least. Laryn was pissed that we'd lost our eyes, so to speak, and she took it upon herself to research how to make the covering over our navigation systems more secure."

"Laryn?"

"She's the head mechanic who works on our choppers. She's a genius with anything mechanical. She's also dating Casper. Although, 'dating' seems like a tame word. They'll eventually get married, but neither is in a big hurry to tie the knot."

Zita liked this. Learning about his personal life. "Is it frowned on for two people who work together to date?"

"Nope. Laryn is a contract employee. She doesn't work for the Army."

"Oh, cool. Are any of your other friends in a relationship?" She wasn't sure why she was asking, only that she was curious.

"Yeah, one. Buck met Mandy on a recent mission in South America. They spent two weeks in the jungle, evading rebels who'd kidnapped a school full of orphans, and they're closer than two peas in a pod now."

Zita had so many questions, but she simply said, "That's good."

"It is."

So it wasn't that he and his friends couldn't or wouldn't date.

It was either Sage hadn't found anyone he wanted a long-term relationship *with*...

Or, as he'd told Carmen, he really wasn't interested in dating.

"And they make it work?" she blurted.

"Make it work?" Sage asked, looking her in the eyes.

Zita wished she could take the question back. Since she couldn't, she soldiered on. "Yeah. I imagine your schedule is pretty unpredictable. With missions and stuff."

"Oh. Well, that's definitely true. But I think if you love and respect someone, you find a way to make things work, regardless of what's happening with work or family or anything else."

He wasn't wrong.

"True."

"Being a set medic can't be an easy schedule either," he mused.

"It's not," she agreed, shrugging. "Most men just aren't willing to deal with me being gone so much."

"*Hmph*."

It was less a word than a breath of sound that escaped his mouth.

Zita was busy wondering what that meant when a shout came from across the set. She whipped her head around instinctively, trying to see where it came from and what was happening.

A split-second later, someone yelled, "Medic!" in a frantic tone.

Zita was moving before her brain could catch up. She grabbed her medical bag that was always by her side and ran behind the camera operators—she'd learned the hard way to never, *ever* cross in front of the cameras, in case a scene was still in play—toward a woman lying on the ground, with two men hovering over her.

She didn't know the woman's name but knew that she was one of the boom operators, responsible for holding the boom mics when needed on set. Kneeling next to her, Zita saw that she was sweaty and clammy, and holding her left arm.

She got to work immediately, asking the woman questions about what happened, where she felt pain, and getting her medical history. She wasn't aware of anyone else around her, all her focus completely on the woman. She vaguely heard sirens in the distance, but she didn't let those distract her either.

Before long, she was joined by two paramedics from a local ambulance company. She'd already inserted an IV and had the leads attached to the woman's chest to monitor her heart rhythms.

She stood back as the ambulance crew took over. They agreed with her initial assessment that the woman was having some sort of heart episode. They put her on a stretcher, removed Zita's heart-monitoring lines, and hooked up their own. Thanking her for her quick actions, and for getting the IV inserted, they moved across the set toward the exit.

Satisfied that the woman would have the best care, now that she was on the way to the hospital, Zita began to clean up the mess left behind by both herself and the ambulance crew.

To her surprise, someone knelt at her side and began to help. Looking over, Zita saw Sage.

"I've got it," she said quietly.

"I know," was all he said, but he didn't stop picking up the wrappers from the sterilized equipment she'd used.

It didn't take long to clean up the area. Then Zita stood, as did Sage.

Without a word, they returned to the seats they'd been using before the emergency.

Zita settled back down, making sure her bag was once more at her feet and ready to go at a moment's notice. She needed to repack some of the things she'd used on the woman, but she always had plenty of needles, gauze, and whatever else she might need while on the set, so that could wait.

After a moment, Sage said quietly, "You were great with her."

Pride flooded Zita's system. It wasn't as if his words were the first time she'd heard such praise. Zita wasn't conceited, but she knew she was a damn good paramedic. She'd spent more than her fair share of time on the front lines and could treat anything from pediatric seizures to gunshot wounds to the gut. She had yet to experience anything on the set of any of the movies she'd been on that she couldn't handle.

"Thanks," she said a little belatedly.

"Staying calm is one of the most important things anyone can do in an emergency."

Zita nodded. She could totally picture this man not getting ruffled in the least when the shit hit the fan when he was behind the controls of his helicopter. "Yeah."

"But it's more than staying calm," Sage said, turning to look at her once more. This time, there was something...*more* in his gaze. She couldn't put her finger on what it was, but the look in his eyes made her tingle in places she hadn't tingled in a very long time. "It's making the person you're treating feel down to their very soul like they're in good hands. Like they aren't going to die. Like you're going to help them. Make the pain go away. Keep them alive."

Zita wanted to argue that the woman wasn't on the verge of death. That even if she was having a heart episode, she wasn't in active defib or anything. But he was right, and she figured he'd had more than enough experience watching military medics or special forces operatives deal with teammates who were gravely wounded.

She'd love to pick his brain about the things he'd seen. Zita figured she could probably learn a lot from hearing what others in her profession had said and done while in emergency situations. But it was unlikely she'd ever get the chance, since she didn't have top-secret clearance.

"You're an easy person to be around, Zita."

She was literally at a loss for words.

No one had ever said *that* about her before.

She was Type A. Didn't like to sit still. Liked to be doing something. Days off had always been difficult for her, because she couldn't simply veg on the couch and watch TV or read a book. She tended to talk too much. Ask inappropriate questions. Fidget. She'd even had one boyfriend tell her that she exhausted him, and he couldn't deal.

So Sage saying that she was easy to be around was a new one. And it meant the world to her. She wasn't sure she entirely believed him; after all, he'd only known her for a week or so, but still. The compliment made her feel all warm and fuzzy inside.

"Thanks," she whispered.

The scene that had been interrupted by the small drama resumed, and Zita turned her attention in that direction, not really seeing anything because she was replaying Sage's words in her head. She had a report to type up regarding what just happened—she was required to document everything she did while on set, partly to justify the cost of her being there, but also for insurance purposes—but she didn't want to leave Sage's side just yet.

For some reason, sitting next to him calmed the constant need inside her to move. Probably why he thought she was "easy" to be around. It was actually all *him*.

For the next ten minutes, Logan filmed the scene where he was being welcomed back by his teammates, and when Zita happened to glance over at Sage, she saw he was watching with his entire being. Meaning, he was leaning forward, his gaze locked on the actors, his hands clenched together as his elbows rested on his thighs. Even his jaw was tight, and Zita could see a muscle ticking there.

She couldn't tell what he was thinking or feeling.

Was he upset? Irritated that the scene wasn't authentic? Thinking about his *own* friends, and a time when he'd experienced something similar to what was being acted out in front of them? She wasn't sure. But she couldn't sit there and pretend he wasn't experiencing some sort of big emotion and not *do* something.

Taking a chance, Zita reached out and put a hand on his forearm.

She felt him jerk under her. He glanced down at her hand, over at her, then turned his attention back to the scene being filmed.

Feeling awkward, as if she'd done the wrong thing, Zita decided she should leave him to his thoughts, find something else to do...maybe go off and complete that report after all.

But as she started to pull her hand away, Sage moved. Putting his right hand over hers where it lay on his arm.

Taking a deep breath, Zita stilled. His palm was warm, and when he squeezed her hand lightly, she closed her eyes in satisfaction.

He lifted his hand a moment later, and she let go of his arm, placing her hand back in her lap. But when she looked at him now, he seemed...less tense. It felt good that she'd been able to help in a small way.

A couple of minutes later, the scene was completed and Henry seemed satisfied that he'd gotten the shots he needed. The production designer approached Sage at that point, asking if he'd look over the pictures of the choppers they'd be using in the extraction scene being filmed in a couple weeks.

Sage nodded and stood. Zita got to her feet as well—she couldn't put off writing that report any longer. She never knew when the next emergency would occur, when her skills would be needed, and the last thing she wanted was reports piling up. That was a good way to forget something, to get details from one episode mixed up with another.

Sage followed the production designer for a few steps before abruptly turning back toward Zita, still by her chair. When he reached her, he said in a low voice, "My friends and I sometimes hang out at a bar slash restaurant called Anchor Point. We've made plans to get together a few days from now. It's nothing fancy, really a hole-in-the-wall place, but...if you're not busy, I'd love to introduce you to everyone. Hang out with you away from the set."

Zita's heart was beating a million miles an hour. Was he asking her out?

No. Not really. Especially since he'd made a point to tell her that all of his friends would be there. And he'd already made it clear he wasn't interested in dating at the moment. But...it wasn't as if she had any plans. After she left the set, all she did was go back to her budget motel and try not to be bored out of her skull. Besides, she'd love to meet his Night Stalker teammates.

She did her best to keep her voice calm and steady. "I'd like that."

"Great." He pulled out his phone. "If you give me your number, I'll text you the details. Address and time and stuff."

Zita felt as if she were in high school all over again, and the boy she had a crush on had asked for her number. She recited her digits to Sage, and then felt her phone vibrate with a text right before he put his phone back in his own pocket.

"You've got my number now, in case anything comes up. See ya later."

"See ya," she echoed.

He once again went to follow in the direction the production designer went, but he turned once more, still speaking in a low voice. "Thanks." He gestured toward the set with his head.

The next time he walked away, he didn't turn back or stop.

Zita's heart was still beating too fast in her chest. He didn't need to thank her for supporting him when he was experiencing something intense while watching a scene, but he had.

Shit. This wasn't good.

Zita liked Obadiah Engle *way* more than she should. Than

was healthy. If she was smart, she'd turn down the invitation to spend more time with him. Come up with some sort of excuse why she couldn't go to Anchor Point.

Telling herself that she could be just friends with him, that she'd be gone before too long, that nothing would ever happen between them because their lives were too different and he didn't want any kind of relationship, casual or otherwise, didn't make the butterflies go away.

The truth was...Sage affected her more deeply than any man had in a very long time. She would probably get hurt by encouraging this...*whatever* this was between them.

But she wasn't going to say no. Wasn't going to back off. She was going to live for once. No matter the consequences, she wouldn't have any regrets. For the first time in what seemed like forever, Zita was going to follow her instincts.

And they were screaming that Sage was a man worth getting to know.

CHAPTER FIVE

Three days later, Obi-Wan was still wondering what had come over him. Why he'd asked Zita to come to Anchor Point. He wasn't looking for any kind of relationship, but there was something about the woman that made his heart beat faster and stirred him deep inside like no one ever had before.

It wasn't just one thing about her either. It was everything he'd observed and learned. The way she stayed calm in the face of other people's anxiety and hysteria when there was an emergency on set. He'd watched her deal with both minor and major issues already. From the woman with the heart episode a few days ago, to a compound fracture of someone's wrist, to a mild concussion, to food poisoning. She was unflappable. And he liked that—a lot. Because that's how he had to be behind the controls of his chopper. No matter what went wrong, he and his fellow pilots had to deal if they wanted to live. If they wanted everyone onboard their helicopters to survive.

He was a problem solver, and he really liked that Zita seemed to be as well.

But it was also her keen observational skills. He hadn't even realized he was getting so worked up while watching that scene with Logan greeting his teammates a few days ago. Not until she'd put a hand on his arm to comfort him.

The fact that she'd realized he was dealing with some intense emotions stirred up by that scene—particularly, the reunion he'd had with Buck, after he'd been missing for two long weeks in the jungle in South America—and had done what she could to support him without making a big deal out of it, soothed him in a way he hadn't even known he needed until she'd done it.

He'd said that she was easy to be around, and she was. But he'd done a lot of observing of his own...and she was also restless. Kind of like him. She didn't like to sit still. Was constantly walking around the set, talking to people, asking how they were, observing what was going on, offering her help.

It was fair to say Zita Darlington intrigued him. And it had been ages since Obi-Wan was intrigued by *any* female. So he'd impulsively invited her to come to Anchor Point.

What he *really* wanted was to ask her over to his apartment. Cook her dinner. Get to know her better without anyone else around. But he was a coward, so he thought the barrier of his teammates—and Laryn and Mandy—would be safer. Maybe he'd discover she had some super-annoying trait he didn't know about yet. Maybe she was a closet lush, an alcoholic. Or too loud and rowdy when she got drunk. Or maybe she smacked her lips when she ate. Or chewed too loudly.

Obi-Wan mentally rolled his eyes at himself. He was being ridiculous. And he couldn't go back on his invitation now regardless. She'd already accepted and said via text that she was looking forward to meeting up with him and his friends tonight.

PT that morning had been brutal. Casper had driven them harder than normal, saying they'd gotten soft with all the meetings they'd been sitting their asses in lately. Obi-Wan wasn't sure if that was the true reason or not. Casper and Laryn had seemed...stressed the last couple of days. Neither was talking to anyone about what might be bothering them, but Obi-Wan hoped like hell they weren't on the verge of breaking up.

That would be awful. He loved Laryn like a sister and thought she and Casper were great together. They complemented each other in a way he'd rarely seen. If those two couldn't make a relationship work, there wasn't a chance in hell *he* could.

So after less sleep than he needed and a grueling workout, Obi-Wan was tired, and kind of grumpy, and irritated about some changes to the script that made the main character sound like a douche. He was confused about his feelings toward Zita when he definitely wasn't looking for a relationship, so he'd planned on staying away from her this morning...but that didn't stop him from buying her usual coffee on the way to the set.

So as soon as he arrived, the first thing he did was look around to see if she was there yet.

Instead of finding Zita, however, he caught Carmen's eye.

Shit.

The second she saw him looking her way, she abruptly turned from the cameraman she was flirting with and headed toward him.

Feeling like he was caught in the crosshairs of an especially dangerous force, all Obi-Wan could do was stand there. For someone who was really good at making decisions on the fly, he was doing a piss-poor job of figuring out where to go, who to talk to, so he could avoid the upcoming conversation with Carmen.

She'd tried several times over the last few days to get him alone, but thankfully he'd always been busy or had someone else he needed to talk to. Since he'd just arrived, he didn't have that excuse at the moment.

Resigned to the inevitable conversation, Obi-Wan steeled himself. He felt bad about having such harsh feelings toward someone he really didn't know and had only talked to a handful of times. But each of those times had been...trying. The woman didn't take no for an answer, and she honestly seemed to think there was no way anyone would turn down any kind of sexual overture on her part.

"Hi!" Carmen said perkily as she stopped in front of him. Well inside his personal space.

Taking an obvious step backward, Obi-Wan nodded at her.

"It's a great day today, isn't it?"

He grunted. His sore muscles disagreed with her. The sand he swore he could still feel in his underwear, even after a shower, disagreed with her. And the fact that he hadn't been able to find Zita yet, so he felt like an idiot holding two cups of coffee, also made him disagree with her.

"Is that an extra cup of coffee? I'd kill for something decent, unlike what they serve on set."

She reached for the cup he was holding in his left hand, but Obi-Wan moved it away so she couldn't take it from him. "No."

He was being abrupt, but he really wasn't in the mood for her. Hell, he should probably turn around and leave. He wasn't going to be a help to anyone today with the way he was feeling. Off-kilter. Irritated. Worried about Casper and Laryn.

Carmen looked taken aback, but she quickly rallied and smiled. "We haven't had a chance to sit down and talk. Get to know each other," she said with a pout. "I'm filming a few scenes this morning, but maybe you could come to my hotel tonight. I'm staying at the historic Cavalier Hotel, near the beach. We could have a few drinks. Hang out."

It took everything in Obi-Wan to keep his thoughts off his facial expression. "Sorry, I can't." He didn't elaborate.

The pout on Carmen's face deepened. "I'm getting the feeling you don't like me for some reason. Have I done something to offend you?"

Obi-Wan was uncomfortable. He wasn't good at this kind of thing. He honestly didn't want to hurt Carmen's feelings, he just wanted her to back off. Not be so aggressive in her pursuit of someone who *clearly* had no interest. "No. I'm just here for the job, that's all."

She stared at him for a long moment. Long enough for Obi-Wan to start feeling annoyed. But again, none of that showed on his face. He was too well trained to let anyone see what he was truly feeling.

"We can be friends though, right?"

"Sure," he answered tentatively.

"Great. And friends hang out together," she said with a satisfied smirk.

Fuck. This woman. She was relentless.

"Carmen!" one of the producers yelled from across the set. "Ten minutes and you're up!"

"Looks like I've got to go. I need to stop by makeup once more and make sure I'm good. I'm not going to give up, Obi-Wan. When I want something, I get it. I haven't gotten to where I am in Hollywood by backing down from anything. And I want us to be friends. *Very* good friends."

Then she leaned into him, grabbed the back of his neck, and kissed his cheek, right next to his lips.

Obi-Wan felt trapped. The firm hold on his neck kept him from stepping back, unless he wanted Carmen stumbling into him. And his hands were full of hot coffee. Not that he would've shoved her away even if they weren't; that simply wasn't the kind of man he was.

His gut churned at the unwelcome kiss. And her long fingernails dug into the skin of his nape, making him shiver—but not in a good way.

The satisfaction in her gaze when she pulled back and smiled didn't bode well for Obi-Wan. As she sauntered away from him, shaking her ass suggestively, he vowed to do everything in his power to avoid being alone with her ever again. He wasn't sure if her words were a threat, or simply those of a spoiled actress used to getting her way.

Instinctively, his gaze swept the room. He was used to scoping out his surroundings. It had saved his life more than once while on the job. He wasn't on an op right now. Wasn't in the middle of a hostile situation. But habits were habits, and this was one he couldn't break.

Instead of finding anyone staring back with nefarious intent, Obi-Wan met the gaze of the one person he *definitely* wouldn't have wanted witnessing Carmen's little game.

Zita.

He couldn't read her expression—that was another way they were alike. But for a split second, he could've sworn he saw disappointment in her gaze. And that killed him. He didn't want her to think he'd encouraged Carmen in any way. That the kiss she'd given him had been something he wanted.

He took a few steps toward her, but someone called her name and she abruptly turned and walked in the opposite direction.

Obi-Wan was left holding two cups of coffee while people milled around him. He felt like he'd somehow let Zita down, even though he hadn't intentionally done anything.

Fucking hell. The day that had started out rough wasn't getting any better.

For the next two hours, he watched the current scenes being filmed, approved the military uniform Logan would be wearing when he shot various scenes later in the schedule, went over the timetable for the mountain shoot in a couple weeks, and even got a sneak peek of some of the footage that had been shot the first day he was on set.

He should've been getting more and more excited about the trip to the western part of the state. Instead, all he could think about was what Zita must think of him after what she'd witnessed earlier that morning. How she probably thought everything he'd told her about not wanting a relationship was bullshit. Maybe even thought he'd played her to make Carmen jealous or something.

It wasn't like Obi-Wan to let his feelings get the better of him. But by the time he was free of his obligations on the set, he was almost desperate to find Zita and explain what she'd seen that morning. Desperate for her to know that he in no way, shape, or form wanted to be with Carmen.

That it was *Zita* he was interested in getting to know better.

If nothing else, this morning had served as a wake-up call. She'd completely avoided him on set, and the odd feeling that he was losing Zita before they'd even had any kind of real relationship was a punch to the gut.

He might not have wanted to date anyone when he'd started this job a week ago, but now Obi-Wan was willing to entertain the idea. But only with Zita.

It was still highly possible they'd get to know each other better and find out they were no more compatible than a bird and a fish...but he wanted to find out.

However, it was obvious she was still trying to avoid him, because she ducked out a side door as soon as he started walking toward her. But Obi-Wan was determined to talk to her before he left today. He didn't want to have any misunderstandings between them. Wanted to explain what she really saw that morning between him and Carmen.

Spinning around, Obi-Wan jogged toward the nearest door. He shoved it open and ran around the building toward where Zita had exited. As he hoped, she hadn't gone far. Had probably just left in the hopes that when she went back inside, he'd have gone for the day, as usual.

Thankfully, she was also alone. She was sitting in the area the smokers used when they came outside, staring into space.

"Hey," Obi-Wan said quietly as he approached.

He hadn't meant to scare her, but she jerked all the same and whipped her head around to stare at him.

He held his hands up. "Sorry, sorry, sorry. I thought you heard me coming."

She shrugged. "I didn't. But it's okay. Shouldn't you be heading back to the base?"

Obi-Wan winced, not liking that she was obviously trying to dismiss him. He sat next to her, leaving plenty of space between them on the bench. The last thing he wanted to do was crowd her, but he needed her to hear him out.

He decided not to beat around the bush.

"What you saw this morning wasn't what you think."

"I don't know what you're talking about," she said, a little too nonchalantly.

"I was looking for you, to give you your coffee, and she took the opportunity to waylay me. *She* kissed *me*. Not the other way around."

"Okay."

Obi-Wan studied her. She wouldn't meet his gaze.

"Zita. Look at me. Please."

It took a beat, but she eventually lifted her chin and met his gaze head on. He could see the anger in her expression. But also...sorrow? She was killing him, and he needed to make this right.

"My hands were full. I couldn't push her away, not without making a scene. And I know better than to humiliate her. She could make my life, and everyone else's around her, completely miserable. She kissed me. I didn't want it or invite it."

"She wants you," Zita said plainly.

"Yes. But she's not going to get me," Obi-Wan said firmly. "There's only one woman on this set I want to get to know. And it's not Carmen St. James."

It took a split second for his words to sink in, and Obi-Wan saw the moment they did. Disbelief overtook the other emotions in her eyes.

He pressed on. "You're the one I asked to come to Anchor

Point. Not her. You're the one I bring coffee to every morning. Not her. You're the one I look for when I first get to the set. *Not her.* Please believe me when I tell you that what you saw, was Carmen doing her best to seduce a very unwilling partner."

"She's famous. And rich."

"Yeah."

"I'm not."

"Neither am I. Is that a problem?"

"No."

"I'm sorry I didn't get your coffee to you this morning. I'll make up for it tomorrow," he told her.

Zita shrugged. "I was avoiding you."

"I know."

She sighed. "I think I owe you an apology. I thought the worst of you without giving you a chance to defend yourself. But you have to understand...I've seen guy after guy fall for her, even when they claim they don't want her."

"I get it. But when I say something, I mean it. Well, except..." His voice trailed off, and Obi-Wan couldn't believe he was going to admit this. But he needed this woman to trust him. To believe him when he said something important in the future.

"Except what?" she asked with a tilt of her head.

"I meant it at the time, but I'm taking it back. I said I wasn't interested in dating anyone."

"You *are* interested in dating?"

"Yes. But only you."

Her eyes widened. "Doesn't that seem a little...premature? Presumptuous? What if *I* don't want to date?"

Obi-Wan held her gaze. "It's probably a little of both. And trust me, it's as shocking to me as it apparently is to you right now. I didn't accept this job with the intention of hooking up with someone on set, or dating anyone I met. But here we are."

"So now you're saying you want to hook up with me? Again, that seems like a one-sided decision."

Obi-Wan closed his eyes for a moment and ran a hand over his head. He was screwing this up royally. "Shit," he mumbled. "I should've stayed in bed this morning."

"Bad day?" Zita asked.

"You have no idea. Look, all I'm saying is that I'd like to retract my statement about not wanting to date anyone. But the only person I'm remotely interested in getting to know better is *you*. I'm not saying we'll fall madly in love and elope and have fourteen babies. But I'm open to the possibility. I don't want you to think I'm going out of my way to ask you to come to Anchor Point and meet my friends without wanting to further our friendship. That's not the kind of man I am. I'm trying to be open and honest here."

For the first time, Zita's shoulders relaxed a little and her facial expression softened. "I'm sorry. I'm being horrible. I...it's just...I've been screwed over more than once, and I'm a little gun-shy about getting to know people while on set."

"I understand. I won't presume to know how you feel, but it sounds a lot like when my team and I are on a mission on a naval ship. We meet lots of people, some very nice men and women, but we're always very careful to keep lines drawn because we're well aware we won't be there very long. And it's extremely difficult to keep any kind of friendship going once we leave those ships. Not impossible, but not easy for sure."

Zita nodded. Then asked, "You haven't had a good day?"

"No. PT was brutal, something's up with my team leader and his girlfriend, and that's concerning. I think I've still got sand in my underwear from this morning, then there was Carmen, the coffee I got for you went to waste, it's gross out here, even though it's much better now than it was when I first got to the set, and I have an afternoon of meetings ahead of me."

"I'm sorry."

Obi-Wan shrugged. "Will you still come to Anchor Point

tonight? No pressure. Just a night away from work, the set, and you can get out of your motel for a while."

"What, you don't think the Ocean Side Inn is exciting?"

"The Ocean Side Inn? Carmen said she was staying at the Cavalier."

"*She* is. Logan and the director too. The rest of us lowly staff are at a budget motel."

That made sense, but it still irritated Obi-Wan. He let it go because it wasn't as if he could do anything about it. "You'll come?" he pressed, really really *really* wanting her to say yes. "I can pick you up if you want. I'm assuming you don't have a car here."

"I don't. Don't need one. The set isn't that far and it's nice to get some fresh air and exercise in the mornings and afternoons by walking to and from the motel."

She was killing him with the non-answers. Obi-Wan didn't press again. Actually, he wanted to beg, but that wasn't who he was. If she didn't want to come to the bar tonight, she didn't want to come to the bar.

"What time?" she asked.

Elation hit him *hard*. "Seven? We usually don't stay too long. Maybe until around ten or so if we're not too tired. But I'm guessing tonight might be an early night."

"Okay."

"Okay?"

She smiled and nodded. "Yeah. I'll wait for you at the main doors of the lobby at the Ocean Side Inn. Seven. Don't be late."

"I'm never late," Obi-Wan informed her. "And thank you. My day's looking up already."

She rolled her eyes. "And, Sage, you don't have to bring me coffee every morning."

"Do you like it?"

"Of course. What's not to like?"

"I'll make sure to have an extra-large cup tomorrow, to make up for not getting yours to you today."

"It was my fault you couldn't find me to give it to me."

Obi-Wan simply shrugged.

"You're different from pretty much any man I've been around before."

"Good." He didn't bother to ask in what way. He hoped she meant it as a compliment, but he wasn't going to push his luck.

The door behind them opened and two men and a woman came out. Both he and Zita stood, surrendering the table to the smokers. They took a few steps away before Obi-Wan said, "Looks like this is my cue to get going. I'll see you tonight. Seven sharp."

"Wait, I know you said Anchor Point is a dive bar, but just to make sure...I'm not going to be out of place in my cargo pants, T-shirt, and sneakers, am I? I don't need to wear cowboy boots or daisy dukes, right?" She was grinning when she said it.

Obi-Wan couldn't stop his gaze from running up and down her body. He admired her physique all over again. She was curvy in all the right places, petite compared to him, which he loved. "What you've got on now is perfect...but maybe let your hair down."

Taking a chance, he reached out and took her hand in his, giving it a short squeeze before dropping it and turning to head for his Jeep in the parking lot.

He looked back once to see Zita standing where he'd left her, staring after him with an unreadable look on her face. The smokers sitting at the table were staring at him as well. He gave them all a chin lift, then turned back toward the parking lot with a small smile on his face.

For a day that had started out so shitty, it had definitely picked up in the last twenty minutes.

CHAPTER SIX

"Wear my hair down...whatever," Zita muttered to herself as she stared into the mirror in the small bathroom at the motel.

She'd spent the last twenty minutes trying to decide what to do with her hair after she'd showered and blown it dry. She actually liked her hair...liked the auburn color...but no matter how hard she tried, it always ended up losing any curl she put in before going out. It was straight as a board. Everyone always wanted the kind of hair they didn't have, and she was no exception. Zita would kill for some natural curl of some sort.

She usually put her hair up in some sort of ponytail, bun, or in a thick braid that fell down her back, to keep it out of her face while she was working.

But Sage's words kept going through her mind. He wanted to see her hair down, and Zita couldn't deny that she wanted to look nice for him tonight. Wanted to make a good impression with his friends. It was obvious they meant a lot to him. That he respected them. So she brushed her auburn locks until they shone and left it down. As he'd requested.

Zita tried to tell herself that this wasn't a date. It was simply her hanging out with someone she'd met at work and wanted to be friends with. Something to do to change things up. Sitting alone in her room every night wasn't the most exciting thing in the world, and she was looking forward to getting out for once. To spending time with people who weren't involved in the film industry. It was cutthroat, and even though she was on the peripheral with her job as a medic, she still felt the stress that came from being on set, constantly competing with others for jobs and attention from those who could further their careers.

But she was lying to herself, and she knew it. Sage intrigued her. He seemed to have his shit together. He was a hotshot Night Stalker. Had a good job. Friends. Was extremely good-looking and fit. And yet today opened her eyes to the fact that he was still very much human.

He'd shared enough of his life and experiences with her that she already knew he was nothing like many of the actors and actresses who starred in the shows and movies she worked on. They would pretend they didn't have anxiety and were completely put together at all times. That wasn't Sage. Not at all.

But seeing Carmen kiss him? Thinking he'd allowed it? That had been a blow.

She'd enjoyed their mornings together, and the attraction she'd felt toward him from the first day they'd met had only grown. So she'd been crushed by that kiss. Had even thought he might've been playing her, lying about his disinterest and simply biding his time until he could get close to Carmen.

Zita felt bad for doubting him...and foolish. She could tell he was sincere when he'd explained that the actress had cornered him. And when she thought about it, Carmen had been hitting on him *hard* since day one. If Sage wanted her, he could have had her ten times by now.

With a little more thought, she realized he *had* taken a step back this morning, to no avail. And his hands *had* been full, holding on to their coffees...the coffee he'd faithfully brought to her every morning for days. It was a sweet gesture, and even though she told him he didn't need to keep doing it, he still did.

Her attraction to Sage hadn't waned. Not in the least. If anything, after today and his explanation of the encounter between him and Carmen, it had grown. And knowing he occasionally got grumpy just like everyone else made him seem more down to earth. More approachable.

Though, Zita had a feeling that, like a certain actress, Sage was *also* used to getting what he wanted, that he didn't often hear the word no...as evidenced by her getting ready to go to the bar he frequented with his pilot friends. But she didn't think he was the kind of man to take advantage or to continue to push if someone truly didn't want to spend time with him.

In short? Obadiah Engle was possibly the most interesting man Zita had ever met. He had more depth than you'd think just looking at him. He had layers, and each one she discovered intrigued Zita more and more. She couldn't wait to see who he was around his friends. Was he a jokester? The rowdy type? Did he have a wandering eye when he'd had a beer or two? Would he want to play pool or darts and be uber competitive? Was he respectful to the men and women who worked in the bar?

There were so many things she could find out about him tonight, and she was looking forward to it more than she wanted to admit.

She found herself ready to go fifteen minutes before seven. It was too soon to go to the lobby to wait, so she paced her small room, trying to work off some of her nervous energy. She still wasn't sure if this was a date. Sage had taken back his adamant assertion that he wasn't interested in dating, but that didn't necessarily mean *this* was a date. He was probably just doing what *she* was doing—seeing if the crazy feelings she had anytime they were together could amount to anything. After all, he was still taking her to a bar where he hung out with his buddies. Not to mention, all those friends would be there as well.

Did a man invite a woman out for drinks, then invite his best friends?

She doubted it. And that thought took some of the pressure off the night for her, which was a relief.

Looking down at herself, Zita winced, realizing her clothing choices might belie her thoughts. She'd clearly gone out of her way to impress Sage, despite trying to convince herself this was a friends thing. Her jeans were tight—and very flattering on her curves, if she did say so herself. She'd chosen a green shirt that she always got compliments on. It was sleeveless with a high neck, and there was absolutely no cleavage showing, but it still brought attention to her boobs, which were currently nestled in a bra that pushed them up and together. The color also looked fantastic with her hair and skin tone.

On her feet, she'd donned her favorite pair of watermelon-colored light canvas shoes with cream polka dots. They didn't match the shirt exactly, but she didn't care. Seeing them on her feet never failed to make her smile.

Taking a deep breath and deciding it was too late to change, Zita grabbed her purse. She'd made sure her phone was charged for the night, she had extra cash, as well as the usual things she carried around...trauma shears, gloves, medical tape, a small first-aid kit, her penlight, glucose tablets, and a pocketknife.

Past boyfriends had made fun of her for carrying that kind of stuff everywhere she went, but Zita had been in plenty of situations where she'd needed to use something. She couldn't turn off her medical knowledge, and she would never sit back and watch someone hurting if she could do something to help.

Putting the strap of the crossbody bag over her head, she left her room on the ground floor and headed down the sidewalk, toward the motel lobby.

She probably shouldn't've been surprised to see Sage already parked there, standing on the passenger side of his Jeep Wrangler, waiting for her...and yet she was. Looking at her phone, she saw he was almost ten minutes early.

Relieved she wouldn't have to pace the lobby, letting her anxiousness about the upcoming night rise, she smiled as she headed for him.

"Hi," she said when she got close.

His gaze ran from the top of her head down to her shoes, then back up. And the appreciation and pleasure in his gaze warmed her from the inside out.

"Hey," he returned. "You left your hair down."

Feeling a little self-conscious, Zita ran a hand down the silky-soft strands. "Yeah."

"It's beautiful. I knew it would be. And longer than I expected."

Her hair *was* long. It went midway down her back and chest, which was why she wore it up when she worked. The last thing she needed was her hair getting in the way of CPR or bandaging a bloody wound.

"Love the shoes too."

Zita smiled. Had she ever had a man compliment her eclectic taste in footwear? No. Usually the guys rolled their eyes or asked if she was trying to relive her childhood. Because Zita had quite the collection of bright-colored canvas shoes. All different brands. The brighter the better. They made her smile. And she needed as many things as possible in her life that made her happy, since her job was damn tough at times.

"Thanks. They're one of my favorite pairs," Zita said, sticking her foot out so he could see it better, and so she could admire the shoe for herself.

"You ready to go?"

"Yup."

Sage opened the door and held it for her as she climbed inside the Jeep. He pulled the seat belt down and handed it to her, which was an extremely polite and caring gesture. It wasn't as if Zita would ever ride in a car without a seat belt, but it was nice of him to assist her in getting it on.

He walked around the front of the Jeep and got behind the wheel, putting his own seat belt on before turning on the engine and heading out of the parking lot.

It was a nice night, and the windows were rolled down slightly, letting in the fresh evening air, but not making it impossible to talk over the sound of the wind.

"How did the rest of your day go?" Zita asked. "I hope it got better."

Sage winced. "Well, if you call being in meetings all day, and Edge spilling his coffee all over me *better*, then yes."

Zita couldn't help but giggle. It was kind of rude to laugh at his misfortune, but she couldn't help it.

He turned to her and smiled, letting her know he wasn't offended by her chuckles.

"He didn't do it on purpose, did he? Edge?"

"No. Of course not. He was reaching for a map on the table and bumped it. Thankfully it wasn't full, but we all still scrambled to get the maps out of the way of the liquid so they wouldn't be ruined. Apparently the table isn't as level as we thought, because the coffee—cold coffee, thank God—made a beeline for where I was sitting and ended up in my lap."

Zita could picture the scene, and her smile widened. "At least tell me you got the sand out of your underwear."

"Finally, yes. Took a long shower after getting home tonight, and I'm pretty sure I got it all...until tomorrow morning, when Casper decides to make us all sugar cookies again, just to be a dick."

That made Zita laugh out loud.

"He's been stressed out for some reason, and none of us know why. And we've noticed that Laryn, his girlfriend, has been cranky as well. Something has to give, because while we respect and admire Casper, we don't like being treated as if we're privates in basic all over again. He needs to lighten up, for his sake *and* ours."

"Will he be there tonight?" Zita asked.

"He should be. When I reminded everyone about tonight before we left base, he said he and Laryn would do their best to be there."

Zita hoped the tension between the team leader and the rest of his friends wouldn't be too awkward. If they had some beef with him, the last place she wanted to be was in the middle of it.

"Buck and Mandy will be there as well. And the rest of the guys."

"Can you remind me of their names?"

"Sure. Pyro, Chaos, and Edge. Casper and Pyro usually fly together, as do me and Buck, and Chaos and Edge."

"Do you always fly with the same person? Are you assigned to them?"

"Not all the time. We can fly with anyone. And we're able to interchange who's the pilot and who's the copilot, as well. We all know the roles and duties of both positions. But we're comfortable in the current configurations, so why switch it up? We aren't assigned, per se, but if we had to choose, those are likely the partners we'd pick. Because they work. And we're all damn good together."

There was so much about helicopters that Zita had no clue about. And the Night Stalkers were even more mysterious. All she knew was that they were the best of the best, and they were sent into dangerous missions around the world. Which wasn't comforting, but it did make her proud of the man sitting next to her. It was hard for her to imagine him being in full gear, dodging bullets and RPGs as he flew in and around mountainous terrain while he dropped off or picked up teams of special forces soldiers. That kind of situation seemed a million miles away from the cozy and intimate atmosphere of his car.

"Did you always want to be a Night Stalker?"

"Hell no. I mean, I've always loved flying, but I wanted to be a commercial pilot." He grinned. "But I got bored in college. One of my friends was joining the Army and somehow talked me into joining with him. It was extremely rash, but it also changed my life for the better. I would've been bored to tears flying planes from one airport to another. There's no bigger rush than being behind the controls of my chopper and swerving around missiles and mountain peaks while successfully picking up our brave men and women on the ground. You probably think that's crazy."

Zita shrugged. "I mean, it's not the same at all, but it sounds a lot like the feeling I get when I come up on a really bad scene, and there are people screaming for help and I have to triage the situation and figure out who needs the quickest assistance. The adrenaline that courses through my veins when I get someone's heart started after being flatlined. When I can stop blood spurting through a severed artery.

"Sometimes, after delivering a patient to the hospital and coming back out to my ambulance and seeing every inch covered in blood, vomit, and other bodily fluids, I wonder why any sane human would do what I do. But then I remember the lives I've saved, the mothers who'll live to see their children again, and husbands and wives who'll get to spend more time with their loved ones. It makes all the yucky stuff a little more bearable."

She felt a little silly when she was done speaking, comparing her job to what *Sage* did. But to her relief, he simply nodded in agreement.

"Adrenaline is a strange thing. What we both do is a little crazy, huh?"

She snorted. "Just a little."

"You like working on the ambulance when you aren't on set?"

Zita nodded. "Yeah. Even though I spend most of my time on sets, and make most of my money there, I find working shifts on the ambulance is a good break from all the travel that comes with a job in the film industry—not to mention some of the egos. Conversely, movie sets are a good way to force me to pace myself. I know far too many paramedics and EMTs who've burned out by working day in and day out on an ambulance, experiencing the extreme highs and extreme lows."

"Where's your home base?"

"Right now, Hollywood. But I've been thinking about moving."

"Yeah?"

"Yes. For a while now. I don't know if you've been out to Hollywood or not, but it's...different."

"I haven't been there. Different how?"

"The drug problem is out of control. And it's not just the homeless who are afflicted. I mean, yes, we go on a lot of calls for people passed out in the streets next to their tents or shopping carts. But it's rich people too. People are shooting up left and right. It's wild. We use more Narcan than you could probably imagine. And yet, the next day, week, whatever, we see the same people, and we have to bring them back to life all over again. I get that addiction is a disease and it's extremely difficult to overcome, but as a paramedic, it's tiring and disheartening."

"I can't imagine. Where would you like to move to?"

"I have no idea. That's mostly why I haven't left yet. And before you say it, I know there are drugs everywhere, but I'd love to find a place where I could use my skills for more than just administering Narcan. Maybe somewhere a little less populated. I don't want rural, because I'd probably be bored, so I'd want to be in a city somewhere. Just not like LA."

"Would that hurt your chances of working on sets?"

"I don't think so. I mean, I can always fly to where I need to be, where a show or movie is filming. I might not get as *many* gigs. For instance, I'd probably no longer get jobs filming in California. And eventually, if I'm not in LA where the unions reps and agents are, I could fade from their memories entirely. But I don't think I'd mind that so much."

"You have family?"

Zita liked this. Liked how interested Sage seemed in her life. Too many dates, she'd been the one asking all the questions and listening all night to a man talking about nothing but himself.

"Nope. I hatched from a pod on an alien world and was dropped off here on Earth."

The burst of laughter from Sage made Zita's lips curl up into a huge grin.

"Knew there was something different about you the first time we met," Sage said, without missing a beat.

"Of *course* I have a family. I mean, I guess there's no 'of course' about it, since some people don't. My parents live in West Lafayette, Indiana. They're both professors at Purdue University. I have a younger brother, Chris. He's married, lives in Monticello, which is a little north of Lafayette. He works at a car factory. No kids yet, but he and his wife are actively trying to change that, according to Chris. Which is way too much info. Thinking about my dorky little brother having sex is enough to make me want to puke. But I know my parents are anxiously awaiting the day when they'll be grandparents. I think they've written me off on giving them any grandkids, so my brother's their last hope. What about you?"

"No siblings. My parents live in Colorado Springs. My dad's an engineer, and my mom hasn't worked...ever? She raised me, and she's involved in all sorts of volunteer work and charity things. I don't think they're super close, but their relationship seems to work."

"Colorado Springs...isn't the Air Force Academy there? Is that where you got your love of flying?"

"It is, and not really. We took a trip to Disneyland when I

was little, and I got to go up to the cockpit and sit in the pilot's seat. I got my picture taken with him, and he gave me the little plastic wings pin they give to kids, and that was it. Seeing all those buttons and levers, and realizing the people who sat up there and flew the plane knew how to use them all, was fascinating to me."

"And now here you are," Zita said with a small smile. "Flying helicopters."

"Yup."

"I have one more question."

"Shoot."

"Do you still have the pin you got that day?"

"Of course," Sage said, looking over at her with a huge grin on his face. "It's in a box under my bed with all the medals I've earned in my career."

Zita had no idea if he was kidding or not, but figured he probably wasn't. "Awesome."

"Yeah. We're almost there."

Looking out the front windshield, Zita saw a building with extremely bright lights ahead and to the right, covering the entire parking area.

"Wow, you could land your chopper right there in the parking lot," she joked.

But Sage didn't even crack a smile. "Mandy was attacked in the lot one night, several months back, and since there were hardly any lights, Buck didn't see it coming. After a large donation by a former SEAL we know, the owner put in the high-powered lights to try to ensure no one else gets attacked on his property again."

Zita felt horrible that her joke was apparently in such poor taste. "I'm so sorry. I didn't know."

"It's okay. And yes, the lights are a little bit overkill, but no one complains. Not even the people living in the houses nearby. I think they're probably relieved, because this neighborhood hasn't been the best at times. But it's slowly getting better."

"She's okay though? Mandy?" Sage had talked about the other woman a few times, and Zita still felt horrible that she'd made such an offensive offhand remark about someone he cared for.

"She's good. Took a bit for her to recover, but she's been amazingly resilient. She's currently long-term subbing at a school on the naval base, but Buck told us the other day that there's a full-time slot opening for a first-grade teacher at the same school next year that she'll almost certainly get."

"That's great."

"It is. She's the kind of teacher I'd want for my kids. Caring, compassionate, and determined to make their school experience a good one."

Sage parked his Jeep toward the back of the lot, under one of the bright lights. He turned to her before he opened his door. "Ready?"

"Ready," Zita told him. And she was. The more she learned about his friends—and him—the more she wanted to know.

Sage nodded and reached for his door handle. Zita did the same, and they met at the front of the Jeep. She could hear music coming from the bar as the door opened and closed, with people entering and exiting. It seemed like a popular place, which was a good sign. In her experience, the more rundown a place looked from the outside, the better the food and atmosphere. And the fact that it was so busy also said a lot about it...all good things.

Even with her nerves, Zita was glad she'd agreed to come with Sage. Not only because she was getting to know him better, but because she loved learning about the soul of a town or city.

The more she saw of Norfolk, the more she liked. There was an interesting mix of military men and women, minorities, income levels. Zita had visited a lot of cities and towns thanks to her career, had seen the good, bad, and ugly, and she felt as if she was a good judge of a location's character. And she got nothing but good vibes from the city on the coast of Virginia.

She shifted her purse around her body and smiled at Sage as he held the door open for her. Taking a deep breath, she walked inside, excited about the upcoming night and meeting Sage's friends.

CHAPTER SEVEN

Obi-Wan was pleased at how things were going so far. He and Zita had talked nonstop on the way to Anchor Point, which was a good sign. He'd been on some dates where he'd had to do all the talking, or where the woman he was with wouldn't shut up, blabbering on and on and trying too hard to give a good impression of herself.

Zita was down-to-earth and relaxed. She was interesting, and funny, and obviously had a good head on her shoulders. He already knew she was a hard worker, which he appreciated and admired. And he couldn't deny that he was physically attracted to the woman.

He knew her hair would be beautiful if she ever let it out of its normal tight bun—and it was. The green shirt she wore complemented the auburn shade, and all he wanted to do was bury his hand in all that hair to see if it was as soft as it looked.

Thankfully, he was able to restrain himself, because that would be weird and probably send her running in the other direction.

They were clicking on a level he didn't experience often when dating. When she'd taken what he'd said about the adrenaline rush he got from flying in extreme situations and compared it to her own experiences, his respect for her grew. No, the two situations couldn't *really* be compared, but just as she probably couldn't imagine what he experienced during *his* job, he couldn't fathom the things she must see on a regular basis.

He hoped she got along with his friends. It would be extremely difficult to date anyone who didn't mesh with the people he spent the majority of his time with, both in and out of work. He couldn't imagine why she wouldn't click with them though. Everything he knew about her told him tonight would go just fine. He hoped.

Anchor Point was fairly crowded for this early in the evening, but looking around, Obi-Wan saw his teammates had taken over one corner of the bar. They'd pushed two tables together so they'd all fit, something they hadn't had to worry about before Laryn and Mandy joined their crew.

"Hey!"

"Glad you could make it."

"Hi, Zita! Cool name."

The greetings came fast and furious, and Obi-Wan quickly made introductions. Since he'd already told Zita about his friends, she didn't seem confused or overwhelmed, which was a relief.

"Hi!" she said with an open and friendly smile. "It's good to meet you all."

There were two seats open next to Casper and Laryn, and Obi-Wan quickly saw that whatever was bothering their team leader and his girlfriend apparently still wasn't resolved. They both looked stressed, although they were holding hands, so he hoped that meant whatever was going on, it wasn't an imminent break-up. He hated to think of them not being together...especially after it took years for Casper to get his head out of his butt and realize what was right in front of him.

There were two pitchers of beer on the table, and the women both had glasses of what looked like iced tea in front of them.

"Beer?" Chaos asked both him and Zita, with a raised brow.

"Definitely," Obi-Wan told him. It was early, so he knew he could have a glass and still be okay to drive Zita home in a couple of hours.

"Zita?"

"Um...I'm not much of a beer drinker. I can go to the bar and order something," she said, sounding uncomfortable for the first time.

"Just tell me what you want, and I'll go get it."

"Oh, I can do it."

"Of course you can," he said with a small smile. "But I'd be happy to do it for you. Unless you aren't ready to be alone with these weirdos." Obi-Wan smiled, letting her know he was kidding.

"Oh, no, it's not that. I'm more than happy to sit on my butt and let you wait on me. I just don't want to be one of *those* women. You know, who assumes the guy should do everything while she sits on her fancy throne and lords over him."

Everyone around the tables laughed.

"It's good for him to be lorded over," Buck said.

"Please, sit on your butt," Casper added. "Boy's gotten soft hanging out on that fancy movie set every morning."

Obi-Wan rolled his eyes. "Whatever." Then he looked back at Zita. "What can I get you?"

"Is that *tea*-tea, or loaded tea?" she asked Laryn and Mandy.

"Just regular tea," Laryn told her.

Zita's brow furrowed slightly for a moment before she smoothed out her expression. "Tea's fine for me too," she told Obi-Wan.

He leaned toward her, holding her gaze as he said, "If you want something with alcohol, get it. Just because the others aren't drinking doesn't mean you have to abstain."

"Yeah, I'm fully planning on getting a lemon drop next, but the kids at school were extra energetic today, and I didn't drink nearly as much water as I usually do, so I thought it was in my best interest to have some tea before any alcohol to make sure I don't get dehydrated."

"Oh, that's smart. Too many people dismiss how a lack of water in their system can really play havoc on their body," Zita said with a nod.

"Always good to have a paramedic around," Edge said with a grin.

"Is it okay with *you* if I have a drink?" Zita asked Laryn. "I know sometimes people feel awkward when they aren't drinking and others are."

She looked surprised. "It's none of my business if you drink," Laryn told her.

"Why aren't *you* partaking?" Pyro asked their mechanic. "You always have a beer or two with us."

To Obi-Wan's surprise, Laryn's cheeks heated. She bit her bottom lip and wouldn't meet the eyes of anyone around the table.

"Laryn? Are you okay?" Buck asked, leaning forward with a look of concern on his face.

"She's fine," Casper answered for her. "We weren't going to say anything, but...you guys are our family. We just found out this week—Laryn's pregnant."

Silence greeted the announcement for a split second—then everyone spoke at once.

"Holy shit, *pregnant*?"

"Congrats!"

"That's awesome...isn't it?"

"Wow! I take it this is a surprise?"

When everyone quieted down, Laryn said, "We were going to wait to mention it. We wanted to have some time to sit with the news, just us for a while."

"This is why you've been so stressed out," Mandy said softly. "You admitted that much to me the other day when I called, but you didn't say why."

"Yeah."

"We're happy. Ecstatic. It's just been a little overwhelming. The change in our plans and all," Casper explained.

"I can imagine," Mandy said. She reached across the small table and took Laryn's hand in hers. "But you're okay? Healthy?"

Laryn gave her a small smile. "Yeah. I'm good. Thanks. And for the record, even though he or she wasn't planned, we couldn't be happier."

"Coulda fooled me," Edge mumbled under his breath.

"Happy, but stressed about everything it's gonna mean," Casper clarified.

"I don't want to *not* be deployed with you guys," Laryn explained. "When the colonel finds out I'm pregnant, he's probably going to take me off the rotation, and I can't stand the thought of Tate, or any of you guys, going anywhere without me there to troubleshoot. That sounds conceited as hell, but I know your choppers like the back of my hand, and there's no one who'll work harder than me to make sure they're battle ready.

"And then there's what will happen after the baby's born. Will I be allowed to be deployed with you at all? Do we even *want* both of us to be deployed at the same time? If we are, what will we do with the baby? It's not as if we can stick them in a kennel like we would a dog. I *love* my job, and I don't want to have to quit."

"I keep telling her that we'll figure it out," Casper said, rubbing Laryn's back lovingly. "We've got some time to make plans before the baby arrives."

"I'm more than willing to help out," Mandy said. "Aunt Mandy will spoil your kid rotten while you're gone, and when you get a little heathen back, you'll wonder where the calm, rational child you left behind has gone."

Everyone chuckled.

"Thanks, Mandy. I told her that my dad will be thrilled to come up and babysit while we're gone, as well. He's gonna dote on his first grandchild. And if Nate's not busy, he'll be willing to help out too."

"Your brother is a SEAL," Laryn said in exasperation. "He's got just as hectic a schedule as you do. He's not going to be able to drop everything to babysit."

It sounded as if they'd had this conversation before. At least now Obi-Wan knew why they'd both been stressed out recently. Having a kid was a huge deal. It would mean a drastic change in their routine. And Laryn was right, their jobs would be a challenge to work around when it came to childcare.

"I might know someone who could help out," Zita blurted.

All eyes turned to stare at her.

"I mean, I know we *literally* just met and all, but there are always actors and actresses on the sets I work on who have kids. And yes, while they have the luxury of bringing them to the sets sometimes, and traveling with them, they can't be by their sides all day. There are women I've met who're professional nannies for babies and kids on set. I've talked to them a little, and often they stay in the hotels, near the parents, so they're always available."

"We wouldn't be able to afford a full-time nanny," Laryn said.

"They aren't as expensive as you think, since room and board are considered part of their salary. I know it might be weird to leave someone in your house, with your child, but if you got to know the person from day one, and trusted them, it could be a solution. Think of it like a rent-a-granny or something."

Everyone chuckled at that.

"That could possibly work. And I could go over every day to check on things," Mandy added. "Maybe take night duty or something."

"I couldn't ask that of you," Laryn said, with tears in her eyes.

"Whatever. Any time I get with your baby will be a blessing, and *I'd* be the lucky one."

"I just don't want to have to quit my job. I want a baby, but I love what I do," Laryn said tearfully.

"I think women everywhere have the same feelings as you," Chaos said gently. "There are enough smart people sitting around this table that I'm sure we can figure something out by the time it might become an issue."

"You're right. I'm just...stressed. Hormones, you know," Laryn said.

Casper put his arm around Laryn and pulled her into his side. She rested her head on his shoulder and sighed.

"And before any of you assholes ask, yes, we're getting married. That was always in our plans, but the baby sped that up a bit. There'll be a lot of doctor visits, to make sure Laryn and the baby are okay, and I want her to have all the health benefits being married to me will give her."

"Doesn't she have those with her job now?" Obi-Wan asked. He wasn't being an asshole, he was truly wondering.

"That's what I told Tate," Laryn said, sitting up.

"So you don't *want* to get married?" Chaos asked, sounding confused.

"Of course I do. I love him. But I don't want to *have* to get married."

"It doesn't *sound* like you have to get married," Pyro chimed in. "You've got health insurance, you're living together, what else will getting a piece of paper give you?"

"Shut the hell up," Casper complained.

Laryn giggled, and the sound was a nice break in the tension that had surrounded the friends.

"I keep telling her that this changes nothing about our plans, just moves them up a little. She's the love of my life, and if something happens to me, I want her and our baby to receive all the benefits that come with being my spouse. You all know as well as

I do that spouses in the Army have more rights than non-spouses."

He wasn't wrong about that. It was possible that if they weren't married, and something happened to Casper while on an op, no one would come to Laryn's home to tell her. Unlikely, but possible.

"And I'm going to officially ask her. It's gonna be uber romantic. And she's gonna remember the proposal for the rest of her days, and tell our kids and grandkids all about how their dad and grampa went out of his way to make the most important question of her life memorable."

"So you have it planned?" Pyro asked with a grin. "Can we help?"

"No, and no," Casper growled.

Obi-Wan chuckled.

"Don't embarrass me," Laryn told Casper with a scowl.

"Wouldn't dream of it."

"And no asking when we're in bed either. Because I'm not telling our kids or grandkids about *that*."

Laughter once more rang out around their tables.

"Please tell me that with the big secret out, Casper's going to be less of a dick and PT won't be quite so horrible from now on," Buck muttered.

"Don't count on it," Casper informed him.

Everyone groaned.

Obi-Wan leaned into Zita once more. He was worried that all this drama was going to turn her off from wanting to hang out with his friends. Her idea of a live-in nanny was a good one, but if it was *his* kid, he wasn't sure he'd trust someone he hired like that with his baby. He'd worry about what was happening the whole time he was gone.

"You still want a drink?"

She turned to him with a sheepish smile. "I didn't mean to start a whole...brouhaha," she said. "All I wanted to know was if it was okay with Laryn if I had a drink."

Obi-Wan smiled at her. She was adorable. And he loved how considerate she was. "I think it's safe to say that she's okay with you having whatever the hell you want. Now, what can I get you?"

"Diet Coke and rum, please."

"You got it." He couldn't resist the urge to lean in closer, until his lips were almost touching her ear, and saying, "Thank you for being so cool with this. I swear it's not usually so...heavy around us."

The hand she placed on his knee felt as if it was burning through his jeans. "It's fine, Sage. Promise. When the medics and I get together while on duty, you'd probably be scandalized at how raw our casual talk is. All about medical procedures and bodily fluids and stuff."

Obi-Wan pulled back and chuckled. "Not much scandalizes me. I'll be right back."

Then he stood and asked if anyone wanted anything from the bar. When everyone said they were good, he headed across the crowded room to get the drink for Zita.

By the time he got back, with both the Diet Coke and rum and a lemon drop for Mandy, talk had settled into more mundane topics. Zita was talking about the film and what she did on set. Everyone was laughing at the story she was telling about the extra she'd had to dose with Zofran, to get her to stop throwing up from nerves after being near Logan Striker.

"Thanks," Zita said with a small smile as Obi-Wan put the drink down in front of her.

"You didn't have to get me a lemon drop, but I appreciate it," Mandy told him.

Obi-Wan nodded at her and leaned back in his chair, one arm resting on the back of Zita's as he took a sip of the beer Pyro poured for him.

"So, tell the truth. Were you weirded out when Obi-Wan told you that we'd all be here tonight?" Edge asked.

"Why would she be weirded out?" Buck asked.

"Seriously?" Edge asked, with an incredulous look on his face.

"Yeah."

"Maybe because going on a date with all your buddies isn't normal?" Edge said.

Buck frowned.

And Mandy giggled.

He looked at his girlfriend, seeming completely befuddled. "I'm missing the joke."

"Dude, you did the same thing," Chaos informed him. "Brought Mandy to Anchor Point on your first ever date—with all of us in attendance."

Buck looked from Mandy, to Chaos, to Zita, then back at Mandy.

"It's okay," Mandy said, taking pity on him. "I wanted to meet all the friends you talked about while we were in the jungle."

"I...It's... I just wanted to share the most important people in my life with you," Buck said, looking exasperated. "I totally should've taken you out to a fancy restaurant or something. Maybe bowling." Both Mandy *and* Laryn giggled at that. "Anything, as long as it was just the two of us."

But Mandy shook her head. "No, Nash. I was happy to meet everyone. I wouldn't have wanted to do anything else."

Obi-Wan glanced at Zita. Had he fucked up too? He was out of practice wooing a woman, and apparently screwing things up right from the start.

"Don't," she said, obviously reading his mind. "Tonight is perfect."

"But—"

"If you'd asked me out to dinner at some fancy restaurant, I probably would've turned you down. I'm not a fancy restaurant kind of girl. And I let you pick me up, sure, but that was about as much leeway as I was going to give you, since you specifically invited me to a casual night out with you and your friends. Besides, neither of us were interested in dating anyone, remember?"

Obi-Wan was well aware his friends were listening intently to this conversation—and that they'd probably give him shit tomorrow. But he didn't care.

"I wasn't. But now I am," he said firmly.

"You are *what*?"

"Interested in dating. You."

He couldn't read Zita's expression, but he wasn't telling her anything he hadn't said this afternoon, in the smokers' area on the film set. He went on.

"Next time, I'll do it right. Maybe we can rent electric bikes and ride up and down the boardwalk at the beach. Or we can do one of those escape rooms or ax-throwing things. I've heard the aquarium is neat too."

"Oooh, we should all do an escape room! We'd break a speed record for figuring out the puzzles!" Pyro bragged.

But Obi-Wan kept his gaze on Zita. He hadn't thought it was weird at all that he'd asked her to come hang out with everyone at Anchor Point. But now, he realized it was probably a bonehead move...because deep down, he'd known even then that this was a date. Hadn't he thought at the time that he'd prefer to cook for her at his apartment, just the two of them?

At least she was being cool about it. And he believed her when she said she would've turned him down if he'd gone the more traditional route.

This dating thing was tough.

"Zita?" he whispered, when she didn't respond, suddenly feeling off-kilter and unsure of himself.

"Me too," she said after a long moment.

"You too, what?" Chaos asked. "You want to date our boy here?"

Oh, for fuck's sake, Obi-Wan was done with his friends. Why he'd thought this was a good idea was beyond him. He should've had this conversation somewhere else, away from his teammates, but it was too late now. But then again, if Edge hadn't brought up the possibility that a group get-together wasn't the best impression to make on a first date, he probably never would've thought twice about what he'd done.

He glanced at Chaos to tell him to fuck off, but a commotion at the front door of the bar had everyone turning to see what the hubbub was all about.

Obi-Wan couldn't believe what he was seeing.

Who he was seeing.

Carmen St. James had just sauntered into Anchor Point as if she were the queen of England, and she was doing her subjects a huge favor by gracing the commoners with her presence.

There was a big man standing right behind her, a guy Obi-Wan had seen on set more than once, but he had no idea what his job was.

Carmen looked around, saw him staring at her—and made a beeline straight for him.

Obi-Wan heard Zita inhale deeply and mutter, "What the hell is *she* doing here?"

But he had no time to do or say anything else before the beautiful actress was standing next to his chair with a huge smile on her face.

KEEPING ZITA

CHAPTER EIGHT

Zita could not fucking believe that Carmen was here. And looking at Sage as if he was some kind of prize at the bottom of a box of kids' cereal.

How the hell had the woman known where he'd be tonight? Did she know Zita would be with him? And Carmen had brought that creepy bodyguard, Silas Graves, who followed her everywhere. She didn't begrudge the actress having someone at her back, but Silas always had a gleam in his eye that made Zita nervous. Like he was looking for a confrontation so he'd have a reason to be violent.

She'd seen him literally knock one of the caterers away from Carmen because she came too close when telling her how much she enjoyed her movies. The woman had gone flying, tripping over a table and knocking all the food to the floor. Silas didn't apologize. No, he'd had a satisfied look on his face as he led Carmen away from the mess.

Zita's hand dropped from Sage's leg, and she schooled her expression so none of her thoughts showed...she hoped. She hadn't known Carmen long, but she'd met plenty of women exactly like her. Spoiled, conceited, and used to getting whatever they wanted because of their money and looks. And just as she'd warned Sage, what Carmen wanted was *him*.

It wasn't as if Zita could even blame her. Sage was impressive. And sitting with his equally impressive friends, wearing civilian clothes, looking relaxed and happy...yeah, there was no way in hell Carmen wasn't going to take her best shot at dragging Sage back to her hotel room.

Tonight, she was wearing a short, tight black miniskirt that looked painted on. It showcased her long, toned legs and left very little to the imagination. If she had to bend over for any reason, she'd surely flash her cooter to everyone in the room. But then again, it was likely if she dropped anything, someone else would pick it up for her. And if she *did* lean over, it would be for the express purpose of having sex.

Her blouse was white and sheer and clearly showed the white bra she wore underneath. Her makeup was done with a heavy hand, and the bright red high heels on her feet pushed her height over six feet. She was dressed more for a night club than a rundown hole-in-the-wall bar like Anchor Point.

But it wasn't surprising that Carmen didn't look one bit like she felt out of place. She'd walked in as if she owned the place, and probably thought she did.

"Hi!" she said perkily. "Looks like we both had the idea of checking out the local nightlife. This place is so...quaint. Is there room for me at the table?"

No one moved for a moment. No one said a word. It was obvious there *wasn't* room. The tables that had been pushed together weren't huge to begin with, and everyone was crowded around in the chairs they'd pulled up, so they could all talk without having to yell at each other.

"Silas? Will you find me a chair?" Carmen ordered, as she turned to the hulking, muscular man next to her.

To Zita's shock, he stalked up to the table next to theirs and growled, "Move," as he put his hand on the back of a chair where a young woman was already sitting. She was obviously out with a group of girlfriends, and they were laughing and giggling and having a good time in each other's company.

Without waiting for her to do as he said, Silas basically pulled the chair out from under her, forcing the woman to either stand and give up her chair or fall to the floor. He walked back over to Carmen and set the chair down with a nod.

"What the absolute fuck?" Sage growled, as he surged to his feet. The rest of the guys around the table did the same, everyone looking pissed beyond belief.

Sage glared at Silas, then picked up his own chair and carried it over to the other table, apologizing to the woman before returning to his friends and Zita. While he was gone, Casper had walked over to an empty table not that far away to get a replacement chair.

"Sorry, this is a private party," Sage told Carmen, not sounding sorry in the least. He gave Casper a nod in thanks and sat down.

Carmen simply pretended like she hadn't heard him, smiled, then pulled up the chair her bodyguard had stolen, trying to wedge it between Sage and Zita. She sat daintily, her knees to one side—which didn't keep her from almost exposing her underwear...if she was wearing any—and shot Sage a seductive grin.

"Hi," she repeated.

Zita was pissed. But she wasn't the kind of woman to make a scene. Though, she *also* wasn't about to move from her spot next to Sage. Their knees were almost touching, and Carmen trying to shove herself between them was annoying at best.

Rude, presumptuous, and fucking bitchy as hell, at worst.

To her surprise, Sage reached out and grabbed Zita's hand, which had been on his knee a moment ago, and brought it back to his leg, placing it on his thigh this time. He kept his hand over hers. She wasn't sure if he was telling her nonverbally not to leave him with Carmen or if he was staking a claim.

It didn't really matter, Zita had no intention of letting the bitch who'd crashed their date have her way.

"What are you doing here?" Sage asked between clenched teeth.

The rest of his friends were silent, watching the scene play out. Probably trying to figure out what was happening. They were also probably a little in awe that Carmen St. James was sitting at their table. Was right there within touching distance. That happened a lot with the actors and actresses Zita worked with. People tended to be dazzled by them whenever they were in close proximity. Outside of Hollywood, it wasn't often people had the chance to be up close and personal with someone famous.

"I heard you were going to be here, and I wanted to see if you'd like some company. It's kind of...lame, don't you think?"

"Who told you I was going to be here? And no, it's not lame. It's laid-back. Relaxing. Which is what most people need after a long day's work."

"It's more fun to blow off steam by dancing to techno music at a club until you're so tired, you fall asleep the second your head hits the pillow. Then again, there are other ways to exhaust yourself that are much more...satisfying." She winked when she said it, and leaned forward, running a hand down Sage's arm.

The same arm that was attached to the hand covering Zita's own, on his thigh.

The nerve of this woman was off the charts.

"How did you know I'd be here?" Sage asked again.

Carmen sat back in her chair with a small smile. "Oh, you know how film sets are...Actually, you probably don't. Nothing is private. Everyone knows everything. Who's sleeping with who, who's allergic to what. Who has the hots for who."

"*How?*" Sage bit out, obviously at the edge of his control.

"My hairdresser's dating one of the set directors, who knows one of the boom operators who was taking a smoke break when you were talking about coming here tonight."

"Ears everywhere," Chaos muttered, loud enough for everyone to hear.

Sage's lips pressed together. He wasn't happy that his conversation with Zita had been passed on to Carmen, that was for sure.

Without warning, he stood, still holding Zita's hand, giving her no choice but to stand with him. He wrapped his arm around her waist and sidled away from where Carmen was sitting. He didn't say a word as he led her away from the table...away from Carmen.

"Sage?"

"Give me a minute," he said between clenched teeth.

Seeing how hard he was working to hold on to his temper, Zita swallowed what she was going to ask—namely, if he was all right; it was obvious he wasn't all right—and didn't resist as he walked them toward the hallway where the restrooms were located.

He didn't stop. Just kept walking until he'd pushed open an emergency door, and they stepped out into the dark night.

There weren't as many lights out here as there were in the parking lot, but it wasn't dark either. There was a bright light over by the dumpsters, which lit up most of the area behind the building.

Sage leaned a shoulder against the building and pulled Zita in front of him. He turned her so her back was against his chest, then wrapped his arms around her, holding them together. Zita put her hands over his and leaned against him. His chin came down to rest on her shoulder, and she could feel him taking deep breaths.

She had to admit, she approved of the way he'd removed himself from a situation that was uncomfortable instead of lashing out. Instead of saying something he might regret. She had no idea if he'd learned that from being in the military, or from being one of the best pilots in the country, but she was impressed with his self-control.

"You know I had nothing to do with her being here tonight, right?" he asked, after a long moment.

"Yes."

"I might've been a bonehead and invited you on a group date, but I wouldn't invite that woman to join us even if my career as a Night Stalker depended on it."

That surprised her.

Zita turned so she was facing Sage. She put her hands on his chest, liking how his arms stayed around her, now clasped together loosely at her back. At any time, she could break out of his hold, but she was happy where she was.

"I'm enjoying our group date," she insisted. "I like your friends. You all complement each other perfectly. I can see why you like working together so much, why you're so good at what you do. It almost seems as if you can read each other's minds at times."

"And I know you didn't invite Carmen. I mean, she admitted that she knew you'd be here because of gossip on set. She's also right that there are no secrets on a film. I'm not sure why everyone seems to want to know what everyone else is doing, but it's always been that way, at least on the movies and shows I've worked on."

He nodded but didn't look any less stressed. A muscle in his jaw ticked as he obviously still struggled with controlling his anger at the unwanted interruption to their night.

"What do you need me to do? Would it make things better if I left? So you and your friends can deal with her without me there?"

"No!" he said immediately, his arms tightening around her, as if to keep her from leaving.

Zita caressed his chest lightly. "Okay. You want *me* to go back in there and tell her off? You can circle around to the parking lot and take off without having to deal with her again tonight."

"You think I'm that big of a coward?"

"Not at all. Just giving you options. I could beat her up. Well, that probably wouldn't go so well for me with Gigantor at her side, but I'm thinking I could get in a few licks before he stopped me." She was kidding, she wasn't a violent person, but she would say whatever it took to get Sage to relax.

He stared down at her for a long moment before saying, "Don't ever put yourself in danger for me. I can fight my own battles."

"I know, Sage. I never doubted that you could. I just...I hate that you're upset. That *she* upset you. She's not worth it."

"She disrespected me, but more importantly, she disrespected *you*. If she heard the gossip, then she knew I was taking you out. And even if she didn't, your hand on my leg should've told her that we were together."

"I'm sure there've been plenty of men who've been swayed away from their dates at the prospect of being with Carmen St. James."

"I'm not most men. And it's fucking rude."

Zita nodded, feeling all tingly inside. When had a man ever been so upset on her behalf? Never. And the fact that he was dismissing a famous actress made it even more meaningful.

Sage took a few more deep breaths.

"So, what's the plan? What do you need me to do?"

"You're doing it."

Zita chuckled. "Sage, I'm not doing anything."

"You are. You're here with me. Letting me have a moment to control my irritation. You're letting me hold you. You're not freaking out that she's here."

Zita could feel herself blushing. Thank goodness the shadows were long out here, so he couldn't see. "What do you think your friends are doing? Or saying?"

Sage chuckled, and Zita could feel it all along her body. Somehow, she'd moved closer without even realizing it, and now she was plastered against his body from thighs to chest.

"They're taking care of it."

"How?"

"Don't know. They just are. By the time we go back in, the bitch'll be gone."

It was Zita's turn to get nervous now. She bit her lip. "She's not going to be happy. She obviously wants you, Sage."

"I'm not some toy to be fought over."

His words startled Zita. Was that what she was doing? What he thought was happening? That two women were fighting over him? She tried to take a step back, but Sage tightened his arms around her. The thought she had earlier about being able to break out of his hold was obviously way off the mark. Though, she wasn't afraid of him. Not even close.

"I know you aren't," she clarified. "But I wouldn't hold it against you if you changed your mind and wanted to go out with her."

Sage chuckled.

"I wasn't trying to be funny."

"And yet, you still were. Zita, if this was a competition, you'd've already won. I'm here with you. I want to *date* you, when that was the furthest thing from my mind a week ago. I can't stop thinking about you when I leave the set, and you're the first person I look for when I arrive every morning. I've never bought a woman coffee, and yet I've done it every morning since our fifth day on set. You've met the most important people in my life, and I'm already trying to figure out where to take you on our first one-on-one date. I don't care if Carmen wants me—*I don't want her*. She's just going to have to get used to disappointment."

Zita pressed her lips together. She knew it wasn't that easy.

Carmen St. James was like a lot of the famous, rich, spoiled actresses she'd met over the years. They all wanted what they wanted, and nothing and no one stood in their way.

Carmen wanted Sage. At least, she wanted what he represented on the outside. She didn't really care to get to know him, or figure out what mattered to him, or what his values were. She just wanted eye candy on her arm for the time she was here in Virginia.

"You ready to go back in?" Sage asked.

"Are you?" she countered.

Leaning down, Sage put his forehead on hers. It was a very intimate position, and Zita was in no hurry to end it.

"Thank you for being with me while I got my shit together."

"I didn't do anything," she protested.

"You did. You didn't ask me a million questions. You trusted me out here, in a dark alley, and didn't freak out. You didn't get all catty and hysterical when Carmen showed up."

"I wanted to."

He pulled back and smiled. "I know. That's why I got us out of there. That, and I didn't want to see her being rude to you any more than she already was. Probably wasn't the best idea to bring you out here in the dark though."

"It's not that dark."

"Mmmhmmm."

"And I've taken self-defense." She didn't know why she was blurting out that inane fact, but there it was. "Also, I'm sure if I screamed, *someone* would come out to see what was happening."

Okay, that was stupid. She had no idea if someone would come looking for the source of a scream or not, but it sounded good right before the words came out of her mouth.

"You're safe with me," Sage said, the look on his face telling her how serious he was.

"I know," Zita whispered back.

"You *will* go out with me again, won't you? On a you-and-me date? Not one with all my buddies?"

She didn't even need to think about her response. "Yes."

"This time we won't talk about it on set, so we don't get interrupted."

"Probably smart."

He stared at her for a long minute, before dropping his arms. "Come on, let's go find out what happened in our absence."

"You really think she's gone?"

"Yes."

"What if she's not?"

"She is."

"You can't know that, Sage," Zita insisted.

He chuckled under his breath once more. "Trust me, Edge was one second away from escorting her out. And I thought Laryn was going to get the heavy-duty wrench she likes to carry in her purse. Not to mention, the owner of the bar wasn't happy at all that Carmen's goon took that chair from right under the poor woman next to us. The entire bar might've been in awe when she walked in, but after just a couple of minutes, they were all ready to physically throw her out."

"How do you know all that? You were giving Carmen a death stare when she was talking to you."

"Because I'm observant. I have to be in my line of work."

"I have to say...it surprises me how upset you think everyone was. I'm sure chairs are stolen all the time in bars."

"Not while people are still freaking sitting in them. And Anchor Point is special. This isn't Hollywood, Zita. No one's impressed by status here. Which is mostly why we like it. My friends and I are well aware that our reputations precede us sometimes, but we're simple men and women who want a place to unwind and just be who we are...much like the rest of the patrons who come here to have a beer and a burger."

Zita liked that. A lot. She was way too used to LA and how

people would bend over backward to suck up to anyone who was even the smallest bit famous, in the hopes it would further their own career.

"I think Anchor Point is my new favorite restaurant and bar."

Sage grinned. "I'm glad you think so." Then he took her hand in his and led her back to the door.

"It would suck if that door locked behind us," Zita said with a smile.

In response, Sage took hold of the handle and tugged.

It didn't open.

Zita's mouth fell open in shock. She'd totally been kidding.

Then Sage laughed and pulled the door open.

Shaking her head at how easily she'd been duped, Zita found herself smiling. It was amazing how just ten minutes ago, both she and Sage were struggling to control their emotions over Carmen's appearance, and now they were both laughing.

Sage walked her down the hallway, past the restrooms and back into the bar. As he'd promised, there was no sign of Carmen or her bodyguard.

Sage held her chair for her as she sat. Then he pulled his own closer than it had been before, grabbing his glass and taking a sip of beer. "What'd we miss?" he asked, after he'd swallowed.

Mandy leaned forward with a smirk, and, after pushing her empty lemon drop glass out of the way, said, "It was *awesome*! Carmen stood, like she was going to go after you, but Laryn hopped up and grabbed her arm, preventing her from leaving. That made her steroid-riddled, puffed-up bodyguard lose his mind, and he took a step toward *Laryn*. Which, as you can imagine, didn't go down well with Casper or anyone else.

"Casper stood, as did the rest of the guys, and they forced Mr. Muscle back against the wall. Then the bartender arrived— you know how big *he* is. But he was acting all gentlemanly, and he took Carmen's hand as if they were at a freaking English ball or something."

Zita laughed at that.

"While our guys were all up in the asshole bodyguard's face," Mandy continued, "the bartender tucked Carmen's hand under his arm and led her away. I think she assumed he was hitting on her—but instead, he escorted her to the door, opened it, and kind of pushed her out! Told her that she wasn't welcome here ever again, and to take her 'skank Hollywood ass' back to where she came from! Said people around here weren't interested.

"Her bodyguard probably would've stayed to get his ass kicked by our guys, but when he saw Carmen get that tiny little shove out the door, he busted his ass to get to her side. It seems to me that if the bitch wants some dick, she should look to her sidekick to get her jollies. Not a guy who *obviously* isn't interested and who, in fact, is on a date with another woman."

Zita grinned. It was obvious Mandy was feeling the effects of the drink she'd consumed in the short time she and Sage had been outside. Then she turned to Laryn. "Are you okay?"

The other woman snorted. "I'm fine. Bitch didn't touch me. But I kind of wish she had, because I would've kicked her ass. She might tower over me, but in those heels and that tight skirt, I would've had the upper hand for sure."

"You're pregnant," Casper reminded her in a low, emotional voice.

"And?" Laryn demanded. "I'm not helpless. Never have been and never will be. I'm also not fragile. I'm not going to break if someone grabs me or pushes me around. I love how protective you are, Tate, but I'm not going to be happy if you spend my entire pregnancy treating me as if I'm made of glass."

"I know, but—"

Laryn held up a hand, palm toward him. "No buts!" she declared.

Zita couldn't help the small chuckle that escaped.

"Thanks, guys," Sage told his friends.

"No need to thank us," Buck said. "Besides, the bartender was the one who actually took out the trash."

"Not that we wouldn't've, but we were more concerned about making sure that fuckhead didn't put his hands on Laryn," Chaos said.

"Are *you* guys good?" Buck asked Sage.

"Yeah," Sage told his friend.

"You going to have a problem on set after this?" Edge asked.

Zita wasn't sure if he was talking to her or Sage, but she answered anyway. "I don't usually see much of her. She's either in her trailer or on set. Unless she falls and conks her head on the floor and requires medical attention, I should be able to keep my distance."

"Good. What about you, Obi-Wan?"

"There's no reason for me to be around her. I've mostly been talking to Logan and the set directors, script people, the director, and the costumers."

"Hopefully she'll be too humiliated to seek him out again," Mandy said, a bloodthirsty kind of satisfaction in her voice. "I know I would be."

Zita wasn't too sure. Carmen was a product of Hollywood. She drastically overestimated her own appeal. The thought that Sage honestly wasn't interested was a concept so foreign, she couldn't comprehend it.

Unfortunately, she would probably twist everything that happened tonight into some sort of scheme on Zita's part to keep her and Sage apart. She hoped not, but she wouldn't be surprised if Carmen became even more desperate and determined to get Sage into her bed.

Doing her best to push the thought away—she'd never been the kind of person to stress about something she had no control over—Zita tried to relax. It helped that Sage's arm was on the back of her chair, and she could feel the heat from his thigh seeping into her own leg, which was touching his.

They stayed another hour, laughing and joking with his friends. Several people sent over free drinks for the table, which Mandy and Zita ended up consuming most of, since the men were driving and didn't want to be impaired, and Laryn was pregnant.

By the time everyone decided to head home, Zita was a bit unsteady on her feet but happier than she'd been in a long time. She had fun tonight. She loved meeting and getting to know the people who were closest to Sage. And Mandy and Laryn were fun to be around, and she'd clicked with them in a way she didn't usually with most women.

After they'd all stood, Mandy gave her a long, heartfelt hug, which felt amazing. Before meeting Sage and his friends, it had been forever since Zita had been touched by another human in a way that wasn't casual or a part of her job as a medical professional. Her family was very affectionate, but she didn't get home to Indiana to see them often enough, something she made a mental vow to remedy as soon as she could.

When it was Laryn's turn to say goodbye, she also hugged Zita, but it was a little more reserved, which went with the tough exterior the mechanic projected to others. Zita couldn't help but hold on to her a second longer as she said into her ear, "I'll see what I can learn about live-in nannies, to help you out when the time comes. I've got some connections, and I swear I'll find you a good one."

When they pulled apart, Laryn stared at Zita for a long moment before nodding.

"It's going to work out. How could it not when you have these amazing friends who all have your back?"

"Friends who'll all be on the same deployment I will," Laryn reminded her.

"Well, you've got me and Mandy too. And while I have no idea where I'll be by the time you have that baby, or when you'll be deployed for the first time after giving birth, I'll do what I can from wherever I am to help you."

"Why?"

Zita shrugged. The alcohol she'd consumed was swimming in her bloodstream, making her a little more mushy than she usually would be after meeting someone for the first time. "Hell if I know. I just know that Sage is a good man. I respect him, and you're someone he would obviously throw down for, which means you're good people. So I want to help."

Laryn smiled. "It sounds so weird to hear Obi-Wan referred to as Sage."

Zita grinned back at her. "It's weird for me to think of him as Obi-Wan. I haven't even seen the movies."

"*What?* Are you kidding me?" Sage asked from behind her.

Turning, Zita smiled up at him. "Nope."

"Change in plans. *Star Wars* movie marathon is now on the agenda. We'll order in."

Zita giggled.

Laryn rolled her eyes. "Not everyone is a *Star Wars* freak like you, Obi-Wan."

"She might love it, won't know until she sees them," was his response.

"Come on. We could stand here all night shooting the shit, and I'm tired," Casper said, putting his arm around Laryn's waist.

"Does that mean PT in the morning won't be as stupid as it has been recently?" Pyro asked.

Casper grinned. "I believe I already answered that question earlier."

"Shit."

"Damn."

"You just had to open your mouth, didn't you, Pyro?"

Zita giggled at how disgruntled all the men sounded. They all made their way to the door, but at the last minute, Zita dropped

Sage's hand and dashed over to the bar to thank the bartender for helping to get rid of Carmen and her sidekick.

He smiled and winked at her. "My pleasure. I hope to see you again soon."

"I think you will," Zita said a little shyly, as she looked over her shoulder at Sage. He was waiting by the door, giving her a moment to talk to the man behind the bar. She headed toward him once again, waving at the girls at the table next to where they'd been sitting, who called out their goodbyes in drunken slurs.

Zita looked back at the bartender, concerned for the women. He correctly read her look right, because he said, "Don't worry. They're in here every other week or so, and their husbands take turns at being designated driver. They'll text one of them when they're ready to go. They'll be fine."

Nodding, and satisfied that the women were in good hands, she made her way back to Sage. His friends had all left the bar by then, and he immediately took her hand in his once more. It felt good. Right. As if they'd been holding hands for months rather than tonight for the first time.

They exited into the cool night air, and Zita saw that Edge and Chaos were still in the lot. They were standing by their cars, shooting the shit.

"They haven't left?" Zita asked Sage.

"After what happened to Mandy, we're all sure to never leave anyone alone in the lot again. Just in case."

Zita felt sad about Mandy's assault all over again, but she loved that the men had changed their routines to look out for each other. Again, that proved what good men they were.

After settling Zita into the passenger seat of his Jeep, Sage gave his friends a chin lift, which he got in return, before getting behind the wheel. As they headed down the road toward her motel, Zita leaned against the headrest and turned to look at Sage as he drove.

"You good?" he asked, obviously feeling her gaze on him.

"More than. You?"

"Perfect."

"I hope things will be okay on set tomorrow. And after that," she mused.

"They will be. I don't do drama. Carmen most certainly got the hint tonight that she's barking up the wrong tree with me. It'll be fine."

Again, Zita wasn't so sure, but she kept her mouth shut, not wanting to ruin the mellow mood. All too soon, Sage pulled into the parking lot of her motel, and she told him what room she was in instead of making him drop her off at the lobby.

She trusted him. Some people would think she was making a mistake, but she'd seen firsthand exactly *how* trustworthy Sage was. If she couldn't trust *him*, she was going to become a nun and move to the mountains of Switzerland and live the life of a recluse.

"What's put that smile on your face?" Sage asked as he pulled into a space in front of her room, and she unfastened her seat belt.

"Nothing," Zita said, not sure how she could explain how funny the thought of her becoming a nun and wearing a habit was.

"I had a good time tonight. Thanks for being a good sport about the group date thing."

"It was great. They put me at ease. Let me have the confidence to get out of the rut I've been in. Thank you."

She stared at him as he leaned forward. *Had* he leaned forward? Was she imagining it? No, he'd definitely moved closer.

Feeling bold, and thrilled that he wanted to kiss her, Zita leaned toward him.

His hand came up and touched her cheek almost reverently, before his lips covered hers.

It was a sweet kiss...at first. But all too quickly, it morphed into something more.

Their mouths opened and they devoured each other. As if they'd known each other for years and this was their first time back together after a long separation.

Zita couldn't get enough. He tasted faintly like beer and all man. He smelled awesome, probably like the soap he'd used before picking her up tonight. His facial hair brushed against her cheeks, giving her already overloaded senses something else to focus on.

He pulled back way before Zita was ready but kept his hand buried in her hair. She hadn't even noticed that he'd gathered her loose strands in a fist at the back of her head as they'd kissed.

"I love your hair," he murmured quietly, slowly loosening his fist, letting the silky strands fall from his fingers.

"It's too straight," she complained.

"No such thing," Sage countered. He stared at her for a long moment, then licked his lips.

The action made her want to kiss him all over again, so she did. The next kiss wasn't as long or as passionate, but it was no less intimate.

Excited butterflies swam in Zita's belly. She hadn't felt like this in years. Probably since she'd made out in her date's car in a well-known spot after Homecoming her senior year.

"It's late," Sage said, after she pulled back to take a breath.

"Yeah."

"You still want to go out with me again?"

"Yes." He'd pretty much already asked her out, but she liked that he was making sure they were both on the same page.

"*Star Wars* movie marathon at my place? If anyone unwanted shows up, we can just refuse to open the door."

"Sounds perfect." And it did.

"I'd say I'll cook for you, but I suck at it. So we'll order something takeout. I have a whole drawer full of menus of places we can choose from."

"Okay."

"And if you hate the movies, we can watch something different."

"I won't hate them."

"We aren't going to be able to get through them all in one night." He sounded nervous, which was kind of adorable.

"Okay."

"Okay."

"I'll see you on set in the morning."

"You will. I'll have your coffee as usual. I'll find you."

Zita smiled at him. Jeez, he was a good man.

She hated when his hand left her hair as she sat back in her seat. Then she reached for the door handle. She felt as if she was floating as she walked to her door. After unlocking it, she looked back at the car. Sage hadn't pulled away yet, was watching to make sure she got inside safely.

She gave him a little wave, then forced herself to close and bolt the door instead of walking back to the Jeep and inviting him into her room. It was too soon for that, and she was enjoying getting to know him little by little.

But there was no doubt the two of them had explosive chemistry. She couldn't see the future, but she hoped he didn't do or say anything that would prove everything he'd shared with her so far was a farce. That he wasn't as genuine as he seemed.

Smiling, Zita dropped her purse on the floor and headed to the bathroom. It was late, much later than she usually went to bed, and morning would come very early. She needed to get some sleep, but even after she'd changed, brushed her teeth, and gotten into bed, the events of the night replayed in her mind.

She could only hope that Carmen wouldn't be a bitch for the rest of the shoot. It would make things extremely uncomfortable, but Zita wasn't going to apologize for something Carmen had brought on herself.

It wasn't too much longer before Zita finally fell asleep, with the memory of Sage's lips on hers running through her head.

CHAPTER NINE

The bitch wasn't going to let it go.

Obi-Wan sighed. He'd hoped Carmen would've gotten the clue that he wasn't interested in anything she had to offer.

And yet, the morning after the incident at Anchor Point, she'd greeted him on set as if she hadn't been kicked out of the bar after her advances toward him were turned down flat. Hell, he'd told her their get-together was a private thing, and she'd totally ignored him.

Not only that, she seemed more determined than ever to "win" him. Which was a joke, because he wasn't a fucking prize in one of those claw machines. She didn't get to decide that he would be her next lay and expect to have him just materialize in her bed as if by magic.

The movie set that used to be an exciting change of pace for Obi-Wan was quickly turning into something he dreaded. And that sucked.

Of course, seeing Zita was a bright spot. And honestly, he still enjoyed what he was doing. Using his expertise to fine-tune the military wardrobe and lingo, and point out things that were just blatantly wrong regarding the helicopters. Obi-Wan was impressed that Grubbner actually took what he said seriously. It was nice to see the man was truly interested in making everything authentic.

The situation with Carmen was why he was looking forward to the next phase of the film. In a week, the entire operation would be moving to the western side of the state to film the bulk of the scenes with Logan Striker. It would take a full week for the transition itself. For the entire production to relocate to the new location, and for the staff and crew to get everything ready for filming again. Obi-Wan was thrilled...as Carmen wouldn't be accompanying the production. Her scenes in Virginia were almost complete, so she'd be returning to Hollywood.

But with the looming change in venue, it seemed Carmen was doubling down on her efforts to get him into bed. Everywhere Obi-Wan went, she was there. Sidling up to him, touching him, fucking petting him as if he were a dog she could bring to heel.

He was done trying to be subtle about not wanting anything to do with her. In the last few days, he'd told the actress more than once that he wasn't interested and to please keep her hands to herself. Even flat-out insisting he wasn't attracted to her. All to no avail.

To make matters worse, Zita had been keeping her distance from them both. She claimed it was to keep the peace on set. To avoid making any waves. And that irritated Obi-Wan most of all, because all he wanted was to talk to her, to be near her, to get to know her better.

It had been five days since their night at Anchor Point, and Obi-Wan hadn't been able to talk to her long enough to plan the *Star Wars* date they'd discussed. It wasn't about the movies, although they were awesome, it was about his eagerness to spend more one-on-one time with the woman he couldn't get out of his mind.

They had each other's phone number and texted every night,

but those conversations were brief and impersonal, and he hadn't found an appropriate time to bring up when they could get together again. For a man who preferred to be the pursuer, he was doing a piss-poor job of it. He needed to get his head out of his ass and go after what he wanted—Zita.

This morning, he'd arrived on set only to be immediately accosted by Carmen yet again. As if she'd been waiting for him—which she probably had. He had his usual second cup of coffee for Zita, and he was determined to get it to her while it was still hot. There were a couple of mornings this week when either he or she had been busy, and by the time they managed to have a second to speak, her coffee was lukewarm or even cold.

As usual, Carmen's bodyguard was hovering not too far from her as she walked toward him with a huge smile on her face. She was in the same dress she'd worn for most of her recent scenes, a modest, navy-blue cotton sheath that went down to her knees, which he'd heard her complain about more than once. She thought it was ugly, plain, and too constricting. In Obi-Wan's opinion, it was classy, making her look exactly as a pilot's wife should—respectable.

"Good morning," she purred as she approached.

"Carmen," Obi-Wan said with a nod, barely keeping his temper in check. Now that Casper and Laryn's secret was out, the stress level Casper had been feeling was reduced, but PT hadn't gotten any easier. This morning, they'd run a half marathon, with the last half being in the sand, which sucked big time. Running in the sand was one of Obi-Wan's least favorite things. It was a great workout, but that didn't mean he liked it.

He was also late getting to the set because he'd witnessed an accident on the way in, and had stopped like the responsible citizen he was to give a statement to the police.

"Guess what today is!" she said perkily.

Obi-Wan took a sip of his own coffee and didn't respond,

wishing she'd get on with whatever she wanted to say so he could be on his way.

"It's my last day of filming! And there's going to be a party for me around three. I know you usually leave around lunchtime, but I thought you could make an exception today and stay to celebrate with me."

"Can't, sorry," Obi-Wan said. "I have to work."

Carmen pouted. "But I was hoping we could go out afterward."

That was it. Obi-Wan was done. "When have I *ever* given you any indication that I was interested in you, Carmen? In fact, I've told you the exact opposite—multiple times. You're beautiful, and successful, and obviously very popular. But I told you from the get-go that I wasn't interested in dating," Obi-Wan said bluntly.

Her eyes narrowed. "You sure seemed interested in dating that weird medic when I saw you canoodling together at that backwoods bar."

Obi-Wan blinked in surprise. Not because of what she said, because she wasn't wrong. He was very interested in... canoodling...with Zita. But more because of the absolute fury in her tone.

She was an actress, could turn the tears on at will. For the first time, Obi-Wan realized what a good actress she *really* was. She'd hidden her anger, jealousy, and irritation over his attention toward Zita extremely well. He'd kind of thought she was an airhead, almost oblivious to the fact that she wasn't making any headway with him at all.

"I can't believe you'd choose *that* instead of *this*." She gestured to her body, arching her back to show off her tits and cocking her hip to the side.

There were so many things Obi-Wan wanted to say, but deciding silence would be the best way to go here, he simply shrugged. Which seemed to inflame her further.

"You're going to regret saying no to me. You have no idea how much influence I have. How many people would bend over backward to do what I want."

Obi-Wan stood up straighter. "Are you threatening me?" he asked incredulously.

"No. Of course not." Her voice had changed. Lost the acrid tone. Now she sounded sickly sweet. As if she was nothing more than the airheaded actress she projected to the world once more. "I'm simply saying you're missing out. I could've given you the world, Obi-Wan."

"I don't want the world. Just my little corner of it. And I'm perfectly happy with where I am in my life right now—without *you* in it, thank you very much."

Her eyes narrowed again, but then her face lost all emotion. It was actually kind of impressive how she could lock down everything she was feeling and project nothing but serenity to those around her.

But Obi-Wan had seen through the smoke screen she hid behind. She'd let her shields slip. Deep down, the woman was poison. Spoiled rotten and used to getting her way. She might not throw a tantrum in front of the cast and crew...but she was planning something. Obi-Wan had no doubt about that. And while she claimed she wasn't threatening him, he'd been around enough to know that when someone was experiencing high emotions, the words coming out of their mouth were usually more true than not.

He sensed movement behind him and glanced over his shoulder to see Silas standing there. Carmen's bodyguard had probably heard their entire conversation. The question was, what would he do about it? It was obvious the man was besotted with his client.

Thankfully, he didn't do anything other than follow behind Carmen when she turned away in a huff and stalked off.

The air around him literally seemed to lighten the second the woman was out of his personal space. Taking a deep breath, Obi-Wan watched as Carmen approached the director after he called cut.

To his amusement, Grubbner didn't even look at her, simply waved her away.

Two rejections in as many minutes probably fanned the flames of resentment in the actress, but Obi-Wan didn't hang around to see what she'd do next. He was done with her. D.O.N.E. After today, the set would be a much more relaxing place. He wouldn't have to be on his toes, wouldn't have to try to avoid running into Carmen.

It didn't take long to find Zita. She was in the makeshift break room that had been set up by catering to provide light snacks to everyone on set throughout the day. Obi-Wan had been impressed on his first day to find not only large tables overflowing with nonperishable snacks—both healthy and not so much—but also several little round tables with chairs. It kind of looked like a café of sorts, but without the specialty coffees and servers.

"Morning," he said, walking over to the small table where Zita was sitting. He placed the coffee he'd gotten for her beside the laptop she was using and took a seat opposite.

"Caffeine," she practically moaned, making Obi-Wan's cock twitch in his pants. He could imagine her moaning just like that, with pleasure, under entirely different circumstances. He was glad he was sitting, and that his flight suit had some extra room in the crotch.

She immediately reached for the cup and took a sip, closing her eyes and moaning for real as the sugary coffee hit her taste buds.

Obi-Wan couldn't take his gaze off her. Couldn't stop his mind from picturing the woman with her hair spread out on his pillow as he watched her from between her legs.

Her green eyes opened and her gaze met his. "Hi."

"Hi," Obi-Wan echoed.

They stared at each other. It felt as if they were the only two people in the world at that moment. Sparks shot between them, an intense connection that felt so right.

Her cheeks pinkened, and she looked down at the screen in front of her.

"Whatcha doin?" Obi-Wan asked, taking another sip of his own coffee, just to keep himself from scooting over next to her and tasting the coffee she was drinking straight from her lips. He couldn't help but remember their kiss in his Jeep. It had thrown him off balance with how amazing it was. So much that he'd kinda taken a step backward, unsure about what the hell he was doing. But after several days of not being able to talk to her like he wanted, like he had the night he'd taken her to Anchor Point, he was over his reticence.

To his surprise, Zita would no longer meet his eyes. She kept them glued on the screen in front of her as if it held the answers to world peace or something.

"Zita?"

She sighed. "Don't read into this, okay?"

"Ooooh-kay," he drawled, truly interested now.

"I was looking at open paramedic jobs in the area. I do it everywhere I work," she added quickly, "just to see what's out there. What other states pay, things like that."

Instead of freaking out over her possibly finding a job she might want in this area, the idea made him feel all warm inside.

Shit, things were moving too damn fast, and he hadn't even really begun to pursue her. It was either a really bad sign...or a good one. He couldn't decide which at this point.

But maybe he was getting ahead of himself. He couldn't deny that checking out the competition, seeing what other companies offered, was a great way to get a pay raise or more benefits from her current employer.

"That's smart," he said. "Find anything interesting?"

She looked up at that. "You aren't upset? Thinking I'm some psycho who'll become a stalker or something?"

Obi-Wan snorted. "I just had the shittiest conversation with the only woman around here who I'd remotely classify as a stalker. If anything, I'd like for you to be a little *more* interested in my lame advances."

She grinned. "Advances? Have you made any?"

In response, Obi-Wan nodded to the coffee sitting next to her. Then said, "And I seem to remember a kiss that knocked my socks off that I can't stop thinking about."

"You too?"

Those simple words made Obi-Wan feel ten feet tall. "Yeah."

"Well, um...not really. I mean, I haven't found anything super-interesting yet, but I just started right before you sat down."

"You thought about working for the government? I know there are some paramedics working for contractors on base. Army and Navy." He wasn't even going to bring up the possibility of working for private security companies that contracted with the military to provide medical support for their personnel in high-risk environments, often overseas. He couldn't stomach the thought of this woman being in some of the awful places he and his team had been on missions.

"Really?"

"Really," he confirmed.

"I might be interested. Honestly, while working as a set medic used to be fun and exciting, as I get older, it's not so much anymore."

Obi-Wan could understand that. Just as he opened his mouth to see if Zita wanted to get together for their movie marathon before they left for the western part of the state, the one woman he didn't want to see again walked into the break area. Carmen. And of course, she was shadowed by Silas.

For once, though, she didn't make a beeline for him. She

actually pretended as if she didn't see him at all, smiling brightly at everyone else and saying good morning as if she was best friends with all the grips, lighting techs, and extras milling about.

"What's up with her?" Zita asked. "I've never seen her in the break room before."

Obi-Wan sighed. "She's pissed at me. Probably trying to make me see what I'm missing by turning down her generous offer of sleeping with her after her going-away party this afternoon."

"Good grief," Zita said with an eye roll. "It's not a going-away party. I mean, nothing special has been planned. Just the usual food that's delivered in the afternoons. She probably ordered a cake to make herself look more important."

Obi-Wan chuckled. "You think *she* ordered it? I'm thinking she had her sidekick do it."

"True. I can't imagine her lowering herself to order anything from anywhere."

"What's up with her bodyguard, anyway? I've never seen one hanging around Logan," Obi-Wan asked.

Zita closed her laptop and leaned forward, her elbows on the table as she gave him her complete attention. "He has one, but it's his own guy from California. A professional who knows how to stay in the background. Doesn't bring any attention to himself like Silas does, who seems to love the spotlight as much as Carmen. And I think his services were provided by a local company. That's often how it works, unless the talent wants to bring their own men or women with them. Sometimes that's the case with ultra-famous actors and actresses. But Carmen, while very popular, isn't quite on the same level as some of the people Henry has worked with."

"Interesting."

"And I think he's sleeping with her too," Zita said, before taking a drink of coffee.

"Seriously?"

"Yeah, the gossip on set really *is* pretty amazing. I overheard two of the boom handlers talking about how they heard Silas telling one of the camera operators all about it."

"Why in the hell would she want to sleep with *me* then? If she's already getting some from Hulk?" Obi-Wan asked.

Zita giggled. "Because you're way better-looking than him. And you're not a blue-collar worker like he is. I mean, a Night Stalker or a bodyguard? There's no competition. Although, now that I think about it...it kind of sounds like a romance novel trope. She probably has delusions of being fought over by the two of you. Or maybe a threesome."

Obi-Wan wrinkled his nose in disgust. "For the record, I'm a one-woman kind of man. Not into sharing."

"Good to know," Zita said with a vague grin.

The sound of a chair clattering to the floor caught both their attention, and when Obi-Wan turned, he saw a woman standing next to a table, her hands around her throat in the telltale nonverbal signal that she was choking.

Before he or Zita could move, Carmen was behind the woman, grabbing her around the sternum. She began yanking at her chest area, screaming at her to "spit it out" as she did so.

"For fuck's sake," Zita swore, quickly jogging over to where Carmen and the choking woman were struggling. They were surrounded by people, everyone staring in disbelief at what was happening, which Obi-Wan knew was pretty normal. He saw it all the time on missions. When the shit hit the fan, a lot of people froze instead of getting away from the danger. Or wanted to watch whatever destruction was happening around them.

Zita grabbed Carmen by the arm and yanked her away from the woman. Carmen lost her footing and stumbled before falling to the floor. Zita didn't waste any time checking to see if she was all right; she put her own arms around the choking woman, placed her hands in the correct position, just above the belly button and under the rib cage—instead of over her sternum—

and proceeded to pull inward and upward on the woman's diaphragm.

She was so focused on dislodging whatever was stuck in the woman's throat, she didn't see the little drama unfolding behind her.

Silas helped Carmen off the floor—then moved toward Zita with a bloodthirsty look on his face.

Obi-Wan got to him just before he could put his hands on her.

"Back off," he growled in a low, menacing tone.

"She touched *Carmen*. Threw her to the floor."

"Because she was doing the Heimlich wrong!" Obi-Wan told him. "Anyone could see that. All she was doing was hurting the woman and wasting time. This is what Zita does. She's a fucking *paramedic*, remember?"

Silas's eyes narrowed. Now he took an aggressive step toward Obi-Wan.

Before he could do anything, the woman who was choking coughed.

Obi-Wan looked at her just in time to see a piece of food go flying out of her mouth and land with a wet plop on the floor. Zita immediately stopped what she was doing and put her arm around her waist, helping her stay upright as she continued to cough.

After a few seconds, the woman's cheeks began to pinken, and she lost the blue tinge that had formed around her lips.

"Oh my God," the woman said between coughs. "Thank you! Thank you so much!"

"Don't talk. Just breathe. You're okay now."

The woman nodded, and just like that, the people around them became unstuck. Telling the woman they were glad she was all right, commenting about how it happened so fast, and thanking Zita for being there and knowing what to do.

"You're kidding me, right?" Carmen demanded. She had her

hands on her hips and was glaring at everyone. "I was the one who reacted first, while the rest of you just stood around looking like idiots! I was doing just fine until Dr. Doody here decided she wanted all the attention."

"I didn't have time to explain that your hands were in the wrong position," Zita said calmly. "You never would've dislodged what she was choking on by pressing on her sternum. That's for CPR, not choking."

"You're a liar! I know what I was doing! I've been trained in first-aid. I was doing just fine until you assaulted me so you could take over."

Obi-Wan couldn't believe what he was hearing. Carmen was pissed she didn't get credit for saving the woman's life? What a bitch.

In response, Zita shook her head in exasperation and walked back toward the table where she'd been sitting.

"I'm not done talking to you!" Carmen sneered.

Zita continued to ignore her.

Silas took a step toward her, and Obi-Wan got between them again. "Don't even think about it."

The look the large man gave him was full of menace and hate. Which was pretty interesting, considering they hadn't shared more than a few words in all the time they'd been on set together. But then again, if the man was sleeping with Carmen—and feeling possessive and protective of her—it was no surprise he believed every word that came out of her mouth. Namely, that she'd been cheated out of the accolades that came with saving someone's life.

Looking over, Obi-Wan was relieved to see Zita heading out of the area. It was taking a hot second, because of how many people were stopping her to thank her and to say how impressed they were with what she'd done.

Obi-Wan hurried after her, looking over his shoulder to make sure Silas and Carmen weren't coming, as well. They weren't. Silas had his arm around Carmen's shoulders but she wasn't leaning into him. She was glaring at Zita as if she hoped daggers would come out her eyes and strike her down where she stood.

The level of hate in her expression made Obi-Wan extremely uneasy. And he was very glad the woman would be heading back to California in the next few days.

Rushing after Zita, he caught up to her outside the small break area. "You okay?" he asked.

She looked at him. "Yeah. Why wouldn't I be?"

"That was intense."

To Obi-Wan's surprise, she laughed. "Sage, this is what I do. The Heimlich? It's like Paramedic 101. I mean, I'm glad the woman is all right and that I was in the right place at the right time, but seriously, it wasn't that big of a deal."

Only Zita would say that saving someone's life wasn't a big deal. Although he supposed that it probably wasn't for her. Just like flying most missions wasn't a big deal for Obi-Wan. He was good at what he did, and Zita was obviously just as good at what *she* did. She didn't hesitate to do what needed to be done in order to help that woman.

"Carmen's not happy," he said unnecessarily.

Zita rolled her eyes. "She's never happy. I don't care. She was honestly hurting that woman more than helping her. If she'd been doing the Heimlich right, I wouldn't have interfered. I would've stood by to help if needed, but I wouldn't have yanked her away. But she wasn't, so I did. I'm not going to apologize for that."

"And you shouldn't. You want to come over tonight for the first part of our movie night?"

It was an awkward transition, but Obi-Wan didn't care. They could be interrupted again, and the right time to ask her out might not come again. He was old fashioned. Didn't want to ask her out over text. Or even over the phone. He could read her expressions face-to-face. See if she truly wanted to go out with him again or not.

Zita stopped walking. She hugged her laptop to her chest and looked up at him. "Tonight?"

"Sure. After today, the set will be closed down for a week while they go and set up in the mountains. It's the perfect time for us to get to know each other better. You *are* going to the secondary location, right?"

"Of course. Are you sure you don't need a break from all this?" she asked, putting her hand up and circling it around, as if indicating the entire set...and herself.

"I do. But I don't need a break from *you*," Obi-Wan said simply.

"Oh, that's...that's nice. Sure. I'd like that."

The tension Obi-Wan was feeling lightened, now that she'd agreed. "Great. I can pick you up at your motel again. How does five sound? Is that too early?"

"No, but is it for you? What time do you usually work until?"

It would be a little tight, and he'd have to leave work a bit early, but he hoped his teammates wouldn't mind. The last mission they'd been researching was scrapped, and hopefully it would stay quiet. His leave started in a week, and he'd be able to give all his attention to the more complicated set and the choppers that would be flown in for the movie. Not to mention Carmen and her sidekick wouldn't be on set, which would be a huge relief for Obi-Wan. And probably everyone involved with the project.

Carmen was a diva, and while a very good actress, she was a pain in the ass.

"Sage?"

"Sorry, we usually work until five, but we don't have anything going on right now, so I'm sure I can leave a bit early. We can order dinner once we get to my place. Sound good?"

"Sure."

"And this goes without saying, but you're safe with me, Zita. Just because we're going to my place doesn't mean I expect anything other than a nice evening getting to know a woman I enjoy being around very much."

"Thanks. I appreciate the reassurance."

"Of course."

"But does that mean we're friends?"

Obi-Wan frowned. "I'd like to think so."

"I mean...are we *just* friends? Because I have to admit, I liked that kiss we shared too, but I wouldn't really consider it a friend thing. And don't think I didn't notice how you had my back when Gigantor wanted to take me out for daring to touch his sugar mama. Thank you for that."

She was joking about what happened, but Obi-Wan hadn't realized she even knew what was going on behind her. He thought she was too focused on the woman choking in her arms. But he should've known she was aware on some level that there was a threat. Yet it hadn't stopped her from doing her job in the moment.

His respect for her grew. In many ways, she was a lot like him and his teammates. Or the special forces soldiers they transported. Even when the shit was hitting the fan, they did their jobs, relying on their teammates to have their backs.

"You're welcome. And we're friends for *now*. Do I want more? Yes. *Hell* yes. Not a day has gone by since we've met that I haven't thought about you. And trust me, that hasn't happened in a very long time. But I don't want a one-night stand."

"Me either. But...we live on opposite sides of the country," Zita said, looking a little upset about that.

"One day at a time, sweetheart. That's all we can do. For now, food, movies, and talking. Maybe a kiss here and there."

"Okay. I can live with that. Five o'clock."

"Watch your six today," Obi-Wan warned. "Carmen was

humiliated back there. At least *she* thinks she was. She's not happy, and I have no idea what she'll do as a result."

"I'm planning on staying out of her way for the rest of the day, for sure. Which won't be hard, since I have a meeting with the producer and the set designer about safety on the secondary set. It's important that Logan not be pushed too hard, physically or emotionally, as he films the scenes where he's on the run and hiding in the woods. Actors and actresses can sometimes get too immersed in their roles and suffer as a result."

This woman...she was good down to her bones. And every time she spoke, it felt as if Obi-Wan was falling harder for her. "That's true. Especially considering what the pilot who actually *was* shot down went through. Okay, if you need anything, or if you need to change our plans, just let me know. I have a short meeting about something in the script, then I'll be headed over to the hangar at the airport to look over the helicopters that'll be used at the next location."

"Thanks for the coffee, as usual," Zita said, holding up the cup in a small salute.

"You're welcome. Good job back there."

"Thanks."

"I'll see you tonight."

"Anything I should bring?"

They were prolonging their goodbye, but Obi-Wan didn't even care. "Just yourself."

"Okay. See you around five then."

"Five."

They stood there for a split second, and Obi-Wan wanted to lean down and kiss her more than he wanted to breathe. But they weren't alone, people were walking all around them on the set, and the last thing he wanted to do was cause more gossip or make Zita feel uncomfortable.

As they stared at each other, she licked her lips as if she was thinking about the same thing he was.

"Bye," he said, as he took a step backward.

"See ya."

Forcing himself to turn around and walk away, Obi-Wan couldn't stop himself from looking over his shoulder after a few steps...and he found Zita standing exactly where he'd left her, staring at him with a longing in her eyes that weakened his resolve not to kiss her. But he hadn't endured years of training in patience for nothing.

He'd get to see her tonight. Spend time with her. Kiss her.

It would have to be enough for now.

Thankful that he'd hopefully seen the last of Carmen St. James and wouldn't have to deal with her harassment any longer, Obi-Wan almost felt carefree as he headed for his meeting with the script supervisor. One week, then he'd get to the most interesting part of his job as military advisor.

Not only that, but he'd have a week off from meetings at the base, a week to spend with Zita. They'd both be working, but hopefully they'd be able to find time—more time than they had in the city—to hang out.

And of course, there was the week before filming began again, when the crew was traveling to the west side of the state and preparing the sets. Maybe he could convince Zita to remain in Norfolk, drive together to the new location. They'd have even *more* time to get to know each other.

Things were looking up, and even with the irritation of Carmen, Obi-Wan was thankful as hell for being where he was. For meeting Zita.

CHAPTER TEN

Zita was irritated. She'd had to deal with a call from a bigwig at the studio who wanted to know what the hell had happened that morning, and why she'd pushed Carmen around. It figured the bitch had called someone to complain, trying to get Zita fired. It wouldn't be the first time someone had tried to say she'd done something inappropriate in regard to her medical care.

She'd been able to mitigate any trouble for herself, but only because several other people who'd been in the break room at the time had already corroborated her account of what happened, including the choking woman herself. Which made her wonder why the asshole had bothered to call her in the first place. If he already knew what happened, why try to intimidate her?

That was just one more reason she was tired of working as a set medic. There was politics involved in every career. Someone's ego. But when she was on the ambulance, she didn't have to deal with *nearly* the amount of shit she did while on set. And yes, while there was still the chance she could be sued for medical malpractice, it was a significantly lower chance than when working with the rich and sue-happy Hollywood set.

She hadn't lied to Sage when she'd told him that she always looked at job openings at set locations. She did, for all the reasons she told him. But this time felt different. She loved the Norfolk area. The vibe was so much different than the West Coast. The people were pretty friendly...and Sage was here.

Which was ridiculous. She'd sworn that she'd never be the kind of woman who uprooted her life to be with a man, and here she was, considering doing just that—and she wasn't even *with* Sage.

But she couldn't deny the attraction, the chemistry on both their parts. Which was why she'd wanted clarification about whether he was just looking for a friend...or a friends-with-benefits situation. She didn't think so, but if he'd backed off and decided he was just interested in a fling, she would've turned down his movie invitation. Zita knew herself well enough to know if she continued to hang out with Sage, continued to get to know him, his friends, his likes and dislikes, she'd end up falling for him.

And if he just wanted to get laid? That would hurt.

Zita couldn't deny she'd felt a spark in her womanly parts that she hadn't felt in years when she realized he had her back while she was dealing with the choking woman. Yes, the people she worked with on the ambulance would do the same thing, but with Sage, it felt different for some reason. Personal. *Very* personal. So his saying that he wanted more than a booty call was a relief.

Which was why she was putting extra effort into her appearance for tonight. This would be the first time, other than when they were in his Jeep on the way to and from Anchor Point, that they'd be alone together. And she was very much looking forward to it.

It was all she could do not to stretch to her tiptoes and kiss him when they'd said goodbye that morning. And she swore she could see the same need in his eyes as well. It boded well for some kind of relationship between them. Zita was enjoying the thrill of the chase though. It felt nice that he was trying to impress her with the coffees. That he was moving slowly, even though it was obvious they both wanted more.

She liked being courted. A lot. Too many men these days wanted to fall into bed to "see if they were compatible" instead of getting to know each other outside the bedroom as a way of finding out the same thing. Zita liked sex as much as the next girl, but she needed more in a relationship. She needed to be able to talk to her partner. Needed to know they had something in common. And so far, Sage was ticking all her boxes...

Except for the tiny little fact they lived on opposite sides of the country.

She scowled, pushing the thought to the back of her mind. Like Sage said, one day at a time. She had plenty of time to worry about the "what-ifs" later, if things between them continued to progress. And tonight was the next step in testing their compatibility. She was actually looking forward to dinner and the movie. She'd never been interested in science fiction, but she had a feeling watching the *Star Wars* movies with Sage would be an experience in and of itself.

A text pinged on her phone, letting her know Sage was pulling into the lot of her motel. She grabbed her purse and headed out the door, seeing that he had indeed arrived.

She waited until he'd parked, then he surprised her by jumping out and jogging around to the passenger side of his Jeep, where she was already reaching for the handle. He opened the door for her and smiled.

Lord. This man. Holding her door open? Wearing form-fitting jeans and a tight black T-shirt? And wearing some kind of heavenly cologne? He'd obviously had more time than he thought after leaving work if he was able to change and take a shower and everything.

After she was settled, and he'd gotten back into the Jeep and started driving toward his apartment, she said as much.

"Casper and Laryn had a doctor's appointment this afternoon, and Buck and Mandy were taking their dog, Rain, to the vet for some kind of checkup. So the rest of us decided we were playing hooky as well. I feel bad, as I've been gone more than I've been around lately, but the thing with our job is that when we're on a mission, we can work twenty-four hours a day sometimes, with no breaks. So our colonel is pretty cool about giving us time off when we're on base."

"I get it. Sometimes I get paid to sleep at the station when I'm on shift, and other times I'm working for twelve hours straight. There's no telling when the shit will hit the fan, so we tend to take our downtime when we can get it."

"Exactly," Sage said with a huge smile on his face.

This was one more thing they had in common, and Zita loved it.

They arrived at a midsize apartment complex in under fifteen minutes. It was four stories high and looked clean and the parking lot was well lit. Zita felt safe, not only in Sage's presence, but because of the location of where he lived. Which was probably a little silly, since bad people could live in the most expensive and fancy places, but there was something about the complex that appealed to her.

Walking into Sage's apartment, Zita hadn't been sure what to expect. Would it be a typical bachelor pad? Would it be as neat as a pin? Was Sage a slob? She was pleased to see it was none of the above. It looked like her own apartment back in California, when she had time to actually live there.

There were photographs everywhere—which Zita made a mental note to check out when she could—the requisite large-screen TV, a comfy-looking love seat, and she absolutely adored the two oversized tan suede chairs, with blankets and pillows stacked up on the seats. There was also a footstool in front of each. They looked extremely comfortable, and she loved that apparently Sage liked to be cozy while watching television.

He had no coffee table, but he *did* have a decent-size table in the small dining area next to the galley kitchen. That space wasn't anything special, but it included the normal appliances, plus a microwave, a coffee machine, and what looked like an air fryer on the counter. Off the kitchen, there was a hallway that had four doors, and a half bath sat off the living area.

It was a fairly large apartment for a single guy, but obviously taken care of, clean and lived in, which made Zita feel more at home.

"It's not much, but it's home," Sage said, after giving her time to look around. "I'd offer to give you a tour, but it's not too exciting. Three bedrooms, two and a half baths, the normal closets, and of course, this room and the kitchen. I've got a designated parking space, which I love, and there's twenty-four-hour security."

"Three bedrooms?" Zita asked. Then immediately regretted the words. Why should she care how many bedrooms the man had in his apartment? It was none of her business.

"I wanted enough room so when my parents came to visit, none of us would feel as if we were on top of each other. They don't have a ton of extra money, so I wouldn't feel comfortable with them staying in a motel when they're here." He shrugged. "They haven't come out too many times, but it's worked out well when they have."

Zita's heart did a little somersault in her chest. Of *course* Sage was so thoughtful. He wasn't the stereotypical macho badass military man someone might assume he was.

"What are you in the mood to eat for dinner?" he asked, walking into the kitchen and opening a drawer. He pulled out a stack of papers and set them on the counter. "These are all my favorite places to order from. Take your pick."

Zita chuckled as she saw the number of takeout menus. She

shuffled through them and decided on an Italian place that had the most delicious-looking picture of a plate of spaghetti piled high with sauce and meatballs. Intellectually, she realized that the real thing probably wouldn't live up to what the picture advertised, but she was starving and craving some carbs.

"Good choice," Sage said with a grin. "I order from here all the time. They know me well. And for the record, their pasta is homemade, which makes all the difference in the world."

After she told him what she wanted, Sage made the call to the restaurant. He could've used one of the food delivery apps, but it seemed the restaurant had their own delivery drivers, and they definitely knew Sage. Whoever he was speaking with seemed to know him personally, because he laughed several times while giving his order.

He hung up and said, "It'll take about thirty minutes or so for them to get here."

"Sounds good."

"And before you think I went overboard and ordered enough for twelve people, Teresa, the owner, was curious as to why I was ordering two dinners instead of one tonight, and when she heard I was on a date, she got all giddy and told me she was going to 'take care of us.' I'm a little afraid of what that means, but most likely it's probably extra bread, meatballs, and possibly even a side dish or two thrown in for free."

"Oh, that's nice," Zita said, secretly more pleased than she wanted to admit that it seemed as if Sage dating wasn't a normal occurrence.

"You want to start the first movie while we wait? They're kind of long. I thought we'd start with the original movies, even though technically they aren't the first ones in the chronological series. The timeline of the films is a little confusing, but my favorites are still the old school ones. They aren't as full of CGI, and they're where I learned my love for the franchise."

"Whatever you suggest."

"Again, the movies are longish, around two hours each, and we won't be able to get through them all tonight, but hopefully you'll enjoy what we get through enough to want to continue watching the others later."

"I'm sure I will. I'm easily entertained, although I don't have a lot of time to watch movies, or read, or catch up on the shows that are so popular these days."

"Same. I like my sleep too much."

Zita grinned. "You too?"

He returned her happy smile. "Definitely. And luckily, I'm a good sleeper. Meaning, I fall asleep fast and can almost always sleep through the night."

"That's awesome. I'm the same. Except maybe after some especially gnarly calls."

He sobered. "Yeah. Sometimes when I get home from a mission that either went sideways or someone got hurt or almost ended badly, I'm the same way."

Zita was having a hard time wrapping her mind around how compatible she and Sage seemed to be. But what was the old saying? Opposites attract? If they were *too* alike, did that mean they would have issues if they actually tried to take a serious shot at dating?

She shook the thought off. It was too early for that. She and Sage were simply getting to know each other tonight. Not planning their wedding and how many kids they wanted.

"Pick a seat and I'll get us some drinks. I've got lemonade, water, coffee, and various flavored teas."

"Oh, I'd love a tea. Surprise me."

He nodded and turned to flick on an electric kettle on the counter, which had been hidden behind the air fryer.

Zita wandered into the living area and looked around. She could choose the love seat or one of the oversized chairs. Both had pros and cons.

She decided on the big chair…because all she could picture was her and Sage sharing it.

When he entered the room with two mugs in his hand, she smiled at him and asked, "Can these oversized chairs hold two people?"

He grinned back before saying, "I don't know. I've never attempted it."

His words made Zita feel all warm and fuzzy. Knowing he hadn't snuggled with another woman in either of his chairs meant something to her. "Shall we find out?"

"Hell yes," he said under his breath. Then he held out one of the mugs to her. "Try this, see if it's to your liking. If not, I can brew something different."

Zita took the cup from him and inhaled the steam coming from the tea. "Mmmm. This smells great."

"Vanilla almond. It's one of my favorites."

Taking a sip, Zita almost moaned. "It's delicious."

His smile grew, and Zita felt all tingly inside. He put his cup on a small table next to the chair where she was sitting. "Scoot over to one side. We'll see if we both fit. If it's not comfortable, when dinner arrives, we can change the seating arrangement."

It was a good idea. This was basically a trial run, which Zita liked.

She scooted over, and Sage lowered himself onto the cushion next to her. Surprisingly, they fit perfectly in the chair. Her thigh was pressed up against his, but the chair was wide enough to accommodate them both comfortably. Sage's body heat seeped into hers, and he smelled really good.

Letting herself relax, Zita leaned against him. He put his arm around her shoulders, which made their position even more comfortable. They both drank their tea and instead of starting the movie immediately, they talked about nothing in particular for a while. It was…nice.

Before they knew it, they'd both finished their tea, and Sage finally reached for the remote. "You ready for this?" he asked with a grin.

"As ready as I'm going to be," she told him.

He clicked quite a few buttons, and then the first movie started.

Zita wasn't much of a sci-fi fan, which was why she'd never bothered to watch any of the franchise, but to her surprise, she found herself getting sucked into the storyline. At least until there was a knock on the door. Sage paused the movie then extricated himself from the chair and went to answer.

Zita met him at the table, and when he started to unpack the paper bags full of food, she could only inhale in appreciation.

"Oh my, it smells heavenly."

"Wait until you taste it," Sage told her with a small smile.

He was right, the Italian food was some of the best she'd ever had. And the owner obviously had a sweet spot for Sage, because there was so much extra food it wasn't funny. She'd even thrown in some cannoli for dessert.

After she helped Sage package up the leftovers, he asked, "Ready for more *Star Wars*?"

"Definitely."

"You're enjoying it?"

"More than I thought I would, if I'm being honest."

"Good. You want to sit with me again or take the other chair or couch?"

"With you," Zita said without hesitation.

They got resettled in the chair, and this time, Zita asked if he'd mind if she put her legs over his. He agreed, and that's how she found herself snuggled into the crook of his arm, feeling full and warm, and safer than she'd felt in a very long time.

As the movie restarted, Zita was quickly absorbed in the plot again. When Obi-Wan Kenobi showed up, she lifted her head and turned to look at Sage with a huge smile...only to find he was sound asleep. His head was resting on the back of the chair and his mouth slightly open.

Zita chuckled to herself. She'd been enjoying the feel of his body against hers and wondering if they'd end their night with more kisses, and he'd fallen asleep. It was kind of hilarious. But she didn't mind. He'd been working extremely hard both on set and at his regular job.

Besides, he'd seen the movie probably hundreds of times. Okay, maybe not that many, but certainly dozens. Not to mention the chair was comfortable as hell, and he'd pulled a blanket over them both so they were cozy and warm. They'd had large amounts of carbs, and if she wasn't as interested in the plot as she was, she would've been asleep from a food coma herself.

Putting her head back down, Zita let him sleep. She could rib him about the character he was named after when the movie was over. She curled even closer to him and sighed in content. Honestly, this was her ideal date. Not Sage falling asleep on her, of course, but good food and being alone with him, instead of being around tons of people as she was most of her days.

As the credits began to roll, Zita was anxious to start the next movie. She needed to know what happened. But she wasn't sure how to operate the complicated remote sitting on the small table next to Sage, and she really didn't want to watch it without him anyway. So instead...she closed her eyes. Tonight had been great, even though Sage slept for most of the movie. She should wake him up, but she hated to disturb his rest.

She decided to let him sleep just a little longer. She'd sit there and rest her eyes for a moment...

She wasn't sure what woke her. All she knew was that the TV was on and she felt disoriented.

"Zita, are you awake?"

"Mmmmm," she mumbled.

"I fell asleep."

Memories returned. Sage. His apartment. The movie. She'd obviously fallen asleep in his arms. "What time is it?"

"One."

Zita frowned. "In the morning?"

He smirked. "Yeah."

"Oh shit!" she exclaimed, sitting up. But Sage kept his arm around her, holding her so she couldn't immediately leap up from the chair.

"Easy. It's okay. You want me to take you back to the motel now? Or do you want to go back to sleep? I have to get up in a few hours and head to base for PT, but when I get back, we could go out for breakfast or something. You don't have to be on set today, right?"

She was still half asleep, but it was hard to believe Sage was inviting her to stay in his apartment while he went to work out. For two people who hadn't planned on anything but a simple movie date, things sure were moving quickly.

"I might go by the set later to make sure everything's okay as they're packing up, but no, I don't have to be there at the regular time."

"So you'll stay? You can stay here in the chair, or you can sleep in a guest room."

"Here," she said, then yawned.

"You want me to get up?"

"No."

"I'm sorry I missed the movie."

"It's okay. But I want to see the next one."

"And the next *Star Wars* junkie has been created."

"Maybe. I'm reserving judgement."

"Thanks for being so cool about this. I didn't mean to fall asleep on you."

"It's okay. You were tired."

"Yeah. You comfortable? Too hot? Too cold?"

"Perfect."

"Good. Close your eyes and get some more sleep. I'll probably wake you up when I have to leave, but just ignore me and go back to sleep."

"M'kay."

Zita swore she felt Sage's lips on her forehead, but she was too tired to open her eyes to see for sure. All she knew was that she was warm and comfortable. She fell asleep with the scent of Sage in her nostrils and a feeling of contentment in her soul.

CHAPTER ELEVEN

"She's still at your place?" Buck asked. "Is that smart?"

"Zita's not going to steal anything. Hell, she doesn't even have a car," Obi-Wan said, feeling irritated with his copilot.

"No, I meant, is it smart for you to get any closer? It's obvious you feel something for her, but she lives in California. It's already kind of hard to have any kind of relationship with us doing what we do, but with someone who lives on the other side of the country? I'd imagine that's near impossible."

His friend was right. A relationship with Zita probably wasn't smart, but Obi-Wan couldn't stop the train he was on now even if he wanted to...which he didn't. He *liked* Zita. Admired her. Wanted to be around her every moment he could get.

He'd been surprised when he'd woken up in the middle of the night from a sound sleep with Zita still in his lap. More surprising was how much he'd enjoyed it. Leaving her to head to the base for PT was actually difficult, which made him realize how much it was going to suck when the movie was done filming and Zita went back to California.

They'd both have some decisions to make about the two of

them, but for now, he was going to enjoy her company when and where he could.

"Obi-Wan?" Buck asked, bringing him back to the present. "What are you thinking about the future for you guys?"

"Honestly? I'm just looking forward to next week, when we're in Fallport for the filming of the rest of the movie. I like being around Zita. She's smart, and beautiful, and the more I'm around her, the more I *want* to be around her. I have no idea what's going to happen after that, but I'm not going to back away from the most interesting woman I've ever met just because I'm afraid of being hurt."

"Wow, that's grown up of you," Edge joked.

"Shut it," Obi-Wan growled.

They were running through the streets of the base; for once, Casper hadn't made them head to the beach, which everyone was thankful for.

"Casper, you and Laryn okay?" Pyro asked.

"We're good," their team leader said. "Finding out she was pregnant was a surprise, but now that we've had a bit of time to process it, we're way more excited than stressed."

"Good."

"As you should be."

"Have you told Nate?"

Nate was Casper's twin, who was in the Navy. They were as close as brothers could be, having that special "twin connection" a lot of them had.

"Didn't need to. He knew something was up and called the other night. Wanted to know what was wrong and who he needed to kill."

Everyone chuckled, knowing the SEAL was probably only half kidding.

"He *did* ask something we hadn't even thought about," Casper added.

"What's that?" Pyro asked.

"If we're having twins."

Everyone went silent for a beat—then as a group, they all burst out laughing.

"Holy shit, that's right, twins obviously run in the family."

"Are you?"

"If Laryn was nervous before, she's probably even more so now."

"We don't know yet. It's still too early. The twelve-week ultrasound is more definitive, so we'll have to wait and see then," Casper said, sounding excited about the prospect.

"I take it you wouldn't be upset if it was twins," Edge said.

"Not in the least, although it'll mean more stress on Laryn. Not only her body and the pregnancy, but thinking about child-care and her job after she gives birth," Casper explained.

He wasn't wrong. It was scary enough to think about what to do with *one* child in deployments, but two? No one wanted to contemplate a future without Laryn as head mechanic on their choppers, but Obi-Wan wasn't sure what the couple was going to do. Zita's suggestion about a live-in nanny was good, but was it actually viable? He didn't know. All he knew was that he was glad he wasn't in his team leader's shoes. Or Laryn's. Having to decide whether or not to give up the job you loved would suck.

But if he and Zita wanted a chance at a relationship, wouldn't she have to make a similar difficult decision? It wasn't as if *he* could move. Well...he probably could. If he asked the Army to transfer him to another Night Stalker team. One that was stationed near the naval base in San Diego. It would get him closer to LA, where she'd continue to get film work. But was that something he was willing to do?

He loved his fellow pilots. They'd fought like hell to be together, and to get special permission to be stationed in Virginia. Would he give that up for a woman?

Before meeting Zita, he would have said an empathetic no. But now? He wasn't sure. And that was a surprising sign that he was already way more serious about her than he was admitting out loud.

The rest of PT went by fairly quickly, although they were all groaning by the end. But working out was a necessary evil to keep their bodies in tip-top shape. They had to be ready for anything, in the air and on the ground. Situations could change on a dime and they had to be ready for whatever was thrown at them.

Obi-Wan had to be back at base by eight for a regular workday, since he wouldn't be going to a movie set. He had a week before it was time to head to the small town of Fallport, on the opposite side of the state. That was where everyone would be staying for the next part of the shoot. They'd travel about an hour into the woods each day, where they'd film the most intense parts of the movie.

The weather was still a little chilly, which deviated from the original incident the movie was based on. It was the middle of summer when the Air Force pilot had gone down, forced to traverse the jungle to safety. But thankfully the director didn't want to deal with extreme summer conditions, content to film in cooler weather.

Obi-Wan's anticipation was high as he drove back to his apartment. It felt...*nice* to know someone was there waiting for him. He'd gotten very used to being alone.

Taking the steps up to his third-floor apartment, Obi-Wan unlocked his door, unsure what he'd find. Would Zita still be sleeping? It was only six o'clock, after all. Or would she be up and having second thoughts about staying the night? Would she be watching TV, having a cup of coffee? He didn't know if she was a morning person or not and was looking forward to finding out.

Or had she called a ride-share and left altogether?

The first thing he noticed when he stepped inside was the smell of freshly brewed coffee...which answered his questions about whether Zita was awake and still in his apartment.

He found her sitting at his table, an open book in front of her and a steaming mug of coffee in her hand. Relief at seeing her there made Obi-Wan's knees weak. She was smiling a little shyly at him when he approached.

"Hi. How was PT?"

Obi-Wan couldn't stop himself from leaning over and lightly kissing her. It felt natural. As if he'd done it a million times. Thankfully, she didn't rear back or gape at him if he had two heads. She simply smiled wider...then licked her lips as if she wanted to taste his kiss. Which was a huge turn-on.

Hoping the gray sweats he had on would hide his erection—and doubting it, because he'd seen plenty of memes and videos on social media from women extolling the virtues of how well that particular article of clothing highlighted a man's dick—he turned and went into the kitchen toward the coffeemaker.

"I hope it's okay that I made coffee."

"Of course it is," Obi-Wan told her. "In fact, it's welcomed. And to answer your question, PT was good. Casper wasn't quite as dickfull as he's been recently."

"Dickfull?" Zita asked with a chuckle.

He shrugged. "Felt more polite than calling him a power-hungry, taking-out-his-worries-and-stress-on-us asshole."

She giggled, and the sound went straight to his cock, not doing anything to make the damn thing go down.

"You find everything you need?"

"In your kitchen? Yes. It's very organized."

"That, but also in general."

"Yeah. I appreciate you putting out the toothbrush for me."

"Of course. I'll jump in the shower quickly and we can go to breakfast before I take you to the motel and head back to base."

"Okay."

Taking another sip of the dark brew, Obi-Wan did his best to keep his out-of-control dick away from Zita's view as he headed for the hallway and his bedroom.

His shower was fast, but not as quick as usual, since he took the time to jack off. It felt wrong and perverted, especially knowing the object of his lust was in the other room, but if he didn't relieve the pressure, he'd probably embarrass Zita, which was the last thing he wanted to do.

Finally feeling as if he could walk without hunching over, Obi-Wan quickly got dressed and headed back out to where Zita was still sitting at his table.

"What were you reading?" he asked, noticing the book she'd had earlier was now gone.

"I hope you don't mind. I looked through your shelves when I got up."

"Of course not."

"It was one on Night Stalkers."

He nodded. "The one by Durant and Hartov? Green cover?"

"Yeah. I didn't get very far though. I wanted to read more about what you do."

Obi-Wan walked over to his bookshelf and found the book she'd been reading, pulling it out and handing it to her. "Take it with you. You'll have some time to read this week, won't you?"

"Yeah. You don't mind?"

"Nope."

"Is it accurate?" she asked with a sparkle in her eye. "I mean, I don't want to waste my time if it's all made up to sell books."

"It's pretty good."

She laughed. "I have no idea what that means. But don't tell me. If I knew half of what you actually did, it would probably terrify me."

She wasn't exactly wrong. The book was fairly accurate, but it left out a lot of the more harrowing things Obi-Wan and those like him did on a regular basis. "You hungry?"

"Starving."

"Great. Because the place I'm bringing you to this morning is awesome. You'll roll out of there."

Zita grinned. "Because that's something every girl wants to do."

Obi-Wan headed for the door, grabbed her purse off the counter on his way. "Damn, this thing is heavy!" he said, surprised. He held it out to her.

She took it with a grin. "A girl's gotta have her things."

"Things meaning your medical equipment, just in case, right?"

"Exactly."

The trip to the diner was smooth, as there wasn't much traffic out yet, but Obi-Wan knew the place he was taking her to would be packed, as it usually was on weekday mornings. It didn't look like anything special from the outside, but the food was top-notch and filling. And a local favorite.

There was a relatively short wait before they were escorted to a booth toward the back of the restaurant. Obi-Wan was tempted to sit next to Zita instead of across from her, but didn't want to scare her off this early in their relationship.

Could he call what they had a relationship? He thought so, but he had no idea what the woman across from him thought.

"Did you go back to sleep after I left?" he asked, after they'd ordered coffee. She'd woken up when he'd attempted to slip out from under her earlier that morning.

"Not really. I mean, I dozed, but as comfortable as your chair is, it's not as comfy without you in it with me."

And just like that, his cock was hard again, damn it. But her words made Obi-Wan feel good. Really good. And hopefully answered his earlier question about whether they were in a relationship or not.

"Not sure that chair will ever be the same for me again either," he told her.

"So...what's good here?"

Recognizing her attempt at lightening the conversation, Obi-Wan obliged. "Everything. Seriously, you can't go wrong with whatever you order. The waffles, the eggs, the omelets, it's all amazing."

After they ordered, Obi-Wan leaned his elbows on the table as he held his mug of coffee in his hands. "So...what can I expect from this next stage in the film? What's it like on location?"

Zita had no problem telling him all about what to expect and how things would go. They would have long days out in the woods, the director would be grumpy as hell, the camera operators, sound department, wardrobe, hair and makeup, grip department, lighting, and everyone else would be doing their best to stay out of the way, and yet still be immediately available for whatever was needed.

It sounded like it would be chaotic as hell, an environment Obi-Wan thrived on.

"But there will also be some down time. And it'll be boring at times, because while there are other actors out there besides Logan, like the ones portraying the soldiers looking for him, most of the scenes are centered around the star. A lot of shots will just be him in the woods."

Obi-Wan nodded. He understood that. This film was different in general, in that the majority of the scenes were just Logan's character and what he goes through alone in the wilderness. He'd seen the script, had gone over it with a fine-tooth comb.

What he was looking forward to most were the scenes with the choppers...naturally.

Their food arrived, and as he'd told Zita, everything looked delicious. She'd ordered strawberry waffles with a side of bacon and a bowl of fruit, and he'd gotten the meat lover's omelet, which was absolutely huge.

As they ate, Obi-Wan's thoughts turned to the film's *other* star. "Carmen won't be there, right?" he asked, wanting to make sure.

"No, thank goodness. She and Logan have a few more scenes to film, but they have to wait for when he gets home and regains his muscle and weight, because they're scenes from the beginning of the movie, before he's on the run in the woods."

"That's good news."

"Absolutely," she agreed. "But I do have some news that *isn't* as good."

Obi-Wan braced. "What's that?"

"Her bodyguard? Silas? He's taking over for Logan's bodyguard. The guy he brought with him from California. I guess his wife was in an accident, and he had to fly back home."

"Well, shit," Obi-Wan said, the food that tasted so good a moment ago suddenly sitting like a lump in his stomach.

"Yeah. But maybe without Carmen around, he'll be less of an asshole."

Obi-Wan merely lifted a brow in response.

Zita sighed. "I know. I said *maybe*."

Making a mental vow to keep his eye on Zita even more, Obi-Wan said, "We can hope."

They finished up their breakfast and as they were leaving, Zita said, "You were right, I feel as if I'm rolling out of here."

They both laughed. Obi-Wan couldn't remember laughing so much around a woman in the past. Zita pulled out protective instincts he didn't realize he had, even as she made him feel... lighter. His entire life had been focused toward his job. On being alert for people acting strange, on watching his teammates' backs. He now felt as if he had a different focus.

Zita.

If he hadn't seen both Casper and Buck morph into the men they were today around their girlfriends, he probably would've been a little more concerned about the unfamiliar feelings he had toward Zita. But since he looked up to and admired his friends, he didn't feel as if he was less of a man for suddenly wanting to do everything in his power to make this woman happy. To hear her laugh.

As he drove toward her motel, he felt a little sad that their time together that morning went by so quickly. He couldn't wait to see her again.

"Want to do this again tonight? The movie thing, I mean?" he blurted.

She smiled shyly. "Yes."

Relief swept over Obi-Wan.

He pulled into the parking lot of the motel and into the spot in front of her room. "I know you're an adult and can look after yourself, but I have to say it. If you need anything, I'm only a call or text away. Okay?"

"Thanks. And yes, I can take care of myself, but it's always nice to know I've got some backup if I need it."

"You definitely have it."

They stared at each other for a moment, then they both moved at the same time, leaning toward each other eagerly.

Their kiss wasn't long, and therefore not nearly as satisfying as Obi-Wan preferred. But he did like the anticipation their kisses made him feel. They were on a path toward being more intimate, he knew that, and he hoped her kisses were an indication she did too. But he was enjoying the journey. The fact that neither were looking to jump into bed simply to scratch an itch.

"I'll be in touch later this afternoon about tonight. About what time you want me to pick you up."

"Okay."

"Thanks for not getting pissed about me falling asleep on you. Or under you, as the case may be."

"Of course. Thanks for being a man I could trust."

"Thanks for staying the night."

"Thanks for the Italian and the tea."

Obi-Wan grinned. They were being ridiculous. Prolonging the inevitable goodbye.

He reached out and put his hand on the back of her neck and pulled her toward him, kissing her again. She came willingly, and the feel of her hand on his shoulder, her fingernails digging in as she kissed him, was a huge turn-on. Proof that she wanted him as much as he wanted her.

He pulled back reluctantly. "Have a good day," he said softly, running a thumb over her swollen and glistening lips.

"You too," she said.

He dropped his hand, and she reached for the handle of the Jeep. He watched as she got out, shut the door, and walked to her motel room. He didn't budge until she'd unlocked the door and turned to wave at him. He gave her a chin lift, wanting nothing more than to join her on the other side of that door.

Forcing himself to look behind him, Obi-Wan backed out of the parking space and headed toward base.

It was going to be a long day. A long week. But his reward at the end of it was Zita.

Tonight, and next week when they would be spending almost all day together on set. He'd never looked forward to spending hours in the woods so much in his life.

CHAPTER TWELVE

Zita had never been so horny. She hated that word. It sounded like something a teenager would use in some cheesy eighties movie. But that's what she was. She'd spent every night but one hanging out with Sage in the last week. He'd asked her to stay in town while the crew packed up the set and moved to the other side of the state, and she'd happily agreed. They'd finished the original three *Star Wars* movies and moved on to the more recent ones. She had to agree with him that the older movies had a certain...something that the newer ones didn't. But she still enjoyed the storylines and was now a total fan.

That could be because of the person she'd been watching the movies with though. Sage took the time to explain things she didn't understand, and he didn't give her crap when she teared up during sad or poignant scenes.

But the best part of the last week was getting to know Sage better. She enjoyed spending time in his company, and the more she was around him, the more she liked the man. She felt giddy pretty much at all times when they were together...and heated, as if her blood was hotter than it should be when they sat together in his big ol' chair. His hand on her leg felt like a brand, and it was all she could do not to rip off her shirt and beg him to have his way with her.

But she was also enjoying the pace they'd set. She felt no pressure to sleep with him. Urgency and desire, yes. Pressure, no.

She hadn't spent the night again, even though she kind of missed waking up in his arms in the middle of the night. She'd never had such a compulsion to sleep with another person before. She preferred her space. Liked being able to spread out in bed. To not have to worry about someone else when she rolled over in the middle of the night. But she was beginning to realize she'd only preferred that because she'd never been with someone like Sage. Someone who made her feel safe simply by being in his presence.

Now, they were leaving for the other side of the state. For a town called Fallport. It would be their home base for the next part of filming. Everything she'd read online about the town made it seem like an awesome little community. A few years ago they were made famous because a paranormal show about Bigfoot was filmed there, and someone from the cast was murdered. They now had an annual Bigfoot expo, and the gazebo in the middle of town had a permanent chainsaw carving of Bigfoot proudly displayed beside it.

They were also known for something called Pickleport, a summer festival complete with a parade and booths and everything a small-town event should have. It sounded like a Hallmark movie town come to life, and Zita couldn't wait to see and experience it for herself.

Almost all of the crew for the movie was staying at the Mangree Motel and RV Park. It sounded hokey and cheap, but the pictures online made it seem charming and quaint. There was even a pool, though it wasn't open yet. The production company had rented out the entire motel for the crew, but Logan Striker and Harry Grubbner would be staying at a bed and breakfast called Chestnut Street Manor. It was really the only "high end" place to stay in Fallport.

Zita didn't feel slighted by that, however. The only other options for the crew were a couple of chain hotels out by the highway, farther away from the quaint little town. And she'd much rather stay at a local establishment that put money in the hands of small business owners than a huge corporation.

Fallport also had one of those big box stores near the main highway that led into town, as well as some chain restaurants, but she was most excited to see the town square and all the locally owned businesses. The bakery, the bar, the used bookstore. And especially the coffee shop. The diner also looked amazing; the stained-glass window in the front was a work of art, and she bet it looked even more beautiful in person.

All-in-all, she was looking forward to this shoot more than any other she'd been on. And it wasn't just because of the location—which was much better than some warehouse where sets had been built—but because of the man she'd get to spend even more time with.

When he'd asked her to stay in town, Sage had also offered to drive her to Fallport, instead of Zita taking the bus the film company had rented. The equipment had been sent out days ago, along with most of the crew. All that was left was transporting the few employees who'd stayed behind in Norfolk, doing online prep for the upcoming on-location shoot.

She took him up on his offer without hesitation. She'd been in a car with Sage several times in the last week, but figured spending a few hours with him on the road would tell her even more about his personality. Did he speed excessively? Did he get overly pissed at other drivers around him? Did he text while driving? All things that would turn her off and might give her second thoughts about getting involved with the man.

Who was she kidding? She was already "involved."

He was the first person she thought of when she woke up

and, because of his habit of texting her to say good night, the last person she thought of before she fell asleep. And she didn't think she had anything to worry about with him behind the wheel of his Jeep. The man was a freaking Night Stalker helicopter pilot. Of course, the two weren't exactly the same, but she doubted he'd be so great at his job, and then be an asshole on the road.

Her bags were packed and she was waiting for him when he pulled up to the motel. She had a goofy grin on her face, but she couldn't help it. She was so looking forward to spending much more time with him this week, since he'd be on the set full-time, rather than spending all day on the naval base.

He was also grinning as he got out of his Jeep and came toward her. He grabbed both her large and small suitcase, making them seem way lighter than she knew they were, and she shifted her backpack and purse on her shoulder as she followed him to the back of the vehicle. His duffel bag was already there. Then he moved to the passenger side and held open the door for her. He'd done that every time he'd picked her up, and it never failed to make her feel all warm and gooey inside.

It was a five-hour trip to Fallport, and everyone involved in the movie had an orientation and logistics meeting later that afternoon. All told, it took six and a half hours to make it to the small town at the base of the Appalachian mountains, after a stop for lunch and because traffic getting out of Norfolk was horrendous. But for once, Zita didn't mind.

She and Sage talked nonstop. She felt as if she knew him even better by the time they were pulling into the Mangree Motel's parking lot. Just as she hoped he knew *her* better, as well. They'd talked about everything from their childhoods, their parents, how she got interested in being an EMT and involved in the movie industry, to how difficult the training and tests were to become a Night Stalker.

She'd also learned more about Laryn and Mandy, and the

awful things they'd been through. She was even more impressed with the two women than she'd been before, and that was saying something. What they'd each experienced was horrific, and Zita was so glad they had men like their boyfriends, who were there for them both during and after their ordeals.

Zita met Sage at the front of the Jeep and they walked into the small office at the Mangree together. There was an older woman behind the desk, and she greeted them with a huge smile.

"Hi, I'm Edna. My husband and I welcome you to the Mangree. We're so happy you're here."

"Thanks! I'm Zita Darlington, and this is Obadiah Engle," she said.

"Hmmm, I've got Zita on the list, but I'm so sorry...I'm not seeing *you*," Edna replied with a frown, looking at Sage.

"It's probably under Obi-Wan," he said.

"Oh! You're right. My husband and I kind of chuckled when we got the list of names. Obi-Wan, like Elvis or Prince. Only one name, huh?"

Zita giggled.

"Something like that. Except I'm not a famous musician."

"And you're not dead," Edna deadpanned, her gaze roaming up and down his body in appreciation.

Zita couldn't hold back another chuckle. Edna had to be in her seventies, and the way she was eyeballing Sage was hilarious.

To his credit, he didn't seem uncomfortable in the least.

"I'm going to put you in room twelve, it's right next to the office," the woman told Zita. "It's nice and safe. If you need anything, you can come here. We've hired a trustworthy young man to work the overnight shift. He's a gamer," she added in a whisper. "Plays Dungeons and Dragons almost all night, says he's thrilled that he gets paid to do what he loves."

"Cool," Zita said with a smile.

"And you, young man, are in room twenty-two."

"That's fine," Sage said.

"It's too bad it's too early for the Bigfoot Expo or the Pickleport Festival. They both take place in the summer, and this place is packed with tourists. But then again, it's probably for the best, as the motel would be all booked up. We're happy for the revenue your movie is bringing to the area.

"There are little fridges in your rooms, and microwaves too. We don't allow toasters or hot plates, as there was a small incident a few years ago where the entire motel almost burned down after a guest left the burner on and placed a few plastic bags too close to the thing.

"We have no restaurant here at the Mangree, but you can't go wrong with Sunny Side Up in town. Or the Sweet Tooth, our local bakery. And I'd be remiss if I didn't tell you that Grinders has the best coffee and fancy coffee-flavored drinks on this side of the state. If you have any questions, don't hesitate to ask. Here are your keys."

She handed over two real metal keys, not the plastic key cards that so many motels and hotels had moved to. Zita took it and smiled at the woman. The Mangree Motel might look like a typical low-budget place to stay from the outside, but the friendliness from the owner made it feel homey and comfortable. She just hoped the rooms were as nice as Edna.

"And we don't tolerate any funny business here," Edna said sternly. "Quiet hours are ten to six, and safety is our first priority. If you see anything hinky, let someone know and we'll contact Simon, our police chief."

"Yes, ma'am," Sage replied.

"Sounds perfect," Zita told her.

Edna smiled. "You two have a good day now. I hear you have a meeting over at the high school gym this afternoon. Have fun exploring the area, but don't be late to your meeting."

Edna was as grandmotherly as Zita could imagine, and she wasn't exactly surprised that she knew their schedule. Small towns were much like the sets she worked on...gossip thrived in places like this.

"We won't. Thanks for the tips," Sage told her.

"You're welcome. If you have any other questions, don't hesitate to come find me."

"Thanks."

They headed out of the office, and Zita found herself still smiling as she looked up at Sage. He also had a small grin on his face.

"I like her," Zita blurted.

"Me too. What do you want to do before our meeting?"

"Go to the square. I want to see all the places I've been reading about online."

"You got it. How about we check out our rooms, put our stuff away, then meet back here in about fifteen minutes? Is that enough time?"

"Perfect," Zita said. And it was. She'd much rather spend her time exploring than hanging out in her motel room until it was time for the meeting.

After getting their bags from his Jeep, Sage walked her to her door, which was a nice thing to do. It wasn't as if he wouldn't be able to see her entering and exiting her room, since his door was down a straight pathway at the other end of the motel.

Zita unlocked her door and walked into her room. It was a typical space, with two beds, a dresser, TV, a tiny table next to the window, and the bathroom toward the back. But it was different in that there were what looked like homemade quilts on the bed, and the walls were bright, not beige and boring. The floor also wasn't covered in industrial carpet, it looked like an easy-to-clean synthetic tile of some sort. It also smelled...good. Really good. Like vanilla, which made Zita's belly growl.

"Wow, this is nothing like I expected," she said.

Sage was standing respectfully at the doorway. He'd put her suitcases just inside but hadn't followed her into the room. "It's nice. Really nice," he agreed. "Hopefully mine will be just as cool. Though I wouldn't put it past Edna to save this room for single women, since it's close to the office and so nicely decorated. And I saw security cameras outside pointing at the entrances to the rooms. It's cool that she's so security conscious."

"I hope your room is just like this one."

Sage simply shrugged. "Doesn't really matter, as I've slept in some pretty awful places. No matter *what* the room looks or smells like, it'll be a step up from some...*accommodations* I've experienced."

Zita frowned. She didn't like the thought of him sleeping in crappy conditions.

"Don't look so worried. I'm sure it'll be fine. Edna and her husband aren't going to make one room beautiful and ignore the rest of them."

She wasn't worried about his room. But she nodded anyway.

"It's going to bother you, isn't it? How about we meet at *my* room in fifteen then? You can see for yourself that I'm not living in a hovel while you're here in room twelve in the lap of luxury."

Zita quickly nodded. She was curious as to what the rest of the rooms looked like anyway, so she wasn't going to turn down the chance to have her curiosity appeased.

She watched Sage turn and head down the walkway. She stepped into her room after he disappeared into his own...but not before he saw her staring, and gave her a big smile and wave before closing his door.

She closed her own door and stood there for a moment before grabbing the larger of her suitcases and putting it on the bed. She had time to quickly unpack and freshen up before she met Sage and they explored Fallport. She wasn't sure which she was looking forward to the most—the tour, or spending more time with the man she was falling for.

CHAPTER THIRTEEN

Obi-Wan grinned at Zita. She was adorable. Everything excited her. Everything seemed new and fun. Her enthusiasm was contagious, and he found he was enjoying himself immensely as they walked around Fallport's main square.

When she'd seen his motel room—almost an exact replica of hers, minus the homemade quilts on the beds—he didn't miss her satisfaction that he wouldn't be sleeping in lesser accommodations. It had been a long time since anyone had fussed over him like she did. It felt nice.

They had about an hour to walk around and check out the small town, which Obi-Wan thought wasn't going to be nearly enough time for Zita.

They started in the northeast corner at a bar called On the Rocks. It wasn't too busy, since it was still early, but it was almost as clean as the motel rooms. There was one waitress, who didn't hesitate to greet them as they walked in, and one bartender behind the bar. The walls were covered in newspaper and magazine articles about Bigfoot and about the paranormal show that was filmed in town. It had a homey feel, and Obi-Wan was looking forward to having a beer or two in the place after filming wrapped.

Next up on their tour was The Sweet Tooth. The moment they walked in, his stomach growled. It smelled like pastries and fresh bread. He was a sucker for bread right out of the oven. If someone created a room spray of baking bread, they'd make a killing. Zita bought a cinnamon roll as big as her head and two blueberry muffins. She also talked Obi-Wan into getting a huge slab of jalapeno cheddar sourdough bread.

They each picked up a cup of coffee at Grinders and sipped as they browsed through Fall for Books, a used bookstore on the corner of the square. And Zita couldn't resist getting a shirt at their next stop, Grogan's General Store, that said 'Fallport: Home of Bigfoot.'

Their tour continued by saying hello to two older gentlemen who were sitting outside the post office, playing chess; peeking into a place called The Cellar; and passing the library and health care clinic.

When they walked by Sunny Side Up, the smells coming from within once more made both their mouths' water, even though they'd already indulged in baked goods from Sweet Tooth.

Last on their trip around the square was Knock 'Em Down, a bowling alley.

With ten minutes to spare before they had to head to the high school, Zita suggested they sit inside the gazebo in the middle of the grassy square, which Obi-Wan had no problem agreeing to.

Fallport was a cute town and well kept. There was no trash that Obi-Wan had seen, and the sidewalks were maintained and not cracked or broken. He could see why the town was so popular with tourists. The lure of Bigfoot might've brought people here in the first place, but they probably kept coming back because of the friendliness of its residents and the charm of the place.

"I thought this place would be cute, but it's surpassed my expectations," Zita said happily.

Obi-Wan couldn't keep his gaze off the woman next to him. He could spend all day with her and still want to learn more... which was exactly what was happening.

"I wonder if we'll get to meet any of the original group of Eagle Point Search and Rescue guys. They're pretty famous, you know," Zita said. "I read online that most of them were in some branch of the military or another. You'd probably have a lot in common with them, even though they're all older than you.

"Oh, and there was also a story I read about a guy who was homeless for a long time here. The citizens built him a tiny home behind one of the businesses in the square. Then he went to Washington, DC, and eventually got a job working at the White House in the kitchen as a baker! He's now married with two kids and comes back here to Fallport every summer for their pickle festival. He also sponsors a scholarship for one high school senior every year and donates money to the food bank. And the food bank is run by the police chief's wife. It's all just so...*cool*!"

What was cool was the interest Zita paid to the town and its inhabitants. "Do you always research a place you'll be working in so thoroughly?" Obi-Wan asked.

"Well, no. But often enough. I mean, you already know I research job markets in different film locations. Fallport's special though. There was even a brochure in my motel back in Norfolk about the Bigfoot museum that opened here. And I did want to look into the medical facilities, just in case. Sometimes when I'm on set, especially in or near small towns, I need to communicate with the doctors and nurses and want to know what kind of experience they have and how big the trauma centers and hospitals are—if there are any at all. Besides, don't you do the same thing? Research the areas you'll be flying into?"

Of course he did. He was being kind of an ass, assuming she didn't do any research for her job, when he and his fellow Night Stalkers spent hours, days, or weeks doing the exact same thing. "You're right. It was stupid of me to assume you didn't do any research."

She leaned sideways and knocked against his arm and shoulder teasingly. "I do research, but I admit that I went a little overboard with Fallport. I had a week of downtime before we came out here. What else was I supposed to do?"

"True."

"We can come back, right? I mean, if we have time? I want to eat at the diner and have a drink at On the Rocks. And of course, get coffee in the mornings from Grinders."

"Of course. Besides, Edna said the motel doesn't have breakfast. So I think everyone staying there will be descending on the diner in the mornings before we head out to the set."

"We'll have to be sure to get here early to beat the rush," Zita said.

Which wouldn't be a problem for Obi-Wan, as he was a morning person. Kind of had to be in his line of work.

Zita looked at her watch and sighed. "We probably should go find the high school."

Obi-Wan nodded and stood, holding out his hand. Zita grabbed it, and instead of letting her go once she was standing, he curled his fingers tighter around hers as they headed for the parking lot, where he'd left his Jeep.

To his delight, she didn't pull her hand out of his grip. And when Obi-Wan glanced at her, he saw Zita was smiling.

The schedule they'd been emailed said after the meeting at the gym, food would be served buffet style, catered in for the cast and crew. Obi-Wan would've preferred to have Zita to himself, but tonight was the official start of her renewed duties.

She'd be "on" anytime the film crew was together. It was going to make for some long days, and possibly nights, when they were filming some of the scenes that took place after dark.

Making a mental note to make sure she stayed hydrated and ate enough, Obi-Wan tightened his fingers around hers.

This next week would be intense, but he was looking forward to continuing to share his military knowledge to make the movie more authentic, as well as spending as much time as was feasible with this woman who'd taken over his thoughts.

* * *

The meeting with the crew who'd be working in the forest was informative, and it made Obi-Wan even more excited to get to the set and see Logan Striker in action once again. The man was a very talented actor, and Obi-Wan had no doubt he could bring the role of the downed pilot to life in a way not a lot of other actors could.

It was late by the time they got back to the motel, and as much as Obi-Wan wanted to invite Zita to his room, mostly because he wasn't ready to say good night to her, he refrained. She needed her sleep, as tomorrow would be a long filming day.

Grubbner had laid out the schedule, and the next three days each would be about twelve hours of filming, give or take, depending on how the scenes went. Day four, the choppers would be brought in, and that was Obi-Wan's big day. He'd already approved the choppers and the uniforms, but he wanted to make sure the pilots chosen weren't amateurs, that they really knew what they were doing.

The only not-so-great part of the meeting tonight was Silas Graves. He'd stood in the back of the room and pretty much glared at everyone. He was Logan's replacement bodyguard for the rest of the shoot, but he didn't act much like a bodyguard. Instead of being alert and monitoring the room and entrances for anyone who might be a danger to the famous actor...Obi-Wan could've sworn most of his attention was on Zita. Which was very odd and concerning.

But Zita being Zita, she'd brushed it off, saying the man had no reason to focus on her, especially since Carmen wasn't there. Everyone knew Silas had developed a crush on the actress, and gossip maintained the two had slept together right up until the day she'd left town. But since she was back in California, Zita was convinced Silas's interest in her would wane. She was almost never around Logan, so his bodyguard had no reason to be worried about *her* any more than he was worried about anyone else.

Obi-Wan wasn't so sure. He'd seen the same kind of intense concentration many times before. In those determined to do US soldiers harm overseas. They'd study the movements and routines of soldiers to determine when and where to strike, either with roadside bombs or a coordinated attack.

Not that he thought Silas was going to put an IED in Zita's path...but since he wasn't sure *what* the man was planning, Obi-Wan vowed to be vigilant at all times. To protect Zita from anything the man might do to hurt her. Just because Carmen wasn't around, didn't mean Silas wasn't still loyal to the woman.

He might've been impressed with how seriously the man took his job, except that loyalty seemed misplaced. He and Carmen had only known each other for a short period of time, and Silas seemed to be taking his job too far.

But then again, it was about the same amount of time he'd known Zita. Obi-Wan was feeling *extremely* protective of the medic...and he wasn't even sleeping with her. Not because he didn't want to—he did, very much—but because he was interested in more than a short-term fling. He had no idea how anything long-term would work between them, considering their jobs and the not-so-small fact that they lived thousands of miles apart, but the protective feelings were definitely out in full force.

Which was why he sat in that meeting watching Silas like a hawk. And why he saw when someone had to elbow the man to let him know the meeting was over, and Logan was about to leave the gym. Silas had to rush to catch up with his charge. Thankfully, he was staying at the Chestnut Street Manor B&B with Logan, so Obi-Wan and Zita didn't have to deal with avoiding him at the Mangree.

Now back in his room, he lay awake in his bed, hands behind his head, staring up at the ceiling. The place was quiet. Almost *too* quiet. He was used to the noise that was a constant around his apartment. Doors opening and closing, cars driving by, the occasional siren. But the quiet here in Fallport and the Mangree was absolute. He couldn't hear cars driving by on the road not too far from the rooms, and his neighbors on either side of him were probably asleep, since they all had to head to the site where they'd be filming early in the morning.

The quiet gave him too much time to think. And the main topic swirling around in his head was Zita Darlington. Her enthusiasm for the quaint town of Fallport was adorable. And the way she'd licked her fingers after eating the cinnamon roll from the bakery was sexy as hell. As was the dot of foam on her lip after sipping her frou-frou coffee drink.

Without thought, his hand went between his legs. He'd just meant to adjust his hard cock, but the second he touched himself through his boxers, Obi-Wan couldn't stop. He closed his eyes and imagined Zita was there. Snuggled up against him, her head on his shoulder as her hand caressed him lazily.

Obi-Wan groaned. He'd gotten off more than once with thoughts of Zita in his mind, but after spending all day with her, laughing, watching her charm Edna and everyone else she met, he felt almost desperate to experience *everything* the woman had to offer. Would she be shy in bed and willing to let him take the lead? Or was she more aggressive? The type to demand what she wanted?

Truthfully, Obi-Wan found both a turn-on. He liked to take control in the bedroom, but he could easily see himself lying back and letting Zita have her way with him. He pictured her straddling him with a lustful look in her eye and a sexy smile on her lips as she took his cock in hand and notched him between her legs.

A groan left Obi-Wan's lips as he lifted his hips and shoved his briefs to his thighs. The material restricted his movements, but he didn't want to take the time to shove them all the way off. He was too close.

Palming his balls with one hand and stroking himself with the other, Obi-Wan kept his eyes closed as he dreamed his hands were Zita's. That it was *her* caressing him, driving him to the brink. It was no surprise that it took no time at all for the familiar feeling of an impending orgasm.

In minutes, the overwhelming feeling of pleasure swamped him. Come shot up his cock and landed on his bare belly, and he imagined Zita's pleased face in his mind as he exploded.

"Fuck," he muttered, feeling as if he'd been turned inside out. If he felt this much pleasure at just the thought of her, the real thing might actually kill him. As much as he wanted to take Zita to bed, to feel her pussy caressing his dick, he wasn't so conceited to be confident it would happen. And he'd never pressure her for something she wasn't ready to give.

But man, did he want that. *Her*. He could still remember how she felt in his arms when he'd woken up in his chair and realized she was fast asleep on top of him. It felt so right. Her body weight against him, her legs over his thighs, trusting him not to take advantage of the situation.

And he wanted that again. Her trust, her looking up at him as he slowly entered her for the first time, lust in her eyes, her limbs pulling him closer and her head thrown back. Her auburn hair strewn across his pillow is the sort of image that would forever be imprinted in his mind.

Shit. His cock twitched once more. He felt as if he was in his early twenties again. Getting a hard-on at the smallest provocation. But this was different. The only person who made him feel this way was Zita. He'd seen plenty of good-looking women on the movie set, but only Zita made his dick stand up and take notice.

Obi-Wan had no idea if this extreme attraction, and need, and want, would dissipate if they *did* end up in bed together. He was half afraid to find out. What if it *didn't* disappear? What if he only wanted her more? Was that a good thing or bad? Honestly, it scared him to death.

Was he ready to be completely besotted the way Casper and Buck were? While he envied his friends and the close relationships they had with their women, it was also terrifying to give another human that much power over you. Losing Laryn or Mandy would destroy his fellow pilots. It would affect their ability to fly, to do something they'd trained their whole lives for. Did he want to be in their shoes?

Yes.

Fuck yes.

But only with Zita.

"Shit," he swore out loud. He could feel the come on his belly drying. The scent of sex surrounded him. He'd never get any sleep if he didn't clean himself up and attempt to stop thinking about the woman who was so close, and yet way too far away at the same time.

Nothing was stopping him from exiting his room and going down to room twelve and knocking on the door. Nothing except for the fact he didn't want to scare her. Didn't want to blindside her in the middle of the night by begging her to let him taste her. Make her come. Shove himself so far inside her body that neither would be able to think straight.

He was a terrible person for getting even harder at the thought of doing just that. They were still getting to know each other. If he did any of the things he was fantasizing about, he'd destroy the trust and camaraderie they were building. Hell, she might not even want him that way.

But Obi-Wan dismissed that thought as soon as he had it. A woman wouldn't kiss a man the way *Zita* kissed him if she wasn't interested in him sexually. She wasn't a tease, her emotions were right there on her face for him to see when she looked at him.

No. He wasn't going to rush this.

With that thought, Obi-Wan swung his legs off the surprisingly comfortable bed and shoved his briefs off. He grabbed them from the floor and walked butt-ass naked to the bathroom. He quickly cleaned the come from his body, yanked his underwear back on, and practically stalked back to bed.

This time when he lay down, he curled onto his side and attempted to think about the upcoming film shoot. About the things he was supposed to review, the uniform Logan would be wearing, and how he needed to check one more time that it was as close to the real thing as Hollywood could get it. About the conversation he'd had with Henry that evening after the meeting, who'd reassured him the chopper pilots were highly qualified and some of the best available.

When his eyes finally got heavy, it was a relief.

But even in sleep, his mind turned to Zita. He dreamed about her all night. About her smile. Her hair blowing in the breeze as she walked toward him across a field of wildflowers in nothing but a jade-green nightgown that dipped low over her tits and only reached her upper thighs.

When his alarm went off the next morning, Obi-Wan wasn't refreshed. And his cock was hard as a rock once more. Sighing, he got out of bed and headed for the bathroom. If he was going to get anything done today—hell, if he wanted to walk normally —he had to take care of his needs. His sexual needs.

Control. He needed to fucking find it. He was a Night Stalker. Known for his legendary control. His ability to stay calm in the middle of absolute chaos. He was focused, reliable, and steady.

But right now, he felt none of those things. Zita had him turned inside out. And Obi-Wan found that he wasn't sorry. Not in the least. His blood seemed to sing with anticipation. With the thrill of the chase. He'd never felt this way, not even right before a particularly gnarly mission, which had always been a kind of high for him.

Zita Darlington had gotten under his skin, and he liked her there.

The big question was...did she feel even one tenth of the same? If not, he was in for a world of hurt. A huge letdown. And that was what had him hesitating to make his feelings for her known. It would kill him if she slept with him, wanting just a "friends with benefits" situation after all.

Because that wasn't where Obi-Wan was headed. He had no idea how they'd make things work, but at this point, he was ready to do whatever it took to have a relationship with the woman.

Casper wasn't going to be happy if he lost one of his pilots. Hell, Buck would be *beyond* pissed to lose his copilot. But Obi-Wan could no more ignore the feelings inside him than he could ignore a wounded SEAL, Delta, or fellow Night Stalker who needed extraction from behind enemy lines.

Taking a deep breath, he stepped under the scalding water of the shower. The sooner he jacked off and got dressed, the sooner he could see Zita.

CHAPTER FOURTEEN

Zita felt...off. She was usually completely focused on her job. On making sure the people on set were being safe, and watching for signs or symptoms of any kind of illness, or if an actor or actress was trying to hide a physical injury. They did that a lot, not wanting to be taken off set or, God forbid, replaced.

But today, all she could concentrate on was Sage.

The man looked and smelled *amazing*. She had no idea what kind of body wash he used, but it wasn't the complementary soap from the motel. It was kind of musky, and with every deep inhale as he drove them to the set, her nipples got harder. It took everything within her not to squirm in her seat, even though she was desperate for some friction between her legs. She was soaking wet, which wasn't something she'd ever had to deal with on the job.

In fact, this morning as she was showering, thoughts of Sage popped into her head, as they did more and more frequently these days, and she found her hand between her legs, stroking her clit to thoughts of him. In her mind, it was *his* finger on her clit. She'd imagined him kneeling in front of her in the shower, holding her hip with one hand, staring at her pussy with that intense gaze he had, and teasing the shit out of her by flicking her clit but not letting her come.

She exploded after imagining herself begging him. In her fantasy, he'd looked up at her with a smirk on his face before lowering his head and licking her to a monster orgasm.

She'd felt weak in the knees after she'd come, and it had taken all her energy to finish her shower and dry herself after turning off the water. The man was lethal, and so far he hadn't done more than simply kiss her.

Although she wouldn't describe his kisses as simple...not even close.

Feeling unsettled about her extreme attraction to Sage, she kind of blew him off once they'd arrived on set. The hour drive to get there had been almost excruciating, since all Zita wanted to do was touch him. Slide over the console, straddle him, rip her shirt off, and beg him to touch her. All of which would've been not only extremely dangerous, considering he was driving on some pretty bumpy and back roads through the woods, but potentially embarrassing if he looked at her in shock and pushed her away.

So to try to put some space between them, and to get her raging hormones under control, she'd bolted the second they'd arrived in the small parking area near where filming was taking place. She'd grabbed her pack from the backseat and made a beeline for the assistant director, asking about the best vantage point for the filming that morning.

Luckily—or *unluckily*, for her—everything was going extremely smoothly. No one was sick, no one had gotten hurt so far, so Zita had nothing to do but stand around with too much time to think.

She was being a coward, and she knew it. Yesterday had been awesome. Sage was a blast to be around. He didn't make fun of her excitement over the smallest things, or her enthusiasm for the small town she'd read so much about. He hadn't even teased her about buying that bigfoot T-shirt she couldn't pass up.

Not only that, she felt safe with him. Safe from anyone who might want to do her harm, for sure—although that wasn't exactly something she worried about on a regular basis—but mostly safe to be herself. To say what she was thinking. To laugh at things other people would roll their eyes at. To eat whatever she wanted in front of him, to tell him her hopes and dreams.

And that was what scared her. What had her freaking out this morning pretty much since the moment she'd seen him. They'd eaten breakfast at Sunny Side Up, where they'd been joined by a few of the other crew members. A welcome reprieve for Zita, because the fantasy she'd had in her shower was still too fresh in her mind for her comfort, at that point.

He'd stopped at Grinders on the way out of town and insisted on paying for her coffee. It was a thoughtful gesture... and strangely, one that had irritated Zita, though he'd bought her a dozen coffees by now. The man was just too good to be true. He didn't complain about driving her around, about the expense of a daily specialty coffee...about *anything*, really.

She shouldn't be running from him, but doing everything in her power to draw him closer. And yet, here she was, avoiding him.

Suddenly, she felt terrible about that. He didn't deserve her cold shoulder. He hadn't done anything wrong. This was all on her. She'd panicked over her growing feelings for the man.

Glancing over toward Sage—she might've been avoiding him, but she had an innate sense of where he was on set at all times— she saw him talking to one of the costume directors, all his attention focused on what the man was saying.

And that was another thing Zita liked about Sage. How she always felt as if she was the center of his world when she was with him. He looked her in the eye when she talked and wasn't constantly glancing at his phone or at everything else around him. Oh, she noticed that he was aware of his surroundings, especially when they were inside a restaurant or something, but figured that was ingrained in him because of his job, and not because he didn't want to hear what she had to say.

Zita decided she was going to go over and apologize to Sage the second he was done with his conversation.

But of course, right after she'd made the decision, one of the grips yelled out in pain after getting his fingers pinched in some of the lighting equipment.

After that, one of the extras had some sort of insect bite that needed tending. Then someone else felt dizzy and almost passed out. And so it went. Her quiet morning turned into a very busy day. No one had any life-threatening injuries but over the next several hours, various cast and crew needed tending to and reassuring.

By the end of the day's filming, which was after eight at night —because Henry wanted to continue filming as the sun set, since Logan was nailing scene after scene and he figured he might as well try to get some of the night shots in while he could—Zita was exhausted. She'd managed to grab food here and there from the catering trailer, but her belly was still growling, she was dirty and sweaty, and she *still* hadn't gotten a chance to talk to Sage.

He'd been busy most of the day too, doing the consulting work he was actually paid for, lending a hand to the film crew when they needed it...actually helping anyone and everyone. Being in the woods had thrown everyone's normal routine out the window, and since there weren't nearly as many staff on hand as there was on a closed set, his help was appreciated.

Tomorrow would be another long day, but Zita was impressed with how quickly filming was going. Logan was doing an exceptional job. He was in every scene, but he didn't look tired in the least. He was grinning at everyone and thanking them for their hard work. He even took the time to speak to the extras who were playing the soldiers hunting for him. He was one of the good guys in the industry, and Zita was pleased there was at least one famous actor on this shoot who wasn't a conceited asshole.

It took a bit of time to get the equipment locked into the trailers brought to the location specifically to store cameras, lights, and other props overnight. And of course, there had to be one more person who needed her attention because he'd stepped on a rock the wrong way and twisted his ankle. By the time she'd finished with the man, sending him on his way with instructions to ice his sore ankle overnight, and a promise she'd get with him in the morning to see if the swelling had gone down, most of the crew had left.

Logan, Silas, and Henry had been the first ones to leave, with the driver who'd been hired to shuttle them to and from the shoots.

Looking around, Zita saw Sage leaning against his Jeep.

Feeling bad that he'd had to wait for her, she walked toward him, going over in her head what she wanted to say.

Except when she approached him, her carefully crafted words went out the window. Instead, she blurted, "I'm sorry I was a bitch this morning."

She winced. That wasn't quite how she'd wanted to apologize.

Sage frowned. "What are you talking about? You weren't a bitch. Not even close."

"You bought me breakfast, and then my coffee, and I leapt out of your Jeep as if it was on fire. I didn't even say thank you."

"You did. When I paid the check at Sunny Side Up *and* when I handed you your coffee."

"Sage, I'm trying to apologize here," she said in exasperation.

"And I'm telling you that you have nothing to apologize for," he returned.

Then he shocked the hell out of her by stepping into her personal space and taking her medical bag from her hand. He dropped it on the ground at their feet and pulled her into his arms.

His hug felt amazing, and even though she wasn't sure she deserved it, she closed her eyes and leaned into him, soaking in the affection he was freely giving her.

"You've had a hard day," he said softly into her hair.

"No more than usual," she replied, still not letting go of him.

The strong clean scent he'd had that morning was gone, but she could still smell the faint traces of his soap. Now, he also smelled like he'd been working out. Sweating. But it wasn't bad. Actually, Lord help her, Zita liked it. A lot.

Taking a deep breath, she pulled back, but he didn't let her go. His arms stayed around her waist. Zita put her hands on his chest and licked her lips. "Did you have a good day?"

"Surprisingly, yes. I went over a few details about the costumes, but most of my work is pretty much done until the choppers arrive. It was fun to watch Logan get so into his character today. And it's amazing to see the inner workings of how a movie comes to life. It's a lot more work than I assumed."

Zita nodded. She'd felt the same way the first couple of movie sets she'd worked on.

"I don't like the way Silas watches you though."

She blinked. It was an abrupt change of topic. "In what way?"

"Calculating. An inappropriate intensity. As if he's thinking way too hard about something."

His words made Zita uneasy, but she shook her head, too tired to think about the bodyguard tonight. "Thankfully we won't be around each other much. Unless he gets hurt, I honestly have no need to talk to him or interact with him at all. If he's holding some sort of grudge against me because of Carmen, that's his problem, not mine. We have a week here, then I won't see him again."

"I'll still keep my eye on him for you."

There. That. Sage was being amazing again. Making her feel

safe once more. "Can we go?" she asked, looking around and realizing they were now the last ones on set, and it was fully dark.

"Of course. Sorry," Sage said, letting go of her and leaning over to grab her bag.

"I can get that."

"I know. I've got it."

He put it in the back of his Jeep as she got into the passenger seat. They were on their way back to Fallport in minutes. The drive back to town took longer in the dark, and by the time they arrived back at the motel, Zita was starving but too tired to think about trying to find something to eat.

Sage pulled up in front of her room and said, "Head on in, I'll be back in about ten minutes."

Zita frowned. "Back?"

"I'm going to grab us some food. It'll probably just be fast food, but we both need to eat."

"Sage, I'm tired. I'm just going to go to bed."

"You need *food*, Zita. You didn't eat nearly enough today. Just nibbled. I'll be quick. It won't take more than ten minutes, then ten more minutes to eat, then you can sleep. Your body needs the calories, the fuel. You'll never be able to keep up this pace for a week if you don't take care of yourself."

Tears threatened. He was being so...kind. And it felt amazing to be taken care of. It had been so very long since she'd had anyone who looked out for her the way Sage was. "Okay. No fries though. Protein. Maybe a chicken sandwich."

Sage nodded. "I've got it. Go in, get comfy, I'll be back before you know it."

Zita was more appreciative than she could say at that moment. She got out of the Jeep, grabbed her bag so she could reorganize it and restock it with the extra medical supplies she had in her motel room, and watched Sage drive off through her room's big window.

She changed into a pair of sweatpants and an oversized T-shirt, then prepped her medical bag for the next day. Surprisingly, by the time she was finished, Sage was back. She heard his Jeep pull into the parking space in front of her room, and she had the door open before he needed to knock.

He had two large bags of food from Sonic. Her belly growled at that moment, making them both smile.

"I have to admit, I ate an order of pickle fries between the restaurant and here," Sage said with a sheepish grin.

"Pickle fries? What are those? And did you get me any?" Zita asked, as he put the bags down on the small table next to the window.

"Thought you said you didn't want any fries," he said with a smirk.

"Yeah, well...I didn't want any *then*, but the second you said fries, it seems that's the *only* thing my belly wants. And if a woman says she doesn't want something, it's a pretty good bet she's lying."

Sage chuckled. "Gotcha. I hope you aren't disappointed, but pickle fries aren't actually fries made out of potatoes. They're pickles sliced to *look* like fries, with a ranch dressing dip."

"Yum!"

"I got several different things, actually, so you could have a choice. I know you said you wanted a chicken sandwich, but so many things looked good. I got a southwest crunch queso wrap, crispy tenders, pretzel twists, a cheeseburger, a grilled cheese sandwich—and of course, the chicken sandwich that you requested."

"All that?"

"Whatever you don't want, trust me, I'll eat. The chicken tenders aren't grilled, but the sandwich is," he said, as he unloaded the bags one item at a time.

"It sounds amazing. What if I want it all?" she teased.

"Then you can have it all. I'll go back and get something for myself."

"I was kidding," Zita told him, not really surprised at his answer. "But can we maybe *share* it all? I kind of want to try everything. That queso wrap sounds awesome. And a pretzel would hit the spot. But I also love their cheeseburgers."

"Of course we can share. Here, you take first crack at the wrap. I'll start on the cheeseburger."

Zita smiled throughout the meal. It felt intimate to be sharing food with Sage. To her surprise, the crazy amount of food was gone quickly, and she didn't even feel stuffed to the gills. She was obviously way hungrier than she'd thought. "Thank you for insisting on getting us dinner."

"Of course. Tomorrow shouldn't be quite as long as today, at least I hope not. I talked to the AD, and he said Grubbner's pleased with all the extra shots they got done tonight, and since rain's in the forecast for two days from now, they'd probably shut things down early tomorrow and do another long day when it rains. Get the rainy scenes done while he can."

"This is the only job where people are actually happy it's going to rain," Zita said with an eye roll. "I hate working in the rain. It's slippery, and often cold, and people tend to hurt themselves more often."

"The rain will also postpone the helicopter scenes another day, as well."

"And you're looking forward to those the most."

"Naturally. I'm gonna clean this stuff up and let you get some sleep," Sage said, as he began to pack the bags with the wrappers from their meal.

Suddenly, Zita didn't want him to go. She still felt bad for that morning. Hadn't truly explained why she'd been so stand-offish and not talked to him all day. Had actively avoided him, in fact.

"Can we talk before you go? Just for a little bit?"

He stopped and stared at her for a long moment. "Of course. Anything you want." He grinned as he added, "It doesn't bode well for me in the future, but I can't say no to you." Sage stuffed the rest of their wrappers into the bag and walked across the room to the trash can.

Zita sat there a moment, replaying his words in her head. It sounded as if he was assuming they'd be *together* in the future. After this week was over. It was everything she dreamed but was afraid to go after. That was what this morning was about, after all. She'd freaked out because he was so...perfect. And she didn't know how things could possibly work out for them.

She stood and walked over to the bed and climbed under the covers. She impulsively patted the mattress next to her. "Sit here with me?"

He did as she asked, sitting against the headboard and stretching his long legs out on the bed next to her.

Zita plumped the pillows under her head and lay on her side, facing Sage, curling her arms against her chest. "I'm really sorry I left so abruptly this morning. And avoided you all day."

"Why did you?" he asked.

At least he hadn't said he never noticed. It was pathetic, but that made Zita feel better.

"What are we doing?" she whispered. "I live in California, and you live in Virginia. We couldn't get any farther apart."

"Hey, you could live in Hawaii," he joked.

But Zita didn't crack even the smallest smile.

"Sorry. You're right. It sucks. Because when you find someone you click with, someone you enjoy spending time with, and with whom you want to spend *more* time, it's awful to think you might not be able to do that. And I don't have any answers for you, Zita. All I know is that I've never felt the way I do right now. I've never looked at a woman and seen my future reflected back in her eyes.

"And how will that work? I have no clue. But I'll do whatever it takes to at least see if what we've got can last. Long-distance relationships suck, but I'm willing to try if you are."

Zita's heart nearly stopped beating in her chest. She forgot to breathe as she stared up at Sage. He wasn't touching her, simply sitting next to her, gazing into her eyes, but she felt their connection as clear as day.

"We don't know what the future holds. I could get injured and chaptered out of the Army. I'd then be free to move wherever I wanted. Or you could get sick of Hollywood and take a chance by moving to the East Coast."

"I'm already sick of Hollywood," she whispered.

He looked at her for a moment, taking that in before nodding. "All I'm saying is that everything in me is screaming to not let you go. To make every effort to see where things between us can go."

Zita swallowed hard. This man was way braver than she was. Putting his thoughts and feelings out there so plainly. But then again, he was already an honest-to-God hero. She shouldn't be surprised at his bravery.

"That's part of the reason why I needed some space this morning. You're too nice. Too perfect. Too...everything."

"Where you're concerned, there *is* no 'too nice.' I want to give you the world, Zita. And if that comes in the form of a simple omelet and a sugary coffee, I'll bend over backward to present it to you on a golden platter."

"And what do you get in return?" she couldn't help but ask.

"Are you kidding?"

"Um...no?" She didn't understand why he sounded so incredulous.

"I get your giggles, your smiles, your kindness, your desire to help others, your honesty, your sexiness, your kisses...I get *you*, Zita."

Suddenly, she couldn't bear the idea of seeing this man walk out of her room. She was way too tired to initiate sex or anything intimate, but she wanted him near. *Needed* him near.

"Will you stay tonight? Not for sex, but just...sleep?"

"I have one question before I'll answer that," Sage said.

Zita nodded and stared up at him, wondering what in the world he could want to know before agreeing to stay the night with her.

"Do *you* want to see where this goes after filming is over? Can you possibly see a future between us?"

"That was two questions," she whispered, her heart beating hard in her chest.

Sage lifted a brow in response.

Feeling as if she was stepping off the end of the ten-meter platform at the university where she sometimes swam back at home, Zita said, "Yes."

"Then I'd love to stay. Can I run to my room and change into sweats, brush my teeth, then come back?"

"Of course."

"You can change your mind while I'm gone," he said, proving once more what a good man he was.

"I won't. Take my key so you can let yourself back in when you're ready."

He studied her for a long moment, then leaned down.

Zita anticipated his kiss, but he merely brushed his lips against her forehead. "I'll be right back. Sleep if you want. I won't disturb you when I get back."

"Okay." As if he'd said the magic words, Zita suddenly couldn't keep her eyes open. She was exhausted, her belly was full, and the man she was head over heels for was going to sleep next to her. Her mind and body were as satisfied as they could get...for the moment.

She heard the door shut behind Sage, and it seemed as if two seconds had passed before she felt the mattress dip and his arm drape over her waist from behind. She snuggled back into him with a contented sigh before sleep took her under once more.

CHAPTER FIFTEEN

Obi-Wan had never felt as…giddy as he was now. In fact, he was pretty sure he'd never felt *giddy* in his life. He'd slept like a rock last night with Zita in his arms. And this morning, after a few minutes of awkwardness, things had smoothed out and he felt closer to her than ever.

They'd repeated their visits to Sunny Side Up and Grinders, then once again made the drive out to the set. It was a much more pleasant day, because not only did they get done way before the sun set, Obi-Wan had been able to spend some time with Zita. She wasn't avoiding him today, and in fact, the shy smiles she sent his way were encouraging.

His cock was half hard all afternoon, and it took all his focus to keep it from getting out of control.

The only problem was Silas Graves. He still stared at Zita way too often and with way too much interest. He didn't attempt to talk to her, but that didn't make Obi-Wan feel any better. At one point that afternoon, he was going to go confront the man and ask what his problem was, but he'd been interrupted by a question about the chorography with the choppers.

Something was up with the bodyguard, and with the way the

hair on the back of Obi-Wan's neck was standing up, he wanted to get to the bottom of the guy's issue before the end of the week.

But for now, he and Zita were headed back to Fallport. Instead of fast food, she'd asked if they could eat at The Cellar. From everything Obi-Wan understood, the pool hall had undergone a transformation in the last few years. It used to be a pretty seedy place, where only the roughest locals hung out. Even though it was still owned by the same person, things had changed, and now it was more respectable. There were pool tournaments, dart enthusiasts met up there regularly to play, and couples even went on ax-throwing dates in the establishment.

Edna, the motel owner, had suggested it was now a good place to eat and have a beer at the end of a long day, if that was their thing. So tonight, Zita had asked if they could eat dinner there before heading back to the motel.

As Obi-Wan had admitted to her the day before, he found it almost impossible to deny her anything. But then again, taking her back to the motel too early wasn't good either, because it was becoming more and more difficult to keep his hands off her.

They pulled into the parking lot in the back of the line of buildings along the square, and he saw that The Cellar was indeed a popular place, if the number of cars in the lot was any indication. As they walked toward the back door, Obi-Wan saw a line of boxes along the wall of the building. When he got closer, he saw each one had a tiny door.

"Oh my gosh! Do you know what those are?" Zita exclaimed.

"No clue."

"They're cat boxes! Like, strays can use them to stay warm in the winter. That's so cool!"

It *was* cool. There were six of the little boxes, and now Obi-Wan noted there was straw in each one. Whoever had put them there was obviously a cat lover, which was kind of awesome.

He held open the door for Zita, and they were greeted by

music, laughter, and the sound of many conversations going on. Looking around, Obi-Wan was impressed. The bar was dim but not dark. He could easily see the four pool tables on a raised platform toward the far side of the bar. There were also three dartboard "lanes" set up on the opposite wall, in a position where it was unlikely anyone would be hit by a stray dart.

Then there were two "cages" where people were throwing axes at large bullseyes. Again, he approved of the safety measures the owner had set up to keep bystanders and patrons safe. All in all, Obi-Wan liked the place. He'd been in his share of dive bars over the years, in various countries, and The Cellar was definitely on the higher end of the ones he'd seen.

"Oh, it's cute!" Zita exclaimed.

Obi-Wan wasn't sure he'd describe it as "cute," but he didn't contradict her.

They saw several familiar faces from the film crew but decided to sit at a high-top table for two, instead of joining some of the other men and women. A waitress immediately arrived to take their drink order and drop off a pair of menus. Instead of the prerequisite skimpy outfits found in so many dive bars—low-cut blouses and short skirts, or cut-off shorts that barely covered a woman's private parts—their server wore skinny jeans and a fitted V-neck T-shirt that bore The Cellar's logo. Sexy but without having to be practically naked.

Obi-Wan ordered a bottle of beer, and Zita ordered a lemon drop martini, which she admitted to wanting to try after seeing how much Mandy had enjoyed hers at Anchor Point. They looked over the menu, and Obi-Wan was impressed with the variety of offerings. Everything from burgers and fries, to healthier fare like salads and grilled chicken and fish. He saw from the menu that food service ended at ten-thirty, but the bar was open until one.

The waitress returned with their drinks and they ordered

dinner. Grilled chicken sandwich with a side of fresh fruit for Zita, and a double bacon cheeseburger for Obi-Wan.

After the server had left, Obi-Wan turned his attention to his companion.

Zita looked tired but happy. A little rumpled, but like the girl next door. She was smiling at him, and he couldn't help but reach for her hand. She gladly wrapped her fingers around his.

"Are you looking forward to the day after tomorrow? To the scenes with the helicopters?"

"Absolutely. I haven't met the pilots yet, but the birds them-selves look good. And the costumes for the pilots are almost exactly what my friends and I wear."

"The movie's gonna be a hit, I can feel it," Zita said, taking a sip of her drink.

"Agreed. I also heard that Grubbner, even though he was upset he couldn't talk to the real-life pilot Logan's portraying, has promised a portion of the box office proceeds will be donated to mental health resources for veterans in the Air Force."

"That's generous of him."

"He's very particular, and a hard task-master, but I can't deny he gets shit done," Obi-Wan said. "And yes, he seems to be generous, and well aware of how hard the people who bring his films to life are working. From the A-list actors and actresses to the extras, and even down to the caterers who supply everyone with food during the shoot."

Zita nodded. "I agree. I've worked with a lot of directors, and he's definitely one of the best. I've heard it was his idea to have base camp here in Fallport, and he was the one who insisted on using the local motel instead of the chain hotel out by the highway."

"And we appreciate the business," a gruff-looking man said as he neared their table. He had a rag in one hand and a stack of empty glasses in another. He had black hair that was a little too long, stubble on his cheeks and chin, and a hard look in his eyes. He also had a scar that disappeared into the collar of the plain black T-shirt he was wearing.

Obi-Wan held out his hand and introduced himself.

The man put the stack of glasses on their table, wiped his palm on his jeans, then shook Obi-Wan's hand. "Whip Johansen. I own The Cellar."

"You do? We love it!" Zita said with a huge grin.

Whip glanced at her and nodded his head respectfully. "Thanks. Honestly, it hasn't always been this way."

"Really? Because it seems extremely popular," Zita told him.

"Yeah, well, that's because of my wife." Whip looked back toward the bar, and Obi-Wan followed his gaze to see a tiny slip of a woman behind the bar. She looked like an actual fairy—not that he knew what the hell fairies looked like, but she had hair so blond it was almost white. She was slender and petite, and she wore a long-sleeve pink shirt with a scoop neck that showed off her collarbones. She seemed almost fragile, and he wasn't surprised a man like Whip kept her behind the bar. It was probably the safest place for her.

"That's your wife behind the bar? She's beautiful," Zita said, sounding sincere in her compliment.

Maybe that was why Whip continued to stand at their table and chat. Because Zita had a way of drawing people in. Encouraging them to tell her all of their secrets.

"She is. And I have no idea why she's with me, but I'll fuckin' kill anyone who dares put their hands on her or look at her sideways. I can deal with a lot of shit, but two things I will not tolerate is abuse of animals or women."

"Oh, you must've put the cat boxes out back," Zita said with a huge smile.

"I did. We've got a bit of a stray cat problem, but the vets in the area are doing their best to help with that. They spay and neuter them for free."

"Cool."

"I met Angelica here at The Cellar. Back when it was a hangout for the not-so-good citizens of Fallport. I admit, this place was a shithole, but I honestly didn't care at the time. I was angry at the world, and I actually liked when fights broke out, because I could take out my aggression on the assholes who thought it was perfectly okay to pull out knives and fight right here in the middle of the joint. Honestly, I didn't care for Fallport either, or for the people who live here. I just wanted their money."

"What happened? How did The Cellar change so much?" Zita asked, leaning forward, totally sucked into Whip's story.

"It's too long to go into before your meals arrive, but suffice it to say, Angel changed my life and made me see things in a different light. Without her, I'd still be the same asshole I used to be."

Zita was clearly extremely curious about how a man like Whip got together with his wife. Obi-Wan had to admit...so was he. Something big had to have happened for him to change so drastically.

"He still doesn't like people though," said the very woman Whip had been talking about, as she cuddled up next to him and wrapped her arm around his waist. She was tiny next to the giant bar owner, and the love in his eyes when he looked down at her was easy to see.

"I keep trying to get him to sponsor Pickleport and to be more social, but he'd rather stay in here and serve beer than mingle with the Fallportians...what we call people who live around here."

"Prefer cats. They're assholes, but they're honest about what they want. Sunlight, food, and to be left alone."

Angel giggled. "Pretty much. Which is why we have about twelve scratching posts in our house, along with at least a hundred and two empty boxes for them to nest in, and about half as many little cat beds."

Obi-Wan chuckled, along with Zita.

"How many cats do you have?"

"Officially, three. But we take care of as many stray ones as we can."

"Now that we have vets in town who give a shit, it's easier to help them when necessary," Whip started.

"That's a story for another time," Angel told him. "I'm out of Clyde's moonshine. Need you to go to the storage room and get me some more."

"Won't let her go in there on her own," Whip mumbled. "It's dark and secluded, and horny assholes think it's a great place to get sucked off."

Surprised, Obi-Wan and Zita both burst out laughing, while Angel rolled her eyes. "The last time I walked in on something like that was ages ago."

"Don't care. You doing okay? Need me to call in Bart to help you behind the bar?"

"No, I'm good. Just need that moonshine."

Whip kissed the top of Angel's head. "On it." He nodded at Obi-Wan and Zita before escorting Angel back to the bar, then heading toward the hallway that led to the bathrooms and, presumably, the infamous storage room.

"Wow, I can totally see him running a less-than-reputable bar," Zita said with a grin.

Obi-Wan could too. It was obvious Angel was the only thing keeping him from being mostly feral. The man had an undercurrent of hostility coming from him. But it just went to show how finding the perfect partner could smooth out a person's rough edges.

And that had Obi-Wan thinking about himself and Zita. She made him feel more relaxed than he'd felt in a very long time. He used to live and breathe being a Night Stalker. Resented his time in the States waiting to be called up for a mission. Would've preferred to live full-time on a naval ship so he could fly every day.

And now? He was finding he liked the down time. Yes, he obviously loved to fly, but he could already feel a shift happening. Like with Zita to fill his days, he no longer *lived* to fly. Which was a huge distinction.

Her cheeks were already flushed just from her single drink, and she was looking around the bar with wide eyes, as if seeing it in a new light after hearing Whip's story...which she probably was, because Obi-Wan was too.

Their waitress reappeared with two plates in her hands. "Can I get you anything else?"

"Two waters, please," Obi-Wan told her, wanting to ensure Zita didn't have a headache in the morning.

The food was as good as the atmosphere and the company. And it wasn't long before both he and Zita were finished and had scooted their chairs closer together. They talked and watched people playing darts for a while before she suggested they try their hand.

Obi-Wan agreed and escorted her over to an empty dartboard.

She was terrible. Most of her darts bounced off the target and landed on the floor. And every time it happened, she simply laughed. She wasn't competitive in the least, whereas Obi-Wan strove to hit a bullseye every time.

They were complete opposites in that regard, and he found he liked that. A lot.

Who was he kidding? He fucking loved it. Zita was cheerful and kind and made friends wherever she went. In fact, she'd already struck up a conversation with the couple playing darts next to them.

To his surprise, the man owned On the Rocks, the *other* bar in the Fallport square. And the woman he was with, Elsie, his wife, used to work as a waitress at his bar once upon a time.

Before he knew it, Obi-Wan and Zita were back at their table, and Elsie and Zeke were joining them. Zita was sipping on another lemon drop, telling her new friends how much she loved their little town. When she told them they were staying at the Mangree, Elsie perked up.

"Don't you just love it there? I lived there for a while with my pre-teen son. It was ages ago, but sometimes it feels like yesterday."

"Edna is awesome," Zita said, clearly feeling relaxed from her drinks.

"Isn't she? She put me and Tony in the room right next to the office, so she could keep her eye on us."

"That's where I am! Room twelve."

Elsie laughed. "Some things never change."

The two women talked a mile a minute, and Obi-Wan was content to sit next to Zita, a hand on her knee, just listening.

"You're the Night Stalker, right? The helicopter pilot?"

Turning to Zeke, he nodded. "How'd you know?"

"Fallport's tiny, and it has a very good gossip network." He grinned. "When you retire, Fallport would hire you in a second for the Eagle Point Search and Rescue team. I'm one of the original members, and let me tell you, a chopper and a pilot on staff would be a huge advantage."

"I don't doubt it," Obi-Wan said. "But I'm not planning on retiring anytime soon."

Zeke nodded. "Don't blame you. Loved my time in the Army, but if I hadn't come here, I wouldn't have met Elsie and Tony, and I wouldn't have the family I have today."

"You've got kids?"

"Three, including Tony."

Obi-Wan's eyes widened.

"Yeah, it's a lot. But Else and I wouldn't have it any other way.

We're here tonight on one of our rare dates. We don't like to go to On the Rocks, since we spend way too much time there as it is. And since Whip isn't the asshole he used to be, this place is a nice change of pace now."

"He told us he's changed a lot, along with this place," Obi-Wan said.

"He did? Wow. He's usually not much of a sharer."

"It's Zita."

Zeke nodded. "Yeah, Elsie has the same effect on people. They just seem to want to open up to her."

Elsie turned to Obi-Wan then. "Zita says you're an amazing helicopter pilot. That's so cool!"

The conversation turned more general then, with all four of them conversing. Before they knew it, Angel made last call for food from behind the bar.

Surprised it was so late, Obi-Wan turned to Zita and saw she had a faraway look in her eyes, and she was kind of swaying a bit on her stool. She looked exhausted. She was on her feet for hours at work, and the newness of The Cellar, meeting new friends, and a bit of alcohol had finally caught up with her. He needed to get her to bed.

And not in a sexual way, although that was never far from his mind. She needed sleep so she could be alert on set tomorrow. She'd said herself that rainy days always meant more work for her, and it would be irresponsible for them to stay out much longer, and have her show up to work at less than her best.

"I think we're gonna jet," Obi-Wan said.

He knew he was right about Zita being at the end of her reserves when she made no complaint. They said their goodbyes to Elsie and Zeke, promising to stop by On the Rocks before they left town.

Obi-Wan was steering Zita to the door when she stopped and said, "Hang on, there's something I want to do."

He watched as she headed toward the bar, where Whip and

Angel were making drinks for the many people sitting at the stools. If anything, the bar was busier now than it was when they'd arrived, which just went to show how popular the place was.

She leaned over the bar, and it was all Obi-Wan could do to take his gaze from her ass. But he did, and just in time to see her hold out some money toward Angel.

At first she shook her head, but Zita seemed to insist, and finally the other woman took it. She smiled, and Obi-Wan could read her lips as she thanked Zita.

When she returned to his side, Obi-Wan said, "I tipped both her and our waitress already," knowing he sounded grumpy but not able to help it.

"Oh, I know, I saw. And you were more than generous. I just wanted to give them a donation for the kitties. The stray ones. It can't be cheap to feed them, and to keep those boxes full of clean straw."

Damn. This woman. She was amazing.

Not able to help himself, he leaned in and kissed her. It was a brief kiss, but he still felt it down to his toes. He found he didn't have the words that would adequately express what he was feeling. So he simply tucked her arm into his own and walked them toward the door once more.

His mind was spinning as he drove the short distance back to the Mangree. He once again parked in front of Zita's door, so she wouldn't have to walk to her room. He grabbed her med bag, knowing that she'd want to make sure it was restocked for tomorrow.

She unlocked her door then turned to him. Obi-Wan held his breath. He wasn't going to presume anything, although there was nothing he wanted more than to be invited in once again.

"Do you want to stay?"

"Yes." He wasn't noble enough to turn her down. "I'll go change and shower and come back. That okay?"

"You could shower here," she said shyly.

"I'll be back," he insisted, knowing that if he got naked in her bathroom, it wouldn't help the state of his cock. As it was, he planned on jacking off before he came back to her bed.

"Here's my key," she told him, holding it out.

Taking it, Obi-Wan once more felt grateful for this woman's trust in him.

He would've been embarrassed by how quickly he was back at her room after showering, jacking off, changing, and getting his things ready for the next morning, but he wasn't. He'd kind of resigned himself to being in a perpetual state of need around Zita—including the need just to be near her.

After a soft knock on the door, he let himself in using her key. Zita was already in bed, lying on her side, breathing heavily. Her hair was damp, and she must've fallen asleep as soon as her head hit the pillow.

Realizing he had a grin on his face, and not caring, Obi-Wan shut off the light she'd left on—probably so he wouldn't trip over anything in the dark—and climbed under the covers behind Zita.

The second his arm closed over her waist, she turned, snuggling into him as if she'd done it every day of her life. He rolled to his back so Zita would be more comfortable. Her head came to rest on his shoulder, and one leg hitched over his thigh, as if she was claiming him.

Obi-Wan was completely all right with being claimed. As long as it was *this* woman doing so.

He was tired too, but sleep didn't come right away. He was enjoying the feeling of holding her. Having her trust him to sleep in her bed and not do anything she hadn't specifically consented to. Smelling her shampoo. Simply being this close to another human being. It had been way too long since he'd had anything like this. And he liked it. Craved it.

But only with Zita. No one else. He was sure being with any

other woman couldn't match the feeling he was experiencing right now.

He finally fell asleep half an hour later, a smile on his face and contentment in his soul. This was what he'd been looking for without even knowing it. If he could feel like this now, before being as physically close as two people could be, he was almost scared of how vital this woman would become if—hopefully *when*—they moved their relationship to the next level.

Scared, but one hundred percent willing and onboard. Zita Darlington could destroy the life he'd known up until now, and he was looking forward to seeing what that was like.

CHAPTER SIXTEEN

Zita was exhausted. As she'd expected, the day was crazy. The rain made everyone cranky and impatient. People slipped and fell constantly, needing scrapes cleaned and bandaged. The bugs were relentless. One of the camera operators had a fairly serious injury when she fell and a jagged stick impaled through the webbing of her hand.

That incident took up a good bit of her time, as she went back to Fallport with the woman to get the stick removed at the clinic, and to make sure it was thoroughly cleaned. Thankfully, once she was cleaned up, the wound was relatively minor, all things considered, and she'd be able to return to her job the next day.

By the time she got back to the set, she had three people lined up she needed to deal with, though nothing life-threatening.

The only good to come from the rain was that it was perfect for the scenes Logan shot that day. Showcasing the miserable conditions he had to suffer through as he continued to make his way toward the border and safety. The rain and clouds made the atmosphere on the set almost spooky, which was perfect for the shots of the extras hunting the American who they *knew* was out there somewhere.

By the time Grubbner called it quits for the day, everyone was more than happy to get out of the wet woods and back to Fallport and the motel.

Sage seemed unfazed though, which might've irritated Zita if she didn't think about how close the conditions were to what he probably experienced on a regular basis. Of course, he probably wasn't standing in the cold rain, but flying through it instead. Which she thought might actually be worse.

Every time she'd turned around throughout the day, Sage was there. With a towel, holding an umbrella over her as she tended to someone. He'd even driven her and the camera operator into town without complaint.

When she'd tried to protest, saying she was sure he had things to do, he'd simply shaken his head, insisting that tomorrow was his busy day, the one with the choppers. So she'd given in and taken the help and comfort he offered.

It was wonderful to have someone at her back. She was used to it when she worked on an ambulance, but not in the same way. Sage was there not because it was his job, but because he wanted to be. Because he cared about her. She loved that feeling.

Zita also loved waking up in his arms...though she'd missed falling asleep in them twice now, because she was already dead to the world by the time he'd come back to her room.

But after two nights, she wanted more than just sharing a bed. It was getting difficult not to move her hands to more intimate places when she was with him. To not tell him how much she wanted him. To hide the intensity of her attraction.

She had the feeling he was enjoying their courtship. That he was old fashioned when it came to dating. And she was okay with that, it was a refreshing change from the men she'd met who took her on one date and expected that was all that was required to get her into bed.

But it was frustrating that he didn't even seem *interested* in getting her into bed...not so much as a single inappropriate touch.

And now here she was, headed back to the motel, her clothes damp, her hair frizzy. Feeling tired, hungry, frustrated and, yes, grumpy, because the man she wanted was acting more like a friend than the lover she desperately wanted.

So when he glanced at her and asked what she wanted for dinner, she sighed. "I'm not hungry. Just bring me to the motel."

"You have to eat, Zita," he said calmly. "I'll drop you off so you can shower and get warm, and I'll go out and grab us something."

Now she could add angry with herself, for not having the guts to tell him she didn't want food. She wanted him to stop tiptoeing around their attraction. To either make a move, or maybe tell her that he'd changed his mind and decided they should just be friends.

But she could hardly hold his reticence against him when she didn't have the courage to speak up either. She was an adult who should be able to go after what she wanted.

And he was being a gentleman, not a horndog. Which she would appreciate if she wasn't so frustrated.

To her horror, tears formed in her eyes, and anything she might've said got stuck in her throat. She turned her head to look out the side window as she tried desperately to gain control of her emotions. All she wanted was to be alone to get her head on straight. To find the courage to tell Sage what she wanted.

Sage didn't say anything, simply drove them to the motel. After parking in front of room twelve, he got out of the Jeep and hurried to her side. Zita had just opened the door when he reached her. He took her head in his hands and tilted her face up. He frowned a little at seeing the tear tracks on her cheeks.

"You're exhausted," he said softly.

"Yes, but that's not what's bothering me," she whispered back.

"Talk to me, Zita. Let me fix it."

He wanted to fix what was wrong? Of course he did.

Taking a deep breath, she met his gaze and said, "I'm tired of being with you, but not *being* with you. I feel as if I'm splintering into a million pieces but unable to do anything about it. I want you, Sage. *Need* you. I don't want to spend another night lying next to you and just sleeping. I want it all—every part of you. But I've been afraid to make my needs known because I don't want to lose you if you're not there yet."

She held her breath, staring at him, with no idea how he felt about everything she'd just confessed.

Emotion flared in his eyes, something she couldn't read.

Then he moved. Lowering his head and taking her lips in a rough, desperate kiss.

She immediately opened for him, grabbing his shoulders.

He wasn't gentle. He didn't nip and nibble; his tongue swept into her mouth and took control.

Zita felt dizzy with relief and met his hunger with her own. The pent-up lust she'd felt from being with him, but not *with* him.

Sage lifted her from the Jeep and set her on her feet, and she barely heard him slam the door shut. He didn't lift his head from hers, simply tilted it so he could take the kiss deeper.

She was lost in him. In sensation. When he finally did lift his head and growl, "Key," it took her a moment to understand what he wanted and why. She fumbled in her purse for the metal key Edna had given her and breathed a sigh of relief when her fingers closed around it. She handed it to Sage, and he took it without a word.

He had the door open in seconds, and then they were inside. He kicked it shut with his foot, locked the dead bolt, then reached for her once more.

There was no hesitation this time, on either of their parts. The kiss was carnal, hotter than anything Zita had ever experienced before. She didn't hold back, tried to let Sage know without words how much he'd come to mean to her. How much she wanted this. Him.

She kicked her shoes off, while he worked on the button of her cargo pants. Her hands were busy trying to shove his shirt up and over his head while not breaking their kiss.

Eventually, he pulled back, breathing hard, eyes kind of wild, and said, "Clothes. Off."

She complied, gladly.

There was a mad rush on both their parts to remove the clothes that suddenly felt too constricting. The second they were both naked, Sage reached for her once more. Surprisingly, Zita didn't feel self-conscious in the least. She was more than ready for this. For Sage.

Their bodies came together with an audible slap, and it felt as if Sage's hands were everywhere at once. She wasn't a passive participant either. Her own hands were attempting to learn Sage's body even as they once again devoured each other's mouths.

She ran her hands over his rock-hard ass, marveling at the tautness of the round globes. Running her hands up his sides, she could feel the muscles in his torso flexing as he moved. Her nipples were hard against his chest, the hair there stimulating her even more. Every time she shifted, her breasts rubbed against his body, ramping up her need.

He was doing his own exploring. One hand was locked around the back of her neck, holding her against him as he kissed her, the other was roaming her body almost desperately. His fingers gripped a butt cheek, then grasped her thigh to pull it around his leg. His hand went to her chest next, to palm one of her breasts. His fingers played with the taut nipple, then squeezed the sensitive globe before he moved down between her legs.

Zita jerked against him at the first touch of his fingers on her soaking-wet folds. She broke from their kiss and gasped, sucking in oxygen in gulps as if she'd just run a freaking marathon.

"Sage," she moaned, hiking her leg higher, trying to give him more room to touch her. But the position was a bit awkward, and her other leg was starting to shake with the strength it took to hold herself up.

Thankfully, Sage realized there was a perfectly good bed right behind them. He put both hands on her waist and turned, spinning her around and practically throwing her onto the mattress.

Zita couldn't help but giggle. She loved being manhandled by this man, because she had no doubt whatsoever that he wouldn't use his strength against her. She didn't have time to think before he was on top of her, his lips once more covering hers. His hand went straight back to her pussy, teasing the wet folds before zeroing in on her clit.

It was too much. It wasn't enough. Zita's head spun, as if she'd chugged three of those delicious lemon drop martinis right in a row. Sage lifted his head, and Zita sucked in a much-needed breath. This was intense, but oh so good. Had she ever felt this needy for someone before? Like if she didn't get him inside her in the next three seconds she'd self-combust?

No, definitely not. She both loved and hated the sensation.

"Sage, more," she whispered, not even sure what she was asking for.

But apparently, he did. Without taking his hand from between her legs, he scooted down and took one of her nipples into his mouth. Zita arched into his touch as electricity seemed to shoot from her chest down to her clit.

He wasn't gentle about what he was doing. Sage sucked hard, used his teeth to stimulate her even more. And his free hand came up, plumping her eager flesh to make it easier to get more of her breast into his mouth.

To her surprise, Zita found that she was on the edge of an orgasm, which had never happened to her before. When she masturbated, she always had to concentrate on her clit before she'd get anywhere close to coming.

But with Sage's masterful hands and lips, she was as close to the edge as she'd been in the past after using a vibrator on her clit for a couple of minutes. It was overwhelming, almost scary— and Zita wanted more.

Her pussy clenched. Wanted to be filled. Wanted to share the experience with the amazing man hovering above her, giving her the ultimate pleasure.

"I don't want to come without you," she managed to stutter.

"No. You come first. Always. In everything. Even this. We'll fly together for sure, but I need this. Need to watch you soar, feel you come on my fingers." His words were spoken against her breast; he'd barely lifted his head. Then he shifted so he was lying next to her, his body heat almost scorching her as he pressed against her side.

His hand between her legs never stopped its ministrations. Zita squirmed, opening her legs wider, needing more.

"That's it. Spread yourself for me. Show me where you need me."

His words were just a little crude, but they ramped up Zita's passion. Using one of his knees, he trapped the leg closest to him against the mattress, holding her open.

"You are so damn beautiful," he murmured. "Look at you. I've dreamed of seeing your hair strewn over my pillow. Having you writhe beneath me just like this. I've wanted you since the moment I saw you. The wait was worth it. *You're* worth it, Zita. Come for me. I want to see you fly."

She wanted to tell him that she'd wanted this forever too. But the words were stuck in her throat. Her vision had narrowed to a small pinpoint as her orgasm grew within her.

"Sage!" she called out, when all the sensations suddenly seemed too much.

"I've got you, let go, Zita. I'm here."

Yes. He was. He was most definitely there. What had it been, like three minutes since they'd walked through the motel door? Zita had no idea. It could've been twenty minutes for all she knew, or thirty seconds. All her focus was on Sage, and the amazing feelings he was coaxing from her all-too-willing body.

One second she was having a mini panic attack, and the next she was coming. Trembling from head to foot and calling out Sage's name as she exploded.

When she was finally able to hear again, and breathe, she realized Sage had been talking to her throughout her orgasm.

"...so beautiful. I can see your come leaking out between your pussy lips. You're *so* wet. You're going to feel fucking amazing, I just know it." His fingers were still between her legs, but he was holding her folds open and he'd sat up a little, all his attention focused on the wetness she could feel soaking the sheets under her.

Then he moved, rolling them until she was straddling him.

Zita blinked; she was still in a post-orgasm haze. "Sage?"

"I don't want to hurt you. You're small, and I'm not. This way, you can take me at your own pace."

Putting her palms on his chest to brace herself, Zita looked down between her legs—and saw exactly why Sage had put her in charge. The man was *big*. Bigger than anyone she'd been with before...which wasn't saying much, as she'd only had three lovers before him. He might not be that tall at only five-nine, but he'd been blessed with an impressive dick. It was long and slender, and Zita knew he'd go deeper than might be comfortable. But she was determined to take him. To make this as good for him as he'd just made her feel.

Reaching down, Zita took him in the palm of her hand, loving the groan that escaped his throat. Sex had always been pleasurable, but not very exciting. Always in the missionary position and over fairly quickly. She had this amazing, sexy man under her, and she planned to make the most of the experience.

Smiling, she looked him in the eye as she stroked him. "How long do you think you can last?" she asked provocatively.

* * *

Obi-Wan licked his lips and tried to think about anything but coming right then and there. Staring up at Zita was like looking at a goddess in her element. He'd pulled her scrunchie out of her hair when they'd started kissing, and now the auburn strands were in disarray around her head. She had sex hair going on, and *he'd* done that.

He had no idea how they'd gotten here. He'd been trying to figure out why Zita was in such a bad mood, why she'd been fucking *crying* for God's sake, and then they were kissing as if they had two minutes to live and were trying to squeeze in the last ounce of pleasure they'd ever get.

And he'd had the privilege of watching and feeling her come in his arms.

This experience was like nothing he'd ever had. It was more intimate, more desperate, and strangely more loving than anything he'd felt before. Watching her come apart was sensual, erotic, and he'd never felt closer to a woman.

Seeing her juices leaking out of her folds had ramped up his lust even more. The smell of sex was thick in the air, and his cock was so hard it hurt. But it was a good hurt. He'd been two seconds away from straddling her and shoving himself into her warm, wet body, but at the last moment realized that might hurt her. So he'd rolled to his back and put her in charge.

He hadn't realized until she was on top of him how difficult it would be to keep from coming prematurely. Seeing her tits sway, her nipples still hard and beckoning for his mouth, feeling the wetness between her legs on his upper thighs, and seeing his cock so close to her pussy, made his control almost snap.

But he grit his teeth, determined to let her take the lead, even though it would be torture.

Then she took his cock in her hand and stroked him, and if he thought he was suffering before, it was *nothing* to how he felt now. Obi-Wan could feel the come in his balls desperately trying to spew forth. It was taking all the control he'd learned over the years not to come all over her hand and belly.

"How long do you think you can last?"

He heard her question as if through a long tunnel. She had no idea how close to the edge he was already.

"Not very fucking long. Please, Zita. Please," he begged, desperately wanting to be inside her. Precome was leaking from the tip of his cock and making it easy for her to stroke him. Every slide of her hand was heaven.

To his immense relief, she went up on her knees and guided his cock to her folds. She bit her lip as she concentrated on the sensation of the head of his dick disappearing inside her body.

They both moaned at the sensation.

Obi-Wan closed his eyes, knowing he'd never feel anything as amazing as this ever again. It was a dramatic thought, as some people would say one pussy was the same as the next. But they were wrong.

He couldn't explain how or why, but Zita's sheath felt as if it was made for him.

Then something occurred to him, and his eyes flew open. "Fuck—Zita, wait!"

She froze, not even half of his cock inside her, and stared down at him with a worried look on her face. "Am I hurting you?"

"Hell no! I just...birth control. I'm not wearing a condom."

"I've got an implant. Are you...is there a reason you need to wear one, other than to keep me from getting pregnant? Because I'm good. I haven't been with anyone in a very long time."

It took a few precious seconds for her words to penetrate his brain. And when they did, Obi-Wan lost the control he'd been holding on to by the thinnest of margins. He forgot what he'd said about her being in charge. About not wanting to hurt her. About anything but being inside this woman as far as he could get. Being one with her.

He reached for her hips and pulled her down on him hard and fast, at the same time he thrust upward.

She let out a little shout as he penetrated her so deeply, their pubic hair meshed together. A strangled moan left his own lips as the perfection of the moment sank in.

"Holy crap," Zita whispered.

"Are you okay? Did I hurt you?" Obi-Wan asked, fear making his voice tremble.

"No, I was just surprised, that's all. You feel amazing. You're so deep!"

"And for the record, I haven't been with anyone in over a year. And I get tested by the Army all the time. If you're protected, we're good."

"We're definitely good," she said.

"Move, Zita. Please." All he could think about was the feeling of her pussy around his dick. How hot she was. How tight.

She gave him a sexy little smile, then tentatively lifted off his cock before sinking back down.

"Yes, more."

She did it again. Then again. Her pace was starting slow but minutes later, she was slamming herself down on him over and over, both of them crying out, their breaths ragged as she rode him fast and furious.

Without warning, Obi-Wan felt himself explode. He couldn't stop it. Couldn't do anything but watch Zita's tits bounce as his cock jerked once, twice, three times, while she concentrated on her own pleasure.

He'd never come inside a woman before—and it was glorious. His come made her even more slippery, sopping, and the resulting sounds were sexy as hell. He held her hips tightly but let her go at whatever speed and depth she needed to get herself off. But after just another few minutes or so, he could tell she was tiring and getting frustrated.

Obi-Wan took over. Now that his own pleasure had waned—although he was still half hard—he could concentrate on her. He pulled her down onto his cock and held her there as his fingers went to her clit. Her legs were spread wide over his lap, and he had easy access to that little nubbin.

"I've got you," he murmured, as he forcefully stroked right where she needed it most.

"Sage!" she exclaimed.

Obi-Wan could feel her inner muscles flexing around his cock as she sat stock still on top of him. He kept up the pressure and before long, he could feel her body begin to shake.

"That's it. Let go, sweetheart. Come on my cock. Let me feel it."

And just like that, she came. The feel of her body taking its pleasure, the tight squeeze all around his cock, made Obi-Wan a little dizzy.

He wanted this. Over and over. Every night. As much as this woman would allow. He was already obsessed and would do anything it took to keep her. To make things between them work. He still had no idea how their future would look, considering their jobs, but he was more determined than ever not to let her slip through his fingers.

When she stopped shaking, Zita slowly collapsed onto his chest like a blow-up toy that had been punctured. She was scalding hot against him, but Obi-Wan had never been more comfortable in his life. As far as he was concerned, she could sleep right where she was forever. His dick was still lodged deep within her body, cocooned in her warmth.

"I'm dead. You killed me," she mumbled into his neck, her breath tickling his skin, making him shiver.

"Sorry I came so soon. I'll be better next time," Obi-Wan told her, a little ashamed at how fast he'd orgasmed.

"Any better and I *will* be dead," she mumbled.

Obi-Wan was smiling like a fool, but he didn't even care. His hands caressed her back gently as he soaked in the intimacy between them. His heart was still beating fast, and he could feel hers against his chest as well. Knowing he'd pleasured her was as much a turn-on as the actual act of orgasming had been.

As she lay on top of him, he heard a strange sound. And when he realized what it was, Obi-Wan couldn't help but grin. "I never did feed you," he said.

"Not hungry."

"Yes, you are," he contradicted.

"Fine, I am. But I'd rather lie here than move."

Truth be told, so would he, but there was no chance he was going to let his woman go hungry because he was too horny to get up. He had all the time in the world to enjoy more moments like this one. Of course, this one was particularly special, as it was their first, but he promised himself it wouldn't be the last.

"I'm going to call On the Rocks, I think they're still serving food. I'll run out and get us something."

Zita lifted her head, and it made his cock shift inside her body. Obi-Wan bit his tongue as he did his best not to thrust into her. She had to be sore, and there was no way in hell he'd do anything to make this moment anything other than perfect.

"Are you sure?"

"Of course. What do you want?"

It was almost painful when she lifted herself off his cock and snuggled against his side. The sheets were wet, and Obi-Wan could feel their combined juices on his groin and thighs. It was an experience he'd never had before but couldn't say he hated. Sex would be messier without condoms, but the benefits far outweighed the disadvantages.

"Cheeseburger with fries. And a small salad with ranch on the side. Please."

Her definitive answer made Obi-Wan grin. She usually tried to eat healthy, but she'd more than earned the guilty pleasure of splurging tonight.

"I need to get up and find my phone. I think it's in one of the pockets of my pants."

She giggled. "We were in kind of a hurry to get undressed when we got here, weren't we?"

Obi-Wan went up on an elbow, and Zita turned onto her back to look up at him. "Thank you for not hiding what you felt. For letting me know you wanted me."

"I thought you'd be upset. I got the distinct impression you liked setting the pace of our relationship."

"I did. But sometimes I need a nudge."

"Consider yourself nudged."

He grinned and leaned down, kissing her soft and slow, a kiss quite different from earlier, when they'd been ravenous for each other. Then he got up while he still could, to find his phone. He called the bar on the square and, to his surprise, Zeke answered. After explaining why he was calling so late—without the explicit details, just explaining that they were on set all day and had only recently gotten back to the Mangree—Zeke offered to drive their food out to the motel, since he was about to head home himself.

Obi-Wan agreed without hesitation. The last thing he wanted was to go back out into the damp night and leave Zita's side. He settled back onto the bed and took her into his arms. "Zeke's bringing our food to us."

"Really?"

"Yup."

"Awesome." She leaned down and kissed his upper chest, then his neck, then moved to one of his nipples.

"I think he saw through my excuse about just getting back, because other crew members are probably at the bar eating by now. But I'm still not sure it would be cool to greet him at the door with my dick hanging out. I need to put some pants on."

Zita lifted her head and pouted.

Obi-Wan chuckled. "After we eat, you can have your way with me. Okay?"

"I'm holding you to that."

"You'll get no protests from me, because I plan on having *you* for dessert myself. I didn't get to taste you. Things moved too fast for me to do everything I've imagined."

"You complaining?" she asked with an adorable tilt of her head.

"Fuck no. No complaints here. You're amazing, Zita. And I'm a lucky son of a bitch."

"Damn straight," she said with a grin.

This woman. She slayed him. And Obi-Wan had no problems with being completely besotted. Not at all.

He got up and put his pants back on, wincing at their dampness from being out in the rainy weather all day. Then he grabbed all the other clothes strewn about the floor, hanging them up in the bathroom so they could dry overnight. It wasn't much longer before there was a knock on the door—and by the shit-eating grin on Zeke's face, he knew *exactly* what they'd been doing instead of eating dinner.

But Obi-Wan didn't care if the whole world knew he and Zita were making love. He wasn't about to hide their relationship.

The food disappeared quickly, as they were both starving, and after Obi-Wan threw away their trash and took his pants off once more, he climbed back under the covers. He made his way down Zita's body until her legs were spread around his shoulders.

Her pussy was a bit swollen, and the smell of her sex made his mouth water.

"Hey, I thought I was going to have my way with *you*," she complained with a grin, as she propped herself on her elbows and looked down her body at him.

"After. If you go first, I won't have the control to be able to do this..." Obi-Wan lowered his head and licked up her slit, stopping at her clit. She jerked in his hold and dropped back down to the mattress.

"Oh, all right. If you must," she joked.

Still smiling, Obi-Wan got to work pleasing his woman.

An hour later, they were both sweaty and completely wrung out. He'd eaten her to another orgasm, then she'd given him the best blow job he'd ever had. He'd stopped her just in time to climb on top of her and take her the way he'd dreamed—hard and fast, her fingernails digging into his upper arms as she moaned and urged him to go even harder.

Zita was made for him, and he was made for her. He was hers. Completely and utterly. He'd do anything for this woman.

That thought should've scared him, but instead, it made Obi-Wan smile with contentment. She was currently lying mostly on his chest once more, snoring lightly. His arm was around her shoulders, holding her against him as he drifted off to sleep.

They only had a few more days on set before it would wrap. They'd both have hard decisions to make, and the only thing Obi-Wan was sure of was the fact that he wasn't going to let this go. He and Zita had a connection not a lot of people got to have in their lifetime. No matter what happened, he'd fight for the right to be her boyfriend. Her man.

Because that's what he was. *Hers*.

CHAPTER SEVENTEEN

Zita was excited about today. Not for herself, because today would be just another day on set for her, but for Sage. Today was the day he'd been waiting for since filming began. It was helicopter day.

He was like a little kid excited about a trip to the zoo. Or to an amusement park. His anticipation was palatable. And it was adorable.

She didn't even care that he was preoccupied this morning, or that he'd sprung out of bed thirty minutes before his alarm was set to go off. She would've liked to have spent their first morning after becoming intimate cuddling a bit more. But while Sage had no problem spooning her and holding her all night, he wasn't exactly a "cuddler."

Zita had no idea sex could be so intimate. She'd obviously slept with the wrong people in the past. Sage was not only an exceptional lover, he was attentive, unselfish, and throughout the night was focused completely on her. It was a novel experience. And she truly felt as if he cared for her. He wasn't in her bed to scratch an itch.

He was bossy and confident, and he had no problem letting

her know what he needed and wanted. But because they were the exact things *she* wanted, Zita was happy to let him take the lead. Even when she'd gone down on him, there was no doubt he was still in charge. Which actually thrilled her.

Making love to Obadiah Engle had already changed her life... but Zita wasn't sure what she was going to do about it. If he asked her, she'd move to Virginia in a heartbeat. Hollywood had gotten old, and she'd been ready for a change for a while now. But was moving across the country for a man the right thing to do? What if this was just a novelty? Something new and exciting that would wane once they saw each other on a regular basis? She didn't think it was, at least not on her part, but would Sage change his mind?

Would she be able to deal with his deployments? Especially knowing how dangerous they were? Would they be able to work around *her* schedule? Would he resent her when she left for a month or more to work on a film set? Trust that she wouldn't stray? Was he the jealous type?

She still had so many questions...but she truly believed they could work through any hardships they might encounter that came with a relationship. Being with someone wasn't easy. It took a lot of work. But Sage was worth it.

Would he feel the same about her?

She hated the unknown, the uncertainty. She wanted to live in the moment, but it was as if a giant clock was ticking in her head. When this job was over, what would happen then? She supposed they could try to make a long-distance relationship work, but the odds of that happening were low. Which made her want to cry.

She liked Sage. Was half in love with him. The thought of leaving and not seeing him again felt like torture. She'd never been so in tune with a man before, and the last thing she wanted was to turn her back on that.

Taking a deep breath, Zita did her best to put all her worries aside. Today was a new day, she was deliciously sore, and everything seemed a little brighter. Of course, it *was* brighter, literally, as the rain had moved on and the sun was shining by the time they made their way to his Jeep to head to the square for breakfast before heading out to the set.

Sage had gone to his room to shower and get ready, saying if he showered in her room, they might not make it to breakfast at all, as he'd be way too tempted to drag her into the tiny bathroom with him.

The man might be focused on the job and excited about his beloved choppers, but he hadn't neglected her. Hadn't made her feel as if the night before meant nothing. After they'd gotten up, used the bathroom, brushed their teeth, and figured out the plans for the morning, he'd pushed her backward onto the bed, shoved her legs apart, and eaten her to another orgasm.

It was spontaneous and surprising, and oh so sexy. When he'd finally picked his head up from where he was kneeling between her legs, he'd licked his lips, still shiny from her juices, and winked at her.

"Nothing like a little pussy to start my day."

Zita had rolled her eyes with a grin. It was a cheesy thing to say, but she couldn't say she disagreed with him. Her body felt both languid and charged up, ready to go. She'd reached for him, but he'd grabbed her hand, kissed the palm, and said if she touched him, they'd never leave the room. Then added that he'd take care of his monster hard-on in the shower.

She might've been upset that he'd turned down her offer, except for the look of desire in his eyes. He couldn't fake that. At least, she didn't think he could.

Zita settled for sitting up and kissing the hell out of him. She could taste herself on his lips and tongue, and it was extremely sexy.

He'd groaned and stood up suddenly, his pants tented from his erection, and said he'd see her in thirty minutes.

Zita had giggled, riding her orgasm high throughout her morning routine. When Sage knocked on her door exactly thirty minutes later, he'd taken her in his arms, kissed her once more—a long, drawn-out kiss that made Zita's toes curl—before grabbing her hand and her medical bag, and towing her toward his Jeep.

They'd eaten breakfast at Sunny Side Up—everything Zita had tried at the amazing diner since they'd been in town was delicious—and then made their way to the set.

Sage turned off the engine and undid his seat belt, but made no move to get out. Instead, he turned to her and said, "This is not a fling."

The five words were said with passion and a seriousness that made warmth flood through Zita. "Good, because I didn't think it was."

"I have no idea how this will go. How we'll make it work. All I know is that I'll do whatever it takes to keep what we have going. I've never met anyone like you, Zita Darlington. You impress the hell out of me. And last night?"

He paused, then finally cleared his throat before continuing.

"I had no idea sex could be like that. Intimate...fun...almost overwhelming. I felt a connection with you that I've never felt before. I have no idea if it was the same for you, but it made me realize how rare it is to find someone you click with the way I've clicked with you. But I also know a relationship is more than sex. Passion fades, but being with someone you look forward to waking up to and spending your days and nights with *doesn't*.

"I want a partner who I can be myself with. I get grumpy and out of sorts. I'm not always very social. I like hanging out at home more than I like going out. People annoy me more often than not. We still have a lot to learn about each other, but I have a feeling nothing I find out about you will turn me off in the slightest.

"If you don't think you can do this...have a relationship with me...please tell me now. Because if I spend more time with you, I'm going to fall even harder than I have already. And if that's not what you want, it'll hurt even more if we drag this out."

He wasn't smiling. Was staring at her with an intensity that was almost scary. But Zita's heart was soaring. He was saying things that she'd only dreamed she'd hear from a man. They were so much on the same page, it was uncanny, because she'd had the same fears more than once this morning.

"Would it freak you out if I said I was willing to move to Norfolk?"

He didn't say anything for a long moment. So long, actually, that Zita's heart seemed to stop beating in her chest.

Then he closed his eyes and took a deep breath.

She didn't dare move, wondering what he was thinking.

When his eyes popped open, he moved quickly, reaching out and pulling her toward him with a hand on her nape. He kissed her *hard*, pulling back just enough to say, "No. It wouldn't freak me out. It would make me the happiest man in the world right now."

"I'm terrified," Zita admitted. "But I can work from just about anywhere. I might not get as many film gigs if I'm not in Hollywood, but honestly, I'm okay with that."

"I don't deserve you," Sage said gruffly.

"I think we deserve each other," she told him. "But I'm not moving in with you," she clarified. "I want my own place. Things have moved fast with us, and I want the time to make sure this is really what we both want."

"It's what *I* want," Sage said with no hesitation whatsoever. "But I understand completely. I hope you aren't opposed to sleepovers," he said with a small grin.

"I'm not." Then she shook her head a little wryly. "Are we really doing this? After only knowing each other for such a short time?"

"I feel as if I've known you forever," he countered.

He wasn't wrong. Zita felt like that too, but she also felt as if she should keep reminding him how fast they were moving, because it wasn't exactly acceptable these days to jump into a serious relationship so quickly. Definitely not acceptable for her to uproot her life and move across the country just to be closer to a man.

Her parents were going to have serious misgivings. And her brother would probably want to have a "talk" with Sage. But Zita had no doubt he'd win them over, just as he had her, simply by being himself.

"I'm yours, Zita. Lock, stock, and barrel. I don't care if everyone thinks I'm besotted. Because I am."

She liked that. A lot. The idea of him belonging to her.

And she wanted to be his in return.

"You ready for today?" he asked, and she was glad he'd lightened the mood a little. Things had gotten intense, and while she was happier than she could even express, it was also a little overwhelming. She'd basically just decided to completely upend her life, and bringing talk back around to the here and now was a relief.

"As I *can* be. You?"

"Oh yeah. I hope the pilots Grubbner got are as good as he says. That they can actually fly."

"I'm sure they're the best...though not as good as you, of course."

He chuckled. "Yeah." Sage sat back, but not before his fingers caressed the back of her neck gently before releasing her. "Can I stay with you again tonight?"

Zita smiled. "Of course."

"Awesome. I should probably tell Edna that I don't need my room anymore, but she seems like the kind of lady who wouldn't take kindly to a boy and girl shacking up together if they're not married."

Zita giggled. "Right? I totally got those vibes too."

Sage stared at her for a beat, and she wondered what he was thinking. But before she could ask, he turned and reached for the door handle, and the spell between them was broken.

Zita got out and grabbed her bag, and together they headed toward the group of people milling about, getting ready for the day to start.

* * *

Sage was in his element. And it made Zita smile watching him with the helicopter pilots. He'd spoken with them at length that morning, and from what she could tell from her vantage point, they were getting along and everyone seemed pleased.

And when the scenes with the choppers were filmed, Zita saw Sage's hands moving as if *he* was in the pilot seat of one of the multimillion-dollar aircrafts. The director had given him a headset, and Zita assumed he was talking with the pilots directly.

She was no expert, but it seemed as if the scenes were going extremely well. That the pilots were doing exactly what both Grubbner and Sage expected them to.

Zita was watching Sage so intently that she wasn't paying attention to anything or anyone around her...so when someone bumped her shoulder, she let out a little screech of alarm and quickly sidestepped to the left.

Looking over, she saw to her surprise that Silas Graves was standing next to her. *Right* next to her. In her personal space. She hadn't thought much about him for the last few days, as she'd been too busy, and she had no idea why he'd sought her out today.

She was quick to realize it wasn't for a social chat.

"You need to stay away from the Night Stalker," he said in a low tone.

"What?" Zita was still trying to get her heart to calm down after he'd scared her so badly.

"Obi-Wan. You throwing yourself at him is embarrassing. For everyone on set. You need to stay away from him."

Zita was so confused. Why in the hell did Silas care if she and Sage were together? "Not that it's any business of yours, but why are you so interested in what I do with my time away from the set? I don't get in your face about what *you're* doing, so why are you on my case?"

She was done being nice. Sage was right, the man had been giving her creepy stares for too long now. He'd also been a total jerk while guarding Carmen, but she had no idea what his agenda was now.

"I'm just warning you. Stay away from the guy...or else."

Zita would've rolled her eyes at the overly dramatic warning, but now that she looked at him—*really* looked—he seemed deadly serious, and the last thing she wanted was to antagonize him. Even though she was surrounded by people, she wasn't sure what he was capable of.

And the man was armed. Did she think he was going to shoot her right here in front of everyone on set? No. But he was bigger and stronger and could certainly hurt her before anyone could stop him. She wasn't going to risk it.

She opened her mouth to attempt to understand where this was coming from, to once again ask why he cared about who she hung out with or dated, but he turned abruptly and walked away.

Zita was kind of freaked out by the out-of-the-blue threat. She hadn't done anything to Silas. Had barely even talked to the man. Carmen? Yeah, they'd had words, but she'd been back in LA for days now. Was thousands of miles away.

Still...could she have anything to do with Silas's sudden interest in her love life?

Possibly.

It was impossible to wrap her head around the fact that a

beautiful, successful actress like Carmen St. James would care about someone like her. A nobody contract employee who happened to be working on the same set.

But then again, she'd had her eye on Sage, and he'd rejected her—for Zita.

Could that be it? Was her former bodyguard sending a message from Carmen? Set gossip had the two sleeping together when she was in town, but if that was the case, if Silas had the hots for Carmen, why would he want to break up Zita and Sage? If he was dating someone else, then Carmen wouldn't have a chance of winning him. Which would leave the way clear for Silas.

So why would he warn her *away* from Sage?

Unless he was *that* desperate to prove his loyalty to Carmen. Prove that he'd do literally anything she asked. Maybe he wanted to move to Los Angeles, and he thought if he did Carmen's bidding, she'd find him a job.

Hell, maybe he was simply an asshole who wanted to harass her.

Zita's head hurt. Nothing made sense. She suddenly felt as if she was in the middle of one of those love triangles on a crime show. One that ended badly for one or more of the players in the scenario.

That, or she was being punked. Was there a camera on her? Would Henry come over in a minute, smiling and telling her that she was being played for the gag reel?

No. He was way too engrossed in the scene he was filming. The helicopters. Hell, *everyone's* heads were turned upward, watching what was going on in the skies. It was the perfect time for Silas to threaten her—if that's really what he was doing; she still wasn't exactly sure—because no one was paying attention.

A shiver went through Zita. She'd never liked the man, and she had no idea what he'd do if she didn't keep her distance from

Sage. Silas didn't say. Had simply said "or else" like a movie villain...which could literally mean anything.

Taking a deep breath, Zita pressed her lips together. She and Sage were starting something amazing. She'd just made the decision to move to Virginia. She wasn't going to be cowed by threats from some asshole she'd just met.

Whatever Silas's reasons, he could shove them up his ass. The filming in Virginia would be over in a few days, and everyone would go back to California and finish the movie there, after Logan spent some time training and regaining the weight he'd lost. Zita wouldn't see Silas or Carmen ever again. She hoped.

If she found out the actress would be on any set Zita was slated to work on in the future, she'd turn down the gig.

Feeling better that it wouldn't be long before she'd see the last of Silas, Zita did her best to silence the voice in her head that said she shouldn't dismiss his threat so quickly. She resented the fact anyone was trying to take away the euphoric feeling she had after her night with Sage. They'd had the perfect evening, this morning's conversation was everything she'd wanted to hear...and now someone was already trying to break them up.

Screw that. Screw *Silas*.

* * *

Obi-Wan felt great. The day was fantastic, his favorite spent on set thus far, which wasn't a surprise since it included the helicopters he loved so much. The pilots were good—not as good as the Night Stalkers, of course, but no layperson watching the movie would know the difference.

He missed flying, and it hadn't even been that long. Being here, watching others fly, reminded him of just how much he loved his job. Enjoyed working with his teammates, how proud he was to be able to deliver and pick up the men and women who put their lives on the line for their country.

What he did wasn't always appreciated, most of the time wasn't even *known*, but he didn't need public recognition, he simply wanted to fly.

He felt bad that he'd been preoccupied most of the day, but every time he'd looked around to find Zita—which admittingly wasn't as often as he would've liked—she was busy talking to someone, or taking a blood pressure, or dealing with other minor injuries that always seemed to crop up on the set.

When he approached her at the end of the day—dusty, sweaty, and tired—he was surprised to see her looking...anxious. He'd seen her exhausted, irritated, happy, worried, and even proud. But not jumpy, like she seemed at the moment.

"What's wrong?" he asked, as soon as he was within earshot.

Her expression immediately blanked and she gave him an insincere smile. "Nothing. It looks like you had a great day."

Obi-Wan wasn't willing to let it go, though she obviously wanted him to. He needed to know what was bothering her. He didn't like that he was in the dark when something was clearly on her mind. Of course, she was entitled to keep her feelings to herself, but he still felt a little raw after last night and this morning, about how much she meant to him.

For a moment, when he'd commented on the lady who owned the motel possibly disapproving of them sharing the same room without being married, all he could think of was Zita standing in front of him wearing a white dress, while they shared vows to love and cherish each other for the rest of their lives.

He'd never, *ever* thought about his own wedding before. It was something he'd always figured would happen or not, and yet this morning, he couldn't get the image of the two of them all dressed up for their wedding out of his head.

Thankfully, she hadn't asked him what he was thinking, because he wasn't sure he would've been able to keep his thoughts to himself. And it was definitely too soon to even think about marriage.

"Talk to me. Please," he said softly, running his hand up and down her upper arm gently.

She sighed. "It's not a big deal. At least, I don't think it is. I handled it."

"What did you 'handle'?" he asked, feeling himself tense and trying his hardest to keep his voice level.

"Silas."

Obi-Wan waited for her to say more, and when she didn't, he frowned. "What about him? What'd he do?"

"It was weird, Sage. He warned me to stay away from you, but he wouldn't say why."

"What the *fuck*?" Obi-Wan asked, his brows furrowing.

"Right? But it's fine. Because I'm *not* going to keep my distance from you. So whatever."

Obi-Wan wasn't nearly as willing to let this go as she was. He turned around, looking for Silas, but Logan and his bodyguard were long gone from the set.

He was already making plans to stop at the B&B and have words with the man who'd dared try to interfere with his relationship with Zita when he felt a hand on his arm.

"Sage, it's *fine*. I don't know why he cares if we're together or not, but I'm not going to let him occupy my thoughts for another second. I'd rather concentrate on us."

She was right...and yet, Obi-Wan couldn't shake the sudden bad feeling in his gut. He'd seen the way the man had stared at Zita most of the week. Not as someone who was interested in her, but in a more calculating way. It was weird, as Zita had said. And weird wasn't good, especially when it came to the woman who meant the world to him.

"Come on, let's go home. Well, back to the motel," Zita urged.

He let her pull him toward his Jeep, but he made a mental

note to not underestimate Silas. He'd keep his eye on him, and the second anything seemed hinky, he'd make sure the man understood that Zita was off-limits.

Obi-Wan wasn't afraid of any of the man's supposed bodyguard skills. Or the firearm he carried. Night Stalker training was intense, and he had the confidence that he could hold his own against anyone, no matter what their skill set.

But Zita couldn't. And that was what worried him. He couldn't always be around to watch over her. Not that she'd want that, but he still wanted to protect her as much as he could.

By the time they arrived back in Fallport, they were both tired after a long day, so Obi-Wan parked on the square and ran into the diner to order them something to go.

The Jeep smelled amazing on the short ride to the motel, and they both eagerly dug into the takeout boxes the second they got inside her room.

What followed was another night of the most amazing sex Obi-Wan had ever had. It wasn't that they did anything wild and crazy, but they didn't need to. Making love in the missionary position while staring into Zita's eyes was more than enough to make Obi-Wan feel as if he was the luckiest man in the world. Feeling her come around him, her pussy squeeze him as she flew over the edge, had him hurtling along behind her.

This woman had changed his life, and he felt like a brand-new man. They had some challenges ahead of them, she'd have to return to California and deal with her life out there, then pack, get to Virginia, find an apartment and a job...it was a lot. Obi-Wan was well aware of the sacrifices she was making to be with him, and he vowed never to take her for granted. Or to dismiss everything that she was changing and giving up to move to Virginia.

Before he fell asleep that night, once more holding Zita tightly in his arms, his thoughts strayed again to Silas Graves. What the hell had the man meant by telling Zita to stay away from him? What was his motive? He had no idea but wasn't going to take any chances. As soon as he got back to Norfolk, he'd talk to Casper and the others. See if they thought the weirdness of the situation warranted a call to Tex. Obi-Wan didn't want to bother the man with something trivial if he could help it. Because he was most certainly busy with more life-or-death situations.

But if there was the slightest chance Zita was in danger, he'd call whoever he needed to in order to make sure she was safe.

CHAPTER EIGHTEEN

It was a wrap.

The movie was done. Well, at least the parts that could be filmed in Virginia.

The rest of the week went by quickly, and the after-party had been held in the square. The entire town of Fallport was invited.

Zita was happier than she could remember being in a very long time, but she still felt a little on edge. Silas hadn't approached her again, but she felt his eyes on her while on set. Every time she looked at him, he turned his head and pretended like he hadn't been staring. It was unnerving...and had begun to worry her.

As much as she loved Fallport, she was glad to be back on the road. She had two more nights in Norfolk before her plane left for LA. It was a weird feeling to be looking forward to going home, just to get away from the weird vibes she got from Silas, while at the same time dreading flying back to Los Angeles because that meant she was leaving Sage.

The last couple of nights had been everything she'd dreamed. Sage was easy to live with...if you could call sleeping in a motel "living" together. Their nights were the stuff romance authors wrote about. Sexy, passionate, and full of talking and closeness afterward.

The more she was around Sage, the more she was sure about her decision to move to Virginia. He obviously couldn't leave, so if she really wanted this relationship to work, it was up to her to cut ties to Hollywood once and for all. And it was time. She was thirty-five years old and she wanted a *life*, something outside just movies and the medical field. She loved both, but she rarely did anything but work. She needed more balance.

And she had high hopes that a relationship with Sage would provide just that. Give her the balance she craved. A family.

It wouldn't be easy. Being with someone in the military wasn't a walk in the park. Especially someone with a job like Sage's. Where he could be deployed at a moment's notice, and he couldn't tell her anything about where he was going or what he was doing or even when he'd be back.

But she was looking forward to trying. To getting to know Laryn and Mandy better. She already liked the two women, and she *had* offered to do everything in her power to be there for Laryn and her baby when it was born.

Smiling, because she liked the thought of being in Virginia and settled before the other woman had her baby, Zita glanced over at Sage. They'd gotten a leisurely start back to Norfolk, and with every mile that passed, it felt as if she were leaving Silas and his weird looks and threats behind. She had no reason to see him again, and it felt like a huge weight was lifted off her back.

"You're coming over to my place tonight, right?" Sage asked.

"If that's okay."

"It's more than okay. Though I have to work tomorrow. I need to go in early, and I'll probably be there until late afternoon. I'm sorry, but since I've been gone, I—"

"No need to apologize," Zita said quickly. "I understand. I've got some paperwork I need to do and some calls to make anyway. I've got two more nights reserved at the motel, thanks to the studio, and if you can drop me off there in the morning, I'll get a head start on closing up my life in California."

"You could stay at my place and do that," Sage offered.

"I know, and I appreciate it. But there's also one more meeting with the producer and some of the assistants mid-morning. To finish up reports and logistics, and I need to give them my report on injuries for OSHA. They booked a small conference room at the motel for that, so I'd have to eventually find my way there, anyway. You can text and let me know when you're done tomorrow afternoon and pick me up on your way home...if that's okay."

"That's perfect. Silas won't be there, will he?" Sage asked.

"Not that I know of. His contract was done when Logan left, so he has no reason to be at the meeting tomorrow."

"Good. Okay. Anything you want for dinner tonight?"

Zita grinned a little mischievously. "I'm still full from all the food at the wrap party last night, and that delicious breakfast we had this morning. I'm kind of thinking on our last day off, maybe we can watch another *Star Wars* movie and test out how easy it is to make love in that big chair of yours."

"Damn, woman," Sage breathed, shifting in his seat.

Zita laughed, because she could see the erection in his pants. "Sorry," she said, not feeling sorry in the least. "I had more than one naughty thought while watching TV with you before we left for Fallport."

"You too?" Sage asked with a smile.

This. This was what she'd always wanted. A partner to laugh with. To tease. Someone with whom she shared amazing chemistry. And Sage was everything she'd ever dreamed about and more. Oh, she had no doubt they'd butt heads over time. But for now, she was loving how easy it was to be with him.

"Thank you for giving us a chance," he said after a moment, his tone now serious. "For being willing to sacrifice so much to move to Virginia. You'll never know how much it means to me.

I'll never take you for granted. Take what you're giving up for granted."

"I'm not giving up anything I can't do here," she told him honestly. "And what I'm potentially gaining is worth moving to the other end of the *Earth*, not just the country."

"Not potentially, what you *are* gaining," he replied almost fiercely. "I'm not going to fuck this up. Not going to make you regret making this decision. I'll spend every day making sure you understand how much you mean to me, and how much I respect and admire you."

"Sage," Zita said softly, feeling overwhelmed with feelings toward this man.

He held out his hand, and she took it immediately, squeezing his fingers as she did. They drove the rest of the way home with her hand in his, Zita feeling as if she'd finally found the place she was always meant to be. By this man's side.

* * *

"Harder, Sage! *More*. Give me more!"

Zita was on her hands and knees in his bed, and Sage was behind her, thrusting in and out of her body as desperately as she was rocking back against him. They'd started out in his chair, but things quickly got out of control as their desires ramped up.

He'd put Zita on his lap, straddling him, but because of the ultra-soft cushion under her knees, she couldn't get the leverage she needed to take him as hard as either of them wanted.

Eventually, he'd growled something under his breath, lifted her off his cock, threw her over his shoulder and brought her to his bed, where he threw her down, turned her so she was on her hands and knees, and slammed back into her.

Which is where they were now, with Zita seeing stars and on the verge of an orgasm so immense, it was almost scary, Sage standing at the end of the bed and holding her hips tightly as he took her.

"Come for me, Zita. I need to feel it on my dick."

His words turned her on even more. But it wasn't until he shifted a hand so his finger roughly massaged her clit that she broke.

She let out a half wail, half scream as her body shook. The orgasm went on and on, until Zita didn't think she'd be able to hold herself up anymore. Sage thrust inside her once more and held still as he groaned loudly. The sound was sexy as hell, making Zita's muscles spasm.

They were both breathing hard when it was over. Frozen in place, as if memorizing the moment. At least Zita was.

Probably sensing how shaky she was, Sage pulled out almost immediately, which sucked, but it was a relief when he gently lowered her to the mattress, turning her onto her back in the process. Then he climbed onto the bed, throwing one leg over her thighs, his arm over her chest, and buried his nose in the crook of her neck.

Zita smiled. She loved being used as a pillow, the way he was doing now. She felt surrounded by him. Warm and replete. Safe.

"Never gonna be able to sit in that chair again and not get an instant hard-on," he mumbled against her skin.

She giggled. "I could always sit in the other chair. You have two, after all."

"No way. It's the most exquisite torture having you in my lap."

Her smile wouldn't die. Zita ran her hand lazily over the arm on her chest. She liked this. No, she freaking *loved* it. Lying here with Sage. Her body tingling from her orgasm, feeling a little sore between her legs and having no doubt the man next to her was meant to be hers.

"Not sure I like you thinking about me and torture in the same sentence," she teased.

Sage lifted his head and stared at her for a long moment. Then said, "I didn't get it. Didn't really understand the connection Casper has with Laryn or Buck has with Mandy. But I do now. I feel like a different man than I was before I met you. More compassionate, more determined to be the best pilot I can be so I can come home to you. So the men and women I transport can get home to their loved ones. So my single teammates can stay alive to find their soul mates. I thought loving someone would be scary. Would change my passion for flying. For serving my country. Instead, it's magnified it."

"Sage," Zita whispered, having no idea if he even knew what he'd just said.

"It's like this missing piece inside of me has suddenly been filled in. That's cheesy as shit, but it's how I feel. I like knowing you'll be with me when I'm on a mission. That you'll be there inside me when the shit hits the fan, because I have a feeling it'll help me concentrate. To do what needs to be done so I can come home to you. It's not frightening in the least. It's...empowering. Makes me even more determined to be the best pilot possible. The best partner.

"I love you, Zita. I...you...*Fuck*. It's impossible to put into words just *how much* I care about you."

"I think you just did," Zita said quietly. She was reeling from his admission. She felt much the same as he did. That he made her a better person, because she wanted him to be proud of her. That she wanted to save other people's lives so they could continue to be with their loved ones. Was that love? She had no idea, as she'd never felt about anyone the way she did about this man. Like if she didn't get to be with him, she'd shrivel up into a tiny little raisin and wither away.

Talk about dramatic...she was being ridiculous. Wasn't she?

Sage shifted and kissed her cheek reverently, before putting his head back down and snuggling deeper into her.

Was he upset that she hadn't said the words back? He didn't

seem to be, but Zita had no experience with this. The words were stuck in her throat. She wanted to say them but something held her back. A sense of self-preservation, maybe?

She was well aware that she was making all the sacrifices in the relationship by quitting her job and moving across the country, but she was all right with that. She *wanted* to move. Was ready for a change. But if Sage decided she wasn't what he wanted after all, that he was wrong about loving her, it would devastate her so badly she wasn't sure she'd recover.

"Sleep, Zita. Stop thinking so hard. This is going to work. I give you my word. You'll see."

Deciding stressing about the future would do her no good whatsoever, Zita took a deep breath and closed her eyes. There was no need to lay all her feelings out right this second. The sex was good—no, it was fan-fucking-tastic—but that was no reason to blurt out that she loved him. She had time. *They* had time. Their life together was just starting. No need to rush things.

Feeling better about the situation, Zita fell asleep within minutes, happier than she'd been in a very long time.

CHAPTER NINETEEN

Obi-Wan felt on top of the world. Last night had been...

He couldn't come up with an adjective to adequately explain what it was. He'd jumped the gun by telling Zita he loved her, he realized that, but wasn't concerned that she hadn't said it back. The woman cared about him, that wasn't in question. But he'd most certainly taken her by surprise, and he never wanted her to tell him that she loved him out of some sense of obligation or because she felt it was expected.

Today would be long for both of them. Obi-Wan needed to get caught up with the team and the meetings they'd had while he was gone. He was also looking forward to getting in the air again. It was only a week, but he couldn't wait to be back in the copilot seat with Buck. Zita had the wrap-up meeting, where she'd be presenting her report on the injuries she'd treated while on set. Then a lot of research to do on jobs and apartments in Virginia. He'd see her again that night, when he went to pick her up to bring her back to his place.

They had one more night together before she'd head back to California to begin the process of shutting down her life there.

He'd miss her like crazy while she was gone, but he'd do his best to be patient, since the end result would be her living minutes away, instead of thousands of miles.

After making oatmeal and pancakes, along with large cups of coffee for them both, he sighed. "About ready?"

"Yeah. It feels weird that we won't be spending the day together. I've gotten too used to looking up and seeing you throughout the day."

She wasn't wrong. "Same. But I'll text you when I can, I want to know how your meeting goes this morning."

"Okay. I think my report is after lunch, but I'll let you know for sure."

"All right." Obi-Wan reached for Zita, wanting one last hug before they got on with their day. She held on to him tightly as they stood in the foyer of his apartment. Things would be different starting today, and he wasn't sure he was ready for it. Like her, he'd enjoyed being able to talk to her whenever he wanted. Seeing her on set. Watching her work. But while it sucked returning to real life, Obi-Wan was also looking forward to it. Getting back to a routine—this time, one that included Zita.

She pulled back and smiled up at him. He gently smoothed a lock of her hair behind her ear. She'd left it down, deciding she'd shower when she got to her motel room.

"Gonna miss you today," she said softly.

"Same. But we'll see each other soon enough."

"I know. We need to go so you won't be late. Casper will kick your butt if you're late on your first day back."

"He's gonna kick my butt anyway," Obi-Wan said with a laugh. "Just because he can. And to make me suffer for not working out for the last week."

"I don't know, it seems to me that you had a great workout last night."

He chuckled. "True." Then he leaned down and kissed her

forehead, before turning and picking up her med bag. He was getting used to hauling the thing around. It wasn't light, and he was impressed all over again by how effortlessly Zita dealt with it while on set. He'd told her she could leave it at his place, but she insisted that even though she wasn't planning on needing her medical supplies, she wanted to have them nearby...just in case.

He drove toward the motel, holding her hand. It was still dark out, and he was definitely going to be late to join his team at PT, but he didn't care. Making sure Zita got into her room safe and sound was much more important.

He parked in front of the room she'd been assigned and hopped out of the driver's seat. He walked Zita to the door and stood by as she unlocked it and reached in and turned on the light. The room was nothing special. Looked exactly like the last room she'd had. Obi-Wan dropped her med bag just inside the door as she pulled her suitcases into the room. Then he took her into his arms, unable to resist, and kissed the hell out of her. Wanting her to know without words that when he'd said he loved her last night, he hadn't been blowing smoke up her ass. Hadn't been caught up in great sex or the aftermath of an amazing orgasm.

They were both breathing hard when he finally forced himself to let her go.

"Damn," Zita breathed.

Obi-Wan grinned. "I'll see you tonight. And will text to see how things are going."

"Okay. Same. I want to know how badly Casper and the rest of the guys are on your case about missing a week of work and PT."

Obi-Wan rolled his eyes. "I can handle them. Later, hon."

"Bye," she said softly.

Obi-Wan went back to his Jeep, and he saw Zita peeking out from the window. She waved, and he gave her a chin lift in return. Then he forced himself to back out of the parking spot and drive away.

* * *

Zita licked her lips and smiled when she tasted Sage there. The man was seriously hot. That hug he'd given her this morning? It had been one of the best hugs she'd ever gotten. Spontaneous and "just because." Being in Sage's arms felt like coming home. Because wherever he was, that *was* home. She'd had the realization as she'd stood in his embrace, simply enjoying the moment.

She figured that was why she wasn't more worried about upending her life in California. She wanted to be where Sage was. It didn't matter if they lived in his apartment, hers, in Virginia or Timbuktu. As long as they were together.

She huffed out a little laugh and picked up her smaller suit-case. She put it on the bed and unzipped it, grabbing her toiletry bag. She put it to the side and continued to rifle through her things, looking for the one set of nicer clothes she'd packed, with today's meetings in mind.

A knock on the door had her looking up. Smiling and shaking her head, wondering what in the world Sage had forgotten, Zita walked over to the door.

"What did you—"

Her words stuck in her throat when she saw it wasn't Sage at the door.

It was Silas Graves.

She didn't get a chance to ask what he was doing there or what he wanted.

His fist reared back and he coldcocked her right in the face.

Zita went down like a rock, one hand going to her cheek in shock. The pain was overwhelming. Shooting through her face and down her body in a wave.

Silas didn't give her a second to recover. He reached down

222

and grabbed the front of her T-shirt in a meaty fist, holding her as his arm reared back once more.

Zita tried to protect herself from the punch that was coming, but she was too slow. Too dazed to cover her face.

This time, the pain was so extreme her body couldn't cope. Everything went dark as she gave in to the excruciating agony.

* * *

When she came to, Zita blinked—and immediately realized the small movement caused her head to throb so badly, she felt nauseous. She had no idea where she was, except it was dark. It was taking every ounce of her control not to puke everywhere.

The pain in her head and face hadn't receded, but eventually she realized she was in a car. More specifically, the trunk of a car. The hum of the motor, the way her body swayed back and forth as the vehicle changed lanes or turned, and the darkness all told her she was in deep shit here.

Doing her best not to panic, Zita slowly reached out, fumbled around where she thought the brake lights should be. She'd seen more than one video about how to escape a trunk if you were locked inside. How to disable the lights so maybe the driver would get pulled over. Or to knock them out altogether and stick a hand out so people in other cars could see her waving for help.

But it was pitch black inside the trunk, and she couldn't see what she was doing. She also had no tools to get the screws off the plates covering the electronic wires for the lights.

Feeling frustrated, Zita decided maybe her best bet was to scream. Perhaps someone at a stoplight would hear her and call the police.

She waited until the vehicle stopped, then yelled at the top of her lungs.

"Help me! I'm in the trunk! I've been kidnapped! Call the police! Please! Fire! Fire! Call nine-one-one!"

She'd heard once that yelling for help usually didn't make people act, but saying there was a fire was more likely to get someone to do something.

Her yelling *did* get a reaction. But as far as she could tell, not from anyone who would help her. Silas—she assumed it was that asshole driving, since he'd been the one to hit her—turned on the radio. *Loud.*

The screaming already had her head throbbing even worse than before. Paired with the sudden pounding music, she couldn't hold back the vomit that had been hovering in her throat.

The amazing breakfast she'd eaten not too long ago came up with a vengeance.

Zita did her best to puke off to the side of where she was lying, but once her stomach was empty, the smell in the trunk only made her misery worse.

Tears formed in her eyes. She wanted to be strong. Wanted to be the kind of person who could save herself. She'd also watched videos of women getting out of zip-ties, escaping their assailants, and basically being kick-ass. And here she was, practically lying in her own vomit, helpless to do a damn thing to save herself.

She still had no idea why Silas had kidnapped her. He hadn't said anything before punching her, and she'd been unconscious when he'd put her in this trunk. She had no idea where they were going.

The tears dripped down her cheeks, causing her more pain when the salty liquid seeped into the open wound on her face from Silas's knuckles.

How long they'd already been driving, Zita had no idea. It seemed like she was in the dark for hours before the car slowed once more. It felt as if they were driving over gravel or maybe on a dirt road. Which scared her all over again. Had he driven her out into the countryside? Was he going to shoot her and leave her for dead? Or worse, bury her body so no one would ever find her?

Zita's mind immediately went to Sage. He'd wonder where she went. He'd definitely look for her, but how would he find her if she was underground? Her parents would never know what happened, her brother would probably go crazy trying to find her.

The damn tears she'd briefly managed to stem started up again. She was overwhelmed and terrified.

She thought she heard Silas talking to someone, but the music was too loud for her to understand what was being said, and when she opened her mouth to yell again, they were moving once more. But much slower than they'd been before.

Licking her lips—and feeling more upset that she could no longer taste Sage on them, than she was that her face was swelling because of Silas's punches—Zita tried to think about her best plan of action for when the trunk opened.

She knew all too well that allowing a kidnapper to take her somewhere wasn't good. She'd been unconscious and hadn't been able to fight Silas when he'd put her in the trunk, but she was awake now. And she wasn't going to die without one hell of a fight. She'd get his DNA under her fingernails; she already had *her* DNA in the form of vomit in his trunk. She'd put scratches on him that no one could ignore.

Anything and everything that would point the police, and Sage, straight to Silas Graves.

It wasn't as if they wouldn't know where to start. He was the only person she'd had trouble with in the recent past. He'd threatened her just days ago with that vague "or else" warning. Thank God she'd told Sage about the encounter. Silas would be the first person he'd suspect in her disappearance.

She was so lost in her head, she almost failed to realize the vehicle had stopped. The music shut off suddenly, and Zita could hear her own breaths in the quiet space around her. She needed to calm down. Slow her breathing. She could do this. She had no choice. She wanted the future she'd been hoping to have with Sage. Wanted to start a new life in Virginia. She didn't want to die.

The trunk latch disengaged, and Zita tensed—then she shoved the lid up hard and fast, hoping to catch Silas's head with it.

To her surprise, no one was standing behind the car waiting for her.

Sitting up, Zita looked around, trying to understand where she was and what she was seeing.

There were weeds and high grass everywhere, along with rusted cars, trucks, and...was that an *airplane?*

Most discerning than the obviously abandoned vehicles, though, was the fact that wherever they were, it was desolate and deserted. No one was around. She could hear the wind blowing and smell the scent of the ocean. It was eerie and terrifying. She'd counted on being able to yell for help, to get the attention of someone, anyone, nearby to help her. She should've known better.

It was obviously still early in the morning. She hadn't been in the trunk for as long as she'd originally thought, which meant she probably hadn't been unconscious all that long either. The closer she was to Norfolk, and Sage, the better.

All those observations were done in seconds—then Silas appeared from around the side of the car.

She didn't have time to catalog anything else or figure out how she was going to escape. When Silas reached for her, she simply reacted, letting out an angry and terrified yell and attempting to punch him in the face. But he was so much bigger and faster. He easily subdued Zita by grabbing her around the neck with both hands and pressing her back down into the trunk.

"Relax, bitch," he growled.

Zita didn't have a chance to take a full breath before his fingers tightened. Her hands flew to his, and she frantically dug her nails into his skin, trying to get him to let go.

He didn't. But he wasn't exactly choking her either. Just holding her down, overpowering her—which pissed her off more, knowing she was so easily controlled. That her attack was so easily repelled.

So Zita changed tactics, aiming for his face. She didn't hold back, doing her best to scratch and gouge as much of his flesh as she could.

Silas growled and straightened his elbows, trying to put himself out of her reach.

In a last-ditch effort, Zita aimed for his eye—and jammed her thumb as hard as she could into the almost-black orb staring down at her.

That worked. Thank God.

He let go with a shout and slammed a palm over his face.

But she lost her advantage, her chance to escape. She was too busy trying to suck air into her lungs and climb out of the trunk at the same time. Being a tough-ass bitch was harder than any crime show or instructional video made it seem.

Silas once again grabbed her by the front of her T-shirt. Zita heard it tear as he hauled her the rest of the way out of the trunk and slammed her to the ground. He kicked her twice in the side before pulling her upright with an extremely tight and painful fist around her upper arm.

"Walk, bitch, or I'll fucking kill you right here and now."

With no choice but to walk or be dragged, Zita stumbled alongside Silas. Looking around, she still had no clue where they were, only that they were surrounded by giant hulks of rusting metal. The occasional car or truck aside, most looked like boats and ships of some kind. Not too far away, she saw water.

Silas didn't slow down. He weaved in and around the big structures as if he knew exactly where he was going, which Zita had a feeling didn't bode well for her.

"Why are you doing this?" she croaked, her voice sounding as if she'd just smoked three packs of cigarettes in a row.

"I warned you. Told you to stay away from him. But you didn't. In fact, you flaunted your relationship. Going back to his apartment, staying there all night. Kissing him like a whore in front of your motel room. All you had to do was leave him alone and you wouldn't be here. But you didn't—so you are."

"But *why?*" Zita asked again. If he was going to kill her for loving Sage, she wanted to know the reason.

And just like that, in the middle of this fucked-up situation, it hit Zita like a ton of bricks. Of *course* she loved Sage. She wouldn't be moving away from everything she knew if she didn't.

It was a hell of a time to come to the realization...when she might not ever have a chance to tell the man himself.

"Why else? Money," Silas told her nonchalantly.

"I'll pay you double what you're getting if you let me go."

Silas laughed. And it was a mean sound, not a humorous one. "There's no way you can pay me double what Carmen is."

Carmen.

Zita had already suspected his threat would circle back around to that bitch. She wasn't happy that she didn't get what she wanted...Sage.

"Not to mention, she's gonna make sure I get the best jobs when I move out to Hollywood. She's got connections. I'll be staying in the hottest motels, driving the nicest cars, and buddying up with the most famous actors and directors in the biz. And getting all the pussy I want."

This man. He was delusional. He had no clue how Hollywood worked. How fickle its inhabitants were. If you weren't one of "them," you were a nobody. And while he might get lucky enough to work for a few famous people, he'd never, ever be on the inside the way he obviously hoped.

"Listen to me, Silas. Carmen isn't going to get you *any* of those things. She's using you like she uses everyone. She—"

"Shut up," Silas growled, shaking Zita so hard her head throbbed anew. Nausea hit her suddenly, and she couldn't stop the puke from exploding from deep down in her gut once more.

"Fucking gross!" Silas cried, as she barely missed throwing up on him.

Vomiting made her throat hurt even more. And her head. And her face. Tears once more streamed down her cheeks and snot leaked from her nose. It was as if her body was attempting to expel anything and everything it had taken in recently.

"You're lucky I'm in a good mood," Silas said almost conversationally, as he force-marched her toward an absolutely massive hulk of a ship. It towered over them like a creature from a horror movie. Emerging from the water and ready to devour anyone who came close. And Silas was dragging her straight toward a rickety-looking plank of wood that led from the dock—if the rotted boards held together precariously could be called a dock —into an open metal hatch on the side of the ship. "Carmen wanted me to get rid of you permanently, you know. Said it would serve you right. Stealing the man she wanted."

"I didn't steal him!" Zita couldn't help but exclaim. Her gaze was glued to the ship. What was Silas's plan? She didn't even want to guess at this point.

"Doesn't matter. She wants you gone, so you'll be gone. I'm no killer, but I *am* going to stick you somewhere you can't escape and will never be found."

As if leaving her to die wasn't the same as killing her himself. He was the lowest of the low. A bottom-feeder. A parasite.

"What's getting rid of me going to do? Sage *still* won't want her," Zita pointed out.

"Once word gets out that you're missing, she'll race back to Norfolk. Throw money at the investigation. Hire searchers. Be there for Obi-Wan. Be his rock. He'll turn to her in his grief, and she'll get her chance to fuck him."

"That's all she wants?!" Zita asked, both pissed off and incredulous at the same time.

Her captor shrugged. "Carmen gets what Carmen wants. And if she wants hotshot Night Stalker dick, she'll get it. One way or another."

Zita was living in another dimension. This was unbelievable. People like Silas and Carmen should only exist in stories and nightmares. And yet, here she was, smack dab in the middle of this insane plot.

"Make things easy for yourself and walk across on your own. You don't want me to knock you out again."

No, she didn't. She really didn't. Zita was shaking from head to toe, but she somehow managed to walk across the board and through the hatch in the side of the huge ship without slipping and falling into the water below. She was no expert, but she guessed they were in a large drydock facility. The ship was obviously decommissioned and likely going to be dismantled for scrap or something. But given all the rust, it had obviously been sitting there for who knew how long, waiting for its fate...much as she was.

Silas might not be willing to kill her, but she wasn't going to let her guard down, because he could change his mind any second. The feel of his hands around her throat as he held her down in the trunk flashed into her mind. It would be extremely easy for him to strangle her if he wanted to.

With his free hand, Silas clicked on a flashlight he must've had in one of the pockets of his black cargo pants. The interior of the ship was pitch dark and eerie as hell. Creaks and groans echoed around them as they walked. Zita was soon completely lost in all the long corridors and passageways. But once again, Silas seemed to know exactly where he was going.

"Have you been here before?"

"Yup. Used to be a security guard here. My buddies and I would play hide-and-go-seek inside the empty boats and ships. I was always the winner."

Good God, the man was bragging about winning a kids' game. Zita's head spun.

"There are lots of good places to bring women, to do whatever you want with them. It's not as if anyone can hear them scream."

He chuckled darkly at his own words, and horror once more rose within Zita. Was he going to sexually assault her too?

She'd thought her situation couldn't get worse; she'd been wrong.

"This is the biggest ship here. It's an old aircraft carrier. Has thousands of rooms, hundreds of nooks and crannies. It's the perfect place to stash you. And it's slated to be towed out to sea next week. To be sunk and made into an artificial reef or some bullshit."

Zita closed her eyes as he dragged her down yet another narrow set of metal stairs. Silas was a monster. He might tell himself that he wasn't a killer, but everything he'd done, from stalking, to hitting her, to kidnapping, to choking her, to working with Carmen, and now *this*...was clearly evidence that he was a psychopath.

The plan to leave her in this abandoned ship to drown when it sank at sea was simply icing on the shit cake he was serving her.

After what she guessed was about twenty minutes, Silas stopped in front of a door. One of many that looked just like it in the long hallway. He pushed it open and abruptly shoved Zita inside. She went sprawling on the hard metal floor, but forced herself to immediately get up and face her captor.

Except he wasn't coming into the room after her. He slammed the door with a loud bang.

Zita ran toward it and grabbed the handle. It didn't budge.

She pulled with all her might, then pushed. Nothing.

"Silas! Don't do this! Let me out!"

She heard nothing but the creaking of the ship around her. She couldn't see anything either. It was completely black. He hadn't left her a light. Zita couldn't even see her hand in front of her face.

Her breathing increased. She was on the verge of a panic attack. She hurt all over, and she'd been left here to die. She knew that was Silas's plan. Carmen's too.

Anger hit hard and fast at the thought of the actress. The bitch actually thought she could fly into town and sleep with Sage when he was vulnerable? Not happening. The man she knew had way more honor than Carmen thought. He also wasn't stupid. He'd know in a heartbeat something was wrong. He'd turn over every rock in town to find her.

But will there be enough time?

Zita did her best to ignore that small voice.

With her arms in front of her so she didn't hit her head on something, on top of all the other hurts she had, Zita did her best to explore the room.

It was completely empty as far as she could tell, except for two metal bunks built into the wall. No sink. No toilet. No bedding. Nothing but metal all around her. Whoever was in charge of dismantling the ship and prepping it to be sunk had done an exceptional job of removing anything and everything that could contaminate the ocean.

Moving slowly, as her muscles were screaming in pain and shaking from the adrenaline rush she'd experienced, Zita sat on the bottom bunk. The chilly metal immediately soaked through her pants. She shivered. But not entirely with the cold.

She was scared. *Really* scared.

But she wasn't dead.

If there was anyone who could find her, she knew it was Sage.

Memories of the hug he'd given her just that morning filled her head, making her feel warmer, even if it was all in her mind. Sage wouldn't give up on her. He'd find her.

He had to.

He had one week.

Seven days before she'd disappear forever beneath the waves, and no one would ever know what had happened to her.

Lying down, Zita refused to cry. Instead, she'd wait. And hope.

CHAPTER TWENTY

Obi-Wan was having a good day.

He enjoyed being back at work. Liked catching up with his friends. And was even happy to sit in meetings that a week ago would probably have annoyed him to no end.

While he'd had a good time on set, had appreciated being asked to advise, it was good to be back in a familiar environment. He'd always be grateful for the opportunity, especially because it had led him to Zita, but he was ready to get into his chopper.

He was kind of surprised he hadn't heard from her this morning. She'd said she was going to text to see how PT had gone. While Casper and the rest of his team had given him shit, claiming a week off had made him soft, Obi-Wan held his own. And working out with his friends felt good. Like putting on a favorite old, worn shirt.

He figured Zita was probably busy. Maybe her report time had been moved up. He'd sent her a text around nine-thirty that morning, letting her know he missed her and asking how her morning was going, but she hadn't replied. In fact, the message hadn't even been read, according to the app. Obi-Wan was a little surprised about that...but again, he assumed she was probably engrossed in her meetings, and it wouldn't be cool for her to be on her phone.

But when lunch came and went, and he still hadn't heard from her, and a second text had gone unread, Obi-Wan was starting to worry. True, he hadn't known Zita long, but she didn't seem like the type to not answer texts, especially not after their amazing last few nights together. Maybe he was reading too much into it, or being too sensitive because she wasn't immediately reading or answering his attempts to connect electronically...but he didn't think so.

"What's up?" Buck asked, able to read his copilot like a book.

"Zita's not answering my texts," he said, bracing himself for his friend to tease him about being pussy-whipped or tell him to chill out.

Buck did neither of those things. "And that's out of the ordinary?"

"Yes."

"Then go check on her."

"I can't just leave," he protested. "I've already been gone a week. We have the meeting with Colonel Burgess in half an hour."

"How serious are you about Zita?" Buck asked, sounding as solemn as he did when they were on a mission and shit was about to hit the fan.

"As serious as it gets."

"Then go. In fact, I'll go with you."

Something within Obi-Wan relaxed a fraction. Not that he thought he'd be walking into any kind of dangerous situation, but his Spidey senses were screaming, and it would be a relief to have his friend at his six.

"I'll go tell Casper that we need an hour. We'll head to the motel, you'll talk to Zita, find out what's up...maybe her phone is dead, or she forgot it in her room before she went to her meeting. Then we'll come back and finish up the day. All right?"

Obi-Wan nodded. "Yes. Great. Thank you."

"You never have to thank me for being there for you. I'll never forget how you and the rest of the guys were my rocks when Mandy was in the hospital after she was attacked. I'll meet you at your Jeep."

It was a little cowardly to let Buck talk to Casper and inform him that they were leaving, but Obi-Wan's mind was in overdrive. He couldn't stop wondering why Zita wasn't answering her phone. He hoped he was simply overreacting. That she'd actually read him the riot act when he showed up to find out why she wasn't texting back.

Putting it like that, what he was about to do seemed like an extremely stupid idea. Zita wouldn't appreciate having to check in with him every few hours in order to keep him from flipping out. She might even decide he was acting controlling or jealous.

But this wasn't about that. Yes, he was concerned about her and why she wasn't communicating, but not because he worried about who she was with or what she was doing. It just seemed out of character for her.

And things between them were good. Really damn good. He felt a rush of adrenaline when he spoke to her—hell, when he *thought* about her. He was ninety percent sure she felt the same way. She could be pulling the wool over his eyes, totally scamming him in some way, but he didn't think so. Her reactions to him couldn't be faked. Her orgasms were real, the way her heart sped up when she was with him, her shy smiles, and even the love he saw in her eyes...they were all real.

And he *did* see the affection in her gaze. For some reason, she wasn't ready to say the words, and that was all right. Things had moved fast between them, but Obi-Wan was patient. He could wait to hear her express her feelings. It was enough that she was just as eager to be together as he was.

Which was a large reason why he was so worried right now. He hoped he'd feel stupid as hell when he got to her motel and found her engrossed in the meeting with the producer and assistants. He'd apologize and make his paranoid behavior up to her later...after asking her to please never ignore a text from him for hours again if she could avoid it, so he wouldn't have to worry about her.

Buck jogged across the parking lot toward him, and Obi-Wan took a deep breath. "Everything okay?" he asked, as his friend got close.

"Yup. Casper said he'd work things out with the colonel. And told us to call if we needed him and the others."

Grateful his team would have his back if he needed them, and praying that he wouldn't, Obi-Wan got into his Jeep and took off out of the lot as soon as Buck was belted into the seat next to him. The trip to the motel seemed to take twice as long as it should.

Obi-Wan parked in front of Zita's room and leaped out. He wasn't sure if she'd be in her room or in the meeting space at the motel, but figured he'd start here. Maybe she'd gotten sick or something after he'd left and was sleeping. He hated to think of her being alone and feeling miserable, but given other options, he hoped that was all this was.

No one answered his knock on the door.

After knocking loudly several more times, and still getting no response, Obi-Wan turned to head to the lobby. He had no idea if it was common for the AAR—he didn't know what these kinds of meetings were called in the film industry, but to him, it seemed like the after-action reviews he and his team had after a mission—to take place at a low-budget motel, but at the moment, it didn't matter if the group was meeting here, in a back alley, or in the most expensive hotel in the city. All that mattered was putting eyes on Zita and making sure she was all right.

The hair on the back of his neck was standing straight up, and he had a gut feeling something was very wrong. He'd only had this feeling a few times in his life, and every other time it had been while on a mission. Ops that had gone as wrong as they could go.

And this wasn't a mission. This was Zita. The woman he loved.

He went straight to the front desk and impatiently waited for the young woman working to get done with her phone call.

"How can I help you?"

"Where's the meeting with the film people?" he asked, not even trying to be polite.

"Um, are you with the group?"

"Yes, I'm the military advisor, and I'm late," he said. It was a half-truth, but he didn't care.

Since he was wearing his coveralls with the patch that indicated his unit, the employee had no problem believing him. "It's through there, to the right, at the end of the hall. Past the swimming pool and the workout room."

She'd only gotten half the sentence out before Obi-Wan was on the move. He stalked down the hall, Buck at his heels, and didn't hesitate to open the door to the meeting room without knocking.

There were about ten people inside, and quickly glancing around, Obi-Wan felt his stomach knot when he realized Zita wasn't one of them.

"Engle! Good to see you. We were just talking about you and what a great job you did. We think this film's probably the most authentic one we've ever done, thanks to you. We'd love to get your perspective on a few things."

Obi-Wan didn't stop to wonder why the producer didn't even seem surprised to see him. Or irritated that he'd barged into a meeting he wasn't invited to. "Have you seen Zita today?" he asked impatiently.

"Miss Darlington? No. Do you know where she is? She was supposed to be here this morning. We skipped over the time slot for her report, hoping she'd appear sooner or later to give it."

"Fuck," Obi-Wan said, turning without giving the men and women in the room another word. Zita wasn't there. Hadn't shown up at all. Now an urgency was driving him. Unlike anything he'd ever felt before. Yes, he'd felt anxious while on a mission. Felt a need to drop off or pick up the special forces teams he transported on a regular basis, but this was different. Zita wasn't a soldier. She was a civilian...who he now couldn't help but think might be in serious danger.

He stalked back to the lobby and to the woman behind the counter.

"I need a key to room one-fourteen."

"I'm sorry, are you on the occupancy list?" the woman asked.

Obi-Wan didn't have time for this. He opened his mouth to tell the woman to give him the fucking key, when Buck put a hand on his arm and pushed him to the side.

"Our friend is in that room, and she missed the important meeting taking place down the hall this morning. We're afraid she's sick or something and want to check on her. We already knocked, but she's not answering. We just want to look inside to see if she's there, sleeping, sick, or something. Maybe you could ask someone from housekeeping to let us in, instead of giving us a key? We just want to check on her. The housekeeper could stay with us the entire time, to make sure we aren't there to take anything or do anything we shouldn't."

He gave the woman an innocent-looking smile.

"Well...I guess so. It might be a few minutes before someone's free to come assist you."

"That's okay. We'll just meet them outside the room, thank you," Buck said, as he took Obi-Wan's arm in a firm grip and pulled him toward the exit.

As soon as they were outside, Obi-Wan said, "Something's

wrong. She should've been in that meeting. I left her here this morning. She was inside her room, the door shut. She could've fallen and hit her head or something. She might need an ambulance."

"Breathe, Obi-Wan, we'll get in there and see what's going on. If we need to call for help, we will."

For good measure, Obi-Wan knocked on the motel door again when they got there, and just like before, no one answered. No sound at all came from inside. As they waited for someone to unlock the door, he paced. And tried to understand what was going on.

"I don't want to bring this up...but what if she's not inside? What's the plan?" Buck asked.

Obi-Wan didn't even want to contemplate that. He didn't want Zita hurt or sick, but if she wasn't inside that room, the possibilities were endless as to where she might be.

"Could she have gotten cold feet and gone back to California early?" Buck asked gently.

"No." Obi-Wan's answer was swift and curt.

"Obi-Wan," Buck started, his tone sympathetic.

"I said *no*, Buck. She didn't leave without saying a word to me. We didn't ask the lady if she'd checked out, but I know to the bottom of my heart she didn't up and leave. She didn't get cold feet. We had plans for tonight."

"All right, if she didn't leave, what other options are there? You know her way better than any of us. Does she have any vengeful exes? Anyone she met here in Virginia who might have a reason to hurt her? I haven't heard about any serial killers or rapists on the loose in this area—no, don't look at me like that. I'm just trying to make the unexplainable, explainable."

Obi-Wan took a deep breath in through his nose as he tried to calm his irritational anger toward his friend. The thought of Zita being targeted by a fucking serial killer or rapist made him want to go on a rampage. He stopped pacing and lowered his head. His hands fisted as he forced himself to calm. To think. He normally had no problem controlling his emotions. He had to in order to be a good pilot.

He had no idea if Zita had a violent ex-boyfriend in her past, as they hadn't really discussed previous relationships. Not that he wanted to know who she'd been with before him. He was a typical guy in that regard, he supposed. He didn't mind that she had a dating history, but he didn't want to know about it.

Then out of the blue, it hit him. "Silas Graves," he bit out, lifting his head and meeting Buck's gaze.

"Who?"

"Silas Graves. He was Carmen St. James's bodyguard, then when she left, he was transferred to Logan Striker while we were on the other side of the state filming. She told me a couple days before we left Fallport that he approached her on set and told her to stay away from me 'or else.'"

"Or else? What the fuck does that mean?"

Obi-Wan didn't have a chance to answer, as a woman pushing a housekeeping cart was headed their way.

"About fucking time," he muttered, knowing he was being an ass but not caring.

Buck took the lead, thanking the woman for meeting them and once more reassuring her that all they wanted to do was look inside the room to see if their friend was there.

The housekeeper looked nervous, but she nodded and held a plastic key card up to the electronic plate at the door. She stepped back to allow them entry, but didn't go far.

Obi-Wan stepped into the room—and all his hopes that Zita was sick or sleeping were dashed immediately. The beds were still perfectly made. Nothing looked out of place. Her medical bag was by the door in the exact same place he'd dropped it that morning. A suitcase was open on the bed, her small toiletries bag sitting next to it. He could picture in his head her putting it there as she searched for something to wear before showering.

Just to be positive she wasn't in the room, even though he knew in his gut she wasn't, Obi-Wan looked in the bathroom. The towels were hanging neatly on the racks and nothing was disturbed.

Whatever had happened, it occurred right after he'd left that morning. Which pissed Obi-Wan off all the more. She certainly hadn't left to go back to California; all her things being in the room disproved that option. She hadn't showered, changed clothes, lain down for a nap before getting ready for her meeting. It was as if she'd vanished into thin air minutes after he'd dropped her off.

Except she hadn't.

Turning to the housekeeper, he asked, "Are there surveillance cameras on the property?"

She looked taken aback. "Yes. In the lobby."

"Nowhere else?" Obi-Wan barked, not able to keep his tone even.

"Not that I know of."

Fuck.

The three of them stood still for a heartbeat, the housekeeper watching Buck and Obi-Wan warily, Buck watching Obi-Wan, and Obi-Wan's gaze searching the room for answers. Answers that weren't there.

Except...

"Stop! Don't move! Don't touch anything!" he exclaimed.

Buck and the housekeeper froze.

"What? What do you see?" Buck asked.

"Blood," Obi-Wan said grimly, as he walked closer to the door and leaned over to inspect what had caught his attention. A dark spot on the carpet. It was small, no bigger than the unit patch on his chest. A few inches wide and long.

He wouldn't even have noticed it if the carpet hadn't been just a shade lighter than the mark on the floor. It could be anything. A drink someone spilled, or something more disgusting, but Obi-Wan got on his knees anyway. He leaned in and inhaled, then sat back on his heels and looked up at his friend.

"It's definitely blood."

"We don't know that," Buck said quietly.

"It is. You and I both know what fucking blood smells like. We've seen enough of it in the past. It's *Zita's* blood. Someone hurt her." The last three words were almost whispered, as if saying them out loud could make them any more true than they already were.

The housekeeper looked completely freaked out now, probably in part by Obi-Wan's statement about seeing a lot of blood in the past. But he didn't care. All his attention was on Buck.

"What do we do?" he asked, in that same low voice he'd used earlier. He felt adrift. Panicked. And Obi-Wan *never* panicked. Prided himself on his ability to stay calm in the most chaotic environments.

"Blood?" the housekeeper asked. "We have something that can get that up without too much trouble."

"No!" Buck and Obi-Wan exclaimed at the same time.

Obi-Wan got to his feet. "Do not let *anyone* into this room. It doesn't get cleaned, no one touches a damn thing. We're calling the cops. Everything inside is evidence."

"Evidence of what?" the housekeeper asked with wide eyes.

"Kidnapping. Assault. Someone took my woman, and I'm going to get her back," Obi-Wan growled.

His mind whirled with the things he needed to do, no longer suffering with indecision. It was as if his brain kicked into overdrive. He needed to contact the police, Casper, talk to the men and women in the meeting where Zita was supposed to be, check with the motel about surveillance cameras.

And call Tex.

Fuck, he should've done that days ago, as soon as Silas had threatened Zita. But he hadn't. He assumed the man wasn't really a threat.

A decision he'd regret to the end of his days. Because in his gut, Obi-Wan knew the bodyguard was responsible for whatever had happened to Zita. There simply wasn't anyone else. People liked Zita. She was friendly and open and everyone she helped had been happy with her skills.

Silas had taken her. Why and where, he had no idea, but he'd find out. Tex could find the man. Check his phone records to see what towers his cell pinged off of that morning. Check traffic cameras, his texts. All of it.

Buck was already on his phone when Obi-Wan stepped out of Zita's room. Taking one last look at her belongings, he ached, wondering what she'd gone through. He didn't think Silas was a killer, but he could be wrong. If the man was willing to hurt Zita —and he obviously had, if the blood on the floor was any indication—there was no telling what else he'd do.

He would pay, Obi-Wan vowed. He'd tell him where the fuck Zita was...*or else*. The man liked to threaten women? Fine. He'd see what "or else" really meant when Obi-Wan got his hands on him.

CHAPTER TWENTY-ONE

What time was it? Shit, what *day* was it?

Being in the dark was disorientating as hell.

Didn't fascist regimes use darkness as a torture technique?

Zita lay on the metal bunk, shivering, afraid to move. She'd gotten up earlier because she had to pee—which was horrible; she'd had to pee on the floor in the corner of the room, since there was no toilet, or bucket, or anything else—and she'd hit her head on the bunk trying to find her way back to it.

She didn't even want to think about when she had to do *more* than pee. Being here was demoralizing, which she supposed was part of the point.

Blinking, hoping against hope she'd be able to see something, anything, Zita sighed when the room remained just as dark as before.

The weird thing about being stuck here was, it wasn't silent. Not completely. The ship creaked and groaned, and she swore she could hear voices now and then. Which was impossible. Unless Silas and his buddies who worked at this scrapyard were kidnapping other women and stashing them deep in the bowels of this aircraft carrier. Which wasn't a stretch, as Silas had pretty much admitted he'd brought women here before.

"Is someone there?" she whispered, feeling comforted by the sound of a voice, even if it was her own. "I've seen the paranormal shows, the ones where they talk to spirits. I don't have that fancy box that lets you talk back to me, but I'm not the bad guy here. I'm sorry you died, I hope it wasn't violent. You should know that this ship is gonna be towed out to sea and sunk. Now's your chance to leave if you can. Find a nice house or graveyard or something to haunt instead."

She laughed, and it echoed around her, making her sound a bit unhinged. And she kind of felt as if she was. Talking to ghosts like they were real. But she had to do *something*. Couldn't just lie there in misery until she drowned. Actually, it was likely she'd die of thirst before this ship was even moved.

Her head hurt. Her throat hurt. Her face hurt where Silas had hit her and knocked her unconscious. Hell, even her arm hurt, where he'd gripped her so hard while dragging her around. But she was alive. The asshole hadn't killed her, and she hoped that would be his downfall. She was alive to tell the cops what he'd done. To testify against him.

To tell the world that Carmen St. James had ordered her to be kidnapped and murdered, just so she could get some dick.

Put like that, it was so utterly ridiculous. The woman was delusional if she thought she could rush to Sage's side and he'd be so grateful for her help, he'd sleep with her, even while distraught over his missing girlfriend.

First of all, who *did* that? What parent, partner, sibling, friend was even *thinking* about sex when a loved one was missing? No one.

Except maybe in Hollywood.

Second, she knew without a shred of doubt that Sage would never cheat on her with Carmen, even if Zita *wasn't* missing. He had too much integrity. And he loved her. He'd said so. And Zita held his words close to her heart.

He wouldn't give up on her. Wouldn't fall for Carmen's shenanigans. Her deceit. He'd see right through her.

Hell, Zita hoped Carmen *did* come to Norfolk. *Did* rush right to Sage's side. She had no doubt he'd make the connection between her disappearance and Silas's threat. And if Carmen suddenly appeared, it would become even more obvious that Silas was behind Zita's disappearance.

Carmen had never been the sharpest knife in the drawer, and she was even more of an idiot if she thought she could get Sage into bed by having his woman kidnapped.

But...how long would it take for someone to find her? It wasn't as if she was stashed in a public place. No, she was inside a freaking decommissioned aircraft carrier, destined to be sunk in the very near future.

Sighing, Zita realized it would be almost impossible for anyone to find her accidentally. Silas would have to admit what he'd done. And she had a feeling he'd hold out as long as possible...at least until this ship was long gone and resting on the bottom of the ocean.

She needed to make her peace with dying, as much as that sucked.

"Any spirits around who'd be willing to be my mentor when I join you? Not any killers though, please. Or rapists. Or misogynistic assholes either."

It was official, she'd lost it.

A tear leaked from the corner of her eye, and Zita dashed it away impatiently. She couldn't afford to lose the moisture in her body by crying. And getting all blubbery wouldn't help her get out of here either.

Remembering a documentary she'd seen once about how cruise ships were built, made her think about the room she was in. Everything was metal. The rooms were probably all little metal boxes. If she could find something to bang on the walls with, maybe, just maybe, someone would hear her. A submarine passing by or someone's dog might find the noise irritating and alert to the area.

Both scenarios were ridiculous and unlikely, but Zita didn't have anything to lose by getting off her ass and doing something to keep busy.

Taking a deep breath, she slowly sat up, putting a hand out to catch herself from falling over from the dizzy spell the small movement caused. Shit. This wasn't good. But she was still alive, and she'd do whatever she could to stay that way.

"I'm here, Sage," she said out loud. "Come get me. I'm waiting."

It felt better talking to Sage than the spirits who may or may not be lurking in the hunk of metal that was her prison.

Slowly standing up, Zita moved to the end of the bunk and began to feel around with her hands. There had to be something she could use to try to call attention to the fact that she was here. Even if no one heard her, it would make her feel better.

* * *

Time was moving too fast. Obi-Wan was well aware of the statistics that said if a missing person wasn't found within forty-eight hours, it was likely they'd be dead when—and if—they were found.

Half of that time had already passed, and no one was any closer to finding Zita than they were twenty-four hours ago. He was frustrated, irritated, and terrified out of his skull.

Yesterday, while Buck called Casper, Obi-Wan had called Tex. Something he should've done way earlier. He wished like hell he could turn back the clock and do things differently. But he couldn't. And here they were.

Tex assured him that he was "on it," but Obi-Wan hadn't

heard from him since yesterday afternoon. Which both pissed him off and stressed him out beyond measure.

If Tex couldn't find Zita, what were the odds that *he* could? He needed the man's investigative prowess to at least give him a place to start looking. He'd given him Silas's name and told him what little he knew about the guy, but would that be enough for the former SEAL to find out where he'd taken Zita?

The police were also investigating—and had picked up Silas—but everyone knew Tex could move much faster than law enforcement ever could. And time was of the essence. Crime scene techs had come out and taken swabs of the blood on the floor, and confirmed that it was human. But of course, the detectives had cautioned Obi-Wan, saying that didn't mean it was Zita's.

But he knew it was.

Knew it in his gut.

There was absolutely no reason for Zita to be gone. He'd bet his Night Stalker career on the fact that Silas had come to her room, hurting her the second she'd opened the door.

Casper had decided—with the owner's permission—to make Anchor Point home base for the search for Zita. He could've chosen the Army base, but civilians weren't allowed and they needed all the help they could get. Once word got out that Zita was missing, had possibly been kidnapped, locals turned out en masse to aid in the search efforts.

It was almost enough to have Obi-Wan smiling. Almost.

But being around so many people, all asking questions he had no answers for, was making him extremely jumpy and irritated. He was grateful for any help he could get, but he had a feeling it was all for naught. Whatever Silas had done with Zita, he'd hidden her well. But was she alive or dead...that was the question.

Obi-Wan wanted to know *why*, but right now, finding her was the priority. It didn't matter what his reason was for targeting the unassuming medic who had a smile for everyone, who did what she could to assist the injured on her film jobs—and beyond. The woman carried medical shit in her *purse*, for goodness sake. She didn't have a mean bone in her body.

And Silas had done something to her. Hurt her. Hidden her away.

Obi-Wan and his friends had huddled in one corner of Anchor Point. All the lights were on in the bar, and it made the familiar space seem decidedly *unfamiliar*. It was just one more thing to make him uncomfortable.

Casper and Edge were talking to the police officers and detectives who were helping them organize the search teams. Chaos and Pyro were handing out fliers with Zita's picture to the volunteers waiting to be told where to look.

And Buck was hovering near Obi-Wan, which he appreciated more than he could say. Buck had his back. In the air and on the ground. They were copilots, partners, and best friends. He knew without Obi-Wan having to say a word how on edge he was. He was there, a silent pillar of support, just as Obi-Wan had been for him when Mandy was in the hospital. He'd spent many hours in a chair by Mandy's side, whenever Buck was forced by their other friends to go home to shower and eat.

Buck didn't say stupid things like, "We're going to find her," or "She's all right," because he knew neither of those things were a given.

Obi-Wan was a realist. Silas Graves was a big man. He could've killed Zita and disposed of her body in a number of ways that would make finding her impossible. He didn't want to believe that was what happened, that the beautiful woman he loved was no longer alive, but he had to face the possibility. And that sucked.

The door to Anchor Point opened, and out of reflex, Obi-Wan looked over to see who'd entered.

To his shock, it was Carmen St. James.

There were two large men at her back, whom he assumed were bodyguards. She looked around, saw Obi-Wan, and headed straight for him.

The very last person he wanted to see or talk to was this woman—and he couldn't shake the sudden epiphany that she was part of this.

Silas had been her bodyguard, they'd spent every moment together when she was on set, and rumor had it that she was sleeping with the man assigned to keep her safe. The same man Obi-Wan suspected had taken Zita.

"What is *she* doing here?" Buck growled under his breath.

Obi-Wan didn't have a chance to respond before Carmen reached them and threw her arms around him.

"I'm so sorry! I got on the first plane out of LA as soon as I heard."

Obi-Wan reacted instinctively. He shoved her away from him and took a giant step backward. "*Don't*," he spat.

Carmen looked shocked. But she recovered quickly. "I know this is stressful. What can I do to help?"

"Tell me where Zita is," Obi-Wan barked.

"I wish I could," Carmen replied, her pout sympathetic. "What I *can* do is donate money to the search effort. What do you need? Horses? Dogs? More man-power? SUVs? Whatever it is, I'll make it happen."

Her words seemed sincere, but there was something...calculating about her gaze that had Obi-Wan's eyes narrowing.

"That would be great," Buck said, taking Carmen's arm and attempting to pull her away from Obi-Wan.

One of her bodyguards stepped between them. "Don't touch her," he said in a low tone.

"It's okay, Joe," Carmen said, patting the man's chest affectionately.

Absently, Obi-Wan wondered if she was sleeping with these new men assigned to her as well. Probably.

"Obadiah is an old friend. It's fine."

The bodyguard nodded and stepped back, but kept his gaze locked on Buck. Who was doing his own glaring in return. Obi-Wan had a feeling it was taking all of his friend's control not to take the man out. And he had no doubt Buck could do it too. They'd all been trained in hand-to-hand combat and could hold their own against the biggest, strongest Navy SEAL and Delta Force operatives. This guy was no match for their skills.

"How about we go somewhere quiet to talk about what's needed. Poor Zita is out there somewhere. I just know it. She's waiting to be found, and together, I know we can do that. You and me."

The worthless platitudes were so fucking irritating. As was her assumption that he'd step one foot outside of Anchor Point. Wasn't he just thinking how grateful he was to Buck for not saying they'd find Zita alive and well? For not making promises no one could keep?

She stepped closer and attempted to put her arms around him again.

Once more, Obi-Wan took a step back, his skin crawling even *thinking* about this woman touching him. Especially knowing that she'd been with Silas. The man Obi-Wan was certain had set this nightmare in motion.

Undeterred, she leaned forward and said quietly, "I've missed you."

What the fuck?

Obi-Wan was done.

He abruptly turned his back on Carmen and walked toward the bar.

He heard a commotion behind him, Carmen calling his name, one of her bodyguards telling Buck to "fucking let go of Miss St. James," but Obi-Wan didn't give a damn.

A couple of police officers passed him on the way to deal with whatever was happening with Carmen. When he reached the bar, he put his elbows on the slick surface and lowered his head into his hands.

He wanted to be alone. No, that wasn't true. He wanted to be with Zita. Wanted to be sitting in his oversized chair, watching *Star Wars*, discussing the movies, the plots, and how the new movies and shows connected to the classic ones. Instead, he was dealing with a woman utterly incapable of understanding the word *no*, who may or may not be involved in whatever had happened to Zita—and was hitting on him while she was missing!

Straightening, he looked around and gestured to the closest police officer.

He briefly explained his suspicions, then said, "She was involved with Silas Graves. Sleeping with him while she was in town filming. Someone needs to question her about why the fuck she just decided to show up out of the blue. Why did she come back? I didn't ask her to. How did she even hear about Zita's disappearance? Some fucked-up shit is going on, and she's up to her eyeballs in it. I *know* she is."

"I'll talk to the detectives," the officer assured him.

There wasn't much else Obi-Wan could do. He needed to get out of there. Get some air. He wasn't brave enough to join one of the search parties, because if he found Zita's body—

He cut the thought off there. No. She wasn't dead. She couldn't be.

He sighed, because now *he* was doing it...giving *himself* platitudes.

What he really wanted was half an hour with Silas Graves. He and his teammates could get the details out of him about what he'd done and where he'd taken Zita, of *that* he was sure.

But the cops weren't going to let him within ten feet of the man. They were currently holding him on some bullshit charge... Obi-Wan didn't know what it was, nor did he care. All he cared about at the moment was fucking finding Zita.

It was time to call Tex back. He'd given him plenty of time to find *something*. Obi-Wan was done waiting.

As if thinking about the man had conjured him out of thin air, Obi-Wan's phone rang. One look at the screen confirming it was Tex.

Wanting some privacy to talk to him, he walked down the hall that led to the bathrooms and kept going, right out into the bright sunshine. He had the fleeting thought that it was weird how beautiful it was outside, when it felt dark and dangerous inside his head. It should be raining, gloomy, a fucking piss-poor day. Instead, the birds were chirping and singing...and it felt like an afront.

Not to mention, remembering the last time he was out here, with Zita, felt like a dagger to his heart. He could almost feel her arms around him, as they'd been when they stood in this very spot and talked. When she'd calmed him down after Carmen had shown up at the bar unexpectantly the *first* time.

"Did you find her?" Obi-Wan asked, the second he opened the connection on his phone.

"No, but I'm finding out some interesting info. Did you know that Silas and Carmen still communicate?"

Obi-Wan didn't, but he wasn't surprised.

Tex didn't give him time to respond, just kept talking.

"They've been texting nonstop since she left. I don't have the transcripts of what they've talked about yet, but I'm working on it. They've also spoken on the phone at least once a day. Except in the last twenty-four hours, when all communication seems to have stopped. As if the idiots think that not speaking to each other for a day will somehow indicate they're both innocent. Also, Silas's phone was turned off for about eight hours yesterday. Starting at four in the morning until almost noon."

"Zita was taken around five-fifteen or so."

"Yeah. So I can't track him using cell towers, but Carmen St. James isn't the only person Silas has been talking to recently.

He's got quite an extensive list of buddies who have questionable morals. I tracked the numbers he's texted in just the last two weeks, and they include three men who were arrested for armed robbery, one for conspiracy to commit murder, two for soliciting underage girls, and another who's currently in jail. Was picked up just last night for fraud."

Obi-Wan grunted. Again, he wasn't surprised.

"Silas was hired by the studio because he doesn't have a record. So when they did a background check, he came back clean. He's had quite a plethora of past jobs as well, mostly security guard gigs. Department stores, a scrapyard, and his latest gig, before being hired as Carmen's bodyguard, was a bouncer for a nightclub downtown."

Obi-Wan was having a hard time keeping his cool. Why was Tex telling him all this shit? The only thing he was interested in was any information on Zita.

"My point being, this guy is shady as shit. He could've used any one of his criminal friends to help him. I'm sending you a picture. Check your texts."

Obi-Wan was two seconds away from hanging up. He needed answers, and Tex wasn't giving him any. Still...he took his phone from his ear and clicked on his text messages.

The picture that filled his screen made him gasp in shock.

It was Silas Graves. A booking photo. Dated yesterday. And the man had obviously been in one hell of a scuffle. He had scratch marks all over his face. As if someone had raked their fingernails down his cheeks. Not only that, but his eye was swollen and bloodshot. He looked like shit.

Zita had done that. He knew it down to his bones. Zita had fought like the devil. He was prouder of her than he could put into words, but the picture didn't lessen his worry one iota. His woman was tiny compared to Silas. If she'd done this kind of damage to *him*...what had he done to her in return?

He heard Tex saying his name through the speaker, and Obi-Wan slowly brought the phone back to his ear. "I'm here."

"That's his booking photo. The cops aren't letting him go anytime soon, not with the evidence clear as day on his face that he's been in one hell of a fight. I have no doubt whatsoever that he took Zita. I'm working as fast as I can to try to get transcripts of his texts and to track down the assholes he spoke to right before his phone was turned off. Oh, and one more thing... Carmen St. James is on her way to Norfolk. She landed not too long ago."

"She's here. Or was. Don't know if she is anymore."

"What'd she want?"

"Me," Obi-Wan said with no conceit. "Said she left as soon as she heard Zita was missing. Offered to help in any way she could. Basically saying she'd throw money at the problem."

"Hmmm. How'd she know she was missing?"

"That was my question too. Rumors fly fast and hard on movie sets, but shooting in Virginia is done, and she's been back in LA for two weeks. And it's not as if the producer who's still in town would call to let her know the set medic has gone missing."

"Unless Silas called to let her know the job was done."

Obi-Wan clenched his teeth. He didn't like the finality of those words.

"Right, sorry," Tex added at Obi-Wan's silence. "And also sorry my warning about her arrival is too little, too late. But I'm on her too, by the way. If she had anything to do with this, she's going down. Don't care how rich or famous she is."

"I'll be in touch again within a couple of hours. In the meantime, have faith, Obi-Wan. Anyone who could fuck up a bodyguard like that is tough as shit. She knew what she was doing. Knew he wouldn't be able to hide his face or explain away those fingernail marks. If the cops can't get him to break, I'll find out his secrets another way...by harassing his so-called friends. Guarantee they won't be so loyal by the time I get done with them. I'll call soon."

That second-to-last sentence was the only thing keeping Obi-Wan from completely losing his shit. Tex was right. Silas might keep his mouth shut, and he doubted Carmen would admit to knowing anything about Zita's disappearance. But the assholes Silas ran with? They'd probably throw their mothers under the bus if it meant getting themselves out of a tight spot.

"Hold on, Zita. We're coming for you. Just keep breathing," he whispered, hoping like hell she was still alive, waiting for him to find her.

CHAPTER TWENTY-TWO

One breath in, hold it for five seconds, then let it out for another five seconds.

Zita had gone over every inch of her prison cell. There weren't any loose pieces of metal, not a single loose screw, *nothing*. She was literally in a metal box with two hard slabs sticking out of the wall. She had nothing to eat, to drink...but far more importantly, nothing to signal that she was here.

She was trying to do everything in her power to keep the panic from taking over.

Silas had led her a few levels down into the huge ship, and then down several corridors. Even if someone knew to look for her in this hunk of metal, it would probably take a week for them to check every room. And she didn't have a week. Not without anything to drink. She could live without food for a while, but not fluids.

All she could do was lie on one of the bunks and breathe. She dozed off and on, but when she was awake, she did her best to ignore her growling belly by counting her breaths. She wasn't ready to give up, but she honestly had no idea how anyone...how *Sage*...would find her.

Also, the longer she was in the dark, the more sounds she heard. And the more she was convinced there were spirits inside this ship. She'd been awakened earlier by the sound of a door slamming shut. Thinking someone was here, that they were searching for her, she'd leapt up and screamed as loudly as she could. She'd pounded on the door, not that her fists made much noise against the thick metal door, but she couldn't simply lie there and do *nothing*.

Except after a while, she realized no one was there. It was just as silent as it had been from the moment she was locked in.

Two minutes after she sat down on the metal bed, slumped in despair, she heard what sounded like laughter. It was high-pitched and eerie, only lasting for a split second.

"That wasn't funny!" she called out, pissed off at the spirits for messing with her head.

Of course, she got no response.

Hours after that—at least, she assumed it was hours—Zita could've sworn she felt a cold breeze against her face. But that was impossible, considering she was way down in the bowels of the ship.

In any other circumstance, Zita might've freaked out at the thought of being surrounded by ghosts. But other than teasing her by slamming that metal door, they didn't feel mean-spirited.

She still thought it was more likely she was losing her mind. That happened when people were put into solitary confinement, or so she'd read. But thinking there were spirits around made her feel not quite so alone.

"Sage is gonna come," she said out loud, needing to hear something other than the ominous creaking of the ship and her own heartbeat. "Wait until you see him. He's gorgeous. Muscular, sexy. He makes me feel beautiful too, which hasn't really happened to me before. He's funny, and smart, and the best pilot in the world. And he loves me."

The last words were whispered.

"I'm still having a hard time believing it. I mean, I'm just me. I'm no one special. And yet, when I'm with him, I *feel* special. Like I'm the most important person in his world. It's a heady feeling. He works really hard, and he's a hero too. He's probably been on lots of ships just like this one. He flies helicopters for a living. And he's damn good at it. He's looking for me. Probably worrying like crazy about where I am. But he'll figure it out. Him and his friends. They'll find Silas, see what I did to his face and know he was the one who kidnapped me. My DNA is in his trunk, and they'll look at his past work history and come check this stupid shipyard. He claimed he was the best at hide-and-go seek—but fuck him! They'll find me."

Zita paused.

"I just wish they'd hurry up."

Swallowing hard, she took another deep breath in, held it for five seconds, then let it out slowly while counting once more to five.

Patience. She just had to have patience.

But there was a giant clock in her head that was counting the passage of time...and hers was ticking. As a medic, she knew exactly what the lack of water would do to her. Exactly how being dehydrated would slowly kill her. It didn't matter how strong she was. How smart, how much she loved Sage. Time wasn't on her side. She knew it, and he probably did too.

Deep breath.

Hold it.

Let it out.

All she could do was concentrate on breathing. One breath at a time.

* * *

Buck was currently trying to get Obi-Wan to eat something, but he was in no mood. Would probably puke if he tried to eat.

Every time he looked up, he saw the clock that sat over the bar at Anchor Point. It was one of those old-fashioned ones. With a huge face and a second hand that ticked along slowly but steadily. It seemed to be mocking Obi-Wan, and he swore he could hear the actual ticking of that damn second hand over the voices and other noise in the room.

He was well aware of how much time was passing. If Zita was hurt, every one of those seconds could mean life or death. It was almost physically painful to stand there and wait for something to happen.

For one of the searchers to find Zita's body.

For the cops to call and say that Silas had finally broken and told them what he'd done.

For Carmen St. James to get a fucking conscience and spill the beans on the plot.

But none of those things had happened yet, and Obi-Wan was about to lose his mind.

Running a hand through his hair, he decided he was done. He needed out of there. Had no idea where he'd go, but he couldn't stay in this fucking room one second longer.

Then two things happened at once.

The front door opened and Obi-Wan's phone rang.

A woman entered the bar with a large black Labrador Retriever on a lead. The dog had a black and orange harness that said *SEARCH DOG* in bold black letters along the side. The woman was wearing a pair of navy cargo pants with the pockets bulging, and a navy polo shirt with a small white logo on the upper left chest. Her brown hair was short, and if he had to guess, he'd say she was about five-six. She wasn't smiling, was instead looking around the room as if searching for someone.

She locked eyes with Obi-Wan, and began walking his way.

Seeing the search dog made him feel even sicker than he was before. He couldn't help but think about cadaver dogs. He had no proof that's what the black Lab was, but he didn't want to even face the possibility.

Turning his back on the woman walking toward him, Obi-Wan answered his phone.

"Found the connection," Tex said without preamble. "Shortly before Graves was picked up, he called one of the security guards he used to work with at the ship scrapyard. As far as I can tell, he hadn't talked to the man in months. Why call him out of the blue, in that case, right before kidnapping someone? I called the detective in charge, he went out and grabbed the man and had a chat with him. He said Graves was on the property early yesterday morning, warned him not to tell anyone. Seems mighty suspicious to me. Then he said Graves was somewhere on the property for about an hour and a half. Claimed he didn't see or hear anything out of the ordinary. Not sure I believe him, but he swears he's telling the truth.

"A deputy from the sheriff's office is coming to Anchor Point to escort you to the shipyard. She's bringing her search dog. You'll need something of Zita's for the dog to scent on. She's there, Obi-Wan—I'd bet my reputation on it."

"Is it...it's not a cadaver dog, is it?" he whispered, not even caring that his voice broke as he asked the question.

"No. It's a scent-driven search dog." Tex's voice was sympathetic and reassuring.

Obi-Wan was relieved, but he still felt dizzy. Could this nightmare be coming to an end? It was the morning of day two, not quite forty-eight hours...but it seemed like an eternity. There was still no guarantee Zita was alive, that Silas hadn't taken her to the shipyard and killed her before dumping her body in the ocean or stashing it in one of the rusted-out metal hulks on the property.

But maybe, just maybe...

He let the thought fade away as he turned to face the deputy. Edge had stopped her from approaching, talking to the woman with a frown on his face. It looked as if they were having an intense conversation. But Obi-Wan was more than ready to stop fucking talking and get out of there. That clock behind the bar was still ticking away too damn loudly.

"I'm working on satellite data, and if I see anything I'll let you know. I'll be in touch," Tex said, before severing their connection.

Obi-Wan put his phone back in his pocket and quickly walked over to Edge and the deputy.

The woman turned toward him and held out a hand. "Jennifer Williams. This is Fred." She gestured to the black Lab sitting at her side. Even the dog looked serious.

"He any good?" Obi-Wan asked.

She nodded. "One hundred and forty-two searches. One hundred and thirty-four successful finds. And before you ask, the eight he didn't find were false alarms, not missing people, so I'm not counting those as failures."

Obi-Wan nodded. "Zita spent the night at my apartment the other night. I can get the pillowcase from the pillow she used."

"Perfect, let's go."

Happy that the woman seemed to be as eager as he was to get started, Obi-Wan strode toward the door.

"I'm coming too," Edge said.

All of Obi-Wan's focus was on getting to that scrapyard. He didn't care if the entire population of Norfolk came along to watch and help. All that mattered was finding his woman.

* * *

It didn't take long for him to stop at his apartment. Jennifer came upstairs with him, leaving Fred in her vehicle, and, after donning gloves, carefully put the pillowcase into a plastic bag. She didn't say much, which Obi-Wan was grateful for. He felt like he couldn't speak; all the words he might've said were stuck in his throat.

Edge followed Jennifer's police vehicle as she drove like a bat of hell out of the city toward the scrapyard. It was by the water, not too far from the naval base. There was a fence around the property and a simple guard shack at the gate. There was an armed police officer manning the gate, and he let them through without hesitation.

Obi-Wan felt a shiver go through him as they navigated the dirt roads on the property. He was a practical man. Didn't believe much in otherworldly stuff. Wasn't a fan of the occult or paranormal. But being here was...spooky. The air seemed different. Heavier.

Everywhere he looked, there were the skeletons of huge, empty ships. Some small, some enormous. There were also airplanes, a helicopter or two, and other military vehicles. Tanks, Jeeps, and sedans. It was a junkyard on crack.

But what *really* caught his eye was the huge aircraft carrier. It was the biggest relic in the yard by far. Now that he was here and seeing it, he remembered reading a news article online about how the ship had finally been fully cleaned out and stripped, all hazardous materials removed, and would be towed out to sea soon, sunk to the bottom and turned into an artificial reef.

It towered over everything else. Even the other big ships in drydock looked tiny next to the mammoth carrier.

"That would be the perfect place to hide something you didn't want to be found," Edge said, almost under his breath.

He wasn't wrong. And that made every hair on Obi-Wan's arms stand up.

"She's there. She has to be," he said after a moment.

"We don't know that."

"Look around, Edge. If you were Silas, and you brought her here, where would you put her?"

His friend frowned. "On that carrier."

"Exactly. Especially since it's slated to be towed out to sea. No one would find her, alive or dead, if she was in there when that happened." The words made Obi-Wan's nausea even worse, but they had to be said. He was a realist. Had faced death more times than he could count. But not the death of someone he cared about. Loved.

Suddenly impatient, he wanted to get onto that carrier *now*. He'd tear the place apart looking for Zita. She was there. He knew that as well as he knew his damn name.

Edge parked and they were out of the car in a heartbeat. Jennifer was just opening the back door to her vehicle to let the Lab out as the rest of their Night Stalker team arrived. Edge had called Casper while Obi-Wan was in his apartment with the deputy, which was more than all right with him. The more eyes, the better. And there was no one he trusted more than his teammates.

They weren't in the air, weren't being shot at or dodging mountaintops, but this situation felt no less dire. That damn clock was still ticking in his head.

There were also several police and sheriff's deputy cars. There had to be at least two dozen men, which made Obi-Wan feel a little more optimistic. It shouldn't take too long to find Zita with that much help...he hoped.

"Give Fred five minutes," Jennifer said, as she opened the plastic bag that held the pillowcase Zita had used two nights before. "He'll find her scent and show us where she was taken. I guarantee it."

Obi-Wan swallowed hard and nodded. He was nearly positive Zita was on that aircraft carrier but...what if she wasn't? They'd waste hours looking when they could know within minutes by giving the search dog an opportunity to do what he did best.

It didn't take five minutes. The second Fred got Zita's scent, he was off like a shot. Zigzagging with his nose to the ground and in the air as he excitedly followed Zita's trail.

As Obi-Wan suspected, the dog headed straight for the huge carrier.

It didn't take them long to arrive at a rickety-looking dock, fashioned together from random lengths of wood. Fred pulled on his harness and leash, obviously wanting to go inside the ship so he could continue the search.

"I'm going with the dog," Obi-Wan said.

No one disagreed.

"We're all going with Fred," Casper said firmly.

"I'll coordinate the search out here," one of the detectives said. "We need to be methodical, not running around inside that ship like chickens with our heads cut off. Six of you," he said, pointing at half a dozen police officers, "go with them. The rest of you fan out. Even if they find the vic, we still need to search the property, build a case against the assailant."

"Zita. Her name is Zita," Obi-Wan ground out.

"What?"

"Not *vic*. Her name is Zita Darlington."

"Right. Sorry. If you find anything, any kind of evidence at all, don't touch it, don't disturb it. Call it in. Tire tracks, bodily fluids, clothing, cigarette butts...if it looks suspicious, call me. The crime scene guys are on their way. They'll photograph and collect anything we find. Let's do this!"

Obi-Wan turned his back on the men dispersing into the depths of the property. For a moment, he wanted to call them back, tell them to join everyone else on the aircraft carrier, knowing they couldn't possibly search the entire thing themselves. But they needed all the evidence they could get to make the case against Silas rock solid.

"The most obvious way in is through there," one of the police officers said, pointing to a small hatch on the side of the huge hull.

"But how did he get her in there?" someone else asked.

Fred chose that moment to bark at a large board lying on the makeshift dock. It blended in, looking like another random piece of wood on the unstable structure, but it was obvious what it had been used for. No one needed Fred's alert to tell them Zita had been on that board.

Edge and Chaos helped him extend it over and prop it up, one end inside the hatch, turning it into a walkway of sorts. An unsafe and wobbly walkway, but still a way inside.

He realized if Zita had been left inside, and she'd managed to find her way out, it would've been almost impossible to get off the damn ship without that board in place.

Obi-Wan's hatred for Silas Graves increased with every beat of his heart. With every second he spent in this place. The thought of Zita fighting for her life, putting those marks on Silas's face before she was forced onto this ship, physically hurt. And he had no doubt the fight occurred here, because no one at the motel had heard a damn thing. It was likely she'd been rendered unconscious upon opening the door, allowing Silas to steal her away with a minimum of fuss.

But once they arrived at the shipyard, she'd obviously fought like hell. Obi-Wan just hoped her resistance hadn't ended in her death. That she'd been hidden away on this fucking carrier instead of murdered outright.

Obi-Wan could picture the scene in his head. His Zita refusing to do what Silas wanted, and the asshole taking great pleasure in telling her all about her impending fate. How the ship would be sunk soon—with her in it. It seemed like something the man would enjoy doing.

"You going to be okay going up that?" Edge asked Jennifer, doubt in his tone.

"Of course. Why wouldn't I be?" she answered, as they watched a few officers go up the walkway first, to make sure things were clear inside and that it was a viable entrance.

"Because you have the dog. And it's not stable," Edge said.

Jennifer laughed. "You're kidding, right? And his name is

Fred, not 'the dog.' He's used to walking on things like that. He's a search dog. It's what he does."

Edge nodded. "Sorry. It's just a long way down if he falls."

"He won't," she said firmly.

As soon as the officers gave the all-clear, Obi-Wan was striding up the board as if it were a wide metal platform, instead of one-and-a-half feet of rotting wood. Fred followed him just as easily, with Jennifer and Edge hot on their heels.

The air inside the aircraft carrier was dank and musty, and it was dark. The second he walked too far away from the open hatch in the side of the ship, Obi-Wan couldn't see a damn thing.

Jennifer reached into one of her pockets and took out a light. She clipped it onto her belt, then put another onto Fred's harness, lighting the path in front of the dog.

"Here," an officer said, handing Obi-Wan a flashlight. It was one of those industrial lights, heavy, the kind that could be used as a weapon if need be. The beam was strong and bright.

"If you're going with us, keep the lights away from Fred's eyes," Jennifer warned. "He'll be in front, but it'll fuck with his vision if he happens to look back to check on me and gets hit in the face with that beam."

Obi-Wan nodded.

It took another five minutes of instructions from the detective who'd joined them on their search of the ship. Everyone agreed not to put all their eggs in one basket, so to speak, just in case—though silently, Obi-Wan put his money on Fred. Still, the officers would stick together and methodically search behind every door as quickly as they could, level by level. The Night Stalkers would go with Jennifer and her search dog.

They were given radios and ordered to check in every five minutes, and required to make note of where they were frequently, so they didn't get lost in the huge ship themselves.

Finally, after everyone memorized where the hatch was, and

how to get out of the ship in case something went terribly wrong, the officers began their search.

Obi-Wan and his team turned back to Jennifer and Fred.

She once more pulled out the plastic bag with the pillowcase from one of her cargo pockets and opened it. Fred stuck his snout into the bag for a brief second to get another sniff of who he was looking for, then lifted his head and scented the air before taking off down a dark hallway to their left.

The Night Stalkers followed close behind Jennifer. Obi-Wan was grinding his teeth so hard he had the beginnings of a migraine, but he ignored it. The only thing that mattered was finding Zita.

Everyone hoped to find her quickly, but they were prepared to search the entire ship if things didn't work out with the dog. Obi-Wan had high hopes, given the way Fred immediately seemed to lock on to a scent.

Fred had a long lead attached to his harness, and Jennifer walked quickly behind him, telling him to "find" and occasionally praising him as he searched. Everyone stayed right on her six, their flashlights pointed at the floor or the ceiling, lighting the area immediately around them as they moved.

The ship was massive. Fred doubled back now and then, as if he'd lost the scent, then picking it up again.

"This is normal," Jennifer explained calmly.

Hearing her voice echo through the empty metal halls was so strange, especially since Obi-Wan had spent more than his fair share of time on aircraft carriers that were full of life.

They went down a few levels, and with every step, Obi-Wan's hatred for Carmen and Silas increased. He couldn't imagine what Zita had been thinking when she'd been forced this far into the ship. She had to be scared to death...if she wasn't already dead.

Obi-Wan forced that thought out of his head immediately.

Updates were coming in from the other search team that they hadn't found anything yet.

Nothing.

Nada.

Zilch.

Zita had to be here. She simply *had* to be. Anything else was unacceptable. Because if she wasn't here, they didn't have anything else to go on. They'd have to go back to the drawing board, try to get Silas himself to give them intel.

And if she wasn't here, it meant Tex was wrong.

Tex Keegan was never wrong.

She was here. Obi-Wan felt it in his bones. He just had to find her.

Jennifer stopped Fred briefly, giving him water from a specialized bottle she'd taken out of another cargo pocket. It had a small tray attached to the nozzle so the dog could drink easily. The Lab had been backtracking for the last five minutes, covering ground he'd already been over, as if the scent in the air was confusing, diluted, something. Obi-Wan wasn't sure how it worked, but it was possible Zita was somewhere near and with all the metal and doors, the dog was having trouble pinpointing which one she was behind.

"I'd like to try something," he blurted.

Everyone looked at him. Even the dog stopped slurping the water and tilted his head, as if he could understand every word he said.

"This ship is completely empty. It's nothing but metal. Our steps are echoing as we walk. Hell, even our voices are reverberating back at us. I want to call out Zita's name." He swallowed hard before saying the next thing on his mind. "If she's conscious, she might hear us, even through the doors. I'm not saying Fred has missed her, but I'm not willing to take the chance. If we call her name, then pause to see if we hear any response, that could speed this up."

Jennifer looked skeptical, and his friends looked...sympathetic. But Obi-Wan didn't care if they thought he was wrong.

He'd do anything to find Zita, even if everyone else thought it was a waste of time and energy.

Eventually, Jennifer shrugged. "Might as well try."

"Let's do it," Buck agreed.

"Right. On the count of three, we'll all yell her name as loud as we can. Then wait to see if we hear a response," he said.

After his search partners nodded, he took a deep breath. "One, two, three... ZIIIIIITAAAAA!"

The sound of all of them yelling was loud, Zita's name seeming to bounce off the walls, ceiling, and floor to echo around them, even after they went silent.

Obi-Wan's heart beat out of his chest as he closed his eyes, hoping against hope to hear Zita's voice calling back.

But after their shouts faded, the ship was just as silent as before.

Shit.

"We'll keep doing it," Casper said firmly. "On each level that Fred spent the most time on. It's a good idea."

Obi-Wan had no idea if his friend was being patronizing or not, but he didn't care.

"Fred...find," Jennifer said, giving her dog the command to resume his search. Once again, the dog was off like a shot. His enthusiastic response kept Obi-Wan from feeling as if this search was completely hopeless. He didn't know the dog, but he assumed he wouldn't be quite so eager if he had no scent of Zita.

So on they went. Occasionally Fred stopped at a door, which they'd open. Always finding nothing but metal slats sticking out of the walls, platforms for mattresses for the thousands of men and women who'd lived and worked on this carrier. At any other time, Obi-Wan would've been fascinated by the history of the place. But all he could think of was the fact that Zita was in one of these rooms. That Silas had left her here to die...if she wasn't already.

No. He refused to believe that. Refused to believe all Tex's hard work, all their efforts were in vain.

As they continued down hallway after hallway, Fred continuing to occasionally double back as if confused as to where the scent was going, Obi-Wan did his best to ignore the eerie creaking of the massive ship. As if it was complaining that they were there, invading the space.

He felt an urge to reassure the ship. To let it know, and any spirits who might still reside within, that they'd be gone soon. Once they got what they came for. Before too long, the ghosts would be left alone in peace, once this ship was resting on the bottom of the ocean it had glided across so many times.

He felt an even stronger urge to beg for their help. To ask for their assistance in locating Zita. To help him find the one person in the world he was afraid he couldn't live without.

Taking a deep breath to try to clear his mind, Obi-Wan quickened his steps to catch up to Fred and Jennifer, who weren't slowing down in the least.

It seemed as if there were miles and miles of rooms to search, but Fred raced by most of them without a second glance. Time had no meaning. How long they'd been inside the ship, Obi-Wan had no clue. And he was completely turned around. It would be difficult to find their way out, but he'd deal with that once he was sure Fred had sniffed every inch of this ship.

Sweat dripped down his temples. He ignored it, other than using his shoulder to keep the salty fluid out of his eyes. It was hard enough to see with only the flashlights to illuminate their way.

Every now and then, they'd stop to yell Zita's name, only to hear absolute silence in return.

It was maddening. Depressing. The worst thing Obi-Wan had ever experienced. He wanted this nightmare to be over.

Then Fred made a snuffling noise. Something he hadn't done before.

He stopped in his tracks. When Jennifer caught up to him, she said, "Fred, find."

In response, the dog barked. Once. Then took off down the hall as if he'd seen a squirrel or something and decided to give chase.

Except there *were* no squirrels down here. Nothing a dog would want to chase.

Praying the dog's reaction was because he'd found Zita, Obi-Wan ran after Jennifer, with his team right on his six.

Please let this not be a false alarm, he silently begged as he ran.

CHAPTER TWENTY-THREE

Zita's ears were ringing. Was that even possible when there was absolutely nothing to hear? Was it her imagination? Probably. Just as it was as dark as night, the creaking of the ship had stopped a while ago. Leaving her in silence. It was worse than hearing the ship moan around her.

Was she dead? Zita didn't think so, but she wasn't sure.

With her right hand, she pinched her thigh, *hard*.

"Ow!" she said out loud, breaking the silence. "That hurt!"

Relief swam in her veins. Right, she heard herself speak, felt the pain of the pinch. She wasn't dead then.

That was good...wasn't it?

Sighing, she wanted to *do* something. Wanted to somehow help herself. But honestly, there was nothing constructive she *could* do. She'd tried to find something to use to bang on the walls, tried to wrench open the door, tried yelling...all with no luck.

This *sucked*.

The only thing she could do was think about her life. About the people who would be upset that she was gone. Her parents, of course. Her brother. A few of her coworkers back in California.

Sage.

It was inevitable that her thoughts turned again and again back to the man who'd made her happier than she'd been in a very long time. Being with Sage was easy. He was considerate and went out of his way to do nice things for her. He was fun to be around. Polite to everyone he met. Sexy. Great in bed. Not selfish in the least. And he was a great friend, which was obvious from watching him around his pilot buddies.

He wasn't perfect, which was good. The last thing Zita wanted was someone who never messed up. Who never said the wrong thing, never embarrassed himself, who didn't seem real.

She didn't want to think about what he was going through right now. Hated that he might be blaming himself for her disappearance. It wasn't his fault, or hers. They hadn't done a damn thing wrong by acting on their attraction for each other. Sage wasn't wrong to say no to Carmen. And they'd taken Silas's threat seriously...they just never expected him to do anything so drastic.

The truth was, sometimes bad things happened to good people. And the fault lay with Silas. And Carmen. She *really* wanted to get out of here so she could tell the cops what Silas had told her about that bitch. How getting rid of Zita was her idea.

It was unbelievable. If she could write—which she couldn't—and she wrote a book where someone was kidnapped and left for dead, simply because someone *else* wanted to have sex, any good editor would call bullshit and tell her to rewrite the thing because that was a ridiculous reason for the big ol' drama in a book.

But it *did* happen. *Was* happening. To her. However, Carmen had underestimated Sage. And how quickly he and Zita had come to care about each other. Even if Carmen showed up in

Norfolk and pulled out all the stops to seduce Sage, Zita knew without a doubt he wouldn't give her what she so desperately wanted.

Sick of her thoughts, and tired of lying on the hard, cold metal bed that reminded her too damn much of what dead bodies were put on in the morgue, she sat up...and immediately felt dizzy.

Shit. Same thing happened the last time she sat up, and she knew it was a bad sign. Zita was trying hard to stay positive, but it was getting more and more difficult. What were the odds that Sage could find her in time?

Honestly? Slim.

She sat on the edge of the metal bunk with her head bowed and tried to breathe slow and even. Not to let her heart rate get too fast. She couldn't control much of anything else, except for her thoughts and what she was doing right this moment. One minute at a time. That's all she had to get through.

As she sat there with her head down, eyes closed, and doing her best not to lie back down and give up completely, Zita thought she heard something.

It wasn't one of the voices of the ghosts she imagined were on the ship. It wasn't one of the creaks or groans that were so familiar by now. It was...

A bark?

That couldn't be right. What the hell would a dog be doing in here? That thought just made her sadder. That another living creature could be as trapped as she was.

But then, by some miracle, she thought she heard her name.

And it happened again.

Shit! She wasn't hallucinating!

Zita shot to her feet—and she had to grab the upper bunk to keep from face planting as the room spun around her.

"I'm here!" she screamed as loud as she could. "Help!"

She paused to breathe, praying she really wasn't dreaming.

That she really *had* heard her name twice…that someone was looking for her.

"Zita!"

If she had any extra moisture in her body, she would've started bawling right then. "Yes! It's me! I'm here! Help me, please!"

Then she heard the bark again. There *was* a dog out there. Zita was confused, but she didn't care if there was a hippopotamus outside the door. She'd been found!

Seconds later, she heard banging on the door to her prison, and she couldn't stop smiling.

"Zita!"

The voice was muted, the metal of the door and the ship doing its best to steal the sound away, but she knew without a doubt that it was Sage.

He was here! He'd found her!

"Sage!" she yelled back.

For a moment, she heard nothing, and she had the thought again that maybe she was asleep and dreaming. Maybe she *wasn't* being rescued. Maybe she'd completely lost her mind down here in the absolute silence and darkness.

Until she heard her name again.

"We're going to get you out, Zita! Sit tight! The door's locked and we don't have the fucking key!"

He was muffled, but it was still so good to hear Sage's voice, Zita's legs gave out. She sat hard on the metal bunk, barely feeling the pain that shot up her spine. He sounded stressed out and pissed way the hell off. But nothing had ever made her happier in her life than to hear his voice.

Zita relaxed. It didn't matter how long it took for them to get her out, Sage wasn't going to leave her. He'd stay right there outside the door until it opened and he could get to her.

"You hear me?" Sage asked.

"Yes!" she yelled back.

Her shoulders slumped, her head falling back, and it suddenly felt as if she was a thousand years old. How much time had passed? A day? Two? A week? She supposed it didn't really matter. All that mattered was that Sage had done the impossible. He'd found her. Many people—men, women, children—weren't so lucky.

Zita was well aware that Silas could've killed her and left her body somewhere to rot. But he hadn't. He'd been cocky enough to think he wouldn't get caught, which was incredibly stupid, because of course he would've been the first person on Sage's radar after his stupid threat in Fallport. How in the world he ever thought he could get away with kidnapping her, she had no idea.

Thank goodness Sage was as smart as he was.

She heard banging on the door, as if someone was trying to break it down. Then swearing and more voices. It seemed Sage wasn't alone, which wasn't exactly a surprise. It wasn't as if he'd wander around this huge hulk of a ship by himself. Maybe his team was out there. Maybe the dog she'd heard was Rain, Mandy and Buck's dog, the one that had found them in the rainforest in South America.

It didn't worry her when quite a bit of time seemed to pass. Yes, she wanted out of the damn room, but again, she knew Sage wasn't going anywhere until he had her in his arms.

One second she was sitting on the bottom bunk, staring into space with a half-smile on her face as she dreamed about what she was going to eat and drink when she got out, and the next, she was almost blinded seconds after an extremely loud clanking noise came from the door.

It flew open, and someone used a flashlight to sweep the room. Even though the beam wasn't pointing right at her, the light was extremely painful after sitting so long in the dark.

Zita whimpered in pain and threw a hand over her eyes.

Then a pair of arms wrapped around her so tightly, it was hard to breathe.

She knew immediately who those arms belonged to. Sage.

She went boneless in his embrace, keeping her eyes shut tightly against the lights she could see dancing behind her closed lids.

Several people were talking at once, but all her concentration was on the man on his knees in front of her. She felt Sage sobbing against her shoulder as he held her. She probably would've been crying as well, but again, she didn't have the energy...or the liquid in her body to do so.

"You're alive," Sage rasped in an agonized voice, as he continued to hold her.

Zita nodded as her arms tightened around him. She hated that he sounded so broken. Didn't know what to do to make him feel better.

"Obi-Wan," a voice said gently, "back up a bit. We need to get a look at her."

For a moment, Sage's arms tightened instead...then he slowly eased away from her.

Zita kept her eyes shut, knowing it would hurt if she opened them.

"*Fuck*, Zita. Your neck... And your poor face!"

She could imagine what it looked like. As a redhead, she bruised easily, and those punches weren't exactly love taps. She also still vividly remembered the feel of Silas's hands holding her down...tightening around her throat.

"I'm okay," she whispered. Then she cleared her throat and said it again, a little stronger. "I'm okay."

"Damn straight you are," Sage said reverently.

Slowly, Zita opened her eyes a tad, just to slits. It was enough to send pain shooting into her head. But she didn't close them again. It felt amazing to *see*. And the first thing she saw was

Sage's face. He was frowning, had dirt on his forehead, but he was still the best thing she'd ever seen in her life.

"Hi."

The stupid word escaped without thought.

His gaze whipped up from where it had been focused on her neck, locking on her eyes. Then he smiled. It was small, and a little strained, but it was still a smile. "Hi," he whispered.

"I love you," was the next thing out of her mouth. Locked in the dark, she'd wished over and over that she'd told him before she was taken. That she'd had the guts to admit it when he'd said those three words to her. It was going to be her biggest regret if she hadn't made it out of the ship before it was sunk. That this man wouldn't know how much he meant to her.

The smile on his face grew. Some of the stress lines smoothed out. "I love you too."

Just then, a cold nose nudged Zita's hand where it was resting on Sage's side. Looking down, she saw a black shape standing there. Definitely not Rain.

"That's Fred. My search dog. He found you."

Zita had to close her eyes once more. She was overwhelmed with gratitude. For Fred. Sage. This woman. Sage's teammates. A few officers in the room. The small space was full. She had no idea how many people there were, but it was a lot. And they were all there because they'd been looking for her. She wasn't sure she deserved all the attention, but she sure was grateful for it.

"How about we get the fuck out of here?" Sage said gently.

Zita nodded eagerly, and reopened her eyes into slits once more. It was getting easier now. The light didn't hurt nearly as much as it had before.

"I hope someone knows where the exit is, because I sure as hell don't," Edge said, sounding grumpy.

Zita couldn't help but giggle.

Giggle.

What a difference a few minutes could make.

"Fred'll show us the way," the woman holding his leash said confidently.

Zita stood, and the room swayed around her. Sage didn't miss a beat; he bent and picked her up. One arm under her knees and the other around her back. Zita immediately snuggled into his embrace, laying her head on his shoulder.

They left the room with Fred in the lead, his handler right behind, Edge on her heels, Zita and Sage a few people back, and followed by a whole host of others. People who'd given up their time to look for her. Zita was overwhelmed with gratitude.

She had no doubt she'd be going to the hospital when they finally emerged from the carrier, but that was all right with her. As long as Sage stayed by her side, she'd be able to get through anything.

CHAPTER TWENTY-FOUR

Obi-Wan hadn't left Zita's side since he'd found her in that fucking rusting beast of an aircraft carrier a week ago. It was hard to believe Silas had locked her in a room knowing the ship would be towed out to sea and sunk.

As far as the prosecutor was concerned, Carmen St. James was as guilty as Silas. She was the one who'd set everything in motion. And for what? Sex? It was ridiculous. Hard to believe.

But that definitely seemed to be her motive. Tex had retrieved a full transcript of the texts she and Silas had sent back and forth like idiots. Yes, they'd both deleted the texts, but everyone knew nothing was ever gone forever on electronic devices.

The entire plot had been spelled out in their communications. How Carmen promised Silas money, jobs, and sex with some of the most beautiful women in Hollywood. And in return, all he had to do was get rid of Zita.

Thankfully for Obi-Wan and Zita—because expensive lawyers could've easily argued that "get rid of" didn't translate to "murder"—she'd been more specific when Silas asked for clarification…saying she wanted the woman she saw as her "competition" *dead*.

If there was anything redeeming about Silas, it was that he hadn't actually killed Zita before stashing her in the empty ship. He also hadn't sexually assaulted her. He'd punched her twice, kicked her, and it was clear without Zita having to say a word that he'd put his hands around her neck as well…but she was alive. And thanks to Fred and his handler, she'd been found in a relatively short period of time.

If Obi-Wan and the rest of the searchers had to go through that ship room by room, the outcome might've been very different.

Silas squealed like a pig when he learned Zita had been found, throwing Carmen under the bus. He'd apparently decided if he was going down, so was she. The coconspirators were currently locked up and awaiting a court date.

It was a huge scandal, and Carmen St. James was most likely done with her acting career. Not to mention, the studio was shelling out a fuckton of money so Grubbner could reshoot all the scenes Carmen had been in, having already replaced the actress. It was possible cancel culture would make sure the movie tanked, no matter the effort Grubbner was going through to salvage it. Time would tell.

But as far as Carmen's career went, no director would dare cast her now, considering how reviled she was at the moment. Not that it was even an option, as she'd be spending some time behind bars. Probably not enough for Obi-Wan's peace of mind though.

Zita would have some stressful times coming up. She'd need to testify for sure, but Obi-Wan was confident she'd be able to handle it as well as she'd handled everything else that had been thrown at her.

She'd been missing for two days. Any longer and things could've been a bit dicier as far as her health went. As it was, she was dehydrated to a dangerous level and had lost almost ten pounds in that short time. She was also struggling mentally. Which wasn't a surprise to Obi-Wan and his friends. They knew the effects that solitude and darkness could have on the human body. It was a well-known torture technique, and it made Obi-Wan sick to his stomach that his Zita had experienced it.

Her family had flown in as soon as they were able. They hadn't arrived at the scrapyard in time to join the search, but they'd met them at the hospital, and had spent every possible minute with her that they could. They were extremely shaken up by what had happened.

Unbeknownst to Zita, Obi-Wan had talked to her parents and brother while she was napping at the hospital. It was a little weird at first, since none of them knew each other, but Obi-Wan hadn't held anything back. He'd told them that he loved Zita more than he could put into words, and that he'd do everything in his power to keep her safe from here on out.

It wasn't the way he'd wanted to meet her family, but he reassured them that he was in this for the long haul, no matter how recently he and Zita had met. After the initial awkwardness wore off, Obi-Wan found that he enjoyed talking to her folks and her brother. They were down to earth and obviously loved Zita very much.

When she woke, her family visited for a while longer, before Zita finally convinced them she was okay. After making her promise to come to Indiana to visit them sooner rather than later, the threesome headed back to their hotel, flying home the next day.

Now, Obi-Wan and Zita were currently holed up together at his place. Colonel Burgess had put him on convalescence leave, and Obi-Wan felt no guilt in using every day of the time he'd been given.

After Zita was discharged from the hospital the next day, he'd brought her straight to his apartment. Someone—he had no idea who, but was grateful—had brought Zita's suitcases to his place, so she had her own things to change into.

And to Obi-Wan's surprise, Pyro had insisted on coming to the apartment with them as well, sleeping in the guest room. In the morning, he was still there, having made them breakfast, and hadn't seemed the least bit inclined to leave. Until getting a call from Casper, reminding him that *Obi-Wan* was on leave, not him. Which made both Zita and Obi-Wan chuckle.

But he came back after work to spend the night again. And after the next workday. And the day after that.

Now, just a week after her ordeal, the sun was shining and Zita seemed better every day, proving her strength and resilience. She was still struggling with what had happened, which was to be expected, but she'd slept through the evening without a nightmare, which was a relief.

Obi-Wan, on the other hand, wasn't sleeping all that great. The first night home, he'd just held Zita and listened to her breathe. One hand on her chest, feeling her heartbeat under his palm. He didn't think he'd ever forget the sick feeling he'd had when he didn't know if she was alive or dead. His fear would fade, as would hers. With time and love, they'd both continue to heal from the traumatic experience. But forget? Never.

After she'd showered that morning—her third shower in twenty-four hours, but Obi-Wan wasn't about to comment on that. She'd been taking at least two a day since her rescue...and he understood the need to be clean after such an intense experience—he asked if she minded Pyro staying with them. She'd admitted that after being alone on that massive ship for two days, having other people in the apartment was a comfort.

He hadn't considered that...but clearly Pyro had. So Obi-Wan took her words to heart, asking if the rest of his team could visit. They were all worried about her and wanted to see for themselves that she was all right. She'd agreed without hesitation, and he'd sent out word that they could come see her whenever they wanted.

Which turned out to be that very evening. It wasn't long after the end of the team's workday before his apartment was bursting at the seams, and as each person arrived, Zita seemed to relax even more. It was a tight fit, but no one seemed to mind that Obi-Wan didn't have enough seats for everyone.

Obi-Wan and Zita were in their usual spot in one of his oversized chairs, where they'd spent most of the last week. The entire Night Stalker team was happy to be stuffed into his apartment, along with Mandy and Laryn. The colonel had even stopped by at one point.

Surprisingly, Jennifer Williams and her dog, Fred, were there too, at Zita's insistence. She said she wanted to thank them properly. So they'd dropped by shortly after the team arrived, and were still there. Fred was lying in the middle of the floor on his back, snoring loudly, which made everyone chuckle.

And Jennifer? She was sitting at the table near the kitchen, with Edge. Obi-Wan couldn't see or hear what they were talking about, but they were definitely getting along pretty well. Which was interesting. The two were about the same height, around five foot six, but that seemed to be where the similarities ended. He guessed Edge was at least ten years older than Jen. She seemed laid-back, while Edge was...not. It was part of the reason for his nickname. He always seemed to be on edge. At work, while flying, and in general.

But surprisingly, his friend seemed pretty relaxed at the moment. Hell, he'd even seen the man smile and laugh a couple of times.

Also, when he'd first met Jennifer, there was something different about the woman that Obi-Wan hadn't been able to put his finger on, too busy worrying at the time. Now, seeing her today, when he wasn't fully focused on finding Zita and could see the woman in better lighting, he realized what it was.

She had no eyebrows. Or eyelashes.

It wasn't a turn-off; it was just different. And there were plenty of reasons why she might be missing hair. He wasn't going to speculate about it...he just hoped it wasn't cancer. The disease was awful, and he wouldn't wish it on anyone.

In the end, her lack of hair didn't matter to Obi-Wan. Not one whit. She could shave off every hair on her body and he wouldn't give a damn. As far as he was concerned, the woman was part of his circle of friends now. How could she be otherwise, when she and her dog had found the woman he loved more than he could put into words?

And Obi-Wan had to admit that he liked seeing Edge looking so comfortable around someone. The man was usually standoffish, and he had a habit of scaring away people who didn't know him personally by frowning and looking pissed off at the world.

Jennifer didn't seem scared. Currently, she was smiling at him, and they hadn't stopped talking since after she'd greeted Zita, saying how happy she was that she was all right.

"Thank you all for coming over tonight. It means more than you'll know," Zita told everyone. "I don't know if Sage has told you, but I'll be moving to Norfolk as soon as I can get my life straightened out in California."

"I'm sure Tex could help with that," Pyro joked.

"He could?" Zita asked, with a tilt of her head.

"Why not? The man is a little spooky with the shit he can do," Chaos agreed.

"What do you need done?" Mandy asked. "Maybe *we* can help you? Make some calls?"

"I need to talk to my boss at the ambulance service I work for, pack my stuff, arrange for movers, get my car across the country, talk to my contact at the agency I work for and let her know that I'll be in Virginia instead of California, research ambulance companies here in Norfolk, turn off my utilities, stop my mail, find an apartment here...Man, it's a lot, isn't it?" she said with a small chuckle.

"I can help with an apartment here," Jennifer said from her spot at the table. "There's an empty apartment in my building and the landlord likes me, so I'm sure if I put in a good word for you, she'd seriously consider you for it. It's totally safe too. Cameras, you have to be buzzed into the lobby, and there's a full-time security guard in the lobby as well."

"I can talk to people at the hospital on base," Buck volunteered. "See what ambulance companies are the best and who they'd suggest you contact."

"And Tex can totally deal with everything to do with moving," Casper said.

"I don't want to be a bother," Zita said a little shyly.

"Trust me, Tex loves this shit. He'll have your entire place packed up and all your stuff on the way here within a week," Casper said with a grin. "Your car included."

"Oh. Wow. Um..."

Obi-Wan kissed her temple. "Say yes, Zita. Let us help you."

"I feel as if you've all helped me more than my fair share as it is."

"Nonsense," Laryn said. "This is what friends do. And we might not have spent a lot of time together, but you're pretty awesome."

"Thanks," Zita told her.

"It's settled. You'll need to talk to your boss and the film person, but leave the rest to Tex. I'll give him a call later," Obi-Wan told her.

At that moment, Casper's phone rang. Which wouldn't be unusual, except most of the people he knew were already in the room. And any other day, it could be entirely possible it was a spammer or his brother...but the ringtone was one every Night Stalker in the room recognized.

Because they'd all programmed their phones with the same ringtone for the same number.

"Shit."

"Fuck."

"Damn."

Obi-Wan tensed. He wasn't ready.

Casper took a deep breath and didn't bother to leave the room to answer the call. Everyone's eyes were on him, and no one bothered to hide the fact they were listening to his side of the conversation.

"Davis. Yes, Sir. Uh-huh. Oh-four-hundred, understood. All right. Out."

It was short and to the point. No one was surprised when, a moment later, Buck's phone rang with the same distinctive ringtone.

"What's happening?" Zita asked, looking confused.

"We're being called in. Mission," Pyro told her.

"Oh."

One by one, the men's phones rang and their conversations with whomever was on the other side, probably the colonel, were equally short and to the point.

Obi-Wan tensed after everyone had received a call but him.

And then it was his turn. He wanted to ignore the ringing. Wanted to tell the colonel to fuck off. That he wasn't leaving Zita. Not when he was still feeling so raw about almost losing her.

"Answer it," Zita ordered. She'd turned in his lap and was staring at him.

He slowly pulled out his cell, wanting to throw a tantrum. But everyone was there. Watching. Waiting to see what he'd do. The tension was thick in the room.

"Engle."

"Obi-Wan, I'm sorry to do this. I know you're on leave, but we need you. This one will hopefully be short. The shit's hitting the fan in Gabon. Libreville, more specifically. The government elections aren't going well, we need to pull the US employees, and it's not safe to do so by ground. We're gathering as many employees and their families as we can at the embassy in the capital city. This should be an in-and-out job."

Gabon was in Africa, the west coast. It was a country that had been on the government's watch list as far as violence went. But an "in-and-out job"...there was no such thing in the Night Stalkers' line of work.

Expect the worst, hope for the best. That was their team's unofficial motto.

"Yes, Sir," Obi-Wan managed to say.

"Oh-four-hundred at the hangar. Wheels up as soon as we can get ready to go after that."

Obi-Wan nodded, but his throat was too tight to say anything. He felt like shit that he was both terrified to leave, but excited at the challenge of the upcoming evacuation. It had been a while since he'd been behind the controls of his bird during a mission, and he was ready to get back to it. But that would mean leaving Zita. The situation sucked.

"See you soon." Then the colonel hung up.

"Sage?"

"I have to go," he said softly. It felt as if they were the only two people in the room. Vaguely, Obi-Wan heard Laryn's cell ring, but he was completely focused on the woman in his lap.

"It's okay. *I'm* okay. You need to go and help whoever it is that needs help. Assistance only you and your friends can offer."

"I don't want to leave you."

"But you have to. This is what you do. There will be times when I have a twenty-four-hour shift, or when I need to leave town to be on set somewhere. It sucks, but it's life. Go. Go be awesome."

This woman. She was amazing. He was in awe of her. She'd

just been through hell, had almost died, and yet she was still encouraging him to leave.

"I know we don't know each other very well...but you can stay with me," Jennifer offered from nearby.

Upon hearing his owner's voice, Fred rolled over, shook himself, looked over at Jen, then at everyone else in the room.

And he made a beeline for Zita, putting his head on Obi-Wan's knee in front of her and whining a little.

"He can tell you're stressed. That you're both stressed," Jen said quietly.

Zita petted the dog's head and looked back at Obi-Wan.

He closed his eyes, everything in him screaming to say no. He wasn't going. But it wasn't in him to disobey his superior officer. Besides, he *wanted* to fly. Wanted to help the people who were probably scared out of their minds.

He nodded.

Zita leaned against him and whispered, "I'm so proud of you."

She was proud of *him*? He was about to burst with the pride he felt for how well she was handling everything that had been thrown at her in such a short period of time.

"You could stay with me too," Mandy said. "I mean, if you don't want to stay here by yourself. Wait—I know! What if we had a sleepover? That sounds juvenile, considering our ages, but I could come here with Rain, if that's okay with you, Obi-Wan? And maybe Jen, you and Fred could join us too? Or we could take turns staying here."

"I'd love that," Jen said. "And Fred loves other dogs."

"Rain hasn't been around them a lot, but I'm sure he'll be fine," Mandy said.

Obi-Wan wasn't upset in the least that the women were planning on crashing at his place. He understood and supported Zita's need to have her own apartment when she moved here permanently, but knowing she'd be in his space while he was gone would make him feel much better about not being there.

"Now that that's settled, we all need to get going. Get a few hours' sleep before we head to base in the morning. Everyone good?" Casper asked, looking around the room.

They all nodded their agreement. Obi-Wan eased to his feet, keeping an arm around Zita as they walked everyone out and said their goodbyes.

Once they were alone, Zita leaned into him and asked, "Are you sure you're okay with me staying here? And with Jen and Mandy coming over?"

"Absolutely. I don't want you to be alone."

"Honestly? I don't *want* to be alone," Zita admitted, making Obi-Wan second-guess his easy acquiescence to going on the mission.

As if she could read his mind, Zita said, "You don't have a choice. I'm a big girl, Sage. I'll be okay."

"I want you to be more than okay," he told her.

"You know what? I'm alive. I'm here. I have you, and our friends. I'm good. I'm *more* than good. I'll miss you like crazy, but you'll come back, and maybe by then I'll have figured more things out with my move here."

"Which reminds me, I need to call Tex."

"It's okay if you don't. I'll see what I can get done myself."

"I'm calling Tex," Obi-Wan said firmly.

Zita grinned. "Okay. But if he seems reluctant, he doesn't have to do anything. I'm sure he's busy helping others the way he helped me."

"Tex is definitely a helper. He'll have no problem doing this for you. For us," Obi-Wan reassured her.

"It doesn't seem real that just days ago, I was in a room on that ship. But you know what? I knew you'd be doing everything possible to find me."

"Damn straight. I love you, Zita. The second you didn't

respond to my texts, I knew something was wrong, and I also knew it had to do with Silas. I'm just so damn relieved he didn't..." His voice trailed off, not able to verbalize his fears that she'd been killed before he could get to her.

"I know. Me too. I thought when he had his hands around my neck that he was going to end things right then and there. But I stabbed him in the eye with my thumb...as you know from what I told the detective."

"And scratched the shit out of his face. That was smart, and I'm prouder of you than I can put into words that you didn't give up."

"How could I give up when I had you to return to?" she said quietly.

"When I get back, I'm going to show you just how much you mean to me. I'm going to lock us in our bedroom for twenty-four hours straight."

"Sounds perfect to me," Zita said with a smile.

The doctor had said that if she felt well enough, sex wasn't off the table, but it was obvious to Obi-Wan from the way she was moving so stiffly that she wasn't ready. Which was okay, he could wait. Would wait as long as it took to love her the way she was meant to be loved.

"Be safe on your mission," she told him.

"Of course. I've got you to come home to. I'm not sure if that will change my mindset when I'm flying, but I don't see how it couldn't. I need to talk to Casper and Buck about it. See how they reconcile the danger of what we do, and doing what needs to be done, with worrying about coming home to their loved ones. And now that Casper is going to be a father, I bet he's even more aware of how much is at stake every time he gets behind the controls of a chopper."

Zita nodded. "You and your friends are damn good at what you do. And I highly doubt you'll do anything differently now that you have girlfriends. Do what you always do, Sage." She grinned. "Be all that you can be."

Obi-Wan chuckled and rolled his eyes. "You know how corny that is, right? Using an Army slogan in your little pep talk?"

"Yup. But it made you laugh, which was my goal. Now...you need to pack. I'll help."

"I'll call Tex first, but yes, I *do* need to pack. I love you, Zita. You're my everything."

"Back atcha, Sage. Come on, let's get you ready to save the world."

"Not the world, just a tiny little portion of it."

"But for the people who you'll be helping, it's their entire world."

She wasn't wrong. Because that's how he felt about her. Getting into that damn room on the abandoned ship and seeing her alive, was like being given the entire world.

He hoped the colonel was right and this mission would be fast. Because he was ready to get back home and start a new chapter in his life...with Zita by his side.

EPILOGUE

Pyro was amped up. He was ready for this mission. He didn't like sitting at home in Virginia waiting to be sent somewhere. He lived for the adrenaline of the missions he and his fellow Night Stalkers were sent on. He'd joined the Army for the adventure, the danger.

Growing up, his life had been tough. He was a foster kid, one of thousands of unwanted children in the US who were shuffled through the system year after year. He'd been well aware that when he turned eighteen, he'd age out, and knew he needed a plan. Somewhere to go. A job. And his way out had been the military. He hadn't really planned on becoming a pilot, didn't really think someone like him—with no connections, so-so grades, and a chip on his shoulder—would ever be accepted.

But his drill sergeants had seen something in him that Pyro never had. The Army agreed. The structure of the military was something he'd never experienced, and he'd thrived. He rose through the enlisted ranks quickly, learning as much about helicopters and other military vehicles as he could through his MOS.

Then he'd met a Night Stalker pilot one day, and he'd apparently impressed the man enough for him to become a friend of sorts. He'd been the one to encourage him to reclassify his MOS and go through the channels to become a Night Stalker, himself.

One of the worst days of Pyro's life was the day he heard that his mentor had been killed while on a mission. He'd vowed right then and there to become the best pilot the Army had ever trained, in order to honor the man who'd seen something in the scrawny former foster kid that no one else had bothered to see.

He'd done that and more. Pyro thought about his mentor every time he got behind the controls of his MH-60 with Casper, his copilot. They were damn good at what they did, and this mission in Africa would be no different.

They were in Gabon, tasked with evacuating US personnel from the embassy in the capital city of Libreville. Tensions had been high in the country leading up to elections for president. Corruption and poor governance were tearing the country to pieces, and just about every political figure and governmental agency engaged in corrupt activities, bribes, embezzlement, forgery, and extortion.

Some people might ask why in the hell anyone would go to the country in the first place, but Pyro admired them. Embassy employees, Peace Corps volunteers, those in the oil and gas industry, security, healthcare and even technology, they were all there trying to help humanity...and make a living while doing so.

He'd been on the receiving end of gracious and kind workers like those trying to make the lives of Gabonese citizens better, and he had a soft spot for them. It wasn't *their* fault the government was corrupt, or the locals had finally had enough and were fighting back, using violence as a way to voice their displeasure.

The mission would be a challenge, because there was no guarantee those fighting the government wouldn't turn their ire against the US citizens being evacuated. Against the helicopters swooping in to rescue them. It had happened in the past, and would happen again in the future. Mobs had a mentality that was unstable and unpredictable. Pyro and all of his teammates would need to get in, load up the evacuees, and get the hell out as fast as they could.

Flying over the capital, Pyro could see smoke rising from dozens of sites across the city. Buildings were burning, and even from his seat in his chopper, he could see the destruction in the streets below.

He and Casper had been assigned to evacuate one of the hotels American citizens had been sent to as they waited for extraction. The original plan, devised that morning, was that two dozen women and children would meet them in a field by a school, not too far from the Radisson Blu Okoume Palace Hotel.

But as they flew over the area, Pyro knew that was no longer an option.

The plan had most likely been leaked by one of the very officials the US was working with to get the Americans out. The field was now covered by dozens of vehicles, preventing the chopper from landing. Not only that, Pyro could clearly see several men standing in the backs of pickup trucks, their weapons pointed at the sky.

The mission was getting more harrowing by the second.

"RPG fired!" Chaos said through the radio. He and Edge were on the other side of the city, attempting to evacuate US officials from the embassy building, and, as they'd expected, resistance was heavy in that area.

"Shit. This is gonna be dicey," Casper muttered.

Pyro nodded but didn't speak, all his attention on the ground, on trying to figure out their next plan of action.

"Look," he said seconds later, pointing at the hotel. It was about seven stories high, and there were people on the roof waving white flags...no, bedsheets...calling attention to their plight. The hotel was surrounded by more vehicles, and there were swarms of people with weapons on the grounds.

Pyro had no idea if they'd infiltrated the hotel yet or not—and if not, he didn't know what they were waiting for—but *he* wasn't going to wait to find out. Every second they delayed increased the threat of violence against the citizens they were charged with picking up.

They'd been flying together so long, Casper and Pyro could almost read each other's minds. They were both on the same page as Casper said, "There. The north side. There aren't any antennas and I can set the skid on the building and hover as you help get as many people as possible loaded."

"They're going to have to leave their shit behind," Pyro said, as they flew closer and he saw that just about everyone had suitcases and bags.

"They aren't going to be happy about that."

"Tough shit," Pyro mumbled. "If they want to get the hell out of here, they'll leave it behind. Make room for everyone on board."

Pyro wasn't concerned about material things. He'd spent the first eighteen years of his life having to leave stuff behind as he was moved from one foster home to the next, many times only able to bring what fit into a garbage bag. He'd learned that he didn't need much. A roof over his head, food, water...those were more important than stuffed animals and clothes.

These people would have to learn that as well. A human life was more important than whatever they had in their suitcases.

As Casper maneuvered their chopper closer to the roof of the building, Pyro looked down and noted that the pissed-off citizens were mobilizing. Moving trucks to the side of the building where they'd be hovering.

"We've probably got about three minutes, maybe more, maybe less," he warned Casper.

"Understood. Get those people onboard, Pyro. Do whatever you have to do."

He nodded. He didn't need his teammate to tell him that. He was more than aware of the danger they were in. The details of what happened in Mogadishu were fresh in all their minds anytime they were on a mission in an urban area. The Night Stalkers who'd lost their lives there were a constant reminder of the dangers of ordinary citizens when pissed way the hell off for one reason or another.

Pyro unclipped his seat belt and prepared to duck into the back of the chopper and open the door to assist people inside.

"Do *not* leave this chopper, Pyro," Casper warned. "I don't give a shit what's happening on the roof. I'm not leaving you here, so if you get out, we'll all fucking go down."

Pyro nodded. He wasn't about to forget what happened when he and Casper had left their chopper in the mountains between Syria and Turkey. How Laryn had been taken right from under their noses. And when Buck had left *his* chopper in the rainforest to find Mandy.

He wasn't going to make that mistake. He was a rule follower. He wouldn't do anything that could possibly hurt his career...and one of his best friends. Because he knew without a doubt Casper was a man of his word. He wouldn't leave without him, would die if he had to.

No one was dying today. Not on Pyro's watch.

Casper lowered the chopper until it was hovering over the edge of the roof, then he shifted the huge machine a few inches until the right skid bumped against the rooftop.

"Go, go, go!" Casper ordered urgently, as he held the helicopter steady on one skid.

Pyro jumped out of his seat and into the back. He grabbed the door and wrenched it open.

Dozens of frightened gazes met his as they huddled around each other. Women, children, and even a couple of men. Pyro gestured for them to run toward the chopper.

To his annoyance, no one moved. They seemed frozen in fear.

Shit. They didn't have time for this!

Just as he was about to lose his temper and scream at them to get the fuck moving, a woman separated herself from the group. At least, Pyro *thought* she was a woman. She was petite. Short and skinny. She could be a teenager but...the more he stared, the more he realized that, no, she wasn't a kid.

She had black hair, was wearing a pair of jeans and a T-shirt, and unlike most of the other women, she had no suitcases or bags. Only a small cross-body purse that Pyro hoped she was smart enough to use for carrying her identification and other important paperwork.

To his surprise, she leaned over to speak to a child who'd been standing behind her. The little girl, who looked like she could be anywhere from five to ten years old, nodded and began to walk slowly toward the chopper.

Her black hair was blowing around her face in the downwash from the rotor blades, and she frowned slightly as she walked toward him. Her head was tilted to one side and her steps were small, but not hesitant.

The woman then turned to the group and began talking and gesturing. Pyro hoped she was trying to convince them to get the hell on the helicopter.

It was a strange scene, a group of women and kids huddled together in fear, while a small child walked almost fearlessly toward the side of the building.

But...there was something about the girl's movements that Pyro couldn't put his finger on at first. She had a serious expression on her face and her brows were furrowed even more now, as if she was concentrating extremely hard. When she got closer, she slowed even more—and put her hands out in front of her, as if she was afraid she was going to run into something.

It hit Pyro then. It was almost unbelievable, but the proof was right there in front of him.

The kid was fucking blind.

She'd been using the sound of the helicopter to guide her, but she obviously wasn't sure how far away it was now, as the sound of the rotors was extremely loud and the wind was whipping her hair around her head like she was in the middle of a tornado.

The *only* thing that could've gotten Pyro out of that chopper was this kid. A blind little girl with more courage in her little pinky than the others behind her had in their entire bodies.

"Here!" Pyro called out. He jumped out of the chopper and took two steps forward to touch the child's hand. She didn't jerk away from him, simply smiled in his direction in obvious relief.

"Hi!" she chirped. "Mommy says you're here to take us away from the scary people."

Pyro had been through some shit in his life. Both as a child and as a Night Stalker. He'd seen the worst of humanity, and what he'd assumed was the best. He'd experienced every emotion under the sun...at least he thought he had. And yet this kid, this tiny human, somehow managed to surprise him.

He wasn't a man who believed in love at first sight, but in that moment, he lost his heart to this brave, sunny, beautiful child.

"Gonna pick you up and put you in the helicopter," he warned, almost yelling to make sure she heard him.

"Okay," was her response, and she held her arms up toward him. Her blank stare was focused over his shoulder, as she obviously had no idea where exactly he was standing.

Pyro gently but quickly put his hands on her waist and lifted her easily into the back of the chopper. "Walk about seven steps forward until you can touch the other side, then sit, knees pulled up to make room for everyone else," he instructed her, instinctively giving her directions she could easily follow without the use of her sight.

The little girl nodded and did exactly as he instructed.

His heart beating hard, Pyro turned back around and saw the girl's mother—he assumed that's who it was, since the girl had said her mommy told her to go to him—was pushing another woman and a teenager in his direction. Seeing the little girl get inside the helicopter safely was apparently what the others needed to become unstuck.

Suddenly, they all ran toward him in a panicked rush.

Pyro braced.

But the black-haired woman was right there too, telling everyone to calm down, not to rush, not to panic. She was also pulling bags out of people's hands and throwing them back onto the roof, out of the way.

Things were still chaotic, and the people around him weren't exactly calm, but without the woman's help, things would've taken a lot longer and been a lot more dicey. It didn't escape Pyro's notice that even though her daughter was onboard, the woman didn't insist she be allowed to get into the chopper before the others. She stayed back to help, to reassure, to organize.

It was going to be a tight fit to get everyone inside the chopper. They were over capacity already and had another six people to load.

"Shit, Pyro. Get 'em on! RPG being loaded at three o'clock."

Pyro's blood ran cold. If that missile hit the chopper while it was a sitting duck on the side of this building, loaded with all these people, they were all dead. He needed to get inside, help Casper get them the hell out of there.

But he wasn't leaving. Not until everyone was onboard. Not until the little girl's *mother* was onboard. The trust the little girl had shown by walking toward him, fucking blind, had left its mark on Pyro.

She needed her mom, and he wasn't leaving without her. Not a chance in hell.

* * *

Will Bowie and Penny be okay? Will the chopper be blown to bits taking out our heroes and all the women and children along with it? (I think you know the answer to both of these questions!)

Getting off that roof is only the first problem Penny has to overcome...but she's lucked out because with Pyro at her side, things will become much easier for the single-mother. Get the next book in the series, *Keeping Penny* to find out more about courageous little blind Bowie, and how dangers await them back in the States!

Scan the QR code below for signed books, swag, T-shirts and more!

Eagle Point Search & Rescue

Searching for Lilly
Searching for Elsie
Searching for Bristol
Searching for Caryn
Searching for Finley
Searching for Heather
Searching for Khloe

*

Box Set 1, Books 1-4
Box Set 2, Books 5-7

The Refuge Series

Deserving Alaska
Deserving Henley
Deserving Reese
Deserving Cora
Deserving Lara
Deserving Maisy
Deserving Ryleigh

Game of Chance Series

The Protector
The Royal
The Hero
The Lumberjack

SEAL of Protection: Legacy Series

Securing Caite
Securing Brenae (novella)
Securing Sidney
Securing Piper
Securing Zoey
Securing Avery

Securing Kalee
Securing Jane

Delta Force Heroes Series

Rescuing Rayne
Rescuing Aimee (novella)
Rescuing Emily
Rescuing Harley
Marrying Emily (novella)
Rescuing Kassie
Rescuing Bryn
Rescuing Casey
Rescuing Sadie (novella)
Rescuing Wendy
Rescuing Mary
Rescuing Macie (novella)
Rescuing Annie

*

Box Set 1, Books 1-4
Box Set 2, Books 5-8
Box Set 3, Books 9-11

SEAL of Protection Series

Protecting Caroline
Protecting Alabama
Protecting Fiona
Marrying Caroline (novella)
Protecting Summer
Protecting Cheyenne
Protecting Jessyka
Protecting Julie (novella)
Protecting Melody
Protecting the Future
Protecting Kiera (novella)

Protecting Alabama's Kids (novella)
Protecting Dakota
Protecting Tex
*

Box Set 1, Books 1-4
Box Set 2, Books 5-8
Box Set 3, Books 9-11
Box Set 4, Books 12-14

Delta Team Two Series
Shielding Gillian
Shielding Kinley
Shielding Aspen
Shielding Jayme (novella)
Shielding Riley
Shielding Devyn
Shielding Ember
Shielding Sierra

Badge of Honor: Texas Heroes Series
Justice for Mackenzie
Justice for Mickie
Justice for Corrie
Justice for Laine (novella)
Shelter for Elizabeth
Justice for Boone
Shelter for Adeline
Shelter for Sophie
Justice for Erin
Justice for Milena
Shelter for Blythe
Justice for Hope
Shelter for Quinn
Shelter for Koren

ABOUT THE AUTHOR

New York Times, *USA Today*, #1 Amazon Bestseller, and #1 *Wall Street Journal* Bestselling Author, Susan Stoker has spent the last twenty-three years living in Missouri, California, Colorado, Indiana, Texas, and Tennessee and is currently living in the wilds of Maine. She's married to a retired Army man (and current firefighter/EMT) who now gets to follow *her* around the country.

She debuted her first series in 2014 and quickly followed that up with the SEAL of Protection Series, which solidified her love of writing and creating stories readers can get lost in.

If you enjoyed this book, or any book, please consider leaving a review. It's appreciated by authors more than you'll know.

www.stokeraces.com
www.AcesPress.com
susan@stokeraces.com

facebook.com/authorsusanstoker

x.com/Susan_Stoker

instagram.com/authorsusanstoker

goodreads.com/SusanStoker

bookbub.com/authors/susan-stoker

amazon.com/author/susanstoker